Murder on the King's Jaunt

The Fourteenth in the Murray of Letho Series

by

Lexie Conyngham

Murder on the King's Jaunt

Lexie Conyngham

ISBN: 978-1-917307-02-4

Cover illustration by Helen Braid at www.ellieillustrates.co.uk

Dramatis Personae

The Murray Household:
Charles Murray of Letho and Isobel, his wife
Augusta Murray, a charming infant
The servants: Robbins, Miss Fitzsimmons, Matthew and Mrs. Mack

Friends and relations:
Alester Blair, Isobel's father, and his manservant Smith
The Balfours, discreet cousins of Murray
Mrs. Helliwell, wife of Letho's minister, a sensible but excited woman
Willie Jack Dundas, unimpressive scion of a powerful family
Andrew Hepburn, wished on the Murrays by Willie Jack
Patrick Armstrong, old friend

Others in Edinburgh involved in the King's Jaunt (those marked with an asterisk had the benefit of actually existing):

*Sir Walter Scott, chief architect of the plaid pageant
*David Stewart of Garth, his assistant
*Robert Dundas, 2nd. Viscount Melville, very much in charge
*John Murray, 4th Duke of Atholl, a frustrated sporting nobleman
*Alasdair Ranaldson MacDonell of Glengarry, a loose cannon

The (mostly) erstwhile inhabitants of the Palace of Holyrood, including:
Mrs. McGregor, who has a nephew; Mrs. Ochill, rarely to be seen; Mr. Musgrave, seen slightly too often; and Helen, a practical servant

The erstwhile inhabitants of New Assembly Close, including:
Mr. Maclean; Mrs. Abernyte and her children; Mrs. Duguid (in the capacity of a maidservant); Miss Groves, a lovely milliner

The staff of Hutcheon & Purvis, publishers: Mr. Hutcheon and his clerk
*Lt. Ewan MacDougall, a valiant naval officer
Mr. Boot, who has a viewing platform at very reasonable rates
*Mr. Trotter and *Lt. Col. Stephenson, whose job it is to refurbish the Palace of Holyroodhouse
*Thomas Mash of the Lord Chamberlain's Office, who believes the job is his
*John Townsend, egregious representative of the Bow Street Runners, an observant and questioning man
Many, many Highlanders and those desiring to appear as Highlanders, and those constrained to look like Highlanders for the occasion
*His Majesty King George IV (cameo appearance)

Chapter One

ANNA OCHILL WAS a horrid old woman.

And ugly.

And not even a real Highlander, almost certainly.

Maria McGregor, or Maria Loudon to her own name, hadn't even seen the Highlands till she married Fergus McGregor forty years ago, but she was a loyal servant of the Crown. Her lips pursed in her wrinkled face, eyes narrowed, at the very thought of Anna Ochill being presented to the King. Here, in Holyroodhouse! It was an outrage. There would be Anna, simpering and flirting, the old hag, and imagining that the King had never seen a beauty like her.

But no: Maria's face cleared like the sun coming out. Anna Ochill would not be meeting the King, not unless she fell off one of the rickety viewing platforms into the Royal carriage. Anna would not be attending a Drawing Room, and curtseying and smiling, for all she had been attending deportment lessons with Mrs. Siddons – deportment! Maria had known from her girlhood how to curtsey in front of a King, and (more challengingly) how to rise and back away again, without tripping over her skirts. And she would show them, even now. For Anna Ochill might not be attending a drawing room, but Maria would be. Maria would do her level best to make sure of that.

'Papa says there's hardly room to move in the town.'

Charles Murray of Letho looked across the breakfast table at his relatively new wife, and frowned.

'In August. I can't think of anything worse, can you?'

There was a pause. Murray did not expect his wife to agree with him on everything, but for some reason this pause made him anxious. Isobel continued to peruse her father's letter from Edinburgh.

'His house is full, too, of course, or will be. He has had letters from all over the country from old acquaintances asking to stay – and you know Papa has a great number of old acquaintances.'

'I didn't think the King's processions were going to be anywhere near George's Square,' said Murray.

'It doesn't matter. Apparently people are charging ten guineas for a space at a window on the Lawnmarket, so what must it cost for a bed? Even assuming you could find one.'

'Maybe I should open up the Queen Street house,' said Murray lightly. 'We could finally afford to sort out the damp.'

Again, there was no immediate response. Murray's anxiety levels rose slightly. Which was a pity, because he was very much enjoying seeing Isobel across the breakfast table, and the dinner table, and across all aspects of his life, generally. And she seemed equally content. He had no wish to suspect that he was being in any way manipulated by her. Surely she could not want to go to Edinburgh in August on the off-chance of a distant glimpse of King George IV?

The papers had been full of it for weeks, as had the regular correspondence of his old friend Alester Blair, Murray's father-in-law. Blair had forsaken his usual summer excursions to friends in the countryside – usually staying a good few weeks here at Letho in Fife – to spend his time in his Edinburgh town house, watching the preparations. There had been meetings and practices, constructions and destructions, and a great number of instructions. Sir Walter Scott, Blair said, was in charge of the whole thing, and there was not a scrap of tartan or a dirk to be had between Aberdeen and Berwick. A mighty muster of His Majesty's unexpectedly loyal Highlanders was to be held, no clan wished to be seen to be outdone by another (except those few who dismissed the whole thing and stayed at home), the jostling for places and positions was outrageous, three quarters of it, according to Blair, comprising ancient traditions made up on the spot by Scott and his theatrical pal Robert Murray (no relation), and the other half invented by the various societies of men claiming pure Highland blood somewhere in their line. And still, as far as Murray could make out, no sane person would put money on whether or not the King was going to come to Scotland at all. He was as likely to go to Austria. Murray, having little interest in the grander side of politics, found he did not care much either way.

'I don't imagine Augusta would have another chance to see the King,' said Isobel, still apparently intent on her father's letter. 'What a thing to be able to tell her grandchildren! But then, who knows what other sights she might see to tell them about?'

'All those crowds would scarcely be suitable for a child,' said Murray firmly. 'She would be terrified. And what if we lost her?'

'Well, no, it would take a deal of planning,' Isobel agreed, laying down the letter and applying herself to her chocolate. She was as careful of Murray's little daughter as he was. 'But at least there would be no trouble over accommodation. One could always retreat to Queen Street and take one's ease in familiar surroundings, away from the crowds.'

Murray sighed.

'I'm not so sure it would be away from the crowds,' he said. 'I too have had applications from acquaintances, though probably not as many as Blair. My cousins the Balfours, for example, are most anxious to take a room or two, if I'm not using the place.'

'Well, you like the Balfours,' said Isobel reasonably. 'And there are only two of them: they would hardly take up much room. What about our neighbours? Has no one local asked you?'

'The Georges are staying with friends,' said Murray. He had been relieved by the news: Mr. George and his sister were all very well for an evening, but he would not have wished to have them stay. 'No one else has mentioned it.'

'The Helliwells might like to go,' said Isobel, as if the idea had only just struck her. 'They only get to Edinburgh for the General Assembly. Mrs. Helliwell would love it.'

'The Helliwells are far too sensible to want to participate in such a daft event,' said Murray. Mrs. Helliwell was indeed sensible, and her husband, the minister at Letho Kirk, was never that keen to leave his own fireside.

'Mrs. Helliwell could have a seat in the carriage,' Isobel

went on mildly. 'And of course you have your own stables, so there would be no problem there.'

'I have no obligations to go,' said Murray, aware that somehow he was on the defensive. 'I'm not a Highlander, by any stretch of the imagination. If the Duke of Atholl were going to round up his clan of Murrays, I don't think my name would even occur to him.'

Isobel shook her head.

'Papa says there's no news of His Grace coming to Edinburgh. You would have no duties, I'm sure. It would only be a question of satisfying your curiosity. Papa has secured a window opposite Oman's Hotel, he says: he is going to watch as much as he can from there, and even the crowds, he says, are an entertainment in themselves.'

'I'm sure he'll have a wonderful time,' said Murray, trying hard not to sound grumpy. He sighed. 'Do you really want to go, my dear?'

'We'll not see the like again,' said Isobel, meeting his eye at last. Blue green and intelligent, her gaze was nothing if not reasonable. And very slightly amused.

'Oh,' said Murray, sinking his head into his hands, 'all right. Let's see what has to be done.'

There was a great deal to be done, as it happened, though now that Murray had a wife a good deal less of it seemed to fall to him. Isobel had been familiar with Murray's household long before there had been any thought of marriage, and was liked and respected by his assortment of servants, so that Murray had found things better run and easier than at any time since his father's old housekeeper, Mrs. Chambers, had retired years before. His butler, Robbins, looked less burdened, and Robbins' own wife, Mary, who had previously been a maid in the household, had less need to leave her young family to come and help out in the big house. The house itself seemed cleaner and brighter, and Isobel had been able to settle the new staff, Mrs. Gilmour, the housekeeper, and Susan Knox, a maid recently arrived from Edinburgh, and the young lad Matthew who had worked, briefly, for her father.

Now there would be decisions to be made about which servants were to go with them and which to stay behind, who was to be sent ahead to open up the house, what provisions might be needed from the estate that would be difficult to find in Edinburgh just now, what clothes would be required – fortunately nothing too formal – whether the places they usually stopped on the way would be too busy to accommodate them. Robbins talked to the coachman, making sure he could arrange to have the stables prepared behind the Queen Street house. Murray wrote to the Balfours, inviting them to join the family for the duration of the visit, and Isobel, amidst her other preparations, had a quiet word with Mrs. Helliwell, much to the latter's delight.

'Good gracious! Well, that has to come down, Mr. Stephenson!'

Mr. Trotter, His Majesty's Upholsterer in Scotland, wore an expression of horror with which his companion, Lieutenant-Colonel Benjamin Stephenson, was all too familiar. Not for Mr. Trotter the battlefield horrors that were an increasingly distant memory for Stephenson. No: it was Stephenson's job, as Surveyor General, to prepare the royal residence of Holyroodhouse for the King's arrival, and in that he had had a great deal to do with Mr. Trotter and his abhorrence of the mouldering, the dusty, the rotten, the flaking, the chewed, the stale … in fact the whole state of the miserable mansion, as if the lowering crags above it were crushing it under their general disapproval.

In fact, their work was almost done, he had thought. It was chance that had brought them through a door that had been repainted, so that everyone assumed it had also been opened and checked behind. This was in the oldest and tattiest part of the Palace, the part apparently built by James IV, but that was a bit before Stephenson's time. He and Mr. Trotter found themselves in a short, airless passage ending in a tapestry of unrivalled hue, the original vile green presumably mercilessly preserved here in semi-darkness. Stephenson, the taller of the two by about a head and a half, handed the lantern to Mr. Trotter and stepped forward, taking the tapestry about the waist and giving it a sharp tug.

Clouds of dust enveloped him, but the tapestry clung relentlessly to the wall. But his action did reveal another doorway behind it.

'Oh, heavens, Mr. Stephenson!' cried Mr. Trotter. 'How did

we miss this? Don't tell me there is yet more of this miserable building?'

But even in the lantern light Stephenson caught that glint in Mr. Trotter's eye. Mr. Trotter liked a challenge. Stephenson tried the door handle, a rattly little yellowed button of ivory that might have come off one of the smaller elephants on the Ark. It turned, clicked, and reluctantly gave, and the door shifted.

'Let me see, Mr. Stephenson!' Mr. Trotter flung out both hands towards the unknown room. 'Let me see how many more yards of red velvet we need! How many more gallons of gilding?'

Stephenson held back the tapestry curtain. Beyond it seemed to be a small apartment – so much of Holyroodhouse had become small apartments, their use granted to various pensioners and random minor courtiers who might once have done a favour to some member of the Royal family, in the hope that the beneficiaries would take one look at the state of the place and demand their favours elsewhere. Any who had been reduced to the point where they were willing to live here had been evicted by Royal command at the end of July, and as far as Stephenson and Mr. Trotter were concerned, were all long gone. The Royal Command had had no such effect on the rats and mice, sadly, but they had made great inroads there, too.

The lantern light showed shuttered windows, and Stephenson stepped, long-legged, around the furniture to reach them. They swung back easily when he unfastened them, showing a small drawing room, a little dusty and bare, but respectable enough. A stale, faintly rotten smell pervaded the place, but it was no worse than there had been elsewhere in the mansion – no doubt a rat or two had found their resting place behind the wooden panelling, and could be removed. Nothing very personal remained, as though the tenant had in fact taken all he could and gone in obedience to the King's command. A further door presumably led to a bedchamber.

Mr. Trotter, already calculating pots of the mouse-brown paint with which he had coated every other wall in the mansion, moved more delicately between chairs and tables, and reached the bedroom door before Stephenson. With a sigh and an almost audible roll of his eyes, he opened it, and looked inside.

Stephenson just managed to catch him before he collapsed on the rush matting, and laid him flat. Then he stood to see what Mr. Trotter had seen.

A woman lay on her back on the floor. Blood blackened her once-white linen, but even without that the state of her face and hands would have told the old soldier that the woman was long dead.

Chapter Two

IN EDINBURGH, ALESTER Blair was in his element, and his joy was complete when Isobel's letter came to say the Murrays were heading for the Capital, too. He insisted that his man, Smith, push him in his wheeled chair all the way from George's Square in the Old Town, down South Bridge, up and over the Royal Mile (lined with anyone in Edinburgh who could knock two pieces of wood together, knocking any piece of wood they could find together to make viewing platforms), down the great ramp of North Bridge and into the New Town. Every street was busy, every corner cluttered with men in tartans of every sett and often several at once, armed with broadswords and dirks and sgianan dubha, crowned with feathers and with every conceivable plant pinned into their headgear with as fancy a clan badge as they could afford, or as their lairds could.

'Look, Smith!' Blair wriggled in his chair, making Smith clutch its handles frantically. 'Holly, juniper, heather, fir, ivy – one might be in a shrubbery! and the plaids! Did you ever see anything like it?'

Smith grunted. Blair was a man who had never shied away from bright colours himself, and Smith might not have been that impressed.

The shops along Prince's Street were swarming with customers, stocking every conceivable item of weaponry, jewellery, cloth and footwear, many of them advertising themselves as replete with the best in London fashion – Edinburgh might be swathing every would-be warrior in Highland dress, but no one wanted to look like a country bumpkin in front of the King. Blair did his best to see inside each one they passed, but the doorways were mostly stopped up with eager buyers.

'Take Castle Street, Smith, would you? It's no steeper than any other, I believe.'

'Yes, sir.' The three broad thoroughfares of the original New Town, Prince's Street, George Street and Queen Street, ran parallel and were braced together by a number of side streets such as Castle Street that ran up from Prince's Street, crossed George Street with a pause to admire the view of the Forth, then plunged back down to Queen Street, where Murray's town house was, on the other side. At the corner of Castle Street, Smith steadied himself and turned the chair, sending a few small boys scuttling for the road. Blair and the chair combined formed a substantial weight, but Smith was strong and put his back into it, and Blair did his best not to jiggle all the way up the hill to George Street, until he heard Smith's sigh of relief at reaching the top. It took some time to find a gap in the carriage traffic, never mind the usual carts and chairs and horses, so that they could cross the road. Once they had, though, there was a new and remarkable sight to behold, and Blair clapped his hands with delight.

On the right hand side of Castle Street, almost at the corner with George Street, stood what seemed to all intents and purposes to be a grand villa, with a central pediment high above ashlar walls, and a rounded bay at each side. Closer inspection, however, showed three front doors, one central and one beside each bay, and these, to a person familiar with Edinburgh, were easily recognised as the entrances to two 'main door' flats and a central staircase accessing flats above. Separate flights of steps over a basement area led to all three doors, though it was currently hard to see them, or the railings that guarded the basement area, for every slab of the pavement or rise of the steps was full of people, mostly in tartan, some queuing patiently, others determined to form part of the spectacle.

'That's Sir Walter Scott's house,' said Blair, unable to resist jiggling again. Smith had tight hold of the chair's handles. They were on the other side of the street, though even here it was more crowded than usual.

'I know, sir, we've come here several times before.'

'I know, I know. Sorry, Smith. But imagine, all that outside the front door!'

Smith must be doing so, for Blair heard a faint groan behind him.

'He'll need a month's holiday after this,' Blair went on.

'He's organising everything! I would have offered to help, but I heard it was only Highlanders he wanted – Davie Stewart of Garth, and the like.' He puffed out loose lips in a sigh. 'I'm sure I could have invented a few ancient traditions as well as anyone.'

'Invented, sir?' Smith queried.

'I think some of the stuff is probably real,' Blair conceded. 'But of course the King likes a bit of pageantry, and Scott has free rein, as far as I can see, to indulge His Majesty. After all, we don't want to be outdone by Dublin, do we?'

'Of course not, sir,' said Smith dutifully. He was an Englishman. 'When's His Majesty arriving, then?'

'Who knows?' Blair admitted. 'I don't suppose even Sir Walter has any idea. He's the King, and I believe he's not in the best of health. It's up to him.'

'Do you think he'll come at all, then, sir?'

Blair sighed again.

'I don't know, Smith, I don't know. But I do hope so. I shall never live to see such a spectacle again – though that could be said whether the King comes or not.'

He was about to tell Smith to carry on down the street when he stopped. A dark carriage, smart but not flashy, had pulled up outside Scott's busy house, and something about it was familiar. As they waited, the footman hopped down and opened the door, and the crowd on the steps to No.39 parted politely. Blair squinted round the corner of the carriage to see two grim-faced men, markedly not in Highland gear, glance around at the assembled tartan-wearers before mounting the steps to Scott's open front door. In a moment they had vanished inside.

'Well,' said Blair. 'Of course. But why look so sombre?'

'Who was it, sir?' asked Smith. 'Do you know the gentlemen?'

'One was Lord Melville, certainly. That is his carriage. The other I am not wholly sure, but I believe it is the Duke of Atholl.'

'Is he not a Highlander, sir?'

'You could say so, I think,' said Blair. 'In fact, if we're being very precise, he is Mr. Murray's clan chief. I wonder if Mr. Murray has been summoned by him? Oh, we might see him in tartan!'

There was another groan from Smith, and Blair decided it was time to move on.

Inside Scott's house the mob was denser than outside, but still Lord Melville and the Duke managed to make their way through by dint of authoritative looks and the occasional shove. A manservant in a startling livery of blue and yellow showed them into a small parlour, chasing out a few other men who had been lounging there.

'I'll fetch Sir Walter at once, your Grace, my lord,' he gabbled. Melville noticed that one of his eyelids was twitching.

'This whole thing is madness, of course,' Melville said to the Duke as soon as the door was shut.

'Complete madness,' the Duke agreed. 'Edinburgh in August! What about my grouse?'

'Nevertheless, we cannot allow it to fail now,' said Melville. 'His Majesty went to Dublin and back in perfect safety. If anything should happen to him in Scotland … the consequences could be dreadful.'

'For you?' asked the Duke, cannily. Robert, Lord Melville, Viscount Dundas, was a man of influence, whose father had been known colloquially as Harry the Ninth, the uncrowned King of Scotland. But if the real King fell, and in Edinburgh, no doubt Melville's career would not survive him by many days.

'For all of us,' said Melville sharply. 'Never mind penal laws and banning Highland gear, imagine what other restrictions London might lay on us if we allowed a – disaster like that?'

'Wonder how Scott's going to take it?' Atholl said, but just then Sir Walter Scott, his face pale and exhausted behind a bright smile, entered the room and bowed. They were going to find out.

The Murray family arrived at the Queen Street house in the late afternoon, relieved and exhausted.

'When can we take the carriage on the sea again, Papa?' asked little Augusta, though she was half-asleep in her governess' arms.

'When we're going home – back to Letho,' said Murray, probably for the eighteenth time since they had crossed the Forth. The queue for carriage space on the ferry had stretched back, he reckoned, two miles from the harbour, and the locals were doing a roaring trade bringing refreshments directly to the carriage door, at rather more than the usual prices. On the south side of the firth, Queensferry had been frantic with people trying to find a bed for the night, the last cheap night's rest before they reached Edinburgh. The Murrays, knowing their accommodation was assured, ploughed on through the cobbled streets and made for the city.

'I think I'd better settle her for the night,' said the governess, Miss Fitzsimmons.

'I'll make sure there's some warm milk,' said Isobel.

'I'll see to that, ma'am,' said Robbins, and nodded to the young manservant, Matthew. Matthew bowed and vanished. Murray chuckled. The novelty of a well-run household had still not worn off, and he could see in Robbins' luminous eyes that the butler was still enjoying it, too. Robbins had tried his best for years, in the face of some substantial challenges, but it had taken Isobel's arrival to sort things out properly – for now, at any rate. Murray had a suspicion that the natural chaos of the household could only be suppressed successfully for a while.

'The Balfours are in the drawing room,' said Robbins, handing Murray a small batch of cards and letters on a plate, 'but say they have no need to be entertained if you are tired from your journey, sir. They have dined out already.'

'Let us change out of our grubby clothes and have a bite to eat, Robbins, and we'll join them. Mrs. Helliwell, if you would rather retire for the night …?'

The minister's wife looked fatigued, but she smiled.

'I'm not done yet, Mr. Murray! A piece of bread and butter and a cup of tea and I shall be fighting fit!'

'Some broth, then, in the parlour in, say, twenty minutes, Robbins?' suggested Isobel. Robbins bowed. The Murrays and Mrs. Helliwell, followed by Miss Fitzsimmons with a deadweight Augusta, climbed the stairs, and Robbins disappeared behind the baize door of the staff quarters, head busy but heart satisfied.

There was hot water in their rooms – a minor miracle – and maids to attend them, or in Murray's case Robbins, slipping quickly up the back stairs when he had delivered instructions to the kitchen.

'All well, Robbins?'

'Yes, sir, though the town is busy. Mrs. Mack is much relieved that so much food has been brought down from Letho –

she'll be very pleased with the baskets that came today, too, sir. Food – well, everything – is very expensive.'

'Any word of the King?'

'Expected any day, sir, or not at all,' said Robbins drily. Murray smiled. Robbins had evening clothes already laid out, and it was not long before Murray was ready to go back downstairs for his broth.

'Anything else of interest?'

'Three of your notes are from Mr. Blair, sir.' He paused. 'One of your notes, sir, was delivered by a servant in livery.'

'I'm sure,' said Murray, trying to ignore the tone of warning in Robbins' voice. 'Whose? Not the Duke of Atholl, surely? I don't want to have to pretend to be a Highlander!'

'No, sir, not His Grace. My lord Viscount Melville, sir. Lord Dundas.'

'Oh,' said Murray. 'Bother.'

Robbins, satisfied that all was in order for now, returned to the kitchens where the tables were littered with all kinds of provisions brought from Letho. Mrs. Mack, the cook, was actually stroking a cheese when he appeared, and stepped back smartly.

'Oh, Mr. Robbins, did you ever see such fine food!'

'Yes, Mrs. Mack, three days ago before we came to Edinburgh.'

'Aye, but not to have to pay Edinburgh prices for it, too! It's like manna in the desert, is it no?'

'Well …' said Robbins, surveying the table. He thought they were doing rather better than the Israelites, but was saved from voicing an opinion by the appearance of Mrs. Gilmour, the housekeeper.

'All well?' she asked.

'I believe so, Mrs. Gilmour,' said Robbins. 'The family will join the Balfours in the drawing room after a bowl of broth and some bread and butter. Matthew is taking hot milk up to the nursery, and after that I'm sure Miss Fitzsimmons would appreciate some broth, too.'

'I'm sure she would, Mr. Robbins,' said Mrs. Gilmour. 'We'll give her an hour or so to settle Miss Augusta. They'll need all the rest they can get to fortify themselves against all that is going on in the town, won't they?' she added cheerfully, then looked at Robbins' face more carefully.

'Did you give the master the notes from – from those gentlemen?'

'I did,' said Robbins. He liked Mrs. Gilmour well enough, but he was not used to talking freely with her yet. That tended to take a while, with Robbins.

'What did he say?'

'He hadn't opened them,' he said. 'I daresay we'll find out all about it, in due course. Let's hope it's nothing too serious, anyway. If the King comes, we'll be busy enough without any distractions.'

Murray kept glancing at the note out of the corner of his eye.

Should he open it at once? Should he fortify himself with broth and brandy first? Should he rip it up and pretend he had never seen it? The most tempting, that was however the option he should not choose. Melville, like his father, was the most powerful man in Scotland. What had Murray done to attract his attention now?

Chapter Three

MUCH REVIVED BY the broth, with Isobel in a dark green evening gown that became her very well, the Murrays and Mrs. Helliwell went up to the drawing room to greet the Balfours. As kin and neighbours they were easy guests, and had been making themselves free of the Queen Street house for a few days already. Murray had always liked them, Isobel and Mrs. Helliwell knew them well, and they were all about to settle down for a comfortable gossip before supper when there was a commotion in the hall below that could be heard even past the closed doors.

'Oh, it'll be Papa!' cried Isobel, and excused herself to go and see. Murray followed.

The steps outside the house were too much for Blair's wheeled chair, but the Murray household was well-used to receiving Blair and in a few minutes Blair's man Smith and Matthew the footman had Mr. Blair up and into the entrance hall and on to a hall chair, while Robbins carried the wheeled chair in and up the main stairs to the drawing room. In a moment, with their breath back, Smith and Matthew followed with Blair himself, presenting him triumphantly in the drawing room doorway.

'Arriving like the Queen of Sheba!' Blair announced.

'Grander than the King,' agreed Balfour, bowing with a grin.

'Oh, the King! He left Greenwich late today, they say,' said Blair. He made his bows to the company while he was on his feet, then, using two sticks, he made his way to a place on a sopha, ignoring his wheeled chair. 'I like a change,' he said.

'Then he really is on his way?' asked Mrs. Balfour. 'Is – is that woman with him?'

'Lady Conyngham?' said Isobel, naming the King's latest,

and very unpopular, mistress 'I hope not.'

'My informants did not know,' said Blair sadly. 'But her husband is, for he's Lord Steward of the Royal Household, so he has to come.'

'I don't know how any respectable Scottish household might be expected to welcome her,' said Mrs. Balfour.

'From what I hear,' said her husband, for everyone was well informed on everything to do with the King just now, 'she had no wish to come to Scotland anyway. She wanted to go with the King to Vienna, but the Foreign Secretary's wife cannot abide her.'

'And such a strange way of spelling their surname!' added Mrs. Balfour, as though that were the final straw in the matter. 'Irish, I suppose.'

'Whether they come or not, either or both of them,' said Isobel, clearly feeling the conversation needed turning, 'the town is *en fête*, is it not? Papa, have you anything new to tell us? Surely not! Everything possible seems to have happened already, apart from the arrival of the King himself!'

'Have you been out, yet?' asked Blair. 'Have you seen all the Highlanders? All the weaponry? There are some that fear an uprising, you know: it's only a couple of years since all that trouble. What if there is some kind of attack on the King?'

Murray shifted uncomfortably. The note from Viscount Dundas seemed to hum in his pocket.

'Everyone seems to be feeling very patriotic,' he said. 'And good-humoured. Not that we saw much on our way from Queensferry – some Highlanders drilling in the gardens – but the way here was packed with carriages of people eager to see the King – and not, I think, to rise against him.'

'Sir Walter Scott has been very clever,' said Blair. 'He has persuaded everyone that King George is the rightful descendant of the ancient Scottish kings, and the clan chief of all of us. It is a remarkable piece of work.'

'But there will be some who will be harder to persuade, I'm sure,' said Isobel, frowning. Her conversational turn had taken a dark edge, and she tried to rescue the evening again. 'Mrs. Balfour, will you play for us?'

Everyone but Blair had taken a turn at the fortepiano by the time Robbins arrived to announce supper, and the footman and

Smith carried Blair back downstairs to the dining room.

After supper, as the others went back upstairs, Murray drew Blair into his library across the hall for a quick word.

'Your talk of an attack on the King seems apposite,' he said. Blair, perched on a hard chair, jiggled his remaining leg and scowled.

'You know of something?'

'I received a note on our arrival from Viscount Melville.'

Blair's eyes widened.

'Again?'

'Well, it has been – what, eight years since his father last sought my help, that one time?[1] And at the time I believed he was so unimpressed by the result that he would never ask me to do anything again. Or recommend me to his son.'

'And you were so upset by the whole business, Charles, that you left the country.'

Murray winced. He had indeed fled, first to Italy, then to India. It had not been a happy period in his life, though there had been some benefits to it.

'And when I returned, the whole thing seemed forgotten about, much to my relief,' he said. 'I have never heard from the Dundases from that day to this. Nor had I hoped or expected to.'

'But what does he want now, then?' Blair was impatient.

'Of course he does not say much,' said Murray, taking the note from his pocket. 'He would be concerned about leaving information around on paper. But he wants me to meet him at Holyroodhouse tomorrow morning, as a matter of urgency, he says. A matter of a possible threat to the safety of the King.'

'Goodness!' said Blair. 'I suppose you're going to go?'

'I suppose I'd better,' said Murray.

The next day was Sunday. Murray felt guilty at inviting a minister's wife to stay with them, and then hurrying off before church to an unspecified meeting, but Melville was clearly an early riser – or was keen to attend church himself. He had summoned Murray for half-past seven in the morning. Murray, in his Sunday

[1] See *Fellowship with Demons.*

best and a state of nerves, decided to walk down to the Palace to calm himself. After all, he was eight years older now, a mature and married man, a father, and not in a position to be bullied even by Harry the Ninth, never mind his son.

He strode through the New Town, up North Bridge and left at the Tron to go down the lower portion of the Royal Mile, where every house and shop was decorated and then covered with stands for viewing whatever there might be to view. Even at this hour of the morning, one or two were lounging on the scaffolding, watching the world go by at its early Sunday pace. Murray suspected they were lookouts, in case something might start happening without the household realising.

The Mile curled downwards, narrow enough for any kind of procession: people could lean out of their windows and drop flowers on the King's head, he reckoned – or whatever else they might want to drop. What had Melville found? And why did he think Murray could help?

The walls of the Palace gradually appeared as he rounded the last corner, the old Abbey and its additions tucked into the flank of Salisbury Crags for shelter. Looking to his left, Murray saw he had not needed to climb up to the Tron: there was a new road now, that seemed to sweep around to Calton Hill, or thereabouts. He might investigate on his way back. To his right, the road that skirted Arthur's Seat, the great extinct volcano that pinned Edinburgh in place, had been marked out now with what looked like lamp stands. Clearly no expense had been spared at all, and Murray wondered who exactly was paying for all of it.

It was twenty-five past seven precisely, according to his own watch, when Murray presented himself to the soldier guarding the main gate.

'Charles Murray of Letho to see Viscount Melville,' he said, slightly louder than necessary. 'I'm expected.'

'Yes, sir, you are,' said the soldier, his accent from the midlands of England. 'Arnold here'll take you through, sir.'

Another soldier, who seemed to have been standing waiting entirely for the purpose, stood smartly and turned to lead Murray into the heart of the palace.

Murray could only remember having been inside the building once before, when he was small. His father had brought him to visit … someone, he could not remember who, who had had a grace and favour apartment here for a few years. The someone had kept two terriers, and Murray remembered being impressed by the number of rats the dogs had chased in the course of their short visit. The apartment had smelled very bad, and it had taken a day or two before Murray had been able to rid his nose of the odour which, now he was older, he knew had been rot and mould and poor ventilation.

But in no part of his memory had Holyroodhouse looked the way it did this morning. There was a very great deal of gilding, on every possible ornament, standing out particularly sharply against walls of a kind of dun colour. Not that much of the dun was visible, for all kinds of tapestries and silks had been hung against them, some of them, Murray suspected, not quite as venerable as they looked. Everything was swept and dusted, fresh matting laid on worn stone floors, bowls of dried rose petals on stands in the corners, fresh flowers in abundance wherever there was room. Murray suspected they had even managed to open a few windows here and there: the place smelled unexpectedly airy.

'Fit for a King, do you think?'

Murray started. The soldier Arnold, guiding Murray along yet another narrow passage, had deposited him at an open doorway and abandoned him. Inside the room beyond were four men, standing about a cluttered little parlour. The one who had spoken was clearly Viscount Melville.

'My lord,' said Murray, and bowed.

'Charles Murray of Letho,' said Melville, turning to the man by the empty fireplace and waving at Murray. Murray gulped, recognising him from portraits he had seen here and there – well-built and strong-looking, with an outdoor face and short grey hair. The Duke of Atholl.

'Your grace,' he said dutifully. His clan chief, said some part of his mind looking for humour in the situation. The Duke, as far as he could see, was not wearing a scrap of tartan.

'And these are Lieutenant Colonel Benjamin Stephenson, Surveyor General,' the tall, thin man by the window bowed like an artist's easel come to life; 'Mr. Thomas Mash, of the Lord Chamberlain's Office,' a sleek, scowling individual doing his best not to touch anything; 'and,' added Melville, as another man, on the diminutive side, suddenly appeared from behind the sopha, 'Mr.

Trotter, His Majesty's Upholsterer in Scotland.' Mr. Trotter bowed low. He had a measuring stick in one hand, and a worried expression on his face. Murray tried, and failed, to work out what it was Melville thought he could do for, or with, this strange selection of men. Melville himself had a look of just about coping with a trying situation. The Duke merely seemed annoyed. Murray waited.

'His Majesty the King left Greenwich yesterday evening,' said Melville, 'and is expected to arrive in Edinburgh on Wednesday. Of course he will not stay here, at Holyroodhouse.'

'Entirely unsuitable,' put in the Duke. Mr. Trotter gave an audible sigh.

'The Duke of Buccleuch has offered the use of Dalkeith Palace for the King's accommodation, but events, of course, in this, er, pageant …' Melville and the Duke exchanged glances. Melville cleared his throat. 'Tradition decrees that certain events should happen here, as the King's residence in Scotland.'

This time Murray was sure that it was the scowling Thomas Mash who sighed. And possibly tutted. The room seemed to abound with general dissatisfaction.

'We had believed the renovation to be nearing completion, when Colonel Stephenson and Mr. Trotter happened upon yet another set of rooms, this one, which had not yet been inspected. And, well, in short …' Melville cleared his throat again, and cast a glare around the parlour which seemed to encompass everyone and everything in it, 'they found a body.'

Chapter Four

'A BODY,' MURRAY repeated. 'That's very unfortunate, my lord.'

Melville snorted.

'You have a way with understatement, Mr. Murray. I want Colonel Stephenson and Mr. Trotter to tell you exactly what they found and how, and then I shall explain to you the precise nature of our … misfortune, and the service we require of you.'

Thomas Mash, he of the scowl and the tuts, spoke up as if he were continuing a discussion that Murray's arrival had interrupted. He had a cultivated voice.

'I still think we should have John Townsend in, my lord. He would know what to do more than any Scot.'

'Do you, Mr. Mash?' Melville's tone was not encouraging. 'Well, we shall see. Now, Stephenson, now, Trotter: tell Mr. Murray what happened.'

'We found these rooms on Friday, sir,' said Trotter, stepping forward neatly. 'It's that kind of a building. There are always rooms appearing from nowhere.'

'I thought you had that architect helping you?' asked the Duke.

'Yes, your Grace, but I think the place is beyond the reasoning of a modern architect.'

'Never mind that,' said Melville. 'What did you find?'

'A tapestry at the end of that short passage,' said Trotter, pointing to the door, 'and the door behind it. The handle looked well used and the rooms were not … unclean. I'd say they had been lived in until recently.'

'Which they had,' said Mash, keen to participate. 'They were the rooms allotted to Anna Ochill, who, along with the other denizens of this – this place, was requested to leave by order of the King on the twenty-sixth of July. She should have done so forthwith.'

'Mr. Trotter, pray continue,' said Melville, not looking at Mash. Had he really said 'Mash'? Murray wondered suddenly. Surely Nash was a more common name?

'Thank you, my lord,' said Trotter. 'We came in here and looked about, and noticed the smell – well, most of the place smells bad, but somehow this seemed worse. I noticed this other door,' he went on, pointing to one side, 'and opened it. And that's where we found her.'

'Her?' asked Murray. 'You mean Mrs. Ochill?'

'We didn't know, sir. We just knew she was dead.'

Murray looked at Colonel Stephenson. Stephenson blinked, and nodded.

'Was this …' how to phrase it? '… an unexpected death?'

'She was above middle years, certainly,' said Melville, quick to understand, 'but I daresay she did not expect a knife in her heart.'

'I daresay not, my lord,' agreed Murray. He hesitated again. 'I take it she's not still in there?'

'Good heavens, no, man!' said Melville. 'We had her removed to a room near the ruined abbey. But she is still there, if you wish to take a closer look.'

'Preferably soon,' said the Duke, with emphasis.

'Before the King arrives, certainly,' said Melville. 'Even though I can't see him bothering to inspect an abbey.'

'Ah … thank you,' said Murray, not quite sure why he was being accorded such particular treatment. 'May I look in the bedchamber? I take it that's what it is.'

The men stepped back to allow Murray to look. The window shutters were open, the bed unclothed, a night table standing open and empty as if the last thing anyone had snatched as they left was the chamber pot. The stone floor, bare of any rugs or matting, bore traces of a dark stain, but if the woman had died there her clothing must have absorbed most of the blood. Or she had been dead when she was stabbed, or she had not died on that spot, said part of Murray's mind, leaping on with an investigation he had not yet really been asked to take up. Even women past their middle years had more blood than that in them.

'Did you see anyone else around this part of the palace?' Murray asked Mr. Trotter. The little man tilted his head to one side.

'It's hard to say,' he said. 'We've had workmen everywhere. And as you can see, we're on the ground floor. The shutters in the parlour were closed and latched, but the ones in here were open.'

The bedroom window was mullioned, though, which would have made it hard for any reasonably-sized attacker to climb in.

'Was the main door locked?'

'No, not at all. The handle was a bit shoogly but the door opened easily. It's just old,' he added.

'Everything's old,' said Mr. Mash in disgust.

'Have you moved anything, or taken anything out of these rooms, apart from the body?' Murray asked. But everyone was shaking their heads.

'Nothing at all,' said Mr. Trotter. 'Though I'd like to get started on them, my lord.'

'I doubt the King will venture this far,' said Melville. 'Right, off you go. Thank you,' he added, as Stephenson and Trotter made their way round the furniture to the door. 'You, too, Mash,' he added. Mash made an elaborate bow, and followed the other two as though they were his ceremonial guard. Melville nodded at the door, and Murray obediently went to make sure it was properly shut. Then he returned to the centre of the room, and waited.

'I said in my note,' Melville began, 'that we feared for the King's safety. I should explain to you how that comes about. Perhaps we could risk taking a seat?'

He tried one of the small armchairs by the fireplace, and the Duke took the other. Murray sat on the sopha. The upholstery was cold, and faintly damp. The last time he had been summoned by a Viscount Melville he had not been allowed to sit at all.

'Mrs. Ochill was not unknown to me,' said Melville, 'though I had only met her once or twice. She was a widow, and was granted use of these rooms some seven or eight years ago, following the death of her husband.'

'Damn' shame, throwing all these people out,' said the Duke. 'Pensioners, and so on. Obligations. Though I wouldn't fancy living here myself.'

Most of them would have gone to stay with family, Murray supposed, if they had any. He imagined few would have had much money of their own. Where had Mrs. Ochill gone, if anywhere?

Melville cast a glance at the Duke, and went on.

'Her late husband, John Ochill, was, in a manner of speaking, in the service of the King. A government man.'

'In a manner of speaking, my lord?'

Melville looked uncharacteristically uncomfortable.

'He was, not to put too fine a point upon it, a spy. Eight years ago he met his end in circumstances which might have looked, to an outsider, like a street robbery that ended badly. To all who knew the nature of his business, it looked like murder.'

He paused, and rubbed at a mark on the upholstered arm of his chair, then inspected his fingertip with distaste.

'We decided that, in recognition of his service, and his sacrifice in the course of it, that his widow should be offered accommodation here, which, as you know, she took up. I had thought that she, too, considered her husband's death to have been an accident, and that she had no very clear idea of how it was that he earned his money, but I may have been mistaken. It may be that she was killed by the same person who murdered her husband. Someone who, by the very nature of that incident, must be believed to wish harm to the King, detriment to Scotland, and serious risk to the Union.'

'And who was that, my lord?'

'We have no idea.'

Thinking that he would really rather be walking to church with his wife on his arm, Murray allowed himself to be led to the ruined abbey, now open to the elements. A wooden hut was tucked against one wall, and may have been used by stonemasons attempting repairs, for there were still some tools inside and a few pieces of newly worked stone outside. It was poorly lit, though, for any kind of work.

The woman lay on a trestle table with a sheet over her. Closer inspection showed dun paint across the foot of the sheet, and Murray suspected it had been used recently to cover furniture during the redecorations. Somewhere along their walk through the awkward passages of the palace Melville had acquired a physician, presumably his own, who must have been waiting for them. Now three men stood around the shrouded form while the Duke of Atholl, making himself useful, wielded a taper to light as many candles as he could find. At a nod from Melville, the doctor lifted the sheet from the woman's head and pulled it right down to rest at her feet in a dun and white heap.

A woman, indeed, above middle years. She lay with her eyes and mouth wide open, as though drawing breath for a scream. Murray saw that there was some damage around her soft lips and eyelids – the famous palace rats? He looked quickly away from her face: it would not do to make a fool of himself in front of Melville, never mind why he had been summoned here.

Her lace cap had slipped a little, showing curling grey hair. She was fully dressed in a gown and boots, as if she had been spending her day in her apartments. Black lace mitts covered the backs of her hands but not her fingers, so that he could see two moderately valuable-looking rings, one on each hand. The folds of her fichu disclosed a necklace, silver, but intricately worked around a small cairngorm. Her killer was not a random house-breaker, then. Or palace-breaker.

'It looks as if she has not been touched, except to carry her here,' said Murray.

'I believe that is the case,' said Melville.

'She has not been dead more than a couple of days,' said the doctor. 'There is not much decay. The rooms were not warm, I take it?'

'The fireplace was bare,' said Murray. 'And the rooms faced north.'

'A couple of days,' repeated Melville. 'Yesterday, or Friday, perhaps? The ninth.'

'A knife wound in her breast,' murmured the doctor. 'Or no, actually, below her ribcage. Substantial bleeding.'

The front of the woman's skirts, which had been grey, was black with blood, as Murray had anticipated. Her hands and her white cuffs – and presumably the mitts, though they did not show it – were badly stained, as though she had clutched at the knife as it went in. Blood had splashed upwards, too, on to her linen fichu, presumably as she fell.

'It was a knife, was it?' Murray asked politely. 'Only it isn't here.'

The woman's blue eyes, wide with horror, seemed shocked

at the idea. The doctor looked up at him.

'Hard to say, in truth, until I look more closely. Or we find the weapon. But something like a knife.'

'We'll have to remove her clothing, check for other injuries,' said Murray. 'Is there a maid here who could help us?'

The doctor blinked. Melville stepped outside, and in a moment returned.

'One will be here shortly.'

They waited. Murray went on with his observation of the clothing he could see.

'She has a tartan sash,' he said. 'Presumably once we undo it we can see what the pattern is.'

'Not that it matters just now,' said the Duke gloomily. 'Everyone's wearing anything.'

'Was she to take a part in any of the celebrations?' asked Murray.

'I can find out,' said Melville. 'It's possible. As far as I remember, the couple did hail from the Highlands, somewhere.'

'What, real Highlanders?' asked the Duke. 'Scott would have had her installed somewhere to add to his pageant!'

'Where was her husband killed?' Murray asked. He assumed that Melville would trust the doctor.

'Here, in Edinburgh. I should be able to find the report for you to peruse.'

'Thank you, my lord. Um … it seems that you want me to find out more about this poor woman's death? Is that the case?'

'Of course. What did you think?'

Murray did not point out that he was not quite sure what to think, bereft, as usual, of any kind of explanation. And at that moment, the maid came in, and he was saved the effort of a reply.

Chapter Five

ONE GLANCE SHOWED that this was not going to be a maid who threw a fit at the sight of a dead body. The woman who appeared and curtseyed in the doorway had the slim figure of a girl, but the candlelight soon revealed a face lined with age and experience, intelligent eyes and a discreet mouth. When asked, she gave her name as Helen.

'Have you prepared corpses for burial before, Helen?' asked the doctor.

'Plenty, over the years, sir.'

'This woman has died a violent death. I hope this will not shock you.'

The maid moved forward to see more clearly. Murray watched her take in first the blood, then the wound, then, slowly, the face.

'Is that no Mrs. Ochill, sir?'

'It is, I'm afraid,' said the doctor, not unkindly. 'Did you know her well?'

'I cleaned her rooms, sir, and brought in her coals and took away her slops – the usual, sir.'

The doctor looked up and caught Melville's eye. Melville shrugged slightly.

'None better, then,' he said.

'Shall I fetch hot water and cloths, then, sir?' Helen asked the doctor.

'Yes, do that.'

Murray waited until Helen had gone out again, then said,

'I'll need to talk to her later, when we're finished here.'

'I'll make sure she's available,' said Melville.

'Can we keep all her clothes and jewellery somewhere safe for now, too?' Murray decided to make his demands now, while he could. 'And I'll need to make a more careful examination of her rooms.'

'Haven't you seen all you need to see?' snapped Melville, then seemed to reconsider. 'Of course. I'll take the jewellery for now, and make sure Trotter and Stephenson don't slap their dun paint over everything before you're finished. But the quicker you are, the better.'

'Of course, my lord.'

Helen returned with a clatter of buckets and a sack of cloths, and she and the doctor set to, carefully removing each of Mrs. Ochill's garments and laying them aside. Melville produced a cloth bag from his pocket and held it out for the jewellery, and Murray made sure he listed each item as it was removed. The maid and the doctor worked almost silently, only a murmured comment or instruction here or there, and there was an air of solemnity and respect to the procedure. In a little while, Anna Ochill lay exposed on the table, and it was clear to see that the wound, by knife or other blade, was the only cause of her death.

'The bruises on her back will be from where she fell when she was stabbed,' said the doctor. 'She had rheumatism in her knees, I believe.'

'She did complain of sore knees when the weather turned,' Helen said quietly, her gaze still on the body. 'She kept worrying about curtseying.'

'Nothing else to be discovered?' asked Melville briskly.

'Cuts inside her fingers, my lord, from the blade,' said the doctor, pointing to the bare hands. 'It's only natural to want to defend oneself.'

'Facing her attacker,' said the Duke, who had not spoken for some time. 'She would have seen him clearly. Taken by surprise? Or was it someone she knew?'

'Your kinsman here will find out, no doubt,' said Melville, gesturing to Murray. Murray tried not to look surprised. 'Well, Murray, I shall send you that report. We'll leave you here now and, as I say, the sooner you finish with those apartments the better.' He was about to leave when there was a knock on the door. Melville stepped outside, but Murray could hear the man from the Lord

Chamberlain's office, Thomas Mash, with his self-important tones.

'My lord! I must ask you to step in. The whole procession tomorrow – the matter of the Honours of Scotland – surely it must be plain even to Sir Walter Scott that this is the prerogative of the Lord Chamberlain? And yet he has taken the whole thing into his hands when –'

'Mr. Mash, if you have questions about what Sir Walter is doing I suggest it would be a better use of your time and mine if you approach Sir Walter with them.'

'But I have, my lord! I have, and he nods and smiles and nothing is done! That is if one can even enter his house, for it is full – full of dogs and Highlanders!'

'Oh!' The Duke poked his head out of the doorway to join the conversation. 'Does he still have that splendid deerhound that Glengarry gave him? Wonderful animal!'

And somehow the door closed behind Atholl and Melville, and Murray was left in the little room with the maid, the doctor, and the corpse of Anna Ochill.

Thinking to kill two birds with one stone, once Mrs. Ochill had been prepared for burial and left in the care of the doctor, Murray asked Helen to accompany him back to the apartments formerly occupied by Mrs. Ochill. If nothing else, he was sure that without the maid he would never have found his way back to them.

'The order to vacate the apartments came on 26th July, I believe?' he asked her, when they had arrived at the dingy little parlour.

'Yes, sir, I think that was the date. We had a deal to do, for of course everyone was moving out at once.'

'Were people upset?'

She made a face.

'Lots of them, sir. I mean, it's not much of a place, when you're in it, but to say you live in a royal palace! That means a lot to some of them. And then, well, not everyone had somewhere to go. And there's not much room in Edinburgh just now, is there? So some of them who had thought they'd be right here, on the spot, when the King came – if the King comes – were awful disappointed. But there were a few thought it was all part of the honour of living here. How many people can say they had to move out because the

King wanted their rooms?'

It was not an angle Murray had thought to look from.

'And what about Mrs. Ochill? What were her feelings on the matter?'

'Well ... she was worried, more than anything. She didn't have anywhere to go. No family, and I think all her friends lived in here.'

'Could none of them have taken her to stay wherever they were staying? With their families?'

'I'm not sure, sir. But she packed up her stuff, or I packed it up for her, and I supposed it would have been the end of July when she ordered a hand cart and went off. She said she'd see me again soon. I think she thought they would all just move back in after the King has gone. But I don't know if that will happen or not, do you, sir?'

'I have absolutely no idea,' said Murray honestly. 'Have you any idea where she did go?'

'None, sir.'

'Why would she have come back?'

'I don't know, sir. Maybe she left something behind? Though I think we cleared the place completely, sir. We gave it all a last look round between us.'

Murray glanced at the aged and warped panelling on the walls, and secret compartments came to mind. But whatever one hid in there would have to be rat-proof, anyway. Perhaps she had just missed the old place. Perhaps she had arranged to meet someone.

'Did she have any particular friends here? Or anyone who came to visit her from outside?'

'As to visitors from outside, sir, not that I know of, but I might not know. She never mentioned anyone regular. Her closest friend in here was Mrs. McGregor. She lived – well, you could almost say next door, I suppose.'

'Were there any enmities amongst the people here?'

Helen's mouth twisted a little, and he thought she was suppressing a grin.

'Oh, aye, sir, from time to time. Some of them are very grand, and some of them think they should have special treatment, or that someone else is getting things they're not getting, you ken, sir?'

'Are they mostly elderly? Are there any younger pensioners here, or families?'

'Mostly elderly, sir. It's as well for them to be in here, when they have no family to look after them. The rooms are nae up to much, as you see, but at least they're fed and cleaned and warmed and kept an eye on, and they have a bit of company. Aye, there's some'll miss it badly, sir.'

'And would you happen to know where Mrs. McGregor has gone?'

He waited for yet another negative, but after a moment Helen beamed.

'Yes, sir! I do. It took me a second, sir, for they're all over the place. She's gone to stay with her nephew – or is it her great nephew? One or the other.'

'Any idea where?'

'Aye, sir, for she was that pleased! He's just at the foot of the Castle Hill, where it meets the Lawnmarket. I dinna mind how many times she's said to me about the great view she'll have when the processions go to the Castle. She said her nephew – or her great-nephew, whichever it is – will make his fortune over the thing, and she'd have a better view of the King from her nephew's window than she would ever have, stuck in here – except for the Drawing Room, of course.'

Murray, about to ask for the nephew's name – or the great-nephew's – paused.

'The drawing room?'

'Aye, sir, it's to be next week, if the King gets here. There's that much to be done for it – and everything else. The trouble is, as soon as we clean something yon Mr. Trotter has it painted, and we have to wait and clean it again.'

'Do you mean the reception for the ladies?' Murray asked, trying to recall all Blair had written to them about the various social occasions planned for the King's visit. 'Was Mrs. McGregor to go to that?'

'Well, sir, yes, I think so. Sir Walter Scott sent word to say that if there were any true Highland ladies staying here in the apartments they were to apply to attend the Drawing Room. Mrs. McGregor showed me the letter with his signature on it and everything.'

'Well, that will surely give her a good view of His Majesty,' said Murray. 'Do you know the name of the kinsman she's staying with? I'd like to talk to her. She might know where Mrs. Ochill was staying.'

'Aye, sir, he's a man named Boot. I think he makes spectacles, or some such. But there canna be many men up the Castle Hill called Boot, can there, sir?'

After poking the damp upholstery of the furniture and testing all the wooden panelling for secret compartments – Murray decided that the general state of the woodwork would have put anyone off using them anyway – he left the apartments and instructed Helen to pass on word to Colonel Stephenson and Mr. Trotter that they could gild and paint whatever they wanted. He wondered if he might later regret his haste, but he had a strong feeling that the apartment could tell him nothing. Helen, on the other hand, might still be useful.

Outside in the fresh air he drew out his watch and opened it. He was indeed late for church, but he suspected that Mrs. McGregor in Castle Hill might still be at her worship, and he wanted to go home and tell Isobel what was happening. He would leave the pensioner until a more appropriate time for calling on a Sunday, and attend to his family first.

He was about to stride over to the gate when another man emerged from the Palace's main entrance, passed where he was standing, then stopped to look back as if inspecting Murray with interest. For once, Murray did not feel he had the advantage of size over the stranger, who wore a straw-coloured wig under a wide-brimmed hat, and a bright scarlet waistcoat. Before he could say anything, the stranger bowed to an angle permitted by his comfortable stomach.

'John Townsend, of the Bow Street Runners, at your service, sir.'

A London policeman? Murray raised his eyebrows.

'Charles Murray of Letho, at yours.'

'I thought so,' said the man with satisfaction. 'I always put my powers of observation to good use, you see, sir. I believe you have been asked to look into the death of that poor woman? Mrs. Ockill?'

'News travels quickly, Mr. Townsend.'

'Of course if I can at any time put my expertise at your disposal, sir,' said Townsend. 'I doubt you have much experience of this kind of thing so far north – battles and so on, no doubt, but a mysterious death is another thing, wouldn't you say, sir?'

'It certainly did not seem to be the result of a battle, no.' The man's smugness was irritating, but he might prove to be useful at some point, Murray thought. 'Do you know anything of the case?'

'It's not my job, sir,' said Townsend. 'But I shall be observing, in the course of my duties, in any case. If I make any observations that might be of assistance to you, I'll pass them on, sir.'

'Very kind of you,' said Murray. 'Until then, I shall bid you good day.'

'Sir,' said the large man, and tried another bow. It was no more successful than the first, but his smile remained, and seemed to follow Murray across the forecourt and out into the Canongate.

He took the new road round to the foot of Calton Hill, finding it as crowded on the Sabbath as he would expect on a weekday. Calton Hill itself was covered in people, he saw, looking up at its uneven slopes. Little clutches of observers stood staring out to sea, waiting, presumably, for the first glimpse of the royal yacht and its escort – if they only left Greenwich yesterday evening the spectators would need a good telescope to see it yet. There were even – good gracious! – tents on the hillside. People must be solving the accommodation problems in any way they could think of.

By the time he reached home in Queen Street, Melville had been busy. In a broad white wrapping on the hall table he found the report into Mr. Ochill's death, with a note reminding Murray, in a manner that called to mind Melville's sternest expression, that it would be much appreciated if this whole matter could be cleared up before the King's arrival in Edinburgh. Murray blinked. Suddenly Greenwich seemed a good deal closer.

Chapter Six

'YOU'VE BEEN ASKED to do what?'

Isobel did not look entirely pleased at the honour conferred on Murray. Murray did not blame her.

'She was murdered in Holyroodhouse, in one of the apartments there. Apparently her husband was murdered, too, in 1814, here in Edinburgh.'

'A family failing, then,' said Isobel. 'What has it to do with you?'

'You know – I've told you – that Viscount Melville, the first one, this one's father, asked me to look into a mystery before. You remember?'

'Yes, the Dundases were involved – some unsuitable girl, wasn't it? But that was long ago. And I thought you told me that Viscount Melville's father was not particularly pleased with the way you did it, or the answer you came up with, or something.'

'That's what I thought. His son must be desperate.'

'Well, if he really is, why can't it wait? I hate to sound missish, but Augusta and I – and Mrs. Helliwell – have come to town to see the King and all the pageantry, and I had rather hoped I might be seeing it all with you.'

'The trouble is he wants it all sorted out before the King arrives,' said Murray. He wanted more than anything to cross the room and take Isobel in his arms, but he had a feeling that now was not the moment. 'The Duke of Atholl was there, too,' he added, hoping to intrigue her.

'Oh, so now you are to do the bidding of your Clan Chief?' she said. 'You've been in Edinburgh less than a day, and already you are turned Highlander!' There was the least twitch of a smile to her lips, but she quickly quashed it. Instead she tapped her fingers on the windowsill, a brief tattoo of dissatisfaction. 'When do they think the King will arrive?'

'Not before Tuesday, they say,' said Murray at once. 'I have two days.'

'After which you will be at liberty to attend any and all of the planned events – so far as Lowlanders are permitted – with Augusta and me?'

'Of course. If I find the killer.'

She sighed.

'Two days. That's not very long, actually, is it?'

'Not really, no.'

'You'll need some help.'

'It would be much appreciated,' said Murray, with feeling.

'We'd better make a start, then,' she said. 'Shall I send word to Papa?'

'Yes,' said Murray, 'and I shall call Robbins. Even if they can do nothing practical, their opinions are of great value.'

'And if we need them later, we won't have to explain it all from the start,' added Isobel sensibly. 'Is that the report Viscount Melville sent you? Then read it now, and be ready to tell us all when we are assembled.' She left the window and went to ring the bell. 'As if my father were not thrilled enough with everything that is happening: this will be the crowning glory for him! But not so happy for that poor woman.'

With Blair summoned and Robbins informed as to their plans, Murray went to his book room to sit in peace and read. In fact, there was little need: Mrs. Helliwell, Augusta, Miss Fitzsimmons and the Balfours had all gone for a walk up Calton Hill to look out for the Royal Flotilla (which Murray prayed they would not see for a couple of days yet), and Isobel was sitting in the drawing room window, sketching odd scenes she could see in the gardens across the road. Murray opened the wrapping again and drew out the report along with Melville's note. He saw there was something additional on the back, which Melville had presumably thought of after the note was folded and sealed.

'Pray call on Sir Walter Scott, 39 Castle Street, to keep him appraised of your progress. He has been informed of the discovery.'

Well, that would be interesting, anyway. Murray turned to the report.

It was not clear who had written the report, nor for whom: Murray was quite sure it had not been some junior officer in the city police, anyway. The hand and the vocabulary were educated, the tone respectful but with a certain liberty of expression. The paper was good, too – perhaps this was an office copy, and not the original. It was dated at the top 'October 6th, '14'. Murray reflected that when these events had happened, the political world was unstable. Bonaparte was on Elba, but not trusted to stay there. He read on.

'We write to inform you,' it began without salutation, 'that one of our associates, John Ochill, was found dead two days ago. Circumstances indicate that this was not a natural or accidental death.

'Mr. Ochill, as you know, had been engaged for some time in the city in eliminating any lingering interest in the Highlands in supporting the French, not something we had considered to be a venture fraught with much hazard. He had for the most part been working alone, as the work was not onerous and as a Highlander himself he might be considered to be, as it were, among his own people. He had not reported to this office for some weeks, and we were much surprised to receive a note yesterday from his widow to announce his death.

'We have consulted with the city police office and have discovered that Mr. Ochill was found in a short alleyway between Rose Street and George Street on the morning of the fourth *instanter* –' Murray broke off briefly. He had not, for some reason, imagined that John Ochill had been killed in the New Town. Secret government work seemed better fitted to the narrow pends of the Old Town. 'He had been stabbed, and appeared to have died quickly and on that spot. The weapon was not present. He was found by a water caddie at dawn, but not identified for some hours as he was not local to the area (he had been living for some years in New Assembly Close off the High Street).' Murray smiled – at least the man had lived in the Old Town, even if he had not died there.

'Our further enquiries concerning Mr. Ochill's death have been markedly unfruitful. No one claims to have seen or heard anything, neither gentry nor merchants nor servants in that immediate area. Mrs. Ochill told our representative that her husband had gone out the previous evening at around seven and was expected back to supper, but never appeared. He gave no indication as to where he was going or whom he might be meeting. A man whose shop has a side door into the alley is sure that there was nothing in the alley when he returned to the flat above his premises at ten. It may be presumed, then, that Mr. Ochill was assaulted after that hour. The immediate area, so far as was practical, was searched for the weapon or any other clues, but without success.

'Mrs. Ochill was persuaded to allow us to examine her husband's cabinet where he was in the habit of keeping his papers. In it we found a list of those he was currently investigating, but no notes as to his intentions on the evening of his death. The list is appended.' Murray checked and found that indeed there was a list of names, glued with some sealing wax to the back of the document he was reading. 'None was staying very close to where his body was found. As far as Mrs. Ochill could judge, although she said she knew little of his work, nothing was missing, either from the cabinet or from her husband's person.

'Note: Mrs. Ochill's circumstances are considerably affected by her husband's death and consequent loss of income. It seems he had made but little provision for her future. There are no children. Might it be possible, in view of the probable circumstances of Mr. Ochill's death, *id est*, in our direct service, to find some small apartment and a modest pension for her? The outlay need not be very great and there is no purpose to her remaining in Edinburgh if something suitable and inexpensive can be found elsewhere.'

Here the writer's limited generosity came to an end, for there was no signature or farewell. Murray was convinced that this was a copy, possibly made up only to send to him for information. The list on the back was in the same hand, which convinced him further – a copy again, by the same clerk. He looked at it briefly, decided he needed someone who knew more about Highland families, locked it in the drawer of his desk and went to find Isobel.

'Has your father replied yet?' he asked when he found her, still drawing at the window.

'Straightaway,' she replied. 'He is coming to dinner: he had an engagement this afternoon.'

'Then I shall go and see if I can find this woman at the foot of the Castle Hill, the one who was friends with Mrs. Ochill at

Holyrood. I should be back in time to change for dinner.'

He kissed the top of her head, then decided that was not quite sufficient. The drawing paper was laid aside for a long moment, before he once again bade her goodbye and Isobel returned, smiling, to observe the scenes outside.

The Lawnmarket, the part of the Royal Mile that led up from the Bridges and the Tron, past the High Kirk of St. Giles, to the foot of Castle Hill, was rarely quiet. The lawcourts and the council chambers lay on either side, the sprawl of little market stalls known as luckenbooths attracted all kinds of trade, the Tron itself was busy with fruit and vegetables, and whatever regiment happened to be stationed at the Castle made its presence felt on a regular basis. Shops lined both sides of the street, half their goods out on the pavement, and tenements towered over them. And that was when no monarch had happened to threaten a visit, and the street had not been earmarked as one of the grand processional routes for the occasion.

Even Murray, tall enough to see over people's heads for upcoming obstacles, found progress difficult. In fact he was stuck entirely for a few minutes at the head of New Assembly Close, where the ill-fated Mr. Ochill had lived – along with the even more ill-fated Mrs. Ochill. He doubted if there would be much to see there now that would help to find out her killer, but there might, he supposed, still be a neighbour in residence. Ochill's murder had only been eight years ago, after all. It might be worth making enquiries, however thorough Melville's report might have been. But first he wanted to find out more about Mrs. Ochill.

Helen, the maid at Holyroodhouse, had been quite right: there seemed to be only one Mr. Boot dwelling at the foot of Castle Hill. Murray was directed to a doorway painted a cheerful green (in honour of the royal occasion, perhaps, for he could smell the paint), but he had to bend low under a rank of scaffolding to reach it. He rattled the risp vigorously to make himself heard over all the noise from the street, and in a moment was admitted and taken upstairs to a small, bare parlour, with hard chairs around the walls.

'This is the viewing room, sir,' said Mr. Boot, bowing once again as he reversed into the room in front of Murray. 'As you can see, the windows are generously sized for access to the viewing platform outside, and everyone can be most comfortable – and if you'll be kind enough to step over to the window, sir, you can see that the views of the street below and to either side are unsurpassed. As a Londoner myself, sir, I am well used to viewing Royal occasions of all kinds and have set up this apartment and the viewing platform just as they would be in the Capital. Every convenience has been thought of, sir, and as near as can ever be to all that is happening below. His Majesty will be able to take a flower from your good lady's very hand, sir – and we have flowers available for the occasion, for a modest sum.'

'Well, that's all very commendable,' said Murray, struggling to keep a straight face, 'but actually it's – I believe it's your aunt I've come to see? Mrs. McGregor, lately come here from Holyroodhouse?'

'Oh!' Mr. Boot's face rearranged itself as he realised he had no customer, then wondered if he could persuade Murray, by dint of his obligingness, to become a customer. 'My aunt McGregor – of course, sir! At once. Can I have the honour of bringing you some refreshments, sir, while you wait? She's a little slow, but we shan't keep you waiting, sir, not at all!'

'I should not wish to incommode you in the least, Mr. Boot: if I may just wait here for Mrs. McGregor that would be splendid. I can admire the view.'

Mr. Boot cast him a quick, anxious glance, perhaps in case Murray might use up some of the view, without paying, before the first procession, but Murray must have looked fairly trustworthy. Mr. Boot bowed again and disappeared. In less than ten minutes, he had returned, bowing again, bringing with him, supported on his arm, a small, delicate woman who, though probably in her seventies, had not outlived her own prettiness. Her hair was as white as her cap, her blue eyes smiled, and she sat straight and neat as a girl when she had made her curtsey. Mr. Boot seemed inclined to linger, but Mrs. McGregor was quite at ease.

'Don't let me keep you back from your business, dear Edward,' she said firmly. 'I shall be quite safe here, I'm sure. Now, then, Mr. Murray, wasn't it? What can I do for you?'

Chapter Seven

'I BELIEVE YOU lived until recently in an apartment in Holyroodhouse?' Murray began gently.

'Yes, indeed! Such a privilege!' said the woman. 'Before I married, you see, I was a seamstress to the late Queen, and when my dear husband died I was offered a place there. Of course my nephew would have taken me in here but at the time his house was not at all suitable, and I was so pleased to be the recipient of such thoughtful charity.'

Her enthusiasm was a little surprising, but then for all she knew Murray had come from some office of state, perhaps to see if she would need accommodation again after the visit. Murray had the impression that she and her nephew might only tolerate one another for a few weeks.

'You knew while you were there, I think, a Mrs. Ochill? Anna Ochill?'

'I did indeed. My neighbour, if you could call it that.' She paused very slightly. 'We were good friends there, you know.'

'Do you know where she is now? Where she went to stay after you were all asked to leave?'

'Well, of course, I should very much have liked her to come and stay here, with me,' said Mrs. McGregor quickly. 'But my nephew … it is not a very large house, you see …'

And your nephew has likely let every room to paying guests for the duration, thought Murray, never mind his viewing platform.

'I quite understand,' he said with a smile. 'But do you know where she is staying? Had she relatives nearby?'

'No, not at all. She is the last of her family, so she told me. A widow, like me.' She gave a pretty little sigh, and blinked up at

Murray.

'Friends, perhaps?' Murray persisted.

'Friends, yes, indeed. Or the friend of a friend. She has a cottage a little outside the town, and room enough for all Mrs. Ochill's lovely things. Not her furniture, of course, but linens and ornaments and – all the little things that make a house a home. Mine are in the cellar, here,' she added, a little bleakly.

'Do you know the name of this friend?'

Mrs. McGregor shook her head.

'I don't believe the name was ever mentioned. No doubt we shall communicate again soon, tell each other all we have seen in these momentous days!'

'Or the direction of the cottage? What road it was on?'

She frowned.

'Now wait … I did hear. I'm not a native of this city, Mr. Murray, as you can tell, and I only know some parts of it. Let me think … it is a name I have heard recently … Keith? Something like that?'

Murray quickly reviewed in his head the towns and villages closest to Edinburgh.

'Dalkeith?' he suggested. Mrs. McGregor's face lit up.

'That's it! How clever of you. Dalkeith – well, the road to Dalkeith, I suppose. Now, where else have I heard that name recently?'

'Well,' said Murray, 'the King is to stay at Dalkeith Palace while he is here.'

'That's it! Good heavens – you don't think Mrs. Ochill is staying there, do you?'

'Mrs. McGregor, I have some bad news, I'm afraid. Mrs. Ochill is dead.'

A curious expression passed over Mrs. McGregor's face, fluid as her nephew's as he assessed a potential customer. Murray had to be quick, but he saw, he thought, shock, sorrow, and satisfaction in quick succession. The first two he could understand, but what was the last about? Almost as soon as it had appeared it was gone again, and a mournful surprise had replaced it.

'Dead? My poor good friend! But what ailed her? She was, I thought, quite healthy when we said goodbye.'

'I'm afraid she was attacked. Killed.'

'Robbed? I'm sure that road cannot be safe. The country has so many hazards.'

'No, she was killed in the town, and not robbed, as far as anyone can judge. Do you know what jewellery she was in the habit of wearing?'

'I do, of course. She wore two rings, one on each hand, and a necklace with a cairngorm in it. She must have considered it very pretty, for she wore it all the time. She had some combs and a pair of bracelets, too, but she would not wear those every day.'

'The rings and the necklace were what she was wearing when she was found,' said Murray. 'And she was in ordinary day clothes – a dark grey dress and white fichu, and black lace mitts.'

'Indeed, exactly as I picture her,' said Mrs. McGregor. 'But who would do such a thing? Who would have harmed her? I have heard people say that there are too many weapons in the town just now, knives and dirks and swords and spears all over the place – but why would anyone attack her? An old woman?'

'I have been asked to try to find out, madam,' said Murray. He waited for a moment, wondering if she might say something more, but she was silent, frowning, and did not share her thoughts. 'When was the last time you saw her?'

Mrs. McGregor cleared her throat, giving herself a little shake.

'The day we moved out, I suppose. Well, the day I moved out, for she was later than me. I went to her apartment to say goodbye, for now. For now! alas. She said we would see each other again soon, and I said yes, indeed, we would sit by the fire and share our stories again. That's what I said. That's what she said,' she added, her gaze shifting and passing over his shoulder, somewhere in the past. An odd way of putting it, he thought, as if she were making herself remember the exact words.

'Well, if anything occurs to you that you think might help me find Mrs. Ochill's assailant,' he said, realising that he was losing her to her thoughts, 'perhaps you could have Mr. Boot send word? Here is my card. I shall be very pleased to hear from you at any hour.'

He left her in the viewing room, staring out through the windows with their convenient access to the viewing platform. He wondered how much money Mr. Boot would make from his enterprise. He wondered just how crowded that room was going to be on the day of the grand procession. And he wondered, most of all, what had been the cause of that little look of satisfaction on Mrs. McGregor's face, at the news of her dear friend's death.

'Let me see the list!'

Blair's curiosity had almost defeated his appetite over dinner, and they were barely back in the drawing room when he could wait no longer. Murray, grinning, handed him the report and attached list from his own pocket.

'Take a look, too, Robbins – is there anyone you know on it?'

But Blair was already handing it to Robbins with a disappointed pout.

'Most of these men are dead. They were all ancient,' he said.

'Robbins?'

'I haven't come across any of them, sir. Except Macdonell of Glengarry, of course.'

'Glengarry? From what I hear, he's mad enough for anything,' said Isobel, pouring a cup of tea for Mrs. Helliwell.

'I'm not sure he's mad, my dear,' said Blair in soft reproach. 'But he does have a very quick temper.'

'Is he in town at the moment? I suppose he must be,' Murray answered his own question. 'He'd have to be involved in all this, wouldn't he?'

Blair tutted.

'Yes and no, Charles.'

'Yes and no?'

Blair sighed, but not, it seemed, at Murray's ignorance.

'It's all this business with Walter Scott's committee and all the people who think they're Highlanders or should be Highlanders or want to be Highlanders for the day. Sir Walter's got the town – the whole country, I believe – in such a state that no one thinks they can be anyone unless they have a tartan and a clan chief – or unless they are a clan chief, and so they're all at each other's throats wanting to lead this procession and bring their tail – you know, all their clan followers or tenants or distant cousins – to that reception, the grander the better. He's done a remarkable job, when you think of what this country was like only eighty years ago, and all the trouble since.'

'A victim of his own success?' Isobel suggested. Blair nodded enthusiastically.

'Exactly, my dear. Exactly that.'

'So where does Glengarry sit in all this?' asked Murray.

'Well, poor Glengarry had been setting himself up for years as the true historian and keeper of the traditions of the Highlands and all the clans. Just the kind of man Scott wanted for his committee. And Glengarry can look – well, quite dashing. I think Scott actually likes the man, and all his old gallantry – it suits Scott's romantic ideas. But the trouble is he's far from a peaceable man to work with.'

Robbins made a soft sound of agreement, and Murray looked over at him.

'I've heard it said, sir, from a man who was once in his service, that Glengarry would start an argument on his own, sleeping by the fire in his own parlour. If you'll forgive the indiscretion, sir.'

'Of course,' said Murray with a grin. Blair nodded again.

'And while Glengarry might be setting himself up as the true historian and keeper of the traditions of the Highlands and all the clans,' he rattled off again as if he had practised it, 'he's not the only one who believes he is. There's David Stewart of Garth – and probably others, but it's Garth who has his seat in Sir Walter's parlour.'

'I think I know what he looks like,' said Murray. 'Isn't he the one who looks like a kindly old professor? Surely he couldn't stand up to Glengarry?'

'I don't know,' said Blair. 'He's a very decent man, and not in the best of health, but he has written some stirring stuff about the rights of the Highlanders not to be evicted from their lands – including lands sold off by your kinsman, Charles, the Duke of Atholl. He can be courageous, but I'm afraid he's quite radical.'

'Which is unnerving these days,' Murray admitted, 'even if he is well-intentioned.'

'Nevertheless, in a duel – which I gather Glengarry is fond of,' said Isobel, 'who would come off best?'

'I'm not sure that he has ever gone as far as an actual duel, my dear,' said Blair anxiously. 'I may be wrong.'

'Didn't Garth write a history of the Highlands, too?' asked

Mrs. Helliwell, who had read as many books as came through the doorway of a country manse, and a few from Letho library, besides.

'He did, and he joined Glengarry's Society of True Highlanders. But he never got on with Glengarry, really,' said Blair. 'Glengarry has been clearing his lands, too, while claiming to be on the side of the Highlanders – which is Garth's principal cause. And mild as he is, he cannot bear Glengarry's sharp temper. I think Scott had some trouble working out how best to employ both of them, but Garth has been much the easier. He is using his military experience to make an army out of the gentlemen of the Celtic Society – some of them older than me!' he added, wide-eyed. 'And they might well need to be well-armed and drilled, for Glengarry claims that the Celtic Society are all frauds without a drop of Highland blood between them, and the Celtic Society says much the same about the Society of True Highlanders, and, well, I have been thinking that it would save everyone a great deal of trouble if both societies took themselves off with their ancient plaids and weapons and fought it out on Leith Sands without involving anyone else, and let us get on with welcoming the King!'

'All of which is very interesting – and a little alarming,' said Murray. 'But my question, I suppose, is this: if John Ochill was investigating treasonous links with the French eight years ago, and Glengarry was on his list of possible traitors, did Glengarry kill Ochill in an alley off Rose Street? And then did he wait eight years to kill Anna Ochill in Holyroodhouse? And if so, why?'

'Was Mrs. – the neighbour, Mrs. McGregor – was she any use?' asked Mrs. Helliwell.

'No, though I think she had more to tell,' said Murray. 'She looked quite pleased that Mrs. Ochill was dead, I thought, though she was otherwise very polite and proper.'

Isobel looked at Mrs. Helliwell, then turned back to Murray.

'Mrs. Helliwell and I could go and see her, my dear,' she said brightly. 'She may talk more to other females.'

'Well, if you'd like …' said Murray, not sure. He could see no harm in it, yet.

'And it would help you solve this before the King arrives, wouldn't it?' said Isobel, playing her ace neatly.

'Oh, well, then, yes, of course,' said Murray. He had barely started to play, but he knew he was beaten.

Chapter Eight

'YOU KNOW WHO she was, of course?'

Murray had never met Sir Walter Scott before, though of course Blair seemed to be an old acquaintance. Scott's parlour seemed to be full of dogs and papers, with no particular precedence given to either, though given all that was going on there must have been some considerable level of organisation to it all. David Stewart of Garth, the kindly man who, unbeknownst to himself had been discussed at Murray's house not an hour before, had greeted them and then returned to his desk in the corner, where, glasses on top of his head, he scribbled and folded note after note, laying them all on a tray for delivery. Scott cast him a benevolent smile now and again, by way of encouragement.

'Do you mean Mrs. Ochill?' asked Blair. 'She was Mrs. Ochill, the widow of a John Ochill. That's all we know, really,' he said, innocently. Murray felt they knew a little more than that, but kept quiet.

'Anna Ochill!' said Scott, as if he had whipped a cover off something remarkable. 'You know? The poetess!'

'Oh, goodness!' said Blair. Murray blinked, remembering.

'Around the time of all our quarrels with Bonaparte – a real delight, at the time. In both Gaelic and Scots – such talent! Such imagery! And yet such poignancy – the sense that our brave soldiers in Wellington's army were going through the kind of thing their ancestors had, too – the echoes of the valiant history of our land. What an irony that she should die just now, and in the very royal palace itself!'

'Was she to be involved in the, ah, ceremonials in any way, Sir Walter?' asked Murray.

'Well, now, I don't know. Let me see … Davie, have you the list of the Holyrood pensioners?' He turned back to them as Stewart of Garth left his notes and began to scrabble through a number of bundles of paper, all bound with string. 'The thing is, we had no idea she was there, or even still alive. No one had heard of her for years – not since her husband died, I should think. Anyway, as you know Holyroodhouse was in such a state it needed to be done up completely for His Majesty's use, and I suppose I didn't quite think about the people living there – evicted quite abruptly, I found. So Davie and I thought well, they could come to the Levee, the men, and the women to the Drawing Room. But they're both quite crowded already, and so we had a kind of ballot.'

'Not quite a ballot,' said Davie Stewart, handing him a piece of paper. 'We didn't want anyone coming who would not …'

'Fully appreciate it,' Scott finished. 'We tried to make sure they were appropriate, you know? So we gave them, well, points, of a kind. Were they of Highland family, were they loyal to the Crown, what kind of service had they done, and was there anything else particular about them that might make their presence particularly desirable?'

'Would it make a good story?' added Davie Stewart, and received a bit of a look from Scott.

'When we found she was Anna Ochill, of course, she was one of the guests selected. Here, here's the list.'

He handed it to Blair first, so inevitably it was rather crumpled by the time it reached Murray. It was a list of names, with notes beside them, and then a number. Mrs. Anna Ochill was at No.20, with the word 'Poetess' beside her. Above her were old soldiers and close Royal attendants. Below her name, though, was a gap with a line across it, and then about twenty further names.

'We could only fit in twenty,' said Scott apologetically. 'The Drawing Room was already pretty full.'

'So the other names, the ones below hers – they won't be invited?'

Scott and Davie Stewart exchanged awkward glances.

'I suppose one will be, now,' said Sir Walter 'The top one,

whoever it is.'

'I'll be arranging the invitation today,' added Stewart. Murray looked back at the list. The next name after Mrs. Ochill's was Mrs. McGregor.

Murray remembered, with a sudden chill, Mrs. McGregor's little look of satisfaction at the news of her friend's death. Was this why? Mrs. McGregor would now be invited to meet the King? Was that enough to kill for?

'Lord Melville says you're to find out how Mrs. Ochill died,' said Scott, 'before His Majesty arrives in Edinburgh. I pray you will succeed. I can tell you, if anything happens to prevent this gala, there will be very many disappointed people.'

'I think that Lord Melville was principally concerned lest anything should happen directly to the King,' said Murray. Scott, already pale, turned grey.

'No! A threat to the King? Who would think of such a thing!'

In a city full of well-armed Highlanders, some cleared from their lands or threatened by it, many whose families had fought for a different king, and been harried by this king's uncle? Well, it might have crossed a few minds.

'No doubt Lord Melville's duty is to consider all possibilities,' said Murray politely.

Scott drummed his fingers on his knee, thinking.

'Tomorrow is the official start of the ceremonies,' he said.

'Before the King has arrived?' asked Murray.

'Oh!' Blair jiggled excitedly. 'The bringing down of the Honours from the Castle to Holyrood!'

Scott gave a gratified smile.

'That's right, Mr. Blair! Exactly. In full accordance with ancient ritual.'

Murray happened to be looking over at Davie Stewart, and thought he saw him roll his eyes just a little.

'Perhaps you would be good enough to ride in the carriage with me, Mr. Murray? I would be much reassured to have you there.'

Murray was alarmed.

'But, Sir Walter, if I am to investigate Mrs. Ochill's death … I am not a bodyguard, sir – I am sure you have men around you who see to your safety much more efficiently than I could.'

'Oh, but think, Charles!' Blair was much more interested in

the ceremonial. 'You would be right there in the midst of it!'

'And if someone threatens the King,' added Scott, 'is that not a likely place to find them? It will be only a few hours, and then you may continue with your investigations – if it does not answer all.'

'I have no tartan, Sir Walter,' Murray tried as his last resort.

'I have a spare kilt,' said Scott at once. 'I shall be wearing trews myself. Unless the Duke of Atholl can furnish you with something in your own tartan? ... No, I suspect he has nothing, either.' He sighed. 'I'll have my servant fetch all you need, and send it to your house. And I shall see you at ten tomorrow morning, at the foot of the Mound. It is His Majesty's birthday, and we shall mark it in style.'

'A Gaelic poetess!' breathed Blair, as Smith pushed his chair, alongside Murray, back along Queen Street.

'A kilt!' said Murray, much less impressed. He had never worn a kilt. Why on earth should he have? He was a Lowlander, and not a military man. Would he have to wear a bonnet? 'Such a waste of time,' he added. 'What am I to do in a procession?'

'I envy you, Charles, my boy. You will be part of history!'

'Is it really an ancient ritual?' Murray asked. 'Stewart of Garth seemed to have his doubts.'

'If it isn't, it will be,' Blair reassured him. 'Sir Walter has everything very well organised. And no doubt everything will go very well, too.'

'I would be better off trying to find out who killed Mrs. Ochill, poetess or not – and why. The King could arrive as early as Tuesday. How has this happened again? Melville has me at his beck and call. It's not so much that I didn't agree to do it, but this time he didn't even ask me!' He tried to think what he should do next, but the pipers were practising in the gardens across the road, and a small crowd had collected to watch them. There was racket everywhere. 'I must go and see if I can find where she was staying, after she left the Palace,' he said at last.

'Do you intend to go this evening?'

'I think I must. The light is good and will be for a few hours yet: if I take a horse and go now, I could be back in time for supper.'

'Then I shall not hold you back, dear boy,' said Blair. 'But I might take advantage of your hospitality and still be at your house when you return, just to hear your news.'

Murray guided his horse along the new road between Calton Hill and the Palace. The evening was light, indeed, but the illuminations around the Palace were already lit, and the stands he had taken earlier to be lights along the road towards Dalkeith were indeed burning brightly, showing him the way. He wondered if he were on the right road, for the road from the Bridges through Newington also went towards Dalkeith, but this seemed the more sensible one to start with. If he had no luck finding the right house – had Mrs. McGregor called it a cottage? – if he could not find it tonight, he would send a couple of servants along here tomorrow while he himself was stuck in the procession. He might have as little as thirty-six hours to solve this mystery. Melville seemed to have high expectations of him.

Mouse was a good mare and dealt patiently with his constantly mounting and dismounting and stopping and enquiring and starting again. Fortunately most of the inhabitants were co-operative, but some directed him one way and some another, and he doubled back on himself a couple of times, fearing he had missed the place. But in the end it was some distance from the town, past the tollbar (he felt like charging the expense to Lord Melville), and along the piece of land called the Inch, notorious for flooding. It was the house at Inch he was heading for, or rather the lodge to the main house, or so his last source had said.

'Aye, the lodgekeeper there is a friend of my friend Mrs. Inkster, you'll no ken Mrs. Inkster, sir, but aye, this grand lady's biding with her, for there's not a soul has a place to stay in Edinburgh this fortnight, be they ever so grand. And they say she's one of the King's old mistresses and he let her stay in Holyroodhouse but now he's coming he doesna want to have her there, for he's bringing yon Lady Conyngham, nae doubt, and the pair would be at it like cats in sack if they met. And my Kate saw the cart go past with the lady on it with all her baggage, and she ran after her and gave her a flower as if she was royalty herself – or one of they theatre actresses that are no better than they ought to be.' She shook her head sadly, and received Murray's tip as her due.

The lodge was a cottage, indeed, single storey, just beyond

the gate to Inch House at a tight bend in the road. The neat park contrasted with farmland on the other side of the road, and the lodge was well-kept, with signs of recent fancification about the place. Murray once again dismounted, drew his horse towards the low doorway, and knocked.

At first he thought the door had blown out. Then he realised that somewhere behind the door, an enormous dog was letting the world know that there was a visitor. He resisted the urge to cover his ears, and stood his ground.

There was some muffled cursing, a loud bang and a squeal of alarm. Then a bolt was drawn back, and then another. The door opened, just a crack, and a pale blue eye appeared.

'What d'ye want?'

'I'm sorry to disturb you,' said Murray, hoping to disarm with politeness, 'but someone told me you have a lady from Holyroodhouse staying here. Is that the case?'

'Whit are you? Some other poetry enthusiast?' She pronounced it 'po'try'. 'She's no talking to any of youse.'

'Is she at home?' asked Murray, just in case. Bodies had been misidentified before, innocently or not.

'She's awa out.'

'When did you last see her, Mistress …?'

'Mistress Duguid to you.' The eye blinked, and squinted. 'Are you no a bit grand to be coming to visit the likes of this place?'

'I do need to know about Mrs. Ochill, madam,' said Murray apologetically. 'It's quite a serious matter – and probably nothing to do with poetry. It's more to do with Holyroodhouse.'

'Oh, aye? Well, I ken nothing about yon place. And I havena seen Mrs. Ochill since Friday, though she tellt me she was going nowhere and would bide in the house, for the streets were no safe for her, or so she said to me. Ha!' The eye blinked again. 'She's no dead, though, is she?'

Murray took a breath.

'I'm afraid she is, madam.'

The eye closed. Then the door opened.

'You'd best come in, then, and tell me all about it.'

Chapter Nine

THE COTTAGE WAS not large – Murray had to bow his head until he was safely directly to a hard chair – and the effect of a tight space was much enhanced by the kists and bags that were heaped along one side of the room. And by a Newfoundland dog, about the size of a donkey, which regarded Murray with little interest and went back to taking up most of the fireplace. There was no fire lit.

'Yon's her stuff,' said Mrs. Duguid grimly. By contrast, she was a small, skinny woman, her face wrinkled and her hair grey, with curls constantly streeling out from under her cap. She perched on the end of a bench, with a couple of baskets taking up the other end. 'I mean, the half of it. The other half's in the back room. What used to be my own bedchamber,' she added, bitterly.

'Now occupied by Mrs. Ochill?'

'And the rest of her stuff. And now you tell me she's dead? How so? Did somebody really kill her?'

'Why would you think so?' he countered.

'Why would you no tell me if they did?'

'All right, yes, she was killed,' he conceded. 'Have you been lodgekeeper here long?'

'Five years, if it's any business of yours.'

She would certainly deter any unwanted visitors.

'How did you know Mrs. Ochill?'

'Did I no work for her and her husband? Till I married, ken.'

'You're married?' He wondered how she fitted a husband into the house, along with the boxes, the dog and Mrs. Ochill.

'Widowed,' snapped Mrs. Duguid. 'My man was valet to Sir William Gilmour up at the big house. When he died they let me bide here.'

'So you worked for them in Edinburgh?'

'Where else would I work for them? That's where they lived. In New Assembly Close, off the High Street. I left not long afore Mr. Ochill died.'

This could be fortuitous, thought Murray. Someone who had known both of the Ochills, around the time of John Ochill's murder.

'What can you tell me about his death?'

'Here, you havena told me about her death yet!'

'True,' said Murray, fairly sure by now that this conversation was not under his control. 'Mrs. Ochill was found at Holyroodhouse yesterday evening by the decorators. She had been dead for a day or two. Murdered.'

For a moment, Mrs. Duguid sat in silence, looking down at her hands, tangled in her lap. It was hard to tell how she was taking the news. The only sound was the Newfoundland dog, snoring gently.

'Do you ken who did it?' she asked eventually.

'Not yet, no. But I've been given the task of finding out as quickly as possible.'

'What are you, then? Are you working for the King, or what?'

Murray smiled.

'No, I'm working for Viscount Melville.'

Her eyes widened, impressed at last. Perhaps it was true – Melville did have more influence in Scotland than King George.

'Are you no the one with the fancy friends, then? Maybe Viscount Melville could help me get rid of this dog, an' all?'

'Isn't it your dog?'

'Mine? In a wee hoose like this, have a dog the size of – did you ever see yon whale they had in display up on Calton Hill a few years ago?'

'I did, yes.'

'Well, when I look at him I'm aye minded of yon whale. The size of him! And I could do with the whale to feed him on, an' all.' She made as if to kick the dog, but slumped back and sighed. 'Makes no difference, anyway.'

'So was he Mrs. Ochill's dog?' he asked, surprised that he had not heard of the creature.

'No, not hers. She wouldna have had room either, and she

always preferred cats. She brought one with her, but it ran off when it got here.'

Murray thought he might never know whose the dog was, but Mrs. Duguid had grown talkative.

'He's another one evicted by the King. It's like the clearances of the Highlands round here just now, I tell you.'

'Where's he from, then?'

'Dalkeith Palace, where the King's to stay – if he ever comes.'

'He's left London.'

'So I hear tell, but there's plenty places to go in a wee boat that are no Leith,' she said cynically. 'No, see, the Duke's still a wee lad, a schoolboy,' (this would be the Duke of Buccleuch, thought Murray hurriedly, not the Duke of Atholl, but the owner of Dalkeith Palace) 'but his uncle Lord Montague offered the place for the King to stay when they decided Holyroodhouse was no good enough for him. From all I hear, the corridors are gey narrow and they were feart the King would get stuck. Anyway, the minute the King shows any sign he might come here, Lord Montague locks up the silver, sends seven-eighths of the servants home, and takes the rest of the household to Barry's Hotel in Prince's Street for the duration.'

'What does that have to do with the dog?'

'Aye, well, that's a good question. Barry's Hotel wasna that keen on having a dog that size come to stay, not when they'd be that busy anyway. And they'd no wish to leave him with the King – I dinna ken, maybe the dog's a Jacobite. So they left him with Sir William, up at the big house. But he has a houseful, an' all, so he tellt the butler to take him into his rooms, but the butler was feart the dog would knock over the decanters, or that he would eat him, or something. The new butler, him that came after my husband, he's only a wee laddie, ken? So they sent the animal down here. And then Mrs. Ochill landed in as well, and see this bench? This is my bed now. Though if you say she's dead,' she added, with a thoughtful expression, 'there's no reason I couldna have my own bed back, is there?'

'None at all, I should think,' said Murray. Another person satisfied at Mrs. Ochill's death. What it was to spread such happiness!

'Now I've told you all I know,' he said. 'What can you tell

me about the Ochills? Why did he die? And who do you think might have killed Mrs. Ochill? For the sooner I get this sorted out,' he said, with an unaccustomed burst of cunning, 'the sooner we can find somewhere for all this baggage to go, and clear it out of your house.' If there was no heir, they would have to roup the goods to pay for Mrs. Ochill's funeral and any debts she might have accumulated, including anything she owed to Mrs. Duguid for accommodation.

Mrs. Duguid met his eye, fully recognising what he was doing. She smiled.

'Aye, I'll tell you whatever I can, right enough,' she said. 'And if you take the dog an' all, I'll leave you my fortune in my will.'

'Let's deal with the Ochills first,' said Murray with a grin, 'and then we can work the rest out later.'

'Well, let's see,' she said, absently rubbing the Newfoundlander's back with one foot. The Newfoundlander clearly enjoyed it. 'I worked for them for a fair while, when I think about it. I went to them the spring after my old master died, and he died at Trafalgar, or soon after. So what was that, then – the year '6? The Ochills had not long been in Edinburgh then, I think. He worked some ways for the government, I never rightly knew what. Sometimes he went to an office somewhere, and sometimes he worked at home but all his papers was locked up the minute he had done with them. It was him made me think maybe you worked for the government an' all.'

Murray raised his eyebrows, and shook his head slightly. She shrugged, and went on.

'It was no an awfy big place, but it was gey respectable – ken, it was the next to top floor. The neighbours was nice enough. There was money to make the place look nice and to buy good food and wine, but I'd no say they were rich, as such. I was the only servant there, not that there was room for much else.' She cast an absent glance around her crowded room, maybe thinking of happier days. 'There's not that much else to say. He worked, she visited a few women about her own rank, of course. And the neighbours, they were friendly, as I say.'

'Was that all? Visited friends and kept the house?' It was enough for some people, particularly if there were children, but other women packed their days with all kinds of interests. 'Did she play? Paint? Embroider? Do charitable work?'

'No … She wrote, of course.'

'Oh, yes, of course!'

'I mean, I suppose she wrote something most mornings. She never talked about it to me, nor showed me any of it, and I never had the impression there was that much of it. But there must have been, it seems. The two of them were that pleased when yon book came out, you'd have thought it was their only son.'

'This is the book of Gaelic poetry?'

'That's right. And things changed a bit then, I supposed. She went out more, to wee soirees, or so she told me. People called to see her that she didna know at all. I heard her talking Gaelic, which she hadna done before, though I kenned she could. Folks would come with copies of the book and ask her to sign them. She would sit there in the parlour talking about her muse – I had to ask her what that was, for I kenned well we had no vermin in yon place. It was wild for a bit – I thought they'd have to get a manservant in, maybe to keep the crowds down.'

'Was it really that bad?' Murray had been out of the country around that time: he had remembered the book when Scott mentioned it, but had no recollection of such a fever of enthusiasm for it. He was not even sure he had a copy himself, which was unusual.

'Aye, well, maybe there was no real lunacy in it,' she admitted. 'But we were kept gey busy for a while.'

'And then I suppose it died away?'

'Then Mr. Ochill was murdered,' she corrected him.

'I suppose that would stop the visiting, for a while. While she was in full mourning, anyway.'

'It stopped everything for good,' said Mrs. Duguid firmly. 'First there was the funeral, and then all the people coming to ask questions about Mr. Ochill's papers, and where he was going that night, and who he might have been seeing, and all that. Not that anything ever came of it, so far as I could see. I was engaged to my Mr. Duguid by then, so I was going to be well out of it all, and I said to the mistress was she no going to look for another maid. She said no, she had no money now, or not what would cover the rent, and she was going to leave New Assembly Close and go somewhere else. And then she tellt me she had a place at Holyroodhouse, and she went there, and I came here, and we scarcely saw each other since till a week ago when she said she needed to stay with me.'

'If she had no money,' said Murray, 'why did she not publish another volume of poetry? And what happened to – I presume she made money from the first volume?'

Mrs. Duguid shrugged.

'Not up to me to say – maybe her muse was ate by a cat.'

Maybe it was the mention of the word 'cat', but the great dog at the fireplace groaned, raised its heavy head, and skittered to its feet on the stone floor, looking about it.

'What's wrong wi' ye now?' Mrs. Duguid sighed. 'See every time he moves something else gets broke.'

But there was clearly something amiss. The Newfoundlander shook its ears, and looked towards the back of the cottage. Murray listened. There was a noise even he could hear, the sound of a sash window edging upwards. He rose quietly to his feet.

He might as well have spared himself, for the dog suddenly drew breath and bellowed. Mrs. Duguid threw her hands to her ears, and Murray ran to the inner bedchamber.

The window was open by about an inch. He stepped over to it in two long strides, head echoing with the dog's continued barking.

Outside, all he could see was parkland, and trees in the distance.

And a lone figure, in dark clothes, running as hard as he could away from the enormous dog.

Chapter Ten

'IT CAN'T BE that difficult, can it, sir?'

Robbins had opened the package sent round by Sir Walter Scott the previous evening, and had now laid out the contents on Murray's bed. There was a scarlet jacket, a pair of creamy hose with a chequered pattern at the top, a collection of belts and straps, a box of assorted metalwork, another box containing a bonnet pinned with the feathers of an eagle in moult and a collection of apparently random greenery, and a length of pleated plaid in a rather scratchy wool and mercifully muted shades of green and blue and black. Robbins' wife was from Lewis. He dearly wished she were here, and not helping to keep things under control at Letho.

'Well, a shirt, anyway. That's the easy part.'

Murray pulled a fresh shirt over his head and straightened it. Presumably one of his own neckcloths would also be satisfactory.

'And the hose, sir. That's straightforward.'

Robbins handed Murray the socks, one at a time. There were laces under the chequered turn downs to keep the tops tight.

'I'm not sure if the jacket will fit,' said Murray, lifting the kilt with care. 'Sir Walter's a good deal smaller than me.'

'So I see, sir,' said Robbins, helping to wrap the kilt around Murray's waist. It was a little on the short side, and Murray, looking at himself in the cheval mirror, felt as if he had not yet begun to dress. 'Maybe you could wear it over your shoulder, sir? And explain that this is the way your section of the clan has always done it - maybe in memory of some battle or other?'

'Robbins, you're growing cynical in your old age,' said Murray with mock severity. He and Robbins were of an age, anyway. 'But you could have a point. This is positively indecent.

Did he say what tartan it was, anyway?'

'Campbell, so it says on the note,' said Robbins.

'I wonder why Sir Walter was to wear Campbell tartan?'

'Shall we try the jacket, sir? Just to see?'

He helped it on over Murray's broad shoulders. Sir Walter was not a slender man, but he was not wide in the same places as Murray, and was, as they had already observed, a deal shorter. The jacket strained over the shoulders, fastened loosely at the waist, and terminated just above the waistline of the kilt. Robbins, his luminous gaze lowered, handed Murray the bonnet, and Murray arranged it on his head. It was slightly too small, and looked as if a dying eagle had landed in a vegetable bed. Murray and Robbins stared at the effect in the mirror for a long moment.

'I'm not a vain man,' said Murray. 'But I don't think I can go out looking like that.'

'I'm not sure I would let you, sir,' said Robbins. He sighed. 'Would there be any chance that the Duke of Atholl might have a wee bit of tartan about, just a length of it? We could do something with that.'

'Do you know where he's staying?'

'Mr. Blair said His Grace has taken Lady Seaforth's house in Charlotte Square, sir. I could send a note now if you'd write it.'

'I'll do it at once. But give me my dressing gown, in all charity, Robbins. I don't even want to see myself in the mirror again.'

Robbins helped him out of the jacket and unfastened the kilt, and Murray managed the rest for himself, composing the note in his head before he sat down at his dressing table. Robbins took it away as a matter of urgency, and Murray went down to breakfast. Isobel was already there, and looked up at once as Murray entered the parlour.

'No kilt?' she asked, wide-eyed.

'No kilt,' he said firmly.

'What a shame!'

'The shame would have been what you would have felt to have been connected with me looking like that,' he said, with feeling. 'Robbins is sending round to the Duke to see if he has anything more … useful.'

'I have a cairngorm brooch,' said Isobel. 'I remembered it

last night. It belonged to my great-grandmother, I think. Quite a large one.' She made a shape with her hands to indicate the size. 'You're welcome to use it if it will help.'

'Thank you, my love – we'll see what the Duke can produce, and if it can be produced in time. I wish I did not have to go!'

'It will be very interesting,' said Isobel, who was, after all, her father's daughter. 'And Augusta and I will come to wave you off.'

'Heavens,' said Murray, 'that a child should have to see her father in such straits!'

But Isobel, heartless woman, just laughed, and poured herself another cup of chocolate.

Within the hour, the Duke of Atholl, clearly not wanting to be disgraced by his kinsman, had indeed sent round a length of plaid somewhat lighter than the Campbell one, but with a red stripe through it.

'It could be much worse, sir,' said Robbins, unfurling it across the bed. The cloth had an elderly, lavendery smell, as though it had been discovered in some ancient kist in a long-forgotten wing of Blair Atholl. Or dredged up from the warehouse of some lesser tartan manufacturer, doing as much business as he could while the sun shone. Murray decided he could put up with the smell for a few hours. He was wearing, now, what came closer to his usual clothes, with a blue coat, and Robbins flung the tartan over his shoulder and scooped it up under the other arm, pinning it on the shoulder with Isobel's great-grandmother's cairngorm brooch. Murray looked cautiously in the cheval mirror. The effect was tolerable.

'I'll need something on my head, though,' he said.

'I've taken the liberty of steaming the bonnet, sir, and removing some of the, ah, adornments.'

The bonnet was still a little damp, but it just about stretched around Murray's head. He tilted it a little, straightened up, and thought perhaps he had the look of a Highland gentleman who had taken on a few more Lowland-like habits. Perhaps he would disgrace neither the Duke, nor Sir Walter, nor his household.

'A dirk, sir?' asked Robbins, straight-faced. Murray shook his head.

'I've no idea where I would put it,' he said. 'But perhaps I'll slip the sgian dubh in my pocket. Just in case.'

Robbins handed him the little knife in its silver sheath. Murray drew it, briefly. It was very sharp.

'Maybe Melville is right to worry,' he said. 'Inviting a host of fighting men into the city, and encouraging them to come armed. I'll be relieved when it's all over.'

'And if there's already been one death,' added Robbins, folding away the discarded hose and kilt, 'who knows but there might be more, sir?'

Robbins' words had not helped. Murray walked with Isobel and Mrs. Helliwell, accompanied by Augusta and her governess, well wrapped up against the blustery weather, up to the head of the Mound, near the great promontory of the Bank, to meet Sir Walter and the rest of the procession, but his head was full of possibilities regarding Mrs. Ochill's death – or rather, the lack of possibilities. What had he learned so far? Very little: the woman's husband had been killed while working for the government, the woman herself had been a poet but had given it up when her husband died. Because of her poetry she had a place at a Drawing Room to meet the King, and now she was dead her friend and neighbour, Mrs. McGregor, would have that place instead. It seemed very unlikely that Mrs. Ochill had happened to go back to Holyroodhouse, perhaps to look for something, and by chance had been killed there: it was much more probable that someone had arranged to meet her there and killed her – someone whom, presumably, she had trusted, or was keen enough to meet that trust was of lesser importance. She had made reference to being in danger and had not gone out much. She had few friends, though she had been the focus of literary salons. She had left a mountain of belongings in a cottage on the Dalkeith Road, and it was possible that someone had tried to gain access to them, only for the Newfoundland dog. And he himself should be going through that mountain now, looking for clues, not wasting his time sitting in a carriage with Sir Walter Scott for some ancient ceremonial that had only been invented last week.

A ring of carriages were already assembled, and pipers were playing as Murray went to join the other gentlemen gathered in the midst of them. Several eyed Murray's outfit, but then everyone seemed to be looking to see what everyone else had found, or conjured, to wear, and no one seemed to disapprove, not even Sir Walter. Most of them were more concerned about the blustery wind that threatened their bonnets. Yeomanry soldiers were waiting on the Mile itself, trying to stand in orderly lines, but buffeted by the crowds already in place. Much less buffeted – in fact, given a wide and cautious berth – was a squadron of Celtic warriors, with alarming heavy studded shields on their backs and a wild look in their eyes. They might be necessary, but Murray thought there was an air of relief about the streets – they had been waiting for so long for this great ceremonial, this royal visit, and now at last something was happening.

Here in the little assembly of participants, yet another duke was being given his orders. The Duke of Hamilton had been granted precedence in this procession, as Hereditary Keeper of Holyroodhouse. Murray wondered if he knew about Mrs. Ochill.

The Duke's carriage led the procession, guarded by yeomanry and Celts, and followed by various escorts. Murray was alarmed to find himself in the next coach along with Sir Walter, with the crowds waving furiously at them. Behind them, so far as he could gather, was a great empty coach that would carry the Honours, the Regalia or crown jewels of Scotland, and as to what came behind that again, he had no idea.

'Have you discovered anything new?' asked Sir Walter as soon as they were alone. He smiled and waved at the crowds, but his eyes were anxious.

'I have discovered where she was staying,' said Murray, 'and where her belongings are. I have found out a little more about her life before she moved to Holyroodhouse. Were you acquainted with her yourself, Sir Walter? She seems to have been a very prominent literary figure in the town, for a short while.'

'I believe I saw her at several salons, back then,' he said. 'My Gaelic is not what it could be, I'm afraid. But her verse in Scots was delightful. I have her book, of course.'

'Have you any idea why she only published one book? Apparently she was impoverished after her husband died. Would it not have made sense for her to sell another one?'

Sir Walter frowned, then remembered where he was and smiled again.

'I'm afraid I have no idea. Perhaps her muse did not perform well for money.'

Her muse again, thought Murray. The one that was eaten by the cat. He smiled at the thought, and found himself waving at the crowd, too. But almost at once the carriage stopped, and jerked awkwardly sideways. There were cries of alarm from the people on either side of the street, and Sir Walter, abandoning his waving, stuck his head through the window and looked up at his coachman.

'What's wrong?'

The coach kept shifting back and forth, but not forwards.

'It's the horses, sir, they're no used to all these people. I canna control them, sir.'

A boy came running to Murray's window, and knocked. Murray pushed it up.

'Sir Walter, sir, the Lord Provost says he'll take you in his carriage, just down a wee bit.'

'Oh, very well,' said Sir Walter, and the boy helped them to dismount while half a dozen volunteers held the horses steady. Sir Walter and Murray, trying to look as much as possible as if this were part of the plan, stalked down the cobbled hill to where the Lord Provost of Edinburgh had his carriage door open for them.

'My, this is exciting, eh?' said the Lord Provost. He turned to Murray. 'I'm no even supposed to be part of this procession! I just came along to see the spectacle.'

They started off again, passing, in a few minutes, Sir Walter's carriage from which the nervous horses had now been removed and hustled away. They had almost reached the narrow entry to Castle Hill – made much narrower by Mr. Boot's crowded viewing platform and its assortment of loyal banners flapping in the wind – when there was a dramatic clatter of hooves, cries of alarm, a clash of metal, and everything stopped again.

Chapter Eleven

'WHAT SHALL WE say to her?' Mrs. Helliwell asked Isobel as they climbed up the High Street towards Castle Hill.

'That's a good question. I suppose it might look strange to go in and question her about Mrs. Ochill again, and even if we are women she might be as reluctant to tell us everything as she was with Charles.

'Could we pretend, perhaps, to be visiting on behalf of the church? The High Kirk? I've always wanted to pretend to be a minister's wife,' said Mrs. Helliwell mischievously. Isobel stared at her, then grinned.

'That might work – do you think you can be convincing?'

'Let's see.'

They had left Augusta and Miss Fitzsimmons behind at the Mound, and made good progress around the backs of the crowds and up the hill. From Murray's description it was easy to find Mr. Boot's house, and as two respectable women they were quickly admitted as visitors for Mrs. McGregor, particularly when they said they came from the High Kirk.

'I don't go there myself,' said Mr. Boot apologetically. 'I go to the English Church – being English, see.'

'That's quite all right, Mr. Boot,' said Mrs. Helliwell graciously. 'But we understand that Mrs. McGregor has previously been in the Canongate parish, and we want to make her welcome here.'

He led them into a small room at the front of the house, the room where, perhaps, he sold his spectacles in ordinary times. It was dark with the viewing platform outside, but by the light of a small lamp they could just about make out the small, neat figure of Mrs.

McGregor, and heard Mr. Boot explain why they were there. Mrs. McGregor curtseyed prettily, and gestured to a couple of chairs.

'I'm surprised you are not up on the viewing platform, waiting for the procession!' said Isobel in a friendly fashion. Mrs. McGregor waved a hand towards the window.

'Goodness, no, madam! My nephew tells me it is not yet ready, in any case, but I have no wish to go out on to that thing. It looks far too dangerous.'

'But you'll want to see the procession going past, won't you?' asked Mrs. Helliwell. It was as good a way as any other to break the ice.

'The crowds are quite frightening, madam,' said Mrs. McGregor. 'I fear being knocked down and not being able to get up. And in any case, it is not the King going past, is it? I was in the Royal Household for many years, and am quite used to spectacle. Besides, I shall be at the King's Drawing Room myself!'

'Will you, indeed? What an honour!' said Mrs. Helliwell. 'How very exciting!'

'That's wonderful,' added Isobel. 'How did that come about?'

'Well, you know I lived in Holyrood Palace,' said Mrs. McGregor. 'I suppose the minister at the Canongate Kirk passed on all our names to the High Kirk and so on. The people who lived there had all performed some significant service for the Royal Household, you see – well,' she added, and frowned, 'most of them had. And Sir Walter Scott said that some of us would be able to go to the Levee on Friday or the Drawing Room next Tuesday, and he made a list.'

'And you, of course, were on the list!' said Mrs. Helliwell, properly awed at this extraordinary circumstance.

'Well … well, yes. I am. My name is on it,' she said firmly. 'I am to go to the Drawing Room, and receive my kiss from the King.'

Isobel and Mrs. Helliwell exchanged glances.

'I think I know someone else on the list,' said Isobel, a little wrinkle of concentration on her brow. 'Now, who was it? A name I had not heard for several years, though it was well enough known at one point. An artist, was it?'

'I have no idea, madam,' said Mrs. McGregor, somewhat

dismissively.

'A poetess! That was it. Her name is Anna Grant Ochill. Do you know her, Mrs. McGregor?'

Mrs. McGregor hesitated. Mrs. Helliwell clapped her hands together.

'Oh, yes! I have read her poetry. Quite lovely – though it was a little while ago. Was she at the Palace, too, Mrs. McGregor?'

'Yes,' said Mrs. McGregor at last, though it was as if the word had been extracted from her forcibly. 'Yes, she was there, madam. She never talked about her poetry, though, I'm pleased to say.' She shifted in her chair, uneasy. 'At one time we were quite friendly,' she added at last. The sentence seemed to say a good deal more than it had set out to do. Isobel wondered if she should press on, or leave it there, but the pause seemed to push more words out of Mrs. McGregor's unwilling lips. They came with a satisfied smile. 'She was to go to the Drawing Room, but she'll not be going now. Nor ever again. She's dead, you know, madam.'

Isobel drew breath to respond to this.

'That's a – ' she began, just as Mrs. Helliwell tried,

'Oh, did you have a falling out?'

And at that moment, any conversation was drowned suddenly in a welter of racket from outside. Mr. Boot stuck his head around the door.

'The procession's interrupted!' he cried, half-appalled, half-intrigued. 'There's a fellow on a horse telling them to stop!'

Isobel and Mrs. Helliwell looked at each other.

'Come on!' said Boot. 'Come on out and watch!'

There was nothing else for it. Mrs. Helliwell and Isobel picked up their reticules, and followed Mr. Boot outside. Mrs. McGregor, still with that satisfied smile, stayed where she was as they left.

Sir Walter put his hands up to his face for only a second, steadying himself, before once again sticking his head out of the window.

'I can't see,' he said. 'Whatever it is, it's too far ahead.'

'I'll go and look, shall I?' offered Murray, keen to be out and doing something practical, anyway. He jumped down from the carriage without waiting for steps, and began to make his way through the borders of the crowd, along the sides of the carriages that had been behind Scott's but were now ahead of the Lord Provost's. He sensed that he was not the only one trying to catch up with the action: around him, other official-looking figures in any number of uniforms and tartans were heading the same direction, hands on sword hilts. Up ahead, by the Duke of Hamilton's carriage, was a horseman. By the way his horse was skittering and his plaid billowing, he seemed just to have drawn to a halt, though the feathers in his bonnet streeled out in the breeze, too. He, or his horse's sharp hooves, had carved a wary little circle of clear roadway. Shouting carried back easily to where Murray and others were just approaching.

'My rightful place at the head of this procession!' the rider was crying. 'You will yield, the lot of you, and fall into place behind me! By birth, right and might, this is my place!'

'Who's yon when he's at home?' Murray heard a woman say beside him.

'He's gey handsome,' came a younger female voice, with a sigh.

'Aye, if you like them mad as rabbits,' said a man. 'Yon's MacDonell of Glengarry – you can tell him by his neb, for it's well out of joint as usual.'

Glengarry? Was this the man John Ochill had been investigating at the time of his murder? Or it could be a son, perhaps. Murray took a good look at the man, whose nose, as it happened, seemed quite straight. If this was typical of his temper, Murray could quite see him stabbing someone, though maybe not anywhere as discreet as a dark alley. No one appeared to be challenging the man, but that did not stop his roaring.

'So get behind me, the lot of you! This is my rightful place!'

Glengarry had almost no need to roar, except that he looked like someone who made sure everyone heard him. Although he was in his middle years, he had powerful shoulders and a firm hand on the reins, his broad thighs in tartan trews steady on the saddle. His face was weathered, his teeth bared in his rage, but there was a gleam in his eye as he glared down at the cowering crowd. He was enjoying himself.

Murray was almost at his stirrup now, pushed the last few paces by the movement of the people around him. There was hardly room on the street for all this performance, but a slightly familiar figure pushed forward. Murray frowned: he had met so many new people in the last day or so. Who was this?

'If it's anyone's rightful place,' said the new man, in a persnicket English voice, 'it's the Lord Chamberlain. It should have been the business of my Office to oversee this whole event. That's the way it was done in Ireland for the King's visit, and that's the way it's done in England.'

For a moment, that astonishing statement took the wind from Glengarry's sails, even as the actual wind threatened to blow his plaid over his head. Murray's plaid was better fastened, if a little less dramatically. It gave him a chance to remember the new man's name – Thomas Mash, of the Lord Chamberlain's Office – of course.

Glengarry, eyes widening madly, drew breath and his sword at the same moment. Mash, clearly unaware of the danger – or simply assuming that no one would ever dare touch an officer of the Lord Chamberlain's Office – stood looking up at Glengarry. Murray, hemmed in by the crowd, could do nothing but try to distract Glengarry from what seemed likely to be a bloody attack on Mash.

'Excuse me,' he called up politely. 'Mr. MacDonell, is it?'

Glengarry spun in his saddle to see who was calling him, scanning the crowd. Murray waved, and Glengarry, catching the movement, frowned, puzzled. At that a reckless but efficient young naval officer seized Glengarry's stirrup on the other side, placing himself between sword and Mash, and hissed up at Glengarry,

'History will not say you were not given your due. History will say you attacked an unarmed man in front of women and children, endangering any life but your own, sir. And I daresay history could tell a few more tales of you, if the truth were known. Now, sir, quieten your horse and leave this place.'

For a moment, it was touch and go. No one else seemed to have heard what the young officer had said, and Murray wondered at it himself. Even the horse seemed to hold its breath. Then Glengarry announced, in a low but carrying voice, rich with drama,

'You will be hearing from my seconds, sir.' And with a swirl of plaid and feathers, he turned. Just for an instant he caught Murray's eye. The puzzled expression returned, then, outrageously, he winked, touched his spurs to his horse's flanks, and rode as swiftly as the crowd would let him, back down the narrow street and away. And again, the procession began to move up the hill.

Murray shook himself and walked down to meet the Lord Provost's carriage. The footman helped him to climb back in, shutting the door. Murray told the others what had happened, but not, for now, exactly what the young officer had said, only that he had stopped Glengarry.

'That was one of the young MacDougalls,' said Scott with satisfaction. 'I must thank him later.'

'Glengarry won't really challenge him to a duel, will he?'

'He probably will, and if MacDougall has any sense he'll ignore it. It wouldn't be the first time. Glengarry is always throwing out challenges,' said Scott, almost fondly. 'And Thomas Mash was there for the theatricals? Dear me! I'm sure they've never seen the like of Glengarry in the Lord Chamberlain's Office, do you think, Lord Provost?'

The Lord Provost laughed, and at last they continued cheerily on their way. This time they reached their place before the Castle unimpeded. Scott seemed unbothered by what had happened. Had he planned the whole scene? Anything was possible, only for that muttered exchange between Glengarry and the young officer. Murray shook his head, and was only left to wonder what was going to happen on the way back down.

The gentlemen, wind-whipped and a little damp, descended from their carriages and approached the closed Castle gate. The walls rose in a smooth curve to either side, impregnable. Murray hoped they had remembered to bring a key.

But no: there was more ceremonial to come. A herald from the Duke of Hamilton's escort approached the gate, and knocked at it with the end of his staff.

'Who's there?', came the reasonable question from within. The herald cleared his throat.

'The King's Knight Marischal comes to receive the Regalia, which are deposited within your Castle, and he demands admission in the name of the King.' Impressive words, which were a little spoiled by the herald coughing at the end. Murray, standing a little behind Scott, saw him smile, and then mouth along with the response now heard from behind the gate:

'Throw open the gates, and make way for the King's Knight

Marischal!'

The gates opened ponderously, and the gentlemen of the procession, Murray among them, made their way up the tight cobbled pathway inside the castle, slithering on the wet stones. For a moment or two they were sheltered, but then rose up out of the sunken laneway into the scouring wind. They battled across to the Governor's House, clutching bonnets and kilt skirts and plaids with frantic fingers.

'Damn well hope there's a glass of brandy in there,' muttered the Duke of Hamilton who had been blown back beside Murray.

'And a good fire, your Grace,' Murray responded, smiling.

Inside, the Regalia or Honours were already laid out on velvet cushions on the dining room table, and the butler was giving the Crown a final rub with a cloth.

'All present and correct, Sir Walter,' said the Governor, and then, indeed, saw to it that everyone was given a brandy. Another followed, and there was some gossip about the daftness of Glengarry and the unpleasantness of the weather and the possible arrival of the King.

'If we've gone to all this trouble to bring this lot down to the Palace,' muttered the Duke of Hamilton, 'His damn-it-all Majesty had bloody better turn up to take a look at it. Though I can't imagine it's his kind of thing.'

They all looked again at the sword, the crown and the sceptre, rediscovered only four years before at the Castle after years of concealment. The crown was fine enough even for King George, Murray thought, but he might find the sceptre a bit plain. The sword was huge, and clearly designed to do more harm than good. He had seen the Crown Jewels in the Tower in London, a veritable treasure house. These were plainer, but more venerable.

'They'll not blow away as we cross to the gate, anyway,' said Sir Walter.

'Though we might,' muttered the Duke.

At last it was felt they should probably make a start, or they would all be late for dinner. Reluctantly they wrapped themselves up again and made for the door.

'We don't want to disappoint our audience,' murmured Scott encouragingly.

The moment the door was opened, a blast of military music nearly knocked them back. They were to be escorted back down the hill by a regimental band. Murray fell into place in the procession again, following the soldiers in their scarlet tunics down the narrow lane and out of the Castle gate. Their carriages were still waiting. The crowds cheered, surging towards them, as if a siege had been lifted and the procession was the conquering army. Murray watched, making mental notes of everything to tell Blair afterwards, as the Regalia was laid tenderly in the carriage prepared for it. The escorts took their places, the gentlemen returned with relief to their carriages, and the whole solemn parade started down the hill, with the people parting, not too promptly, to let them through.

This part of the road was narrow at the best of times. Now Murray almost wondered how the carriages were to get back through, with the press of humanity and the wooden scaffolding tight on either side. He tried to look up from the carriage window, riding backwards as he was. Faces and waving arms everywhere, mouths shouting meaninglessly in the general racket, flowers falling from outstretched hands. The beat of the band in front, the glare of the pipes on all sides, the cries of 'God Save the King!' – the street throbbed with noise. This was a friendly, enthusiastic crowd, Murray thought: what would an angry one be like?

Somewhere ahead the front of the procession must already have reached the slightly broader Lawnmarket. In a moment they would be there themselves, if they could squeeze through. Nearly there …

'That's us,' said the Lord Provost, who must have been thinking the same way and was facing forwards. Feeling like a cork in a bottle, Murray stared out as they passed the last rank of scaffolding. That must be the one outside Mr. Boot's house, he thought. Mrs. McGregor is probably up there.

He tried again to look upwards to see if he could see her, but he was too tall to see properly through the small windows. But he did see that the legs of the scaffolding were oddly slanted. And they were moving.

'No!' he cried, scrabbling for the carriage door. 'Look out!'

But he had barely opened the door, the carriage still moving slowly onward, when the first screaming bodies began to land around them on the hard, cobbled street.

Chapter Twelve

SCOTT'S FACE WAS a picture of bewilderment and alarm as Murray slid from the moving carriage. The rest of the procession seemed to be unaware of what had happened behind them: the carriages carried on, the escorting soldiers, yeomanry and Celts kept moving down the hill. At the foot of the Castle Hill, the road was now completely blocked by the fallen scaffolding, and the people who had been upon it and below it. As the sound of pipes and drums died away, it was replaced by cries and groans, awful to hear.

Murray steadied himself and tried to assess the scene properly: unfortunately he had been at similar sites before, and knew that those making the most noise were probably least in need of help. Already some of the crowd were running into the broken structure, trying to find those crying out, possibly endangering themselves, too. He saw that some of the scaffolding poles were simply weighing people down, while others were still supporting parts of the structure. A couple of sturdy men, one in the uniform of the city police, stood by looking shocked, and he nudged them to help him.

Between them they had shifted half a dozen heavy poles before Mr. Boot appeared at his front door, now in the midst of the destruction. He gaped in horror.

'It wasn't finished. I kept telling them it wasn't finished. It wasn't safe,' he kept repeating, until Murray could reach and shake him.

'Did two women call at your house today? To see your aunt.'

Boot, not unreasonably, looked bewildered.

'Yes,' he stammered. 'Yes, they did. But they went away ages ago.'

Murray prayed he was right.

'Get people clear,' he said loudly. 'Is there anyone in your house who could boil water? Fetch bandages? Get them working.' He could hear, somewhere beyond the mound of poles and boards, someone at the other side trying to do much the same thing, and in a few minutes the police officer and a couple of soldiers who had been supposed to be holding back the crowd were also organising space for the wounded, blankets, hot water, and competent nurses.

In some ways it had looked worse than it actually was. There must have been thirty or forty people on the scaffolding – Mr. Boot was of very little use in terms of numbers, though most of them must have come through his viewing parlour. Though he was doing his best, he still endlessly repeated,

'It wasn't finished. It wasn't safe.'

A sheet of canvas lay near the foot of the wreckage, presumably one of the great banners with loyal phrases that everyone seemed to have raised. If it had caught the wind, it might well have helped to bring down the scaffolding, like a sail capsizing a ship. Murray took one end while the police officer seized the other, intending to roll or fold it out of the way. When they saw the figure underneath, they pulled the canvas clear and knelt down at once.

It was a woman, Murray saw: a woman with white hair, and wearing what was probably her best silk gown for the occasion. She had been crushed under who knew what weight of planks and people, and even though she lay on her stomach it was clear she was dead. Carefully, as if he might cause her more harm, Murray turned her over. Her face was unharmed, and he recognised her at once. It was Mr. Boot's great aunt, Mrs. Ochill's erstwhile neighbour, Mrs. McGregor.

'At least I have your cairngorm safe,' Murray said to Isobel, drawing it from the pocket of his waistcoat and handing it to her. 'The Duke of Atholl's plaid is wrapped around some poor injured passerby, I'm afraid. I wonder if I'll ever see it again?'

He was not yet quite sure what he was saying. He was exhausted, and his ears still rang with the noise. His gloves were ruined and his hands raw with lifting the wreckage, and the bonnet that Scott had lent him looked as if it had been abandoned in a ditch and then used as a football. He had a bruise across one shoulder from where, as they had tried to ease the last unsteady portions of the structure to the ground, a plank had slid loose and just missed his head. Isobel was holding a cold compress to it with one hand, and had wrapped her other arm around his back, her cheek on his head.

'When we heard the crash I didn't know what to think,' she murmured. 'We were with Papa, just up from the Mound. And I thought well, if something terrible has happened, I don't want Augusta to see it – but I had to know.'

She had left Augusta with Blair and Mrs. Helliwell and run up the Lawnmarket, but when she had seen he was unharmed she had turned to help with the injured. She was as tired as he was, and as filthy. Robbins and Isobel's maid were preparing baths for both of them, before they could even think of joining their guests for dinner.

'Did you find out anything from Mrs. McGregor?'

'There was a tight rivalry for an invitation to the King's Drawing Room,' said Isobel wearily. 'She was pleased Mrs. Ochill had died and she could go instead. They had had a falling out. But whether or not she killed her …'

He slipped his arm around her now, holding her tight.

'The procession didn't stop,' she said. 'It just carried on. I suppose it would have been even more of a muddle if it had stopped, though.'

'Yes,' said Murray. 'Best to get at least one group of people and horses and everything well out of the way. I hope Scott was happy with the day.'

'It was certainly not without impact,' said Isobel. 'People will remember it.'

Blair had joined them for dinner, too impatient for a full account of the day to wait any longer. He sat open-mouthed at Murray's account of the falling scaffolding, the death of Mrs. McGregor – Isobel and Mrs. Helliwell reported more fully on their conversation with the late seamstress – and the intervention of Glengarry.

'He is a very peculiar character, by all accounts,' said Blair at last.

'And the only one left of those John Ochill was investigating, eight years ago,' added Murray, finding that a bath and a good meal had revived him considerably. 'If it is him. When did his father die?'

'Oh, years ago,' said Blair. 'Glengarry was only a boy when he inherited. It would have been him in Edinburgh in 1814, if there was a Glengarry here. I think he started the Highlanders Society the next year, or thereabouts.'

'So John Ochill was investigating that man …' said Murray, fitting the horseman of today with the dead government man of eight years ago. 'I wonder had he found anything? Would Glengarry have been sympathetic to France and Bonaparte?'

Blair shrugged expansively.

'By the time he was born, the Jacobites were a thing of the past – as much as they ever are,' he said. 'I think Glengarry was educated in England. But what that says as to his sympathies by Bonaparte's time I have no idea.'

'I'll have to send a note to Sir Walter, and explain what happened,' said Murray. 'And apologise for the state of his bonnet. Though Robbins thinks he can revive it, to some extent. As for the Duke's plaid, well, I don't know. Another apologetic note, I suppose. Or I'll go and see him myself in the morning.'

'If you go this evening,' said Isobel, 'he'll see how wretched you look and feel more sorry for you.'

Murray grinned at her.

'True. But today is Monday and the King might arrive as early as tomorrow, and I need to find out something – anything – about Mrs. Ochill's murder. I had half-thought that Mrs. McGregor might have done it, in order to push herself up the list and be admitted to the King's Drawing Room.'

'She might have,' said Mrs. Helliwell, as usual keeping quiet until she had something to say. 'I have heard so many people in the last day or so desperate for a close sight of the King, that I could well believe someone might kill for it.'

They were still in the downstairs dining room, and so in a

good position to hear the risp rattled at the front door, and Robbins' footsteps on the tiles as he went to open it. Whoever it was was brought in, and left to wait as Robbins slipped into the dining room and approached Murray.

'A young gentleman, sir, with an introduction from Mr. William John Dundas.' He handed Murray a folded paper.

'Excuse me,' said Murray to the others, and opened it.

'Dear Charles,' read the note, 'The bearer is a respectable young fellow who once worked for my brother Harry and is now employed by the Lord Chamberlain's Office in a very lowly role. He has been summoned to Edinburgh to assist with the celebrations and has nowhere to stay. I wondered if you might have a half-inch of space left? I declare if he came to us we would have to hang him up in the corner press, for the rest of the house is taken.

'Please forgive the intrusion. Isn't this all extraordinary? A plaid pantomime!'

'Yours in friendship,

'Willie Jack.'

Murray looked up at Isobel.

'Have we any room for another guest?'

Isobel raised her eyebrows.

'Is he a large man?'

Murray looked to Robbins.

'Not very, ma'am,' he said. 'And quite slim.'

'If Miss Fitzsimmons were prepared to share with Augusta, we could just about fit him up on that floor,' said Isobel. Miss Fitzsimmons did not usually dine with the family, so was not present to ask. 'Will you check with her first, please, Robbins? I don't want to impose on her.'

'And bring the young man in here – what's his name? Just like Willie Jack not to say.'

'Hepburn, sir,' said Robbins. 'Shall I lay another place?'

'See if he's dined, first. We'll take his measure, if that's all right with everyone?'

In a few minutes, the young man Hepburn was seated at the dining table, looking rather flushed and overwhelmed, while Robbins had sent a maid to ask Miss Fitzsimmons if she would oblige.

'I'm so sorry, sir,' said the lad. His dark hair was tousled and his eyes wide, but his manners seemed to be in place. 'I'm afraid Mr. Dundas might have been hasty in his kindness. I don't want to put you to any inconvenience, sir.'

'How was it that the Lord Chamberlain's Office could send you here and not arrange somewhere for you to stay?' asked Isobel, not uncharitably.

'Oh, they did, madam. They had a room – well, a bed in a room – for me on the High Street. I stayed there the last two nights. But unfortunately the scaffolding outside the house fell down today, and the man who owns the house, his aunt was killed, and the windows at the front of the house were all broken and the rooms full of glass, and so the people who had the front rooms were put into the back and the last people who had arrived were told they had to leave, and one of them was me.'

'Not Mr. Boot's house?' asked Murray. Surely the scaffolding could not have collapsed in two places today.

'That's the man, yes,' said Hepburn. 'Do you know him, sir? I'm sorry to be the bearer of bad news if you are acquainted.'

'Only slightly,' said Murray, 'and I knew about the scaffolding.'

'I hope you were not injured?' said Isobel.

'I was out to meet my superior, Mr. Mash,' said Hepburn. 'He was trying to make sure that the procession this morning was successful, but of course all kinds of things went wrong. He says it should all have been in the hands of the Lord Chamberlain's Office, but there seemed to be some misunderstanding, from what I can gather. Anyway, it was only when I came back up the hill I found the state of the place, and the state of Mr. Boot. So I went to see Mr. William Dundas – I think he told you I once worked for his brother? I knew he would be able to find me somewhere to stay.'

The idea of Willie Jack Dundas, whom Murray had known from boyhood, being a person of influence to whom one might turn in a crisis was new to Murray. He caught Isobel's eye and smiled.

'I hope Mr. Boot was uninjured. He seemed to be shocked, but otherwise unharmed, when I saw him,' he said.

'Oh, Mr. Boot was fine,' said Hepburn. 'But they're confused about his great aunt – Mrs. McGregor. She was found under everything, in the street, but she was supposed to be inside the house. She'd told Mr. Boot she wouldn't go out in the street today for a King's fortune. Yet there she was, under the scaffolding – and she knew it wasn't safe. The only thing he could think was that someone must have made her go out there.'

Chapter Thirteen

'THAT WOULD BE a strange thing, would it not?' said Murray, after a moment. 'What is Mr. Boot thinking?'

'I'm not sure, to be honest,' said Hepburn. 'I've barely met the man. But he seemed to think it was very odd, that she should have gone out at all, and that she should have stood there. She didn't really trust the scaffolding, he said.'

That much was true. Mrs. McGregor had told him that herself. And even if she had felt a sudden urge to see the procession, she would hardly have stood under the scaffolding, where she would have had no view at all. What had she been up to? Whatever it was, she could answer no more of his questions, anyway. He needed to go back to Mrs. Duguid's cottage and look at Mrs. Ochill's things. He would have to go this evening, unless he could think of anything that might be more useful or urgent.

He drifted away, allowing Blair, Isobel, Mrs. Helliwell and Hepburn to converse among themselves. That cottage on the Dalkeith road was going to take up a good deal of time, particularly if many of the boxes and kists had papers in them. Was there something else he should be doing?

But then he remembered the figure running, the man that the Newfoundland's barking had apparently scared off. He seemed to have been trying to open the window of the room that Mrs. Ochill had so briefly occupied. Mrs. Duguid had not seemed particularly concerned, and he supposed that the Newfoundland had some advantages when it came to household security. But could the man have been looking for something connected with Mrs. Ochill? Something he had hoped to find in Holyroodhouse, or even on Mrs. Ochill's person, but had not succeeded? He was not sure what he could say about the man's appearance – young, by the turn of speed he had managed, quite slim, not above five and half feet tall, with dark hair worn a little long. The man had been clutching his hat, for fear of losing it in his flight. Notably, perhaps, just at the moment, he had not been wearing tartan. But as to his face, Murray had not even caught a glimpse. He would ask Mrs. Duguid if she had seen him again.

But before he went out along the road to Dalkeith that evening, he would have to call on the Duke of Atholl and apologise for losing his Grace's plaid. He sighed. At least he had not lost Isobel's cairngorm brooch.

Robbins appeared, and murmured in his ear that Miss Fitzsimmons was perfectly happy to relinquish her room for the visit of young Mr. Hepburn, and was already removing her belongings to make space for him. Murray told Hepburn, and suggested he send to Willie Jack's for his baggage.

'If it's all right, sir, I'll go back to Mr. Dundas's and send the bags, rather than have them sent. I must report back to Mr. Mash this evening. But I hope not to be kept too late.'

'Just make sure Robbins knows as best you can,' said Murray. 'He'll see to it that you are not locked out.'

He rode up to Charlotte Square after dinner, thinking that he would be riding on to Mrs. Duguid's cottage afterwards. The stables were full, but one of the stable lads agreed to keep an eye on his horse. Inside, he was told that the Duke was indeed at home, and after a moment he was ushered in.

'Ah, Murray!' said the Duke, 'I hope the plaid was useful?'

'Good evening, your Grace,' said Murray, then, noticing the Duke had a visitor, added 'Your Lordship,' as his heart sank. Melville was once again to be witness to his stupidity. He opened his mouth to form an apology for the missing plaid, then noticed it over the back of a chair. 'Ah, yes, thank you very much for its use, your Grace. I see it has arrived back safely.'

'Yes, indeed.' The Duke poured a glass of brandy, and handed it to Murray. He nearly dropped it in his surprise. 'A bright young lad brought it down from the High Street. He was not sure where you lived, but knew the pattern, so he brought it here with grateful thanks from his mother. Apparently you wrapped her in it after that dreadful accident with the scaffolding?'

'I had intended to fetch it myself, your Grace – it was good of her to send it back.' He could not judge whether or not the Duke was mocking him, and Melville's face was as straight as ever. But it was he who went on.

'From all I hear you did good work there, Murray. We heard about it down at Holyrood when the procession arrived with the Regalia. I'm still not clear why Scott wanted your company today, but I think we should be grateful you were there.'

'A number of people tackled the wreckage, my lord, including a very sensible police officer.'

'We were fortunate anyway that so few were killed or injured.'

'The dead included Mrs. Ochill's neighbour from Holyroodhouse,' Murray said, glad that they had no intention of pursuing any misuse of the plaid. 'I had spoken to her only yesterday.'

Melville met his eye.

'Do you believe that to be significant?'

'I'm not sure, my lord. With Mrs. Ochill dead, this woman would have been the next in line to attend the King's Drawing Room next week. And she had declared an intention of not going out into the street this morning, and knew the scaffolding had not yet been secured, yet she was found in the street, under the scaffolding.'

'Over-excited at the prospect of seeing the procession?' suggested the Duke, ironically.

'She could have seen nothing from where she was, your Grace.'

'I hope you're not suggesting that someone is removing the guests from the Drawing Room list one by one?'

Murray suppressed a smile.

'I think it's more likely, your Grace, that Mrs. McGregor – the dead woman – knew more about Mrs. Ochill's death than she told me. Perhaps she knew more than she realised. That is, if her death really was not directly due to the falling scaffolding.'

Melville nodded.

'Well, we know Mrs. Ochill's death was not an accident, anyway. What progress have you made there?'

'I have found where she was staying, and called there. Her

hostess was an old servant who was able to tell me something more of Mrs. Ochill's life before her husband's death and her removal to Holyroodhouse. She was a poetess. Sir Walter Scott knew her slightly.'

'Of course he did,' said the Duke. 'If anyone so much as rhymes two words together on the subject of Scotland, Sir Walter will have dined with them.'

Murray felt much the same way about Blair, and this time allowed himself to smile.

'If we follow the line that her death had something to do with her husband's murder, even though that was eight years ago, then I should question the neighbours in New Assembly Close and speak again with the old servant. But there are more general lines to follow, too. Do you think the workmen will still be at Holyroodhouse at this time of the day?'

'They haven't finished painting yet, so they had better be,' Melville growled.

'I shall go down there shortly, then.'

'But what about John Ochill's investigations? Surely that really would be the only reason for her death?'

'Some kind of revenge, my lord? I looked at the list you sent, the copy of the one Ochill was working through. Of those he might have been observing or questioning that night, to judge by where he was killed, only one remains alive.'

'And who is that?'

'Alasdair MacDonell of Glengarry, my lord.'

'Oh.'

The Duke and Melville looked at one another.

'Another unfortunate incident this morning,' said Melville. 'Did you see anything of that?'

'I saw a good deal of it,' said Murray. 'He made speed past all the carriages and up the hill to the head of the procession, and stopped the Duke of Hamilton's carriage. He was shouting about his hereditary right to lead the procession. He even drew his sword, though he did no harm with it.'

'Hereditary right,' muttered the Duke. 'How can he have a hereditary right to lead a procession that Scott made up on the grounds of a good bottle of claret six weeks ago?'

'Maybe Scott promised it to him,' said Melville. 'Scott has

a soft spot for the scoundrel.'

'He threatened Mr. Mash, the man from the Lord Chamberlain's Office,' Murray went on, 'but a young naval officer seized his stirrup and somehow persuaded him to leave. Though he threatened the young man with a duel.'

'Oh, he would,' said Melville.

'I have very little acquaintance with him,' said Murray, 'but he seems wild and violent enough for anything.'

'You're suggesting he might have killed Mrs. Ochill?' said Melville. 'He certainly could stab someone.'

'But eight years later?' the Duke queried. 'Hot revenge, yes, certainly. But cold?'

'I can't see him sneaking in, planning something like that,' said Melville after some consideration. 'He's impulsive. And he likes people to notice him. If he thought he were justified, he would shout his guilt from the rooftops.'

'Do you think he would, though?' countered the Duke. 'There's little honour in killing a woman, elderly and unarmed and without friends to defend her.'

'Is honour important to him, your Grace? I'm trying to get a clear picture of the man.'

'Oh, certainly,' said the Duke, and Melville nodded agreement. 'The honour of his clan, and of himself, in terms of battle and birthright and stuff like that. Honour that enhances glory. True Highlanders, all standing together – but led by him. The kind of honour you'd see at the theatre, usually,' he added drily.

'I did think it looked like a bit of a performance,' said Murray, remembering the swirling plaid, the outflung sword. 'So you think it unlikely he would have killed Mrs. Ochill?'

Again, the Duke and Melville looked at each other, frowning.

'Is he the only person you have found to link John Ochill's death with his wife's?' asked Melville.

'So far, yes.'

'Then perhaps keep him in mind,' said Melville. 'If Mrs. Ochill's death was not connected to her husband's, it seems to me a remarkable coincidence.'

'Like that other woman dying under the scaffolding?' said the Duke.

'Hm,' said Melville. 'Well, Murray, if you're lucky this breeze will keep the King back a little longer, and maybe keep the crowds off the streets, too. Can you let the minister at the Canongate Kirk know if there will be enough to pay for a funeral? And keep me informed – though once His Majesty arrives I do not expect to be at home very much.' He sighed, and the Duke with him. Their presence would be expected at court whether they approved of Sir Walter's pageantry or not.

Dismissed, but in a friendly fashion, Murray went to retrieve his horse, feeling obliged to tip the stable lad more than usual in Edinburgh's current economic climate. The boy did not object.

Murray rode up Prince's Street and took the new road round the hill to Holyroodhouse, still enjoying the novelty of it. Calton Hill above him was still covered in tents, and the smell of cooking fires wafted comfortably down to him. He hoped the tents were all well-anchored, or there would be a few cold bodies in the morning.

Holyroodhouse was again illuminated like a northern Vauxhall Pleasure Gardens, with lamps in the windows, too, to show that the decorators were still hard at work. They, too, would be praying for the wind to hold back the King's arrival. This time the stable boy took Murray's horse into a much less crowded stable and seemed genuinely pleased to welcome it, talking to it at once. Murray explained his presence to the soldier at the door, and went inside to the maze of dun passages and gilded rooms to see if he could discover any useful information, to point to Glengarry or to anyone else.

Chapter Fourteen

MR. TROTTER AND Colonel Stephenson, who seemed unable to exist outside each other's presence, were in a broad reception room at the back of the Palace when Murray found them. Mr. Trotter looked drained, living on his nerves. Colonel Stephenson, veteran campaigner as he presumably was, looked stoical. Neither could be called happy, and Murray's arrival did not appear to cheer them one bit.

'I'm trying to find out if anyone here saw anyone last Thursday or Friday who should not have been here – or even anyone who saw Mrs. Ochill coming into the Palace,' said Murray. 'I'm quite happy to talk to people while they work, if that helps.'

'That would be best,' said Mr. Trotter, fiddling with his measuring tape. 'We haven't a moment to spare, you know. I think anyone who would have been here on Thursday or Friday would still be here now. We barely go home to sleep. Would you say, Mr. Stephenson?'

Colonel Stephenson nodded. He was making notes in a notebook that seemed almost full, and extra pieces of paper, thick with writing and carefully corralled with pins, stuck out here and there. He looked like a man who could keep track of several things at once.

'Did either of you see her?' Murray asked, before he lost them to their work. 'Or see anyone who shouldn't be here, or was unexpected?'

'I didn't see her,' said Mr. Trotter at once. 'Did you, Mr. Stephenson?' Stephenson shook his head. 'I would have remembered her. As to someone unexpected, that happens almost every day. We have had so many people through here in the last two weeks that it's a wonder there's room to do anything. What do you think of this room, Mr. Murray? It's to be an audience room next week, if His Majesty arrives. A Levee. Does it look grand enough to you? I'm not sure. Everyone says use more gilding, but I think too much is sometimes too much, if you see what I mean.'

There were red velvet curtains at the back of the room, and three women knelt on the floor, stitching their hems, clearly listening to the conversation.

'I suppose once everyone is in here, all in their finery, it will look splendid. I mean,' said Murray, thinking he had sounded too dismissive, 'that it seems to me to form a perfect setting for the King and his court. They would not thank you for outshining them, would they?'

'No, exactly. Dun and gold, with touches of red velvet. That's my idea. With all this tartan about, it's hard to find anything else that sets it off well. Heavens! Did you order more dun paint?'

Stephenson nodded, still writing.

'I hope it arrives in time,' said Murray. 'So may I speak with your workmen?'

'Yes, yes, of course. Go on, Mr. Murray. I hope you find your man, or at least more about your woman, so to speak. Mr. Stephenson, we had better see what has been done in the Gallery, had we not?'

'Oh, before you go, Mr. Trotter – I wonder, are you acquainted with Alasdair MacDonell? Glengarry?'

'Acquainted with him, no, certainly not, Mr. Murray. But I know who you mean, if that helps.' He fidgeted again with the end of his measuring tape, and Murray thought he was gritting his teeth.

'Have you seen him here recently? Around here, I mean?'

'Mr. MacDonell? Here? Between him and that pompous interfering creature Mash, we have hardly had a day's peace, have we, Mr. Stephenson? Mr. Mash telling us that's not the way they do it in England, Mr. MacDonell telling us it has to look – and presumably smell – like the hall of Highland chieftain, Mr. Mash bringing us silk cushions, Mr. MacDonell waving axes around – it is all very distracting and quite disconcerting, and if anyone expects us to have anything at all ready before his Majesty sets foot on the quay at Leith, they would be better leaving us in peace! Wouldn't they, Mr. Stephenson?'

Mr. Trotter's voice had grown higher and higher through the course of this statement, until he almost squeaked. Stephenson lifted his gaze from his notebook, looked at Mr. Trotter, looked at Murray, and nodded.

'Thank you, Mr. Trotter. I'll leave you in peace,' said Murray, and let them go presumably to the gallery. Once they were clear, he turned to the maids sewing the velvet curtains, as the first of the workers he was to question.

He talked to seamstresses, painters, gilders, carpenters and general labourers, to gardeners arranging displays of plants, to polishers scrubbing at the fire irons, to men sweeping floors and women wiping windows, even though it was growing towards dusk. Nobody was of much help: most of them were strangers to the palace, brought in to do a specific job at an unlikely speed in unfamiliar circumstances with unfamiliar colleagues. Few of them had any idea who was allowed to be there and who was not. He skirted round the locked room where the Regalia was being guarded for the night by a party of silent Celts, but all of them were new to the palace. There was only one detail he had occasionally come across from one or two of the more thoughtful workers, which he had noted in his mind. But he felt he needed more.

At last he found himself in a set of ancient kitchens and storerooms, made dark by the lowering hill behind them. There, trying to take some rusty stains out of a length of white linen, was the maid Helen who had helped with Mrs. Ochill's body. He was glad to see her.

'D'ye mind if I work on, sir? This has to be ready for Saturday and if the weather stays like this it'll be hard to dry it.'

'Of course.' He sat where she had pointed and was glad to take the weight off his feet.

'I hear you're going round asking about strangers in the palace, sir. Is this to do with Mrs. Ochill?'

'It is, yes. Anyone here who shouldn't have been here last Thursday or Friday.'

'Aye. I thought to myself you'd be coming back with more questions, you or one of the other gentlemen.'

'I'm afraid so,' said Murray. 'And like the rest of you, we're trying to get the matter cleared up before the King arrives.'

'I dinna ken what we'll do with our time once he's away

again!' said Helen. 'Anyway, I've been thinking, and I'm sure everyone else has told you the place has been full of the world and his wife ever since the residents left. But mostly we – I mean the permanent staff, like me – we've got to know a lot of them. There've been a few high heidyins sticking their noses in – if you'll forgive me, sir – like Lord Breadalbane and Lord Melville and yon fellow Glengarry – I mean Mr. Macdonell, sir,' she added, not at all contrite. 'Lord Melville's very sensible. But I canna see any of them slipping into some woman's apartment and killing her, can you?' She met his eye, as though she really did want to exchange opinions on the matter.

'Probably not,' said Murray, cautiously.

'Anyway, the only person I could think of who I didn't know but I saw him round a couple of times, and he wasna with anybody else, was a young fellow dressed like a shopkeeper, maybe – one of the better shops – or he could have been a clerk. He had a sheaf of papers with him both times I saw him, as if he was making notes, as he might well have been, for all I ken.'

'Can you say anything more about his appearance?'

'Well, he had dark hair, and he wore it over his collar. He was shorter than you, sir,' she went on, assessing him even though he was sitting down, 'and not so broad about the shoulders. I dinna ken that I could say much about his face, though, for he was always sort of sideways on to me. He looked nervous, but then I think most of us do in here, just now. In case we dinna get it all done in time, you ken, sir?'

Murray did indeed.

'If you think of anything else, about him or about some other person you remember, will you send me a message?' He handed her his card. She glanced at it competently before slipping it into the pocket of her apron.

'Aye, sir, I'll do that.

'Have you remembered anything else about Mrs. Ochill herself?' he asked.

'Only that I've heard it said she was some kind of a writer, afore she came in here. But I never saw much sign of it.'

'You never saw her writing? Or heard her talk about it?'

'I canna mind her ever saying anything about it at all, and I never so much as saw her writing a letter, sir.'

'Odd. She had a book of poetry published, a little while before she came here,' said Murray. 'She was quite famous for a while.'

'Aye, well, in here she was just like everyone else, sir,' said Helen philosophically. 'I daresay it comes to everyone in the end.'

Not usually until you're dead, thought Murray. And yet she was right: Anna Ochill seemed to have stopped living, at least as a writer, when she came in here – when her husband died. Could she have been afraid of drawing attention to herself, after what had happened to her husband? Could she have known what he was doing that night, and where he was going? Yet she had never said, certainly not to the government men who had tried to investigate his murder. Surely a secret was safer if it was shared?

But perhaps it had not been a government secret at all. But in that case, what on earth was it, and how was he, now that both Ochills were dead, ever to find it out?

It was too late to call on Mrs. Duguid tonight. It was too late for supper, but if he were lucky Robbins and the cook would have made sure there was something kept for him. He wondered who else had been at supper, as he rode slowly home. Mrs. Helliwell and perhaps the young man Hepburn, probably. The Balfours were mostly out, visiting various friends around the town. Blair might well have stayed, hoping for some more excitement, or he might have had Smith wheel him home to the Old Town in his chair, letting him see all that was happening on the streets. Some of the windows, he noticed, had pretty cut out illuminations with crowns and thistles, or lions and unicorns, or patriotic sayings, modest echoes of the great banners on some of the grander businesses and public buildings. Scaffies were sweeping the streets, for at least the third time that day. Edinburgh would surely never be as busy again, but it was looking its best and for a moment he felt quite proud of it. He hoped the King would arrive and be thoroughly impressed by his northern capital.

'Ah, there you are!' said Isobel when he presented himself in the drawing room. She and Mrs. Helliwell were cutting shapes out of paper, while Blair snored delicately by the fire. No one else was to be seen. 'If I had known I would see even less of you here than at Letho, I should never have suggested we come!'

But she was smiling a welcome, and stood up to go and take him by the hand.

'Let me call for a dish of food for you,' she said as she settled him at the table. 'Only be careful not to brush any of these little pieces off the table!'

'Mrs. Murray and I are constructing our own illuminations for your windows,' Mrs. Helliwell explained. 'My dear husband would tell me that the Devil makes work for idle hands, but I have to say it makes a pleasant change from sewing.'

'How has the evening been?' asked Isobel.

'Tiring,' he said. 'And I never even reached the Dalkeith road. I have been talking to everyone who is at work at Holyroodhouse, and I think I shall never get the smell of paint out of my nostrils.'

'Oh, a parcel came for you,' said Isobel. 'It's on the windowseat – very soft, like a scarf.'

'Oh,' said Murray, and suffered his tired feet to take him over to the windowseat to look.

Wrapped in brown paper was the Duke of Atholl's plaid, with a note.

'Your need is greater than mine,' it read. 'Consider it yours. I daresay you'll do it credit. Good luck. Atholl.'

Chapter Fifteen

HE HAD PLAYED the forte piano for an hour or so while Mrs. Helliwell and Isobel cut their papers, letting his mind wander along with the music, allowing his breathing to slow. As a consequence he had slept fairly well and woke early, the feeling of urgency still upon him but at the same time a sense of purpose that made the urgency seem more controlled. He rose and pulled on his dressing gown, opening the shutters to see what the day had to offer. He was pleased to see that the sharp wind still blew: perhaps he was being granted a little more time. Perhaps the King would lose heart, turn about and go back to London. And what would Edinburgh do then?

But if the King were still valiantly progressing up the coast, he could still arrive late today or early tomorrow. Murray rang the bell for Robbins, and spent the waiting time arranging his plans for the day in his head. No pageantry for him today, he hoped.

'I have taken the liberty of sending the kilt and the rest of the trappings back to Sir Walter Scott,' said Robbins, shaving Murray neatly. 'Except for the bonnet, which is still not quite as I would like it, sir.'

'I'd say it's not quite a bonnet, but if you hold out hope for it then I must be optimistic, too,' said Murray, as Robbins wiped the blade. 'And I may need it again. You saw the Duke's plaid?'

'I did, sir. It has been brushed and laid out.'

'Thank you.' He paused as the blade was applied again. 'I shall go and see Mrs. Duguid again today. If the minister of the Canongate Kirk should happen to call, please tell him that I believe there will probably be enough for a funeral when the goods are rouped, and he should go ahead, but please to let me know the day and hour.'

'Very good, sir.'

'I might call on Mr. Boot on the way. Oh, and I shall make a visit to New Assembly Close off the High Street, see if I can find any of the Ochills' old neighbours there.'

'Would you like me to attend, sir?' asked Robbins. 'It is possible I might be able to speak with some of the inhabitants there more easily than a gentleman might.'

'True – that method has worked well before, hasn't it?' said Murray, smiling at Robbins in the mirror. 'But let me see: I'm not sure when I shall be there. Unless I go there first, and then carry on to the Inch.'

He considered, while Robbins finished the shave. He was not particularly looking forward to a return to Mrs. Duguid's crammed cottage, but yet … where would he be more likely to find information faster? The chances of all the neighbours in New Assembly Close being the same as they were eight years ago felt slim. Was there something else he should be doing? Somewhere else he should be looking? There was no family, and he had spoken to the only friend who had been mentioned. What about the young, dark-haired man at Holyroodhouse, and perhaps also at Mrs. Duguid's cottage? He was certainly someone of some interest, but how was he to be found? Murray had asked the sentries on duty at the doors of Holyroodhouse but they could not remember anyone at all suspicious requesting admittance. Everyone, they said, had had a good reason to be there. So who had he been, when no one inside the palace had recognised him? What had been in his sheaf of papers? Something important, or were they just a blind? If it was the same man, he had been a good deal bolder in going into the Palace than he had been facing the Newfoundland dog at the cottage. But no one had clearly seen his face, and there must be hundreds of young men in Edinburgh matching his vague description. Perhaps even thousands, just now.

If no one at Holyroodhouse could tell him anything of the man, he supposed he would have to go back to Mrs. Duguid's after all. The man might have come back. He hoped that if he had, Mrs. Duguid was safe. But the dog, no doubt, would have protected her.

'No,' he sighed, 'I'll go to Mrs. Duguid's this morning, call on Mr. Boot if I can on the way, then come back here for dinner. After that, if you are not too busy, we can go to New Assembly

Close.'

'Aye, sir.'

'I hope our new young guest is not giving any trouble?'

'Mr. Hepburn, sir? No, not yet. He was late back last night, and very apologetic, but he had warned us beforehand. If he's very busy no doubt we'll not see much of him.'

'I must go and see Willie Jack,' said Murray, remembering where Hepburn had come from. 'I haven't seen him for ages. Maybe when all this puzzle is sorted out.'

He stood, and tied his neckcloth, and Robbins helped him into waistcoat and coat.

'Breakfast, sir?'

'Yes, just a piece of bread and cheese – I want to be on my way. Can you see to it that Mouse is saddled and ready?'

'Sir.'

Murray rode along Queen Street with a smile on his face: he had looked in on Isobel before he left to tell her his plans for the day, and had had the pleasure of some minutes of wifely conversation of the kind he had never enjoyed with his first wife, Augusta's mother. He felt as if it had set him up for the day.

Mr. Boot, dressed in black, was overseeing the reconstruction of his viewing platform.

'It wasn't my fault,' he said, as soon as he saw Murray. 'I told people it wasn't ready. I told people it wasn't safe.'

'I'm sorry about Mrs. McGregor,' said Murray.

'She would have wanted it put back up. She knew it was a good opportunity.' Mr. Boot seemed determined to be defensive this morning.

'I wondered if, before the viewing platform fell, you happened to see anyone behaving oddly around the place? Irresponsibly, perhaps?'

'Only the ones climbing up when I told them it wasn't safe. It wasn't finished!'

'Did you see anyone near your aunt? Do you know what she was doing under the scaffolding?'

'Now that's odd,' said Boot, distracted for a moment from his own concerns. 'She'd said she wasn't going outside at all yesterday morning. Thought the crowds were too alarming. But then when I went to look for her she wasn't in the house. I asked the missus, and she said someone had come calling for her – for my aunt, I mean – and taken her outside.'

'A friend? Someone your wife knew?'

'She said not. Business, she thought, from the look of him. She couldn't hear what was being said, with all the noise outside, but she said Auntie looked puzzled, sort of screwing up her face, and then it was as if she'd placed him, and she went outside with him quite happy.'

'Is your wife at home?'

'No, she's with the neighbours. Two of the women next door are in bed after the platform fell on them and she's helping to look after them. The least we can do. But I did say it wasn't finished. I said it wasn't safe.'

Murray went next door to find Mrs. Boot, who was stirring broth over a hot stove. Murray thought he recognised some of the scaffolding planks broken up and stacked as fuel beside it.

'Well, I don't know who he was, sir,' she said, when Murray asked her. 'Someone Auntie knew. I never heard his name.'

'Did you see him clearly? What did he look like?'

'Nothing out of the ordinary, tell you the truth,' said Mrs. Boot. 'Never seen him before to my knowledge, sir. Young man – I thought maybe the son of a friend? Grandson of a friend? Come to fetch her to take her somewhere she could see the procession. I din't think she recognised him at first, sir, then she realised who he was, that kind of a thing.'

'So a young man. Colouring? Build?'

'Lord, I wasn't looking! I was trying to see past him to see if the procession was coming down yet. They were an age up at the Castle, sir, and it was too cold for Auntie to be standing outside for long. Let me think … well, he didn't take up much of the doorway, so I suppose he was slim. Young, like I said. Not over tall,' she said, glancing up at Murray taking up space in the kitchen, 'but not short, either. Colouring, well, he wasn't fair or ginger. But he was against the light, such as it was. I think he was dark-haired, sir, but I could well be wrong.'

'Did you hear him speak?' asked Murray, hoping perhaps for an accent, but Mrs. Boot was shaking her head.

'In all that racket? You must be joking, sir. I couldn't have heard myself speak.'

Outside, one of the boys helping the workmen handed him back his horse and was appropriately rewarded. Murray rode off again down the Lawnmarket, then turned on to South Bridge for Newington and the direction of Dalkeith. The road through Newington was usually littered with rubbish these days, the rapid spread of the population too fast for the scaffies to keep up, but Murray saw with pleasure that the proximity to the route between Dalkeith Palace and Holyroodhouse had done what no act of Council could have done, and the streets were clean. The carriages of merchants and lesser lawyers carried them smoothly from their new villas into the city, to offices and businesses and perhaps to see if the King had arrived.

Once on to the Dalkeith road itself he was able to make better speed, and it was only a quarter of an hour till he reached the sweeping corner where the gates of Inch House stood open, the parkland windswept beyond, and smoke being ripped from the chimney of the little lodge where Mrs. Duguid lived. The great echoing bark did not shock him this time as Mrs. Duguid opened the door with a sigh, but the dog came to greet him like an old friend.

'Are you come to take away all this stuff?' asked Mrs. Duguid.

'Not yet, but it shouldn't be long,' he said. 'May I come in and go through it? Then I think someone will come from the Canongate Kirk to take it to roup for her funeral expenses.'

'Ken the funeral's from here this afternoon?' she said.

'Is it? Right, I'll try to be here.'

'That'd be grand. I doubt it'll be crowded. Och, it's hard to think she's dead, all the same,' said Mrs. Duguid, in a moment of mild grief. 'Sixteen years I must have kent her, or thereabouts. And she wasna a bad mistress, on the whole. Here, if you start with these bits here I can pass them to you on the table and put them back over there, and we'll ken where we are with it.'

It made sense, and the order pleased Murray. He took the first basket and began to go through it.

'She must have had her faults, though?' he suggested. Robbins would be better at this bit. The basket held only table linen, most of it rather worn.

'She wouldn't spend a shilling if sixpence would do,' said

Mrs. Duguid, handing him another basket and removing the first one. This one held cutlery, more than Mrs. Ochill could ever have needed in her quiet little apartment. 'She was that pleased when she sold her book, for the money it would make her.' The next three boxes held crockery, none of it of much note.

'But they were well enough off, weren't they?' he asked. 'Before Mr. Ochill died, anyway.'

'Oh, aye, I think so. The food was always good quality, that was one thing. But then he liked his food. Ate like he was starving, but never a pick on him: he was thin as a rake.'

The next bundles were curtains and cushions. Murray could picture them in the little room in Holyroodhouse, brightening up the dusty sopha and chairs. She must have made it cosy, anyway.

'Did she say anything to you when you last saw her? Last Friday, didn't you say?'

'Aye, that's right. She'd had a letter come for her, redirected from the Palace, I think. She said she'd have to go out for it was to do with her money.'

'I don't suppose she left the letter behind?'

'She did not, for she said she had to take it with her to show it was her. I was surprised she said that much, to tell you the truth. She wasna a confiding person. Ken, sometimes you work for someone and you wish they would leave you in peace and stop talking to you, but she said almost nothing.'

'Did they talk together?'

'Oh, aye. I'd say they were gey fond of each other, though it would have been hard to find another who cared so much for him. I think this one's glasses,' she said, setting a box down with an ominous tinkle. 'Aye, they talked to each other.'

'About his work?'

'Not so much, no,' she said, frowning in an effort to remember. 'He would tell her what direction he was going and when he hoped to be back, that was all. Even when he came home he didna say "well, that went well" or "what a day!". But he would ask her what she had been up to – not that it was ever very much – and they would talk a bit about books and things. It wasna exactly an exciting job,' she said frankly. 'Last box for this room.'

She hefted it on to the table. It held fire irons and coal.

'Can I use that?' she asked. 'If she'd stayed I daresay we'd have burned it here.'

Murray hesitated. She was probably right, and it did not seem she would have much recompense for her trouble. He nodded, and she lifted it down to the fireplace beside the slumbering dog, then went into the bedchamber for the next box.

'You're fairly getting through these,' she said. 'Here.'

She thumped another basket down on the table, and he opened it. Inside were five prettily bound copies of the same book.

'*A Gaelic Garland*, by Anna Grant Ochill'.

Chapter Sixteen

THE BOOKS WERE almost the only things of interest in the whole collection. Mrs. Ochill had folded her clothes neatly with lavender bags between them and packed them into the kists now in the bedroom. Bedclothes were there, too, and bed hangings, and a nightstand and chamber pot, and a box of boots and shoes, and a bag of undergarments and stockings, in which, if Mrs. Duguid was to be believed, nothing unusual lurked. There was a large reticule which contained headache pills, liniment and sundry other products to make life more comfortable for the older woman. He was beginning to think there were no papers whatsoever when he finally came upon a writing slope, tucked inside a box of gloves and mufflers as if there had been nowhere else for it to fit. He drew it out and laid it on the windowsill where the light was best, and opened it up.

If he had expected some kind of magical indicator of the murderer, or even of the motive, he was to be disappointed. The slope contained the usual pens and ink and a few papers of various ages. One was a copy, signed by the minister, of the Ochills' marriage lines: she had been a Grant by birth, Murray saw. They had been married in the 1780s, in a parish called Aberchalder – he could not at once call to mind where that was. Two were personal letters, each one marked 'Final letter' – one was from her mother and one from apparently a brother. There was a written contract for her book of poetry, for which she had been paid quite a generous amount, Murray thought. He noted the publisher's name and decided to go and see them – it was a business called Hutcheon & Purvis, on Rose Street in the New Town. The last few pieces of paper were accounts rendered by a tea merchant and a confectioner, dated some months before. He took note of the names but thought he would only call on them if all else failed. She was hardly likely to have been murdered over a cup of tea or a sweetmeat.

'I'll take the books and the writing slope,' he told Mrs. Duguid. 'As for the rest, if you're content, I'll let the session clerk at the Canongate Kirk know that it's ready to be sold. You're quite sure she never mentioned relations? She had no visitors called Grant, for example?'

But Mrs. Duguid was already shaking her head.

'She'd that few visitors I'd remember,' she said. 'Was she a Grant, then?'

'It seems so.'

'Aye, well, it takes all sorts,' she sighed. In the main room, the great dog lifted its head, and echoed the sigh at three times the volume.

'Have you seen that young man again? The one that ran away yesterday?' Murray asked, wrapping the writing slope in a piece of cloth to protect it.

'Not to my knowledge,' she said. 'I barely saw him yesterday. He could run, anyway, could he no?'

'Helped by your friend here,' said Murray. 'He's a fine guard dog.'

'Ach, it's all in the bark. He had me awake an hour around midnight last night, telling the neighbourhood some story or other. I'm scared he'll have the roof off. Is that all you're wanting, now?'

'If you think of anything else that might be useful, will you let me know?'

'I suppose,' she said, but he thought she probably would.

He rode back into the town and over the spine of the High Street towards the New Town. The King had clearly not yet arrived – he heard from a passerby that a signal had been received to say he was waiting at anchor in the mouth of the Tweed until the gale would subside – and the city seemed to be holding its breath. Welcoming banners flapped in the wind, premature flower garlands tumbled away spilling petals on damp streets, and workmen cursed as they made doubly sure the miles of scaffolding were finally secure. Murray rode down the North Bridge and through St. Andrew's Square towards Queen Street. From there, in the distance he could see the choppy waters of the Forth, Fife's grey hills rising beyond.

He should have stayed at home in Letho. But he could not go back now: he could not disappoint Melville as he had disappointed his father, nor the Duke, either. And even though he still had no notion of playing about with tartans and chequered hose, he had to admit he was interested to see how everything would work out. Would the King be pleased? Or would the whole city be mortified?

He was home much earlier than he had expected, and now that he knew that Mrs. Ochill's funeral was to be that afternoon he needed to change his plans.

'Are you still willing to come to New Assembly Close, Robbins?' he asked, securing Mrs. Ochill's writing slope and books in his own book room. 'You must be busy just now.'

'The manservants we have brought are very reliable, sir,' said Robbins, with a look. The manservants at Letho had both been left there for a reason: William hated coming to Edinburgh, and Daniel was definitely not very reliable. If Robbins liked this new pair, found by Isobel, he would be able to delegate tasks he would never trust to Daniel. Murray was enjoying seeing how much more relaxed Robbins looked. Isobel had been a blessing all round. Once he was changed for the funeral, he went to look for her in the drawing room upstairs, where she had a good view of the gardens across the street.

'I hope I'll be back for dinner,' he said. 'How many will we be? Is Hepburn not joining us?'

'I don't believe he's back yet,' said Mrs. Helliwell. 'Whatever he's up to, the Lord Chamberlain seems to be working him very hard.'

'If he's working for Mr. Mash, I'm not quite sure what he's doing,' said Murray. 'Mr. Mash seems intent on criticising all the work Sir Walter is doing, but he has no right to interfere, much as he would like to.'

'Strange he thought he needed an assistant, then,' said Isobel. 'The Balfours are out again. And my father is entertaining his own guests, though he might come here for supper, and keep us company if you are to desert us again.'

'He seems to have a houseful,' said Mrs. Helliwell.

'He'll miss them when they go,' said Isobel. 'He really does love the company. Have you made any progress, my love?' she asked.

'Very little,' he said. 'There's a young man with dark hair who seems to have been busy about the place – or about the various places – but no one has seen his face clearly or knows who he is. He could be almost anyone.'

'And Mrs. Ochill's possessions?'

'One could furnish a reasonably sized apartment with them, of course,' he said. 'But as aids in solving a mystery they were sadly lacking. I found copies of her book, and the address of her publisher, so if the old neighbours I hope to find shortly are of no use, he will be my next target. I may have to go and see him this evening, if I can find him: I only have the address of the office, of course.'

'He'll be in the street directory, no doubt,' said Mrs. Helliwell.

'Of course – I suppose he will,' said Murray. 'They've taken to putting in both the business address and the home now, haven't they? I suppose more and more businessmen are no longer living over the shop.'

'Oh, there's a message for you from the minister at Canongate Kirk,' said Isobel, 'though from your attire I think you must have received the news already. He says they're burying Mrs. Ochill this afternoon – he mentioned that they wanted to get it done before the King arrives and the Canongate is even more busy.'

'That's very reasonable,' said Murray, 'and yes, that's on my list of things to do before dinner. If I'm lucky,' he added, with a sigh.

Back in his book room, he found the latest street directory. Mr. Purvis, of Hutcheon & Purvis, lived in Newington – no doubt in one of those smart new villas with nowhere to put his household waste – but Mr. Hutcheon appeared still to live at the business in Rose Street. He wondered which he should tackle first. Presumably Hutcheon was the senior partner, if he were listed first. But what if he were old, or retired? Purvis might have more idea about what was going on in the business. But then, Murray was interested in things that had happened eight years ago. Perhaps Hutcheon, if he had been there longer, would be a better source of information. In fact, he thought, if he went there first he might catch both men before the business closed for the day – and then he and Robbins could go on to New Assembly Close.

'We're going to see a printer first, Robbins,' he announced as they met in the hall, ready to go.

'Very good, sir.'

Rose Street was a narrow street, almost a mews, tucked between Prince's Street and George Street in the New Town. It did give access, via lanes to the right and left, to stables and back doors for the premises on both main streets, but Rose Street also housed plenty of businesses in its own right. Hutcheon & Purvis lay between the side streets of Frederick Street and Hanover Street, on the corner of one of those access lanes. If nothing else, King George should feel at home in this part of the town, where nearly every thoroughfare was called after someone in his immediate family.

The office of Hutcheon & Purvis was in a smart stone building, too small, Murray thought, to hold much in the way of printing equipment.

'Well, exactly, sir,' said Mr. Hutcheon, as he showed Murray to his office. Robbins remained in the outer reception room, where a bespectacled clerk regarded him anxiously. Mr. Hutcheon went behind a well-polished desk, and stroked his ginger whiskers. 'We are publishers, not printers. There are printers we use, but they are a – well, another business.'

A lesser business, he means, Murray thought. He had offended the man.

'I apologise for my ignorance,' he said as he sat on the seat indicated. 'I should have realised. But you are the man who deals directly with writers, are you not? Buys the text of the book from them?'

'That is correct.' Mr. Hutcheon beamed to see what a ready pupil Murray was. 'We are the ones who enable their art to flourish, who encourage their talent, fostering the tender shoots of literature and enabling them to grow into mighty rivers of words.' His smile froze very slightly, realising his own mixed metaphor. Murray wondered if he had aspirations in the literary field himself. Mr. Hutcheon cleared his throat. 'May I ask, sir, if you are here to consider working with us on your own volume of poetry? Or a manual on land improvement, perhaps? That is a very popular field just now – ah! Field! You must excuse the word! Quite unintentional.'

Words seemed to escape him, fleeing in different directions. Murray hoped his publications were more controlled.

'No, I'm afraid not. I'm making enquiries about a woman by the name of Anna Ochill, who sold a book of poetry to you some eight or ten years ago. *A Gaelic Garland*, I believe it was called.'

'Oh, yes, Mrs. Ochill! She was quite the sensation for a while. The flower of many a literary salon – though perhaps not the full garland.'

'I'm sorry,' said Murray, 'I'm not sure I quite understand.'

Mr. Hutcheon's beam turned to a kindly sorrow.

'It is the fate of some writers, unfortunately. They come to us with something they have been working on perhaps for years, honed to perfection, written and rewritten, the substance of all their hopes and dreams. And we buy it and render it into a charming volume, good paper, a choice of covers, and it perhaps sells very well, with help from family and friends. Our margins, you understand, sir, can be lamentably slim.'

'But I understood that Mrs. Ochill's book sold very well indeed,' said Murray. 'Sir Walter Scott mentioned it.'

'Ah! That busy man! He can be very kind to new authors. But no, you are right, Mrs. Ochill's *Garland* sold very well indeed, without much help from friends and family, as I remember. But then the next thing happens, you see.'

'And what is that?'

'The public have read the book, met the author, relished the conversations with their learned friends over the meaning of this, or the stirring feelings inspired by that. But they exhaust that book eventually, and want another one. And the author, for whatever reason, cannot oblige.'

Chapter Seventeen

'AND THAT WAS the case with Mrs. Ochill?'

'It was.' Mr. Hutcheon shook his head sadly.

'Did she speak with you about it?'

Mr. Hutcheon hesitated, pursing his lips slightly.

'Not as such, no,' he said at last. 'She sent me a letter, intimating that she would not be requiring our services again.'

'Could she have gone to another publisher?'

Hutcheon shifted in his chair.

'If she did, I never saw any sign of it. But you must understand, sir, that her circumstances had changed. This was shortly after the death of her husband, as I heard.'

'But surely as a widow she would be more in need of an additional income than less?'

Hutcheon at last looked wary.

'May I ask why you are enquiring about the lady, sir? I'm afraid I thought you were interested in knowing about her work – was I mistaken?'

'Not entirely. I am indeed interested in the progress of her work.'

'Then is it the lady yourself you seek? Because I can tell you at once I have no idea where she is. She left her abode after her husband's death, and never told me where she had gone.'

'I can tell you where she went,' said Murray. 'She went to live at Holyroodhouse, as a pensioner of the government. She was found dead there last week.'

'Oh!' Mr. Hutcheon's eyes widened, and he rubbed at his whiskers as if he found it soothing. 'Oh, my! I had no idea.'

'Lord Melville is having enquiries made into the

circumstances, and as a consequence of that and the death of her husband, I would be much obliged if you could tell me anything you know about the couple, their lives or their characters.'

'My word,' said Hutcheon, and Murray could see that his hand was shaking. 'I'm not sure that I am the man to help you, all the same. Do you mean to say that her death was – was not natural?'

'I do.'

'My word,' said Hutcheon again. The whiskers attracted more attention. Hutcheon looked genuinely agitated.

'When did you last see her?'

'Before she sent me the note,' said Hutcheon. 'About eight years ago, I suppose it was. Just after her husband died, as I said.'

'Could you say that you knew her well?'

'No, I could not. I met her husband about … maybe half a dozen times, and I met her perhaps a little less – three or four times. He negotiated the business, and she came to sign the contract, with him.'

A thought came to Murray.

'Was there any sign of coercion? Do you think he was making her publish the book?'

Hutcheon frowned, thinking back, concerned at the thought.

'I can't remember clearly,' he said, 'but I had no impression of that being the case. She seemed delighted at the arrangement. I saw her at a couple of salons afterwards and again I would have said that she was pleased at the book's reception and happy to talk about her writing.'

'And Mr. Ochill? Had you known him before he came to do business with you?'

'No, not at all. He walked in one day, just has you have, and asked to speak to either Mr. Purvis or me. Mr. Purvis does not come into the office so often,' he added. 'I dealt with Mr. Ochill.'

'What was your impression of him?'

'Quick,' said Mr. Hutcheon, unexpectedly. 'He was sharp – knew all the questions to ask, made sure his wife was receiving her due, went through the contract like a lawyer and I'd say knew every word of it by heart. And I don't think he missed a thing in the office here, either: his eyes were everywhere.' He shuddered a little, and Murray had the impression he had hoped to hide it. But then he leaned forward, intent. 'You might wonder why I remember a man from nearly ten years ago, with whom I had a few dealings over one book. I did not like him, Mr. Murray. Not at all. Mrs. Ochill was perfectly, um, ordinary. But Mr. Ochill – no, I did not like him.'

There was little else Mr. Hutcheon could tell. He had never been to the Ochills' flat, nor met or heard reference to any of their family or friends, and had not heard from or seen Mrs. Ochill since that last note. Given that Edinburgh was not a large city, Mrs. Ochill seemed to have disappeared with great efficiency.

'Did you see where we were, sir?' asked Robbins as they made their way east along Rose Street.

'Where we were?' Murray was confused.

'I think you said, sir, that the lane that Mr. Ochill was found in when he was killed – was it not something like Caroline Place?'

'I think it was, yes.' Murray stopped, looking back towards the publishers. 'Don't tell me that's it.'

'I think it is, sir. The sign is a bit tattered.'

'Then Ochill, whom Mr. Hutcheon did not like, was found at Mr. Hutcheon's back door. There's a thing. Well spotted, Robbins. Did you find out anything else?'

'The clerk who was there just now was also there that night: he was an apprentice then, and slept in the shop. Mr. Hutcheon has a flat upstairs, but he comes and goes through the shop.'

'I take it he remembers that night?'

'Oh, yes, he does, sir. He said there was a stramash, as he put it, in the lane – not much of one, though, for he had been asleep and it woke him but then he was not sure, really, what he had heard. He was wondering whether or not he should go out to look, and had in fact put his glasses on, when Mr. Hutcheon returned home and said good night to him as if nothing was out of the ordinary. So he assumed that it wasn't, and went back to sleep. But then he heard the water caddy cry out the next morning, and he went out then, being up and dressed – I'd say he was a cautious lad – and there was the man dead.'

'Did he recognise him?'

'I don't think he looked too closely, sir. It was only later he discovered they knew him.'

'Strange that Mr. Hutcheon, though he mentioned Mr. Ochill's death, did not say that it was there that he had been found.'

'Indeed, sir.'

'Although he did not seem to have taken to Mr. Ochill. In fact, I should say he was afraid of him. I wonder if Mrs. Ochill was, too?'

'Their servant should be able to tell you that, sir. If it might help to find Mrs. Ochill's killer.'

'Yes … she did not mention it. In fact, I'm sure she said the couple were on good terms. But as to finding the killer, I'm not sure she cares too much about that. Though her own life might be in danger.'

'Perhaps we'll find out more from their old neighbours, sir,' said Robbins optimistically, as they crossed a banner-bedecked Prince's Street towards North Bridge.

In the stair where the Ochills had lived, there were eight flats, a little self-contained hamlet on four floors. One of the ground floor flats was empty, and apparently had a severe problem with damp. The other ground floor flat and one on the first floor were full to bursting, apparently, of two separate and not particularly friendly Highland clans, or rather a dozen or so lowly followers, hastily wound about with tartan and summoned to Edinburgh to make their clan chief look important. They were young men, buoyed up by the excitement of the occasion and slightly better paid than usual, and there had been fights, the neighbours reported, in the close at night. At this time of day they would all be asleep, and would know nothing of the Ochills, anyway. A young wife with a baby on her hip in the other first floor flat, her eyes heavy with lack of sleep, said she and her husband had only been in residence for a year and half, and if they wanted to know anything from as long as eight or ten years ago, they needed to go upstairs to the top floor and speak to Mr. Maclean.

Murray and Robbins climbed the worn stone steps with care. They were kept very clean, except for some rubbish left by the clansmen after their convivial night, but the steps were uneven and there was not much light. It was a familiar setting: Murray had probably visited a hundred tenements like this in his time, and had even briefly stayed in one. There were rules to living here, with set days for your turn to clean the stairs, or to do your laundry, and woe betide those who did not abide by them.

There was a little more light at the top of the stair from a window in the roof, and they could clearly see the polished front door before them with its own risp. Robbins raised his eyebrows at Murray, and stepped forward to rattle it. In a moment, the door opened, and a severe manservant, twice Robbins' age, stood grandly in the centre of the doorway.

'Murray of Letho to see Mr. Maclean, if he will be so obliging,' said Murray. 'I am not expected.' The manservant took Murray's proffered card, peered at it, and laid it on a brass plate.

'Please to step inside, sir. I will ascertain if the master is at home.'

'I know the top flat is always the grandest,' Murray murmured, 'but this is quite a step up from the ground floor. I wonder what he thinks of the young clansmen?'

Robbins' eyebrows twitched at the thought, but at that moment the manservant came back.

'Mr. Maclean will see you now, sir.'

Murray, leaving Robbins behind in the hallway, was led into a parlour which seemed to perform most of the social functions of the flat. It was long, with three narrow windows along one side, and a fireplace at each end. A black oak dining table with matching chairs lined up against the wall took up most of one end, while a gathering of venerable seating and small, three-legged tables cluttered the other end in a comfortable fashion. The room was pleasant with woodsmoke and a vase of fresh roses on the table. Only the fire at the comfortable end was lit, and the armchair nearest it was occupied by an elderly gentleman in a green silk banyan and matching smoking cap, his slippered feet up on a padded footstool. There was a cat curled on his lap, which paid no attention to Murray's arrival whatsoever – in fact, for a moment he thought it was a fur muff, until one paw emerged in a luxurious stretch.

'Mr. Murray!' said the gentleman, sharp blue eyes assessing Murray from top to bottom. 'Please forgive my not getting up. I'd blame old Ferdinand here, but in truth getting up is something I'm able to do less and less these days. Will you take a glass of wine with me?'

'I'd be delighted to, sir. Thank you for seeing me at short notice.'

'I'm pleased to be visited at all! So many of my friends are long dead. Tell me – Murray of Letho? In Fife? Would I have known your father?'

'Quite possibly, sir. He died, I'm afraid, some sixteen years ago now.'

'That's what I thought. He practised law, then went off to tend to his estate, wasn't that the way of it?'

'It was, sir.'

'I practised a little law myself, in my day,' Maclean admitted, with a smile. 'Do you?'

'Not at all, sir. I mostly concentrate on the estate.'

'Ah, a countryman! Splendid. I liked it myself when I was younger, but the town is warmer. But you cannot have come here to reminisce with me about a youth you did not share. How may I help you?'

'I'm trying to find out about the inhabitants of this stair eight or ten years ago.'

'Are you now?' Mr. Maclean raised his glass to Murray, who reciprocated. 'About anyone in particular?'

'I'm trying to find out more about the death of John Ochill, who I believe lived here.'

'John Ochill? Well, well! Now, he was a nasty piece of work!'

Chapter Eighteen

MR. MACLEAN TOOK a reviving sip of wine, manipulating the glass with long, careful fingers.

'No, I was not the least surprised that someone murdered him. I'd happily have disposed of him myself in wilder days. I was surprised they never caught the fellow, though.'

'Why not, sir?'

'Well, it wasn't as if it was just left to the police officers. There were all kinds of interested gentlemen making polite enquiries. I daresay you're one of them, back again?'

'Maybe I am,' smiled Murray. 'Viscount Melville has asked me to look into a few things.'

'Viscount Melville? I should have thought he would be far too busy at present to revisit a corpse nearly a decade cold.'

'He might have been,' said Murray, 'only that as it happens, Ochill's wife has just been murdered, too.'

'Has she, indeed?' Maclean made a face. 'Now that is more of a tragedy. I often wondered what had become of her.'

'She left here soon after the murder, I believe?'

'Almost indecently soon. I wondered if she owed the rent, but apparently not. But she flitted, all the same. A cartful of belongings at night, and she was off. I never saw her again. Had she gone abroad?'

'Had she ever talked of going abroad?'

'She barely talked at all. No, she had not mentioned such a scheme to me. But to disappear like that …' He tailed off, revisiting the past with a frown of worry. 'Where did she go?'

'To Holyroodhouse, as a pensioner,' said Murray.

'To Holyrood? So near? But then it couldn't have been a

government man who killed him …'

'What do you mean, sir?'

Maclean took the decanter, which the manservant had left, and held it out to Murray. Murray nodded, and Maclean refilled both glasses before coughing a little. His cheeks were a little flushed, perhaps not only from the wine.

'I saw Mrs. Ochill once after her husband's death and before she vanished,' he said. 'I was able to get about more then, and I was coming up the stair from the main door early in the evening, though it was already dark. I surprised her on the stair. She was on her landing, with a candle, staring down towards the door – they lived on the second floor. I could see her face quite clearly in the candlelight. She looked terrified out of her wits.'

'Did she say what had frightened her?' asked Murray.

'No. She backed quickly into her own flat and shut the door. I'm not even sure she saw who I was, though I spoke to her. She did not reply. I came on up here and thought little more of it, until I heard she had gone.'

'So what do you think had happened?'

'I think,' said Maclean, 'that she believed that whoever had killed her husband, almost certainly for political reasons, unpleasant as he was, was also coming for her – probably because she knew who they were. And from what you have now told me I am convinced of it. Though I should like to know how they took all that time to do it. But then … perhaps they had only just found her.'

'It seems likely that that is the case, sir. Tell me, did you know the couple well? Even if you did not care for Mr. Ochill.'

'As well as one might know close neighbours. They had a servant, a woman, but neither she nor they were what you might call gossips.'

'Had they any particular friends here? Or that you knew about?'

Maclean shrugged.

'Let me think,' he said. 'Apart from me, no one in this stair now was here then. Alas, tempus fugit! There was an old woman lived on the ground floor, the one that's empty now, but she's long dead. A couple of brothers in the other ground floor flat, both now married and with places of their own. On the first floor … let me think. A young couple – that flat always seems to have young couples in it – but he joined the army and she went back to live with her mother while he was away. Who was opposite them? Oh! That's right: a young milliner. Across the landing here was old Lady Farquhar, a charming lady but I'm afraid quite mad, by the end. And on the second floor, well, the Ochills on the other side, beneath Lady Farquhar, and under me there was a widow with her two children. I think she died, too, and then her children left, but I don't know where.'

'Do you remember anyone's names? Apart from Lady Farquhar, of course.'

'Names … no, I'm not sure that I do. I must apologise. People come and go here. The milliner may have been Grieve? Graham? Grove? And in fact, now that I come to think of it, those children went abroad. To India, if I'm not mistaken. That's right.'

He had shifted from vague to definite very abruptly. Perhaps more of his memories would return, now he had been prompted.

'And the Ochills were not particularly close to any of them?'

'No, not at all. No one liked Ochill much, I think, and Mrs. Ochill just went out very little.'

'Did you have the impression that they were a happy couple? I know these things are hard to judge from the outside, and you might not wish to say, but if I can find out anything that might help me to discover her killer …'

'Viscount Melville would sleep easier in his bed while the King is here, is that it?' Maclean asked with a laugh.

'There is an element of that, sir, yes,' Murray grinned. 'And therefore so should I.'

'You might be better advised to keep to your estate, and leave Edinburgh to stew in its own juice,' said Maclean, half-seriously.

'I might indeed. But I'm here now.'

'Well … yes, I should have said – with all the provisos you mention, that they seemed like a happy couple. I should have been very surprised, for example, to discover that she had murdered him. She seemed very upset by his death.'

'And then very frightened.'

'As you say. As, perhaps, should you be, Mr. Murray. Someone who waits eight years and then pounces and kills, like my Ferdinand here, must be a ruthless man indeed. He might not like to have anyone enquiring after him, however politely.'

He could not help a little shiver as he thought afterwards of Maclean's words. Outside the stair it seemed brighter and safer, but he was glad, nevertheless, to see Robbins emerge from the doorway.

'Any joy at the other flats?' he asked.

'I spoke with Mr. Maclean's manservant first, sir. A very respectable individual. He remembered the Ochills well enough, though he didn't have much to do with them. But he did tell me something interesting, sir. A young man was enquiring for the Ochills recently, only a few days ago. He went up to Mr. Maclean's flat and spoke with the manservant. Of course, he had no idea where Mrs. Ochill had gone, but he did remember that her servant had gone to live at Inch, and since the young man seemed honest and well-dressed he gave him that direction.'

'That is indeed interesting. I don't suppose the honest and well-dressed young man left his name at all?'

'No, sir.'

'Ah, well. What about the other flats, then?'

'None of them was here when the Ochills were, sir,' said Robbiins, following Murray out of New Assembly Close. The High Street was as busy as ever, the coffee houses just as full of lawyers and their friends, and soldiers and Highlanders tried to march smartly between the viewing platforms. They were too far down the hill to see whether or not Mr. Boot had made much progress with his.

'Did any of them know the names of the people they had taken over from?'

'There's a caretaker in the other top one, sir, because Lady Farquhar who was there has died, and the estate is complicated. The Ochills were on the second floor under her and that flat has a family in it now, a father and two daughters. The maid said she didn't think the family knew the previous occupants at all: they have come in from the country because the young ladies are of marriageable age.'

'And the other second floor flat?'

'A lady on her own, sir. She was out, but the cook was happy to talk. She's been with the lady in various Old Town flats for years. They took this one on from a Mr. and Miss Abernyte, after their mother had died.'

'Oh! A widowed woman and her two children. From the way Mr. Maclean described them, I had pictured much younger children.'

'Miss Abernyte is a cripple, sir, and so they wanted to find somewhere else where she would find it easier to go in and out. The cook said she had met the two, and that Miss Abernyte was a lovely young lady but so unfortunate. The family had fallen on hard times, though they had been wealthy.'

'The Old Town is such a mixture,' said Murray. 'Two brothers on the ground floor have apparently risen in the world since then. And further down?'

But Robbins described the lower floors much as Mr. Maclean had, except that he had discovered that the young milliner's name was Groves.

'It should be easy enough to discover her from the street directory, if she is still a milliner,' said Murray.

'Unless she is married, sir.'

'She might keep her maiden name for business, if her husband was happy for her to continue. We'll see. As to the others, well, we have the Abernytes' name now, and that is not a common one. Perhaps Viscount Melville's many helpers would be able to discover the names and whereabouts of anyone else on the stair when the Ochills were there.'

'Where to now, sir?' asked Robbins.

'Mrs. Ochill's funeral. It's starting from her old maid's cottage at the Inch. Let's go over this. I feel I am working in two directions at the moment, and I'm not sure what I'm gaining in either direction.'

They turned right down South Bridge, the wind whipping at their collars and coat tails, and headed for Newington and beyond.

'First there's what Mrs. Ochill was when she died, who she knew, and where she was. She lived a very retired life, and anyone of her old acquaintance seemed to think she had left town altogether. Her only visitor seems to have been Mrs. McGregor, a Royal seamstress, now dead. Apart from the maid Helen at the palace I haven't spoken to anyone else who knew her there – perhaps I should be working on that. When she was evicted from the palace, she took her belongings and went to stay with her old maid, Mrs. Duguid. A young, slim, dark-haired man was seen trying to gain access to the cottage there, and was also perhaps seen with a thick sheaf of papers around Holyroodhouse – or at least someone of that description was seen and has not been accounted for. I have not yet found anyone who saw his face clearly, or it may be their faces.'

'Annoying, sir.'

'Indeed. I don't know why she had gone back to her old apartment, or the exact time of her death – not even the exact day, in fact. It could have been Thursday or Friday last. She was stabbed, but the weapon was removed. She did not appear to have been robbed – she was wearing several items of reasonably good jewellery.'

'I thought, sir, that you said she had gone into Holyroodhouse claiming poverty after her husband died?'

'A good point, Robbins. Yes, she did, or that's what she told a number of people. Yet, indeed, she had good jewellery and some possessions she could well have sold, if she had been in desperate straits. I believe she also paid her rent on leaving New Assembly Close, so she was not in debt.'

'Living within her means, perhaps, sir.'

'Yes, perhaps she was just being careful. Or perhaps … perhaps she made more of her poverty because she wanted to be somewhere she could feel safe?'

'Safe, sir?'

'Yes … let's go back to when the Ochills were living in the Old Town. He was working for the Government in some semi-secret capacity, looking into the matter of support for Bonaparte amongst Highlanders who might have had Jacobite sympathies in earlier years. He was not, by two accounts, a particularly pleasant character, but he and his wife seem to have been happy together. She comes across as pleasant but not very sociable, often seen writing. Eventually her husband approaches Hutcheon & Purvis with a view to having his wife's book of Gaelic poetry published. She comes in and happily signs the contract, and thereafter enjoys some popularity amongst literary circles in the town. Then her husband is murdered –'

'Outside the back door of Hutcheon & Purvis, if you'll forgive me, sir.'

'Of course, that's important – or it's important we should remember it. Yes, he's murdered outside their premises, and apparently at the back of the house then occupied (and perhaps occupied yet) by Alistair MacDonell of Glengarry, one of the people, if we believe the list we were sent, who was being investigated by Ochill himself. So, Ochill dies, other government officials investigate but find nothing conclusive, and his widow, apparently terrified – according to Mr. Maclean – writes to her publisher that she will publish no more, and departs at night with all her belongings for a grace and favour apartment at Holyroodhouse, and oblivion.'

'Where she is later murdered.'

'Exactly, Robbins. So the link with her husband's murder seems clear, doesn't it? Am I leaping to conclusions?'

'It looks likely, sir. I don't think you are.'

'So she's safe in the Palace for eight years, and the minute – well, only a day or so after – she leaves, she is dead. Was it Glengarry, who is mad enough for anything? Or was it someone else – this young, slim man with dark hair?'

Chapter Nineteen

MRS. DUGUID'S COTTAGE was not exactly large, but it was quite large enough for Mrs. Ochill's funeral party.

By the time Murray and Robbins arrived, quite close to the appointed time for departure, the party consisted of Mrs. Duguid, the assistant minister from the Canongate Kirk, the beadle from the same Kirk, and a few of the servants from Inch House, brought in to make up the numbers. The rest of the space was taken up by the coffin and the Newfoundland dog, both of which were at least officially in the little bedroom. The dog, however, preferred the company of the living, and kept pushing his way back out again to slump in his usual place by the hearth.

The assistant minister was a young man and clearly anxious about the dog but determined to be brave, and he sat by it on a low stool, patting its head awkwardly. The beadle, who had probably been to many more funerals than the younger man, had made himself comfortable close to the table where the refreshments were laid. Mrs. Duguid was enjoying a good gossip with her fellow servants. They all looked up in surprise at the arrival of Murray and Robbins.

'Oh, you again!' said Mrs. Duguid. 'Still, it's not as if we've too many mourners here. This is Mr. Murray, who's supposed to be finding out about Mrs. Ochill's death.'

The minister stood and bowed, as, slowly, did the beadle. The servants shuffled to their feet, sorry to be interrupted.

'Archibald Sallow,' said the minister. 'This is Mr. Cooper, our beadle.'

Murray settled in a chair just vacated by one of the servants, as indicated by Mrs. Duguid. She filled a cup with ale and plonked it down next to him, then gave one to Robbins with similar ceremony. Robbins found a place to stand near the bedroom door, out of the way.

'Did you know Mrs. Ochill well?' Murray asked Mr. Sallow. The minister, who had taken the chance to escape the dog and slipped into the beadle's chair while the beadle was standing, shook his head.

'I never met her,' he said. 'Did you, sir?'

'No: I was asked to investigate her death just after her body was found.'

'Aye, it had been there a few days, they said.' Mr. Sallow swallowed.

'Since Friday, we believe. Did you know her, Mr. Cooper?'

Mr. Cooper had glared at the stool beside the dog and decided it was not feasible for him to sit on it. He had taken up a position on the other side of the bedroom door from Robbins, the pair of them looking like sentries.

'Never met her in my life, to my knowledge,' he said heavily.

'I wonder where she went to church, then?' said Murray. 'If she did.'

'Oh no: could she have been a Papist?' The minister looked aghast. 'I can't bury a Papist in the kirkyard!'

'She wasna a Papist,' said Mrs. Duguid. 'When she lived in New Assembly Close she went to the High Kirk every Sunday. I went with her myself.'

'Then perhaps she still went there?' suggested Sallow.

Murray shook his head.

'If she did, no one who used to know her in the Old Town ever saw her, as far as I can tell. I suspect she did not go to church at all, for she kept very much to herself.'

'Hiding,' added Mrs. Duguid, with a knowing nod of her head.

'From what?' asked the minister, alarmed again.

'From whoever killed her, I suppose,' said the beadle. 'Would that not make sense?'

'I suppose … but who was that? Mr. Murray, have you found out? Surely there can be little mystery about it?'

'Aye, well, they never found out who murdered the woman's husband eight years gone, did they?' said Mrs. Duguid, not unreasonably. 'If it's the same fellow – and why would it be someone else? – then he's gey clever at hiding, is he no?'

Everyone looked at Murray.

'I think he must be,' he agreed. 'I haven't found him yet, anyway.'

'But surely, in the Palace,' said Mr. Sallow. 'Surely it must be easy to find someone there? There must be people all over the place. How could someone go in and kill someone else? In a royal palace?'

'There were people all over the place, certainly,' said Murray. 'But that is part of the problem: no one knows who was where. And the place is full of little corners, particularly in the older part. I'm afraid it's not obvious at all.'

'But that's terrible!' said the minister. 'That there should be a murderer wandering around our parish – around the Palace – unchecked! For eight years, did you say, Mrs. Duguid? Eight years!'

'Well, to be fair,' said Mrs. Duguid, 'he wasna wandering about the Palace and your parish eight years ago, Mr. Sallow. He would have been up in the New Town then.'

Mr. Sallow stared at her.

'I'm not sure that's much comfort, Mrs. Duguid! If he was wandering anywhere in the town it would have been too close. After all, he would not have to wander very far to go from the New Town to the Old, would he?'

'If he's no killed anybody in eight years, though,' put in Mr. Cooper, 'maybe he's no so dangerous as all that. It might be into the next decade before he strikes again.'

'Well, I'll no be here,' said Mrs. Duguid firmly.

'You never know the minute, Mrs. Duguid,' said the beadle. 'You could live till you're ninety, or I could be digging the grave for you tomorrow.'

At this they all nodded solemnly, the minister in particular.

Mrs. Duguid looked disgruntled, as if the beadle was not according with her plans.

'Is it no time she was kisted and away?' she asked, jerking her head in the direction of the bedroom.

'I suppose,' said the beadle. 'Mr. Sallow, are you ready to say a prayer or two over the coffin?'

Mr. Sallow did not look ready at all. Murray wondered how many funerals he had attended as minister. He drained his ale cup and looked regretfully at it, then rose from his chair, taking a Bible from his coat pocket. The rest of the company rose too and one of the servants reached for a hammer and nails. In a few reluctant moments they were crowded into the tiny bedroom, or standing in the doorway. Murray, being tall, stayed at the back. The dog lifted his head at the movement, and scrambled up to sit directly behind Murray, breathing heavily. The minister, who could hear the dog but not see it, glanced at Murray and looked unsettled.

He had marked his place in the Bible and read two appropriate passages with care and some skill. Not yet experienced enough to pray extempore, he then drew out two fresh-looking sheets of paper, and read out a couple of short prayers. With an audible sigh of relief, he signalled the servant to nail down the coffin lid, and remained with head bowed as the beadle hurried the servants into position as bearers. The others parted, the dog took the hint and shifted, and the bearers wiggled the coffin out of the cottage, nearly losing the mortcloth a couple of times in the process. Leaving behind the minister and Mrs. Duguid, and the dog, the short procession set off, back towards the toll gate and the town on the long walk to the Canongate Kirkyard.

Mr. Cooper paced steadily, like a monument in motion, behind the coffin, keeping an eye on the bearers as they passed Cameron Toll and began the long, slow ascent where the cottages and houses drew gradually closer together, and the rocky protuberance of Arthur's Seat rose on their right. Round its whin-golden slopes, on the western side, nestled Holyroodhouse: they were almost taking Mrs. Ochill home.

Yet the whole procession, small as it was, felt wrong. All about them, moving almost with them towards the centre of the town, were cheerful people in incredible outfits, bedecked with feathers and plaid and glinting weaponry. To have a coffin in the midst of this, however modest, seemed very peculiar. It took a while for people to notice their group and fall into respectful silence, bonnets in their hands, before they hurried off to Calton Hill or the Royal Mile or wherever they hoped the spectacle would be best just now.

'Strange, is it not?' Murray remarked to Mr. Cooper who had fallen back beside him. Only Robbins followed in any official capacity, though they had gathered one or two additional mourners who had trailed behind out of curiosity.

'Aye, sir. Very strange.' The beadle eyed Murray sideways, and seemed to decide that he had no objection to being seen walking alongside a gentleman of respectable bearing. 'Mind you, it sounds as if the whole matter is odd. Why would anybody murder a wee old woman?'

'Why, indeed?' said Murray. 'Some of her neighbours must have worshipped at Canongate Kirk, I suppose, even if they are scattered now. Did you never even hear her name mentioned? Did you know, perhaps, her close neighbour Mrs. McGregor? She had been a seamstress, I believe.'

'The English woman? Aye, I ken her. She came to us, not to the English Church.'

'Did she never mention Mrs. Ochill?'

The beadle tutted.

'I canna mind, sir,' he said. 'All Mrs. McGregor has ever talked about lately is the King. The King this, and the King that, and making way for the King's visit, and where he'll say his prayers next Sunday, if he ever turns up, and the King's yacht, and King's Levee for the gentlemen, And worst of all, the King's Drawing Room for the ladies.'

'She is an enthusiast, is she?' asked Murray sympathetically.

'The whole thing's madness, sir. The town in uproar, and I doubt if he ever left London he'll most likely turn and go back.'

'You're not going to the Levee yourself, then?'

The beadle gave a dry laugh, then remembered where he was.

'But see, ken, sir, them that lived in the Palace were in a ballot to go to the Levee or the Drawing Room, depending. There was a list given out, and Mrs. McGregor was just one name under the line. She isna going, but she almost was, and it's driving her mad. That and living with her nephew, for he's trying to get compensation for her being moved out of her apartment, and she's that mortified by him asking the King for money that she's scarce speaking to him.'

'She seems to be a troubled woman,' said Murray, revisiting in his memory his interview with Mrs. McGregor yesterday. She had clearly not been open with him, but then he had landed in, a complete stranger, with news of her friend's murder. What could he expect? But the impression she had given Isobel and Mrs. Helliwell was of a jealous, bitter woman, delighted at the convenience of Mrs. Ochill's death.

'She's a bit of a nuisance, sir,' said Mr. Cooper loftily. 'If she's told me about this list once she's told me a dozen times. See, the next woman up is some poetess, long forgotten, she says, who never did a hand's turn for the royal household, whereas she worked for them for years. I told her she should act with more decent Christian modesty as becoming a woman of her station, and be grateful for what she had. That stopped her complaining – but only for a day or so.'

Poor Mrs. McGregor, thought Murray. No sympathy anywhere. And soon, no doubt, the beadle would be digging her grave, too.

At last they reached the lower levels of the High Street, and climbed once again up between tall, pressing houses and busy, tartan-swathed citizens to the gateway of Canongate Kirk on their right. Now the beadle led the way again, guiding the bearers, tired now, round the bulk of the kirk itself and off to the back of the building where a new grave was cut and waiting. Murray and Robbins steadied themselves on the muddy ground, heads bare and bowed for the brief ceremony of interment. The beadle produced a small flask of whisky which was shared by all the mourners and the two grave-diggers, and at last the men all replaced their black hats, and parted, and Murray and Robbins headed for home. And Murray felt he had learned nothing from the whole experience.

Chapter Twenty

'MACDONELL OF GLENGARRY would be a good deal easier to find, sir,' said Robbins, practically.

'True,' said Murray. They were passing Barrie's Hotel now on Prince's Street, with Oman's Hotel behind them: both of them would be packed with impatient gentry just now. 'Glengarry is the only person who was definitely near Ochill's murder scene eight years ago, if Ochill was right, and definitely at the Palace around the time of Anna Ochill's murder. If he were really involved with Bonaparte in 1814, maybe supporting the escape from Elba, I could see why he might have been defensive then. But to go to the trouble of killing Mrs. Ochill now, when the war is long over? And why would he think that Mrs. Ochill knew anything about it, anyway?'

'Maybe he was taking revenge for something, sir. Maybe Ochill did him more harm than we know.'

'But how? What did he do? And how was Anna Ochill involved?'

'I don't know, sir.'

'Of course you don't, any more than I do.' They reached St. Andrew's Square, and again the view of the Forth reproached Murray. 'The King is as far as the mouth of the Tweed. He could land here tomorrow. And I know hardly anything more than when I started. Melville's father was disappointed in me the last time I did anything for him: what will his son say this time, when my ignorance could be putting the King in danger? And why did he cause me to take this on in the first place? Oh, it's all ridiculous, Robbins. I want to go back to Letho and forget about everything.'

'But then if something did happen to His Majesty, sir?'

Murray sighed.

'I know, I know. I must do my best, regardless. And look at all I might miss if I returned to Letho.'

He gestured ironically at the banners on the buildings, the streets crowded with sightseers, the busy shops selling plaids and weaponry, the Celtic Society gentlemen drawn up in elderly ranks on the grass in the centre of the square, the pipers playing different tunes at opposite corners. Robbins' mouth twitched, and they made their way home in thoughtful silence.

Abernyte was indeed not a common name at all. Murray found the young man in the street directory, designated 'clerk', and with an address in the Pleasance. He wondered when Mr. Abernyte – Robert – dined, and thought it was likely to be around the middle of the day. In addition, he was probably out at work, wherever he was a clerk. Murray decided to go after his own dinner, which was not too far in the future.

'Are we to have you at home on any evening while we are here?' asked Isobel, when he told her of his plans. 'Augusta will have forgotten what you look like.'

'Is she upstairs now?' asked Murray.

'I believe they are not long returned, yes.'

'Then shall we go up now?'

He took her hand and went with her up to the nursery, where a brisk three-quarters of an hour playing with a wooden Noah's Ark delighted everyone concerned – not least Miss Fitzsimmons, as Augusta was now quite ready for a nap.

Dinner, however, had been a time to bring Blair up to date on such progress as had been made in the investigation. Murray was almost ashamed to share it, it seemed so thin. Yet Blair was prepared to make the most of it.

'And Ochill's body was found right outside the publisher's door? And he never saw it?'

'It was dark,' said Murray, 'and I believe the body was over to one side, against a wall. Still, the coincidence is striking.'

'If it is one, dear Charles, if it is one.'

'May I ask,' said young Hepburn politely, 'what it is that you are talking about? Who is Ochill, and when did he die?'

'Eight years ago. Sorry, Hepburn,' said Murray. 'I should

have explained. The body of a woman was found by the decorators at Holyroodhouse, and Viscount Melville – who is I'm sure in all other ways a sensible man – has for some reason seen fit to expect me to find out the murderer, ideally before the arrival of the King.'

Hepburn's eyes widened.

'Is this something you do often, sir? Are you connected with the police office? For you know we have several very experienced Bow Street Runners here to assist with matters during the King's visit.'

'It has been my misfortune to encounter several cases of sudden death,' said Murray, 'and my good fortune, you might say, to bring the perpetrators to some form of justice. Usually with the invaluable advice of Mr. Blair here, and others present.' He smiled at Isobel, and at Robbins. Hepburn looked as if he had never come across such a thing before, and appeared to struggle for a response.

'Then you must be as busy as I, sir,' he said at last, knocking a knife off the table with his sleeve. 'His Majesty is expected to arrive at Leith tomorrow. Do you think you will succeed? For I am quite sure that the plans of the Lord Chamberlain's Office cannot possibly all be completed in time.'

'I wonder how Sir Walter Scott is feeling this evening?' said Mrs. Helliwell.

'He is the reason, of course, why my master Mr. Mash is so concerned,' said Hepburn earnestly. 'The Lord Chamberlain's Office is accustomed to arranging all manner of events involving the King and other lesser dignitaries. Mr. Mash cannot understand, as he has told me, why such responsibilities should have been placed in the hands of an unpractised romantic like Sir Walter Scott, when Mr. Mash himself was quite prepared to travel to so remote a place as Edinburgh in order to oversee everything himself, at no small personal inconvenience. Mr. Mash is a much-respected and experienced official, and is not used to having his advice and recommendations ignored so completely.' Hepburn looked about the table and seemed surprised to find everyone gazing at him. He turned quite pink, and bit his lip. 'I – I'm sorry. Perhaps I have spoken out of turn?'

'You show great loyalty to your master,' said Blair kindly. Everyone else, relieved, nodded and murmured agreement. 'No doubt you are a great asset to him in his difficult task.'

'I try to be, sir,' Hepburn mumbled, almost knocking over his wine glass.

'Would you like Mrs. Helliwell and me to find your milliner?' Isobel asked. 'Miss Groves, was it not?'

'It was. If you feel you have the time and inclination, then any extra information we have on the Ochills at New Assembly Close would be very useful.'

'Shall we consult the street directory after dinner, Mrs. Helliwell?' said Isobel, and they grinned at each other. Mrs. Helliwell seemed very pleased that she had accepted the invitation to Edinburgh. Murray gestured to Robbins to clear the fish plates, and the conversation shook itself and changed direction.

Hepburn had disappeared off to his work again after dinner, and Murray set off on foot to the Pleasance, hoping to find the young man Robert Abernyte. The address was easy enough to discover, near Bell's Brewery, whose sweet smell scented the street. Murray walked along it, noting the right tenement, then strolled on. It struck him that this was very near to Holyroodhouse, and he wanted to take a look to remind himself just how close they were. He had hardly taken a dozen steps along the street when he was suddenly aware of galloping hooves, and before he could turn, something hit him hard from behind, spinning him against a wall and knocking his hat from his head.

He heard a cry, half alarm, half anger, steadied himself, and turned to see what had hit him.

'What did you think you were doing? You stepped out right in front of my horse!'

Murray looked up into the handsome, furious face of Alasdair MacDonell of Glengarry, his plaid flung out behind him and his bonnet dramatically askew.

'Perhaps I was not expecting anyone to be riding quite so violently along a city street,' he said. He had located his hat, but just for the moment thought he would let it lie. The street was going round in circles, and looking up at Glengarry was as much as he could manage. For a moment he thought that Glengarry's anger would flare out, but instead the man laughed.

'You are quite right. I was moving a little quickly. I think you have surprised my mare.'

'Not half as much as she surprised me, I can assure you,' said Murray. Now the shock was passing, the pain was making itself felt: the horse's shoulder had made contact with Murray's arm, the one that had been bruised by the scaffolding pole. His hat looked a long way away.

'Wait – do I know you?' asked Glengarry. 'Weren't you in that damned procession, up on the High Street?'

'I was, yes.' Murray was not sure whether to be pleased or not at being recognised.

'What kind of a Highlander are you?' Glengarry's question sounded light, but Murray was sure it was serious.

'No kind at all,' he said. 'I am from Fife. Murray of Letho, sir, at your service.'

'MacDonell of Glengarry, as I seem to remember you know. I admire your honesty, at least, sir,' said Glengarry. 'Too many pretending Highlanders in Edinburgh just now. Yet you were wearing a plaid, I think?'

'I was asked to by the Duke of Atholl.'

Glengarry's eyebrows rose, and he nodded. Murray seemed to have passed some kind of muster.

'I'm sorry if I injured you,' said Glengarry, gracious at last. He swung a leg over and slid off the horse, bent in one elegant movement and retrieved Murray's hat, giving it a shake before handing it back. They bowed, in Murray's case very warily.

'No doubt you were in a hurry, sir,' he said. 'You must have a great deal to do just now. I believe you have even been busy preparing Holyroodhouse for the use of His Majesty.'

'Holyroodhouse? Oh, yes: terrible place. Or at least it has been allowed to decline to a terrible state,' said Glengarry, without apparent concern. 'They have done a tremendous amount to it. Are you involved?'

'Only peripherally, sir. I am a little acquainted with a woman who lived there, in one of the grace and favour apartments. She had an invitation to be at the King's Drawing Room next week. A Mrs. Ochill. I wonder if you have ever come across her?'

Glengarry shrugged.

'I don't believe I know anyone of that name,' he said. 'Was she one of the beauties they are lining up to impress the King?'

'She is an older woman, sir. Her husband died some eight

years ago, murdered, in the New Town. His body was found in a lane to the north of Rose Street.'

'How unfortunate for her. She must have been an unhappy woman,' said Glengarry. 'Well, if you are quite well, I'm afraid you must excuse me. I am, as you surmised, in rather a hurry. Delighted to make your acquaintance, Mr. Murray, and apologies again for the painful manner of it.'

He made use of a low wall to mount again, raised his hat to Murray, and rode off at a more decorous trot. Murray found himself pondering on two things. The first was that he hoped he himself would be able to mount and dismount so smoothly when he was Glengarry's age. The second was to wonder why Glengarry had spoken of Mrs. Ochill in the past tense, when Murray had not mentioned that she was dead.

Robert Abernyte was not yet home from his work, but was expected at any moment, according to a very young maid at the ground floor flat. She showed Murray in anyway, taking his card.

'I'll tell Miss Abernyte that you're here,' she said, and skipped away with assurance. In a moment she was back, and ushered Murray into the front room looking on to the street.

'Mr. Murray,' said Miss Abernyte. 'Please forgive me not rising to curtsey, but as you can see I am unable to.'

'I am sorry to disturb you, Miss Abernyte,' said Murray, bowing.

'Not at all. I lead a dull life, and it is pleasant to have a new visitor.' She gestured him to a chair, and asked the maid to bring refreshments. 'It will only be tea, I'm afraid,' she said. 'We rarely have much in the way of sweet things in the house.'

He took the chair she indicated, doing his best to take in the room, and his hostess, without seeming nosy.

The place was furnished well, if a little shabbily, and there were several shelves of books in an alcove, all of them well-fingered. Miss Abernyte had been reading when he had arrived, her couch as close to the window as could be to catch the best of the daylight. She herself was no more than thirty, he thought, and with a cultured air. Her face was remarkably pretty, her complexion as fine as any lady invited to the King's Drawing Room, and her hair, though not elaborately dressed, was thick and glossy. But he could see that she suffered some disfigurement, for her left hand and arm were thin and useless, and her left leg, from what he could judge, was similarly afflicted, probably from birth. When the maid returned, she poured the tea and handed a cup and saucer to Murray and then to her mistress, making sure Miss Abernyte had the saucer steady before she let it go.

'To what do we owe the pleasure? Or are you only in search of my brother, Mr. Murray? He should not be much longer.'

'I had hoped to speak with both of you,' said Murray. 'It concerns a tenement in New Assembly Close where, I believe, you lived previously. Is that the case?'

'That dreadful place!' cried Miss Abernyte at once. 'If you are come to tell me it has burned to the ground, I should be delighted!'

Chapter Twenty-One

THE STREET DIRECTORY had been applied to again, and when Mrs. Helliwell and Isobel discovered that the only Miss Groves, Milliner, lived almost behind them in Thistle Street, they felt they had time after dinner to make their visit.

Miss Groves was happy to receive them, and not at all surprised at two new apparent customers.

'There's been all sorts in here these last weeks,' she said, seating them on a chaise longue in her narrow parlour. Bonnets, caps and other headware lined the walls on pegs and on shelves. Though she was not a small woman, Miss Groves moved delicately amongst her merchandise, and was discreet in her assessment of Isobel's and Mrs. Helliwell's bonnets. 'So many lovely ladies! Is it for a specific Royal occasion, ladies? Or something suitable for watching events from an hotel window?'

'Oh, the latter,' said Isobel. 'Something different, to help us join in with the celebrations.'

'How lovely! Have you any colour in mind? Madam?' She turned to Mrs. Helliwell. 'I see you know how well that rich brown looks on you, but have you thought of it in this pretty new shape?' She lifted an airy bonnet from a shelf. It was dark green, but adorned with yellow daisies. 'This trim would be lovely with the brown, and very appropriate, don't you think? Just charming.'

There was some discussion of the idea. Mrs. Helliwell was keen: Isobel knew she had been looking for something to remind her of her visit, and a fashionable bonnet, once every few years, was not beyond her.

'You came highly recommended,' said Isobel, watching Miss Groves measure Mrs. Helliwell's grey head. 'And I can see why. Have you been here long? For I had heard that you were in the Old Town – New Assembly Close, was it not?'

'That's right,' said Miss Groves easily. 'But it's been years since I came down here. Six, maybe seven years? I was so lucky to find such a good place, and everything just as I would like it.'

'You have a very pretty establishment,' said Mrs. Helliwell encouragingly.

'Thank you, madam. I like my ladies to think they might have happened upon a lovely little chamber of magic here, where all is prettiness and anything lovely might happen.' She sighed happily. 'May I ask who it was who recommended me?'

'It was a Mrs. Ochill,' said Isobel. She picked up a bonnet almost at random, wondering if anything lovely might happen. 'What about this blue one, Mrs. Helliwell? What do you think?'

'If you'll forgive me, madam, that blue is a touch too bright for your delicate complexion and the lovely shade of your hair. Perhaps this one?' Miss Groves found something nearer what Isobel would have called cornflower, a shade she wore a good deal. Miss Groves was right: it was much better than the more skyrie blue of the first bonnet. 'Yes, Mrs. Ochill was one of my neighbours,' she said, as Isobel examined the effect in a small mirror. 'I'm honoured that she should have thought of me after all these years. What a lovely thing to do!'

'She is elderly now,' said Isobel, 'and a little frail, and I have only known her a little while. What was she like then? When she was younger and more herself?' She assumed a kindly, concerned look, implying that Mrs. Ochill's mind was touched by advancing years but that she was being well looked after.

'Well, now, she was lovely. She and Mr. Ochill were a lovely couple.'

Concealing her surprise, Isobel pressed on.

'I'm sure they were much loved neighbours there. Was it a good stair to live in?'

'It was, yes,' said Miss Groves. 'The Ochills were great friends with the Abercrombies – no, the Abernytes. Mrs. Abernyte was a widow, and so sweet with her two children there.'

'I suppose Mr. Ochill could act as a protector,' Mrs. Helliwell suggested. 'Widows can be so vulnerable.'

'Well, really, it was Mr. Maclean on the top floor who took

Mrs. Abernyte under his wing. I think he was a little fond of her, you know? He was very good to her and the children. I wondered if they were kin, perhaps, but I think they weren't. I think he just cared for her. And she was lovely. And then after she died, poor thing, he helped young Abernyte find a job, I believe. Which was just lovely, as he was so keen to support his mother and sister. They were all devoted to each other – so charming! Such a close little family. Lady Farquhar on the top floor was lovely, too, just delightful, though of course very frail then.'

'Were you there when Mrs. Ochill lost her husband?'

'Oh!' Miss Groves' eyes filled easily with tears. 'Yes, yes I was. What a terrible time that was! Mrs. Abernyte was too ill by then to help her with much, and Mr. Maclean … he was so lovely about it … and I … well, we did what we could, in the circumstances. But I wasn't surprised when she moved away, really. Her heart was broken. It was a tragedy, a real tragedy. Like when Mrs. Abernyte died. That was a real tragedy. Oh, dear, such memories! And such lovely, lovely people. Lovely people.'

'If I hear the word 'lovely' once more this evening,' said Isobel when they were clear of the flat, 'I may not be responsible for my actions.'

'Oh, she's a sweetheart,' said Mrs. Helliwell. 'And her bonnets are delightful. I am very much looking forward to my new one – and I'm sure when you receive yours you will be just lovely!'

In a main door flat on the Pleasance, Miss Abernyte almost at once corrected herself, with a small apologetic smile that warmed her pretty eyes.

'No, I am much too harsh on poor old New Assembly Close. Forgive me, Mr. Murray! We had an unhappy stay there but in fact the neighbours were very kind. I should not even pretend to wish them harm. It is only that we moved there when my father died and we were ruined: we had to sell our lovely home and most of the contents. What you see here is all that was left. And then when we were just beginning to learn the ways of our new life, and Robert had just finished as much schooling as we could afford, and was able to make a proper living for himself and for us, my mother fell ill and died. We moved here not long afterwards, to leave the worst of all those memories behind us.'

'Then I am very sorry to bring them back for you. Perhaps you would rather I left?'

'Oh, no, Mr. Murray. No, please forgive me and my self-pity. We are so very fortunate in many ways, and Robert and I at least have each other, and a secure home, and a great lesson to be grateful for all we have. No, if we can be of assistance – I do not even know yet what it is you want or need! And here is Robert,' she added, glancing out at the street. 'Between us we should be able to help you.'

In a moment there was scuffling and voices in the hall, and a flurry at the doorway as a young man entered the room, his coat still halfway down his arms and a half-smile of puzzled welcome on his face. He could hardly have been anything but Miss Abernyte's brother, though their colouring was different: her warm brown hair and blue eyes surrounded a face the same shape as his, though his hair was darker and his eyes brown.

'Robert Abernyte,' he introduced himself with a bow, finally freeing his hands from the coat.

'Charles Murray of Letho,' said Murray, on his feet to greet his host. 'I must apologise for disturbing you on your return from work, and in the course of an enquiry which I now understand might be uncomfortable for you, or at least bring back unwelcome memories.'

'Good heavens, what is it?' Robert stepped over to kiss his sister's head, laying an affectionate arm on her shoulder, then flung himself into a chair. 'A cup of tea, Minnie, and I shall be fit for anything.' The maid left to fetch another cup and saucer and a pot of hot water.

'He wants to ask us something about New Assembly Close, Robert, and I told him it had not been a happy time for us – what with our reasons for being there and then Mamma.'

'That much is true,' said Robert, now leaning forward. 'But it is probably not what you came to find out, sir. What do you want to know?'

Murray set aside his cup and saucer.

'Where did you move from to live in Edinburgh?'

'A place called Melvaig,' said Robert Abernyte at once. 'Near Gairloch.'

'Quite a distance, certainly,' said Murray. 'Miss Abernyte says the neighbours were kind to you in your trials. I wonder what you can remember of them? Perhaps specifically of a Mr. and Mrs. Ochill?'

'The Ochills? Yes, I remember them,' said Robert.

'Mrs. Ochill was a quiet woman,' said Miss Abernyte. 'She called on us more than on others, but she was not very sociable. I believe our mother returned her calls, but I could not, of course.'

'She was a poetess, I believe?' said Murray. The twist of Robert's mouth told him what Robert thought of that, but Miss Abernyte glanced up at the shelves of books.

'I am very fond of poetry, myself,' she said, 'but I don't believe we ever acquired a copy of Mrs. Ochill's book. That was not long before we left there, of course. Our mother was not well.'

'And Mr. Ochill? Were you acquainted with him, Mr. Abernyte?'

'I met him on the stair, of course,' said Robert Abernyte, 'but he was much older than I. I would have been nineteen or twenty when we left there, would I not?' He checked with his sister. 'Yes, barely a man! And Mr. Ochill of course was a good deal older. He may not even have been aware of my existence, in the way the older sometimes are not, while the younger always notice the older. For my part, I would have preferred not to attract his attention in any case. He seemed an unpleasant man – no, that's not quite the word. Uncomfortable, perhaps? I mean he made me feel uncomfortable, as if he knew things or could see things that no one else could. I heard he worked for the government, but I have no idea what it was he did.'

'Did you ever see visitors go to their flat? Friends, or perhaps work colleagues?'

'No, never that I can recall. You could not accuse the Ochills of leading a riotous life, certainly. It was a quiet stair, for the most part. I suppose we were lucky enough to find a place there.' He exchanged a look with his sister. He seemed more reconciled to their time there than she had been.

'Were they on good terms with other neighbours?'

'It was more that they weren't *not* on good terms, really,' said Robert. 'Old Mr. Maclean on the top floor, he could be a grumphie, but I don't remember any particular argument.'

'He was always very kind to us, Robert,' said Miss Abernyte. 'When Mamma was ill, remember the fruit he sent her? And the wine? He really is a kind man, Mr. Murray. Have you spoken to him? He had probably been there longer than anyone. Like me, he didn't go out very much, but his manservant told him everything that was going on.'

That had been the impression Robbins had had of the manservant. Murray sat back, thinking. He liked this young pair, and was glad he had found them to speak to, but in a way they were not the most useful of informants. Robert at the time of Ochill's death had been exactly the age when young men pay more attention to their own world than to anyone else's, unless the other person should happen to be a pretty girl, and Miss Abernyte could not have been out and about to see things for herself, had she been any more observant.

'Do you remember much about Mr. Ochill's death?' he asked, without much hope. Miss Abernyte shrugged one shoulder.

'I remember that night,' she said, 'because Mamma had a very bad turn, and we were trying to nurse her and go for help and all the rest. So when those men came the next day to tell us he had been killed and to ask us what we knew, I could tell them nothing at all – in fact, I had been sound asleep when they came. It was an awful thing to happen, though. I kept the news from Mamma for several days, fearing she might relapse with the shock. Poor Mrs. Ochill!' she added dutifully.

'Aye, no more poetry for her after that,' added Robert, shaking his head sadly. 'No more money.'

'And we know how that feels, don't we, Robert?

'But things are looking up!' Robert cried suddenly, beaming at her. At once she grinned back. It was as if the two had a pact, when gloom descended, to pick each other up as quickly as possible. They had had enough to face, after all in their young lives.

'Where is it you work, Mr. Abernyte?' Murray asked.

'I work for a lawyer in South Clerk Street,' said Robert at once, with a degree of pride. 'I am soon to be a senior clerk, if all goes well!'

'I hope it will,' said Murray sincerely. 'Tell me, though, have you anything to do with all these preparations for the King's visit?'

'No, none at all, only that I helped to fix a banner over our door on South Clerk Street. The King might come in that way from Dalkeith, you know. The streets are swept every few hours, just in case!'

'Or anything to do with Holyroodhouse? With the refurbishment, perhaps, or with a client who lived there?'

'No, not at all. Ours is quite a small firm, though growing quickly! We would have no clients of that standing, not yet.'

'Our' firm – Murray smiled to himself. Young Robert was ambitious, anyway. But he had had to ask about Holyroodhouse, for here, at least, was a slim young man with dark hair who had known John Ochill at the time of his murder.

He had left soon after, with the maid handing him his hat and gloves with some misgivings.

'I gave it a brush, sir, but just look at it!'

'Oh, goodness!' said Robert, who had followed Murray out into the hall. 'What happened, sir?'

'I had a collision with a horse at the corner down there.'

Robert was shocked.

'I hope the rider stopped! I'm sure it was one of these mad Highlanders, was it not?'

'In a way, yes,' said Murray with a smile. 'It was MacDonell of Glengarry. And he did dismount and apologise.'

'Glengarry?' Robert repeated. 'I'd be careful, sir, if I were you. He's a dangerous man.'

'So I gather. He tried to stop the procession on Monday – goodness, only yesterday! The one fetching the Honours from the Castle. Did you see it? Perhaps you were there: I think three quarters of Edinburgh was in the High Street.'

'Ah, no, sir, I was nowhere near that. My employer says that if the King actually lands we may go and see him, but otherwise we have plenty of work to do!'

'Ah well, I daresay there will be plenty more to see. Good day to you again, and thank you for all your help. I hope I have not disturbed too many unhappy memories.'

'Not at all, sir. My sister and I are very happily settled, as you see.'

Yet Murray still had some misgivings as he walked back to

the New Town. Miss Abernyte had been older than her brother, and so more aware, perhaps, of what had been happening in that tenement in 1814 and before. Was there more she might have told him, if Robert had not come home when he did? Would it be worth another visit, later, during Robert's work time? Or perhaps ... perhaps Isobel might call on her? After all, there were probably things Isobel would think to ask that he had not. He wondered more idly which lawyer in Newington Robert worked for so promisingly. His own father, also Charles Murray, had had a wide acquaintance amongst the lawyers of the town, and Murray's was therefore almost as wide amongst their children, many of whom were now lawyers, too. He hoped that Robert had chosen an employer from amongst the best of them, and that his career would prosper now after such dark beginnings. After all, he had a charming sister to look after.

'I fear it will take some work,' said Robbins, hands working round the desolate brim of Murray's hat. 'Did you suffer injury yourself, sir?'

'A knock to my shoulder, unfortunately,' Murray admitted. 'The same one I hit yesterday. I saw a few stars, I can tell you!'

'Will you want to go down to supper, sir, or would you prefer to rest and I shall bring something up?'

'No, no, I'll go down. Better to keep moving.'

'Aye, sir.'

It hurt, though, to change his shirt and coat, and he hoped that if Augusta were brought down to say good night that she would not wish to be lifted and swung in the air as usual. His whole right side was tender. But there, it could be worse: what must it be like to be as Miss Abernyte was, one side crippled from birth? It must have been a relief just to move to a flat on the ground floor and feel more a part of the world. It was unlikely she would ever marry, or cease to be dependent on her brother. And if he married, she would no longer even be mistress in her own home. Yet the pair of them seemed optimistic, devoted, determined to look to the future. He found he not only liked, but admired them, a little.

At the supper table, Isobel and Mrs. Helliwell told him and Blair of their visit to Miss Groves and her lovely romantic view of the stair in New Assembly Close.

'A little fairyland in the Old Town,' said Isobel. 'But we

have ordered two charming bonnets.'

'Then your visit was not in vain,' said Murray. 'I wonder at the idea that Maclean on the top floor was so attached to the Abernytes. They called him an old grumphie, actually.'

'And what were they like?'

Murray was ready to report on his visit, and on his encounter with Glengarry, but he had barely drawn breath when Robbins appeared with a note for him. He read it quickly, then read it again, out loud.

'"To Mr. Murray of Letho. I believe you are in the service of Viscount Melville regarding the safety of His Majesty on his forthcoming visit. It has come to my notice that there is planned an attack on the King during his progress from Leith to the Gate of the Town, which will endanger his safety and perhaps his life, not to say the reputation of the city of Edinburgh. I trust you will know what to do with this information to ensure the King's security." There is no signature.'

'Endangering the King's safety?' echoed Blair. 'Oh, Charles, my boy, what are we to do?'

Chapter Twenty-Two

'PASS IT ON to Viscount Melville,' said Isobel at once. 'It cannot be your task to search for some vague danger all the way from Leith harbour to – to where? Anywhere in Edinburgh? Surely there are other people already doing this kind of thing? There are soldiers all over the town!'

'Quite right,' said Mrs. Helliwell. 'This is surely a responsibility too great for any one man, Mr. Murray.'

Half reluctantly and half with relief, Murray concurred.

'I shall send it on to Viscount Melville at once. I wonder who sent it, though, and why they should have sent it to me?'

'No doubt someone you have spoken to in the last day or so,' said Isobel briskly. 'Let Melville sort it out.'

Murray read through the note once more, then asked Robbins to fetch pen and paper.

'I had better put it in a cover for Melville, anyway,' he said. 'I wonder why he writes "the Gate of the Town" like that. See?' He turned the note around so that each of them could look.

'Oh,' said Mrs. Helliwell, 'I think I saw that today! Don't you know about it?' she asked Blair, as the most likely to know what she was talking about. He looked puzzled for a brief moment, and then light dawned.

'Oh! The great Gate at Picardy Place! Is that what you mean? What the writer means?'

'What great Gate?' asked Murray.

'Oh, it's more theatrics,' said Mrs. Helliwell with a smile. 'So that the King knows he has actually arrived in Edinburgh, Sir Walter has caused a great gateway to be built at the top of Leith Walk in Picardy Place. You know, the other end of this street.'

'Yes, yes,' said Murray, 'but what do you mean, a gate? Surely they have not actually put up a real gate?'

'No, of course not,' said Blair, jittery with excitement at the thought. 'You'll have to come and look at it, Charles. It's a great wooden structure covered in painted canvas, like a stage set –'

'Exactly like a stage set. That's what it is,' said Mrs. Helliwell, as pleased with it as Blair. 'That actor-manager at the Theatre Royal had a hand in it, by all accounts.'

'And it looks like a great city gate, and that's the way the King's carriage will come up from Leith and then there will be keys presented to him and then he'll be driven round into the very end of Queen Street then up and through St. Andrew's Square and down on to Prince's Street and then up past Oman's Hotel and towards Calton Hill and down and round on the new road to Holyroodhouse,' said Blair rapidly, all on one breath. Murray wondered if he had had sight of some of Sir Walter's plans and had memorised them. No doubt, anyway, that the statement was accurate: Blair had a wonderful memory for details like that.

'It's all just like a huge play, isn't it?' said Isobel. 'I've filled three sketchbooks already just from watching the street outside, and another from yesterday's procession. I feel I could publish a book afterwards.'

'What a wonderful idea!' said Mrs. Helliwell. 'And Mr. Murray has just met a publisher!'

'Who might have been involved in a murder,' Murray reminded her. 'I think I'd rather look elsewhere just now.'

'By the time I might be ready to publish, you'll no doubt have worked out whether or not he is guilty,' said Isobel, almost reassuringly. 'Let's just see what happens, shall we?'

Murray took a moment to write a note to Viscount Melville and wrapped it around the anonymous paper, handing it all to Robbins to arrange dispatch.

'Thank you, Robbins. For immediate delivery.'

'Sir.'

'His Majesty is supposed to be arriving tomorrow,' said Blair.

'He is, isn't he?' said Murray flatly. 'I don't feel as if I am anywhere near sorting this out, and yet I have been running about the place, finding things out … just the wrong things, or useless things.'

'It was only the day before yesterday that you were given this commission,' Isobel reminded him. 'I think you have done a very great deal in the time you were given. A woman with no friends and few acquaintances, dying on an undetermined day for no clear reason – what did Viscount Melville expect from you? Miracles are thin on the ground these days.' She cast an apologetic look at Mrs. Helliwell, minister's wife, but Mrs. Helliwell nodded.

'He seems to have expected far too much,' she agreed sympathetically.

'And yet there must be something more I can do. This gate: it is intended that the King should go through it, is it?'

'Yes, I believe so,' she said. 'It is certainly large enough.'

'From the note,' said Murray, 'it seems that the writer believes the threat is somewhere between the harbour and the gate, not further up than that.'

'Yes, but Charles,' said Isobel, 'there is no evidence that this threat is anything to do with what you have been charged with investigating. How could the death of a woman in Holyroodhouse be connected with some attack planned on, say, Leith Walk? He is the King: there must be any number of people and factions who would like to frighten or harm him, or unbalance the state in some way. The place is full of Highlanders – how many of them had fathers and grandfathers out in 1745? How many were harried by the Duke of Cumberland, the King's uncle? How many were involved in that business only two years ago, causing trouble? How many madmen are there who will do anything to attract attention to their cause, however ill-conceived? There is little chance that a murderer in one place is the same as an attacker in another, is there?'

Blair nodded sadly at his daughter's words, and looked to Murray. Murray took a moment to consider.

'You are quite right, my dear,' he said. 'Everything you say is true. All I can offer is that someone sent me that note – sent it to me. As you said yourself, it is likely that it came from someone I have been speaking with since Sunday morning when all this business came to light. Someone I have met has thought it best to tell me about this threat, and the people with whom I have spoken have been connected with the Ochills or with Holyroodhouse. So I think there is a chance that the two threats are indeed linked. And in any case,' he added with a smile, 'what better way to spend an hour or so on a summer evening than to go and inspect a fake gateway? I have no other lines that I can follow, at this time of the night, anyway. If the King arrives tomorrow I have done all I can think of. In the morning I shall go and see Mrs. Duguid again, to find out if that young man has been back, but for now, shall we take a walk after supper?'

Isobel sighed, but grinned back at him.

'Oh, very well,' she said. 'I should know by now that if someone gives you a task to do, you will not leave it until it is done. I seem to have married a terrier!'

'A Newfoundland dog would be more restful,' said Murray, remembering the one in Mrs. Duguid's cottage. 'I am sorry, my dear. I should be able to deter intruders with one bark, and never shift from my own hearth while I do it.'

The earlier damp wind had eased somewhat and the four of them, along with Smith pushing Blair's wheeled chair, enjoyed the fresh air as they walked along Queen Street towards the top of Leith Walk. The remarkable structure of the gate was visible long before they reached it, standing splendidly in the midst of Picardy Place, the focus of many on similar promenades as the populace made their own inspections of the King's proposed route for the next morning.

'Good heavens,' said Murray, 'it must be thirty feet tall – and then the fortifications on top!'

The ubiquitous workmen were climbing around the fake gateway, which had a large arched aperture fit for a grand carriage, but currently blocked by a wooden gate in two parts, one still off its hinges. The front of the gateway seemed to be complete but the back, facing Murray and his party, was causing vexation for the workmen as they tried to drape it with lengths of painted canvas. Whether the canvas was wet from the weather or too freshly painted, it was clearly heavy and awkward and there was a good deal of shouting going on, with men on the ground, men on the fortifications, and men inside the great wooden framework, trying to undo unintended folds and creases as the canvas swayed and cracked.

'You have to see it from the front, though,' said Mrs. Helliwell, eyes bright with suppressed amusement. She clearly did not feel her journey from Fife to have been in vain. She urged them round the outside of the gateway and down Leith Walk a little, then told them to turn around. The gateway loomed above them, painted like a stage fortress with grey and cream stonework. A line of shields had been arranged above the opening with the Royal shield in the central position, a little larger than the rest. Murray had no wish to enquire as to the authenticity of the others. The direct line to the gate had been roped off to each side, and an arrangement of trees in pots had been created just before the gate, as though one were approaching the city through some picturesque Highland wilderness. As they watched in awe, one of the workmen erected a flagpole at the top of the battlements, and Murray was startled by a loud and heartfelt groan from a man next to him, looking in the same direction.

'See yon flagpole?' said the man, eager to talk to someone. Murray was about his height, which no doubt helped. 'See that? I'm supposed to be up there the morrow, playing my pipes for the King.'

'That's a great honour,' said Murray.

'Oh, aye, sir. Sic a great honour, that's what they tellt me. Hang on to the flagpole, lad, says the officer, and you'll be grand.'

'You don't think it's safe?' asked Murray.

'See yon scaffolding fell down up the High Street? I doubt this is no better.' He took a breath, happy to have found a ready audience. 'See the size of me? Well, I'm twice the size of most of they workmen up there just now. They've a wee door, a wee tiny door, made into the frame round the back, ken. I've nearly to go on my knees to get through it. Then they've made steps – well, you'd be safer climbing a tree. And then there's a hatch, to keep the rain out. And I've to squeeze through that, with my pipes an' all, and stand up on yon roof. The floor's that thin you could near spit through it. That's if I'm no blown to my death on the street in front of the King's aun carriage - or worse still, straight into it and land on him. Then it'd be the Tower for me,' he said darkly. 'But at least it's better built.' He heaved another sigh, added, 'Good evening to you, sir,' and wandered mournfully away.

'Did he say there are steps inside the gate? Actual steps?' asked Blair.

'No, Papa, you cannot possibly ask Smith to carry you up there,' said Isobel firmly.

'I suppose ...'

'Mr. Blair, I fear you and I are not nimble enough to avoid greatly inconveniencing the workmen,' said Mrs. Helliwell. 'We must just appreciate the spectacle from down here – and I for one never saw anything like it!'

'You are right, Mrs. Helliwell,' said Blair, though Murray was sure he would have talked his way in had he only still had both legs. He himself looked up thoughtfully at the construction, wondering whose fanciful idea it had been. Tomorrow, all being well, the King himself would ride in his carriage through that make-believe gateway. If he had not been attacked on his way here from Leith, would this be a prime position for an attempt on his life?

Chapter Twenty-Three

ON WEDNESDAY MORNING, Murray rose and immediately went to see what the weather was like. The previous evening had not been too bad, only a little damp and breezy as they returned from their inspection of the grand gateway. This morning, as though the weather were determined to prove that it was not August, was both blustery and soaking. Rain struck the window so hard Murray almost jumped back, and the view of the Forth trailed in long lines down the glass. No beplaided yeomanry practised today in the gardens opposite. The street was almost empty. Murray's heart leapt with joy – was this another reprieve? In weather like this, surely the Royal Yacht would stay safely at the mouth of the Tweed, half into Scotland, half still in England, symbolically, anyway. But there were steam ships too in the flotilla. The King might be transferred to one of those, and arrive even faster than expected.

He opened the shutters properly, decided to leave Robbins in peace for now, and sat at a table by the window where he had placed Mrs. Ochill's writing slope and the pretty copies of her book of poetry. Had he exhausted all their possibilities? He opened the writing slope again and stared at it. Was this where Mrs. Ochill had written her poetry? The thin, golden brown leather was worn, certainly, and the slope itself had seen a long and useful life: the hinges were a bit loose, and the lock was broken though the catch was still secure enough. Someone had told him that the Ochills were not quick to spend money, and this seemed to be evidence of that, unless she had kept the slope for more sentimental reasons. Had she written while she was at Holyroodhouse? He had not found any poetic scribbles there amongst her possessions at Mrs. Duguid's. Had he missed something important? The possessions might already be off with the session clerk of the Canongate Kirk to be sold. He should have been more thorough. Yet he would have thought she would have kept any such papers in her writing slope, or perhaps in a notebook, and he had looked at all the volumes that were there. Perhaps she had left them with someone for safe keeping. Perhaps she had thought them of no value at all, and had burned them in the hearth.

He sighed, and opened the writing slope once again to confirm what he had seen at the cottage. Yes, the letters. Yes, the receipts. He laid them out on the table beside the slope, and stared at the empty compartment, as if it would take life and tell him something vital.

It was lined with worn green baize, balding and a little grubby with ink stains and the kind of dust that always seemed to find itself in the corners of such containers, and could not be removed. He noted it, and then saw that the baize was lifting away around the edges, more on one side than on the other. He caught an edge between thumb and finger, and gently pulled.

There was no glue holding down the baize across the bottom of the compartment. He pulled the baize right back to reveal the bare board of the slope's base, and a single piece of paper. He stared.

'Death to the Fat Hanoverian!' proclaimed ink so black it seemed still to be wet. 'Give us Reform!'

He sat back in shock, then glanced quickly about him, heart beating fast. This was a seditious pamphlet – well, only one page, a handbill really, but still – and for such things there could be harsh punishments. The last man found printing them had been transported to Australia, and that pamphlet had not urged the death of the King. He would have to take this to Melville, at once. Taking one last, long look at it – it was one sheet, and the paper was so cheap and thin that the ink showed straight through to the back – he took pen and ink and wrote a note to Melville, signed it, and sealed the illicit handbill, tightly folded, inside it. Then he addressed it to Melville, just in case it went astray before he could deliver it. Then he caught his breath.

He rested his chin on his hands and stared at the slope, letting his mind wander. What did he really know about Mrs. Ochill? All that he had been told so far had left his impression of her flat and almost characterless. She was nicer than her husband, not very sociable but moderately friendly. He was a government agent, and

Murray had had no reason to believe that she was not similarly a loyal citizen. Was she not? Where had she found the page? Particularly as she rarely went out. Had someone delivered it to her? A friend? Or – the page had not looked old, but it had been carefully hidden – had someone given to her years ago, before she went to the Palace? Could it have been something to do with her husband's investigations – a piece of evidence she had agreed to hide for him, or which he, unbeknownst to her, had hidden in her writing slope, and he had then been killed before he could retrieve it? But there was nothing on the handbill to say who had printed it – he had at least checked that before he had wrapped it up safely. Or had he? Should he look again?

He tapped his pen on the table, thinking. Then he lit a candle, heated a knife blade in the flame, and slid his own seal off the package for Melville. He drew out the illicit sheet, and studied it intently. The first bold line of printing was clear. The second had, as was common enough with cheap printing on cheap paper, smudged a little. The tail of the second 'R' in 'Reform' was blurred. He looked more closely.

No, he saw, it was not blurred. It was more delicately done than he would have expected, but under the tail of the letter were two very tiny, italic initials – 'A.C.' Someone had been prepared to take credit for this, however discreetly. Someone was either quite stupid, or was taking this seriously.

He added a postscript to the note and wrapped the paper up again, more carefully this time, and used the reheated knife blade to reseal it. A.C. It was a common enough combination of initials. It might even have stood for something other than a person's name – a something Club, perhaps? Nothing came directly to mind. Unless … Mrs. Ochill had been Anna Grant.

He drew another deep breath, reflecting again on what he knew of her. She was not a spender of money. She was a poetess, who had written for years, suddenly published, then stopped, apparently. Her maiden name was Grant. She had no known relations surviving – mother and brother evidently dead, anyway, for her last letters from them were preserved in the writing slope. Her husband, less pleasant than she, had been murdered and at that point she had been frightened, and had left her accommodation to live at Holyroodhouse, at short notice and, apparently, at night. She had been murdered, too, and had not been robbed. Had she been an agent of sedition? How could he find out?

The only people she seemed to have considered more than slight acquaintances were Mrs. McGregor, now also dead, and Mrs. Abernyte, the mother of the pair he had visited yesterday – and she was dead, too. And perhaps Mrs. Duguid. Murray rubbed his eyes. Was Mrs. Duguid in danger? Even with the Newfoundland dog at her side?

The theory was that whoever had killed John Ochill had waited eight years to find his wife and had then murdered her. But why? If John Ochill had been killed in connexion with his work, what could that have to do with Mrs. Ochill? Unless the killer were simply vindictive. The best suspect, if it had been to do with Ochill's work, was Glengarry – no doubt he could have been investigating other men that night, but Glengarry was the only one on his list known still to be alive and to be in Edinburgh. But if it were not to do with his work, then what on earth could the motive have been? And was it relevant that his body had been found just outside the publishers who had produced his wife's book of poetry?

Murray sighed, and looked at the five small volumes he had set down just beyond the writing slope. They were, as he had noted before, very prettily bound in blue cloth, with a gold embossed pattern of sprays of leaves and flowers on them, long sharp leaves and little flowers arranged around a single stem. '*A Gaelic Garland*', read the title, and underneath it said, 'Anna Grant Ochill'. He lifted and flicked through the first four copies, but his Gaelic was only good enough for him to recognise a few words here and there. The opposite pages had presumably the same poems in English. None was longer than twenty lines or so, and Murray read three or four, quickly. They were good, he thought: the imagery was striking, though the subject matter was not particularly varied, describing a bird singing in a tree, or a cat playing with a leaf, or raindrops on flower petals. They were, he thought, very suitable for a lady, and charmingly restful. She had had some talent, then, anyway.

There was nothing extraneous in any of the first four volumes, but the fifth was different. The first four might never have been read until now, the page edges fresh and clean and the binding unblemished, though the pages had been cut. But the fifth showed some signs of wear. He opened it and flicked through the now-familiar contents, and a page drifted out, falling to the floor. Wincing at a stab of pain in his shoulder, Murray picked it up and unfolded it. It was a letter.

'My dear Mrs. Ochill,' it began, with only the date above it – 2nd. September 1814. 'You will be surprised to hear from me and I hope you will forgive the liberty I take to write to you now. I had no idea, until I came across this delightful little volume, that you were still alive, or I should have written long before. I trust your publisher will do me the service of forwarding this letter to you as of course I have no idea of your address.

'It has long seemed to me that the rift which divided our respective fathers was of little service to us, and that we would have done better to abandon it when they were both dead. I know your father died some years ago, and my own father, who was very dear to me despite his sometimes uncertain temper, is dead these ten years. Had I known that you were alive and in the country I should have written at once, and laid before you my intentions of burying any hatchet that might remain to us.

'Like you I am a married woman now, and for all I know you too have family, as I have – two fine boys and a darling daughter. I hope you have been equally blessed.

'I intend to write my address clearly at the foot of this letter, my dear Mrs. Ochill, so that there can be no reason for you not to reply to me and to tell me, if it is the case, that you also wish to be reconciled and to forget our beloved but foolish fathers' unfriendliness.

'I wish you, in any case, every success with your charming publication – may it be the first of many! – and hope before long to hear from you. I remain, as always, your loving cousin, M. Grant.'

Below that, Mrs. Grant – who seemed to follow the older fashion of retaining her maiden name after marriage, unless she had married another Grant – had indeed written her address with some weight and clarity, almost ripping through the paper. Drumnadrochit, in the Great Glen – perhaps the place of Mrs. Ochill's own birth. A living relative, when everyone thought she had none. But then, perhaps Mrs. Ochill had been less interested in reconciliation than Mrs. Grant. Or perhaps she had thought her cousin only approached her now because of her new-found fame. But then why keep the letter?

He stood and stretched, cautiously shifting his right arm, and rang for Robbins. When the servant arrived with his hot water, Murray handed him the letter.

'What do you think?' he asked, when Robbins had handed it back. He sat to be shaved.

'I think, sir, that Grant is a good Highland name, and that there might well be many of them in Edinburgh just now.'

'That is a very good point. You're right. But how might that fit with her husband's murder in 1814?'

'What if the rift wasn't really healed, sir? I mean, what if this cousin, this M. Grant, was only trying to find out where Mrs. Ochill was in order to take some kind of revenge? We know nothing of the quarrel, sir: it could have been a very serious one.'

'True. Yes, you're right again.' He paused as Robbins worked with the razor blade. 'I have her address, of course. I could write to her. Or perhaps it might be better to write to the local minister. If need be, he could break the news of Mrs. Ochill's death, and might perhaps advise us as to the nature of the rift. I wonder how long it would take for a letter to reach there?'

'I doubt you won't have a reply before the King arrives, anyway, sir.'

'No,' Murray sighed, 'you're probably right. Again.' He thought about it. 'I was going to go back and see Mrs. Duguid this morning. I'm a little concerned about her safety – I think I might have been rather careless of it – and I could ask her if she knew anything of the correspondence or the rift. She was probably away from the household by then – it's dated early October and Ochill was killed not long after that – but Mrs. Ochill seems to have spoken to Mrs. Duguid more than to anyone else I have met.'

'Mrs. Duguid might have read her correspondence, sir. Some servants cannot be trusted.'

'Just at the moment I don't care too much about how she discovered the information, as long as it's accurate,' said Murray. 'And as long as Mrs. Duguid is safe. Perhaps I have relied too much on that Newfoundland dog to protect her.'

'Will you require your horse, sir?'

Murray tried to rotate his shoulder.

'Not today, I'm afraid. I shall walk. The streets are so crowded that I shall be almost as fast.'

'Maybe not today, sir, in this weather. Though apparently Calton Hill is just as busy as ever.'

'Hm. Well, I wish them no harm of their drenching, but I hope they see nothing of interest today. My cloak, then, Robbins, please, and hat. And can you see that this is delivered to Viscount Melville, please?' He handed over the well-wrapped handbill.

'Aye, sir.'

Indeed, by the time Murray left the house the town was full of people, though more of them were under umbrellas than before. The streets smelled of wet wool, wet horses and damp woodsmoke, and it felt more like October than August. October was when John Ochill had been killed, a dark night, no doubt, for a dark deed. And on another October night Mrs. Ochill had packed her belongings on to a cart and flitted to Holyroodhouse. Who had she feared, and had the same person caught up with her at last? Her cousin, or some Bonaparte-sympathising Jacobite?

His thoughts went round in circles all the way to the Cameron toll, round and round but never reaching any useful conclusion. If this dreadful weather held, at least the King was unlikely to arrive – and if he did, surely there would be less temptation to parade him openly through the streets? He might be safer. But Mrs. Ochill had been killed indoors, at Holyroodhouse where the King was going to spend so much time. Was Isobel right? Was the warning Murray had received yesterday unconnected with Mrs. Ochill's death? Would he ever know?

He was already approaching the Inch, and the kink in the road where the gateway to Inch House stood. He could barely see the lodge yet, for trees obscured it. But he was suddenly aware of a sound, a cry that chilled him to the bone. It was the sound of an immense dog, howling. He snatched off his hat, and ran towards Mrs. Duguid's cottage.

Chapter Twenty-Four

HE FOUND MRS. Duguid slumped against her own open front door, a long smear of blood trailing down its fresh green paintwork. Over her stood, in a dramatic pose that Glengarry would have been proud of, the Newfoundland dog, howling at the sky. The dog completely blocked the doorway, but there was just room for Murray, heart racing, to crouch by Mrs. Duguid, pull off his gloves, and feel her throat for a pulse.

He had barely touched her grey skin when she jumped and batted him away sharply.

'Get off me!' she cried. He sat back in surprise. The dog barked once in evident relief, sat back in the doorway and licked his lips lavishly.

'I beg your pardon,' said Murray. 'I was checking to see you were alive.'

'Alive? A course I am! Wait … what just happened?'

'It looks as if you hit your head on the door,' said Murray. 'Quite hard.'

She straightened and looked around, startled to see the trail of blood.

'Was that me?' she asked. 'That'll have to come off before the King rides past.' She reached up to the back of her head, and gave a little squeak of pain. Her fingers came away bloody.

'Do you remember what happened?' Murray asked.

'Wait now till I think.' She stared at her fingers for a moment, until Murray handed her his handkerchief, folded into a pad. She applied it to the back of her head with some care.

'The fellow there started barking,' she said, 'and I heard someone at the door – this door, ken?' she added, as though he might be confused. 'And there was someone. He was a young fellow, well enough dressed, respectable looking, ken?'

Murray nodded encouragingly. He could ask for more details later.

'I asked him what he wanted – my, this is sore – and he asked if Mrs. Grant lived here. I said I knew nothing of a Mrs. Grant, but I dinna think he believed me, for he shook his head and said I was to be sure he didna mean her any harm. I said it was nothing to me, for I lived in the place on my own and before me here there'd been old Dod Farrell and if he was Mrs. Grant in his spare time then it was news to me. But the young fellow was having none of it, and he went to pull something out of his pocket. Well, as to what happened next I'm no just entirely sure. Whether it was that this one,' she put a hand out to the dog, 'took against him, or took a liking to him, or thought he was going to attack me, I dinna ken, but he leapt out past me and barked at the man. Just the one bark ken? And I think the man turned to run, but all I can guess is that in the rush this one shoved me against the door by accident. The last thing I remember seeing is the young fellow's heels about my eye level, heading off towards the gate.'

'Can I help you up, Mrs. Duguid?' Murray asked. 'You'll be getting cold down here. And wet.' He had forgotten the rain, and she did not seem to feel it. He helped her to stand. 'I wonder what he intended to leave for Mrs. Grant?'

'Well, it would have been no good him leaving it here. There's no Mrs. Grant here, like I told him.'

'Hm,' said Murray. 'I wonder. Did you know that Mrs. Ochill's maiden name was Grant?'

'Was it? Are you coming in or are you just going to stand there in the rain?'

'Thank you.' He followed her into the cottage. Mrs. Ochill's possessions had gone, leaving the room much more pleasantly proportioned. The dog resumed his place by the hearth, sinking breathily to a prone position as if he had had a particularly exhausting morning. Mrs. Duguid sat down with her hand still to the back of her head. 'Is there hot water? Can I make you a cup of tea?'

She looked up at him in dismissive surprise.

'You're a gentleman. You canna make tea.'

But Murray had already pushed the kettle back over the fire

and taken the teapot from the mantelpiece. The small dresser, now accessible again, held cups and saucers of various patterns, perhaps rejects from the big house in the past. He made sure to heat the teapot, found a jug of milk in a little scullery, and presented the finished article to her. She sipped it suspiciously.

'Where did you learn to do that?'

'I have occasionally had to fend for myself. And you are in need of a hot drink for the shock, I think.'

'Huh,' she said, but drank the tea.

'Mrs. Ochill's book was published under the name of Anna Grant Ochill,' he said.

'I didna read it.'

'No … Did she ever mention any relatives at all? Even dead ones?'

'I tellt you afore she didna.' But she frowned, perhaps at the thought of dead relatives. Had it triggered a memory?'

'Or perhaps relatives with whom she was no longer on good terms?'

'Wait now. Let me think. This is that sore … but if there's any notion of something I've forgotten, no doubt that dunt on the head will have shaken it loose. Wait now. Where was it she was from? Somewhere up, way up in the Highlands. She could speak Gaelic, ken – well, that was part of the book, was it no? And I asked her if she still had friends or family up that way. "I have not," she said, "for my mother is dead and my father is dead, and there is no one else there worth my attention, not any more." Ken, I thought it was an odd way to put it, "worth my attention". But if you think she had relatives she wasna speaking to, that would explain it, I suppose.'

'It would, I think.'

'And do you think that's the reason she's dead, then, sir? Someone came down from yonder and finished her off?'

'It's a possibility,' said Murray, 'though I wonder. You said the young man who called was trying to deliver something to Mrs. Grant – as if he believed her still to be alive?'

'I suppose so.'

'Then perhaps I am wrong. Can you tell me what he looked like?'

'I could tell you what his heels looked like. A very nice pair of brown knee boots.' She paused, thinking. 'Well, he wasna as tall as you, but he was taller than me. Slim, young – ken, all the men look young to me these days, but he'd not have been past twenty-five, I'd say. Dark hair, very nice, and I think he may have thought so, too, for it was on the long side. He had a green coat on, and brown gloves … was there anything else?'

She was asking herself, so Murray kept quiet. He could see that she was doing her best to picture the man in her mind.

'He took his glove off, his left glove, to reach into his pocket,' she said at last. 'And I'm almost sure there was a ring on his pinkie. Ken? His wee finger. There was just a glint, I thought. But the light's no good this morning, and maybe it was a raindrop instead.'

'Silver or gold?' asked Murray.

'Gold,' she answered at once, then looked up at him. 'Aye, it was a gold ring.'

Reassured now that Mrs. Duguid was in danger from little except perhaps the over-enthusiastic devotions of the Newfoundland dog, Murray left her warmed and dried, with her head no longer bleeding. He had offered to fetch someone to sit with her but she had declined the offer, saying she was so glad to have her house back to herself again she had no wish to share it with anyone for now.

He walked back round towards Holyroodhouse and the new road by Calton Hill. As he drew nearer to the centre of the town, he could sense a rising excitement, and felt his heart sink. He jumped as a cannonade of shots rang out, heavy and dull, from the top of the hill above him. Irresistibly he joined the flow of the crowds about him, taking the muddy path up through the scrub of trees at the foot of the hill, curling up with everyone else around the hill's steep side. The masses at the top were thick around and on top of the walls of the observatory, and even more people lined up on the upper slopes, all gazing in one direction, out over the Forth. Murray made use of his height, tried to make sure he was not obscuring anyone else's view, and squinted into the wet rain to see what he could see.

'Good day to you, Mr. Murray,' came a gruff voice from about his own head height. He glanced around. The splendid form of a Bow Street Runner adorned the hillside, his scarlet waistcoat gleaming.

'Good day, Mr. Townsend. Keeping an eye open for London pickpockets, are we?'

'Watching and observing, Mr. Murray. Asking questions.' He scanned the crowd pointedly. 'Always observing, always asking, always finding answers. I hope, sir, that your own investigations are just as successful – though of course, as I said before, my expertise is at your disposal at any time.'

'I'd hate to take you away from your own work, Mr. Townsend. A crowd like this must provide ample opportunity for those skilled English thieves.'

'Indeed, sir, indeed. I shall be on my way. Guard your own pockets, sir: take a tip from me.' He lifted his broad-brimmed hat briefly from his yellow wig, and made his usual attempt at a shallow bow before moving off. Murray turned his attention back to the sea.

The waters were grey sprayed with white, with the coast of Fife a darker grey beyond. But no one was looking at the water. The Firth was full of craft, ships and boats of every size. Anyone with a rowing boat or a fishing smack or the little packet boats that ran up and down the coast, all of them were there, full of waving flags. In the midst of them a flotilla of yachts had almost reached the little island of Inchkeith, and around them their escort of steamships were firing salutes and performing some complex manoeuvre as the warships currently in the Forth fired back. Up here on the hill they could almost taste the gunpowder as the miniature Trafalgar was acted out below them. Murray found that his heart was skipping. Down there, on one of those yachts, the King – the actual King – was waiting to land at the harbour of Leith, really, genuinely, coming to visit Edinburgh. Would he like it? Would everything be ready?

Would he be safe?

'We need to get down to Leith!' cried a man nearby. 'He could come ashore any minute!'

The crowd was divided. Half stayed to drink in the remarkable spectacle before them, as much as they could see it through the driving rain, and the other half, now urgent and slithering on the worn path, were heading down for Leith Walk. Murray was caught up with them and before he could think straight he was down and into the street, nearly swept away. On the street were soldiers, pedestrians, grand carriages – he caught sight of Lord Melville alongside a miserable, gingery-haired, red-eyed man that Murray thought might actually be Robert Peel, the new Home Secretary. In a small carriage sat Sir Walter Scott, who waved at Murray though his expression was a curious one: that the King had finally arrived and he was now going to meet him must have a strange effect on anyone who had done so much to prepare for this moment. Everyone moved slowly but inexorably towards the harbour: it would have been a strong man who could have made any progress in the other direction. Murray did not resist, but let himself be steadily swept along with them, hands thoughtfully guarding his pockets, until they reached Picardy Place. When he saw the great fake gateway he managed, in the broader space of the junction, to break free and stagger off towards Queen Street and home. The rest of the crowd surged on, wet but excited.

'It's so wet! Such a shame,' said Isobel when she saw him drying off in his room. 'I wonder if he will even land today?'

'The high heidyins are off to see him, anyway,' Murray told her. 'I think I saw Robert Peel.'

'I wonder how many more of the Government are here?' said Isobel. 'No doubt someone who wanted to do harm could injure someone else of significance, even if they did not reach the King himself. I've been thinking about that note you received, Charles,' she went on. 'I tried to talk myself out of it, but I fear you are right: it most likely does have something to do with what you are investigating. With that poor woman's death.'

'But what?' he asked, both pleased and alarmed that she agreed with him.

'That I don't know,' she said. 'And if they, whoever they may be, have access to Holyroodhouse, why would they take the risk of an attack between the harbour and there? Why not wait until there are fewer people around and everyone is a little more relaxed?'

'As to that, I suppose it would be much easier for any assailant to disappear into the crowds,' said Murray. 'For a few minutes there I thought that I might never been seen again, and I had no wish to hide.'

Isobel went to the window, and stared out at the rain.

'We are not looking our best, are we? Any intending assassin would be wiser to stay indoors. Well, it is dinner time, or very nearly: if the high heidyins have met the King at Leith I suppose nothing will happen until after they have all eaten, anyway. Shall we do the same?'

Chapter Twenty-Five

IT WAS AN hour or so after dinner that word came definitely, by the strange osmosis that occurred amongst the households of Queen Street, that the King would not land today but would wait to see if the weather were better in the morning.

'There is a great deal of wet livery and soggy feathers,' Blair remarked when Robbins brought the news, 'not to mention muddy skirts and breeches. I doubt if they will all be dry by morning, but the coal merchants may do well enough out of the matter. Poor Smith is trying his best with my boots, but I doubt he will succeed.'

The rest of Blair, who had been everywhere in his chair that day, had been kept dry under his voluminous waxed cape and hat, from beneath the brim of which he had observed all the toings and froings at Leith.

'Sir Walter and Melville and Robert Peel and the Duke of Hamilton all went across in a boat and were taken up into the Royal Yacht,' he had told them, and was quite happy to tell them again. 'Peel looked quite ill. They stayed for dinner – not Peel, but the others. Sir Walter will not sleep tonight for the excitement! If only the weather improves now, and the King comes ashore, he will be quite content. I believe all will be well.'

'Unless someone attacks the King,' murmured Isobel.

'At least we have another reprieve,' said Murray. 'No assailant is going to wait about in this rain on the offchance of injuring the King or anyone else. I have a little more time to consider what else I could or should do. There's the mysterious young man with dark hair. But then there's also Glengarry. As I've said before, we have a definite link between him and John Ochill, and a definite sighting of him at Holyroodhouse around the time of Mrs. Ochill's murder. But how do I find out more? I can hardly go up to the man and ask him if he killed both of them. He would laugh in my face.'

'And challenge you to a duel,' added Isobel, seriously.

'What about the young man you told us about, the one who stopped Glengarry when he tried to interfere with the procession up to the Castle?' Blair's face brightened at the thought. 'He seemed to know something about Glengarry, didn't he? Isn't that what you said?'

Murray thought back to the confident young officer who had seized Glengarry's stirrup, spurs and all. Glengarry had threatened him with a duel, but he seemed unconcerned. What was it that Sir Walter had said his name was?

'I'm trying to remember. Something about knowing something Glengarry had done, wasn't that it?' He scowled, and held out his cup for Isobel to refill with tea. He felt he needed it.

'He was a naval officer, was he not?' asked Blair.

'He was …' Murray pictured his bicorne hat and dark blue coat, his handsome face with dark-fair whiskers and a complexion that spoke of warmer climes, probably in the course of his naval service. 'Let me think. It was only the day before yesterday, after all. Monday, wasn't it? Too much in my head …' He pressed his fists to his temples, thinking hard. For once Blair managed to keep quiet, Isobel and Mrs. Helliwell hushed, and Robbins stood silent.

'MacDougall, that's what his name was,' said Murray at last. 'Sir Walter said he was one of the young MacDougalls. I don't know anything about them, do you?' He looked first to Robbins and then to Blair.

'Are they the orphans, sir?' Robbins asked Blair. Blair nodded.

'I think so. Three brothers, all in the Navy. I have no idea which one is at home just now. Good lads, by reputation, all of them.'

'That's what Sir Walter implied, certainly. I don't know which one this would have been, either. He challenged Glengarry – I don't mean to a duel, I mean he challenged the right Glengarry was claiming, to be at the head of the procession. I have no idea where MacDougall came from, but he was there at Glengarry's side. This was while Glengarry was trying to wave his sword at that fellow Mash – Hepburn's employer in the Lord Chamberlain's Office, you know? He said something about Glengarry going to be remembered for threatening Mash in front of women and children, then he said – let me get this straight – he said, "I daresay history could tell a few more tales of you, if the truth were known." Something like that. Then he sent him off as if he were the senior and Glengarry a mere private soldier. Or whatever the Navy has. And Glengarry went, too, only shouting back about the duel when he was well clear. He had met someone as confident as he, I think, and he had no idea how to react.'

'"If the truth were known",' Blair repeated. '"A few more tales of you, if the truth were known". Do you think he did know?' He turned his wide blue eyes to both of them in turn. Robbins cleared his throat.

'I could tell you where he's staying, sir, as it happens. He's just along the street.'

'Is he, indeed?' Murray sighed, thinking of the rain. He was pleased, though, to find something to do that might be of use. 'Then I shall call on him. It might be that now the King has actually finally arrived Viscount Melville will decide there is no further point in my investigation, but I should like to pursue it, all the same. As long as there is a chance of solving the mystery. We still have two possibilities, the dark-haired man and Glengarry. So if you direct me to young MacDougall's lodging, Robbins, I might catch him after his dinner before he goes out for the evening.'

But when Murray arrived, already sodden, at the address Robbins had given him, the gathering of young men who collectively answered the door shook their heads all at once. Murray had the distinct sense of the boredom of youth in want of something to laugh at and some fair female company. He remembered it himself, distantly.

'He moved on with his friends,' they volunteered.

'Where did they go?'

Some of them shrugged. One thought it was the Grassmarket, and another that they had gone to keep guard at Holyroodhouse, but this was dismissed very quickly. Several thought the Castle was likely, but had no real evidence. They all seemed to be naval officers, and only very slightly familiar with Edinburgh.

'Do you know there is the Theatre Royal at the end of Prince's Street?' he asked them helpfully. 'I believe they have *Rob Roy* on this evening.'

'Have they?' came several voices at once. 'A play!'

'I never thought to find such a thing in North Britain,' said a spotty youth. 'I thought it wasn't allowed.'

'We're a little more liberal now than we used to be,' said Murray with a grin. 'In Edinburgh, at least.'

'A play! Shall we go, gentlemen?'

'I should think so! Thank you for the advertisement, sir!'

'Can I leave my card?' asked Murray, before they could all disappear into the night. 'And if any of you should find out where MacDougall is, or meet him, perhaps you could let me know or at least ask him to call?' He was half-shouting now over the sound of boots and coats and cries for hats and gloves, but he had the sense that a few of the sharper ones had taken in what he had said, at least. Whether anything would come of it, he had no idea, but he left at least half a dozen cards, just in case. Then, with the rain trickling dismally down the back of his collar, he walked home again.

It was certainly not a night to entice Murray or his household out to the theatre to see a play they had all seen before, even Mrs. Helliwell. Murray wished the young officers joy of it but called for hot punch and settled down with Isobel, Mrs. Helliwell and Blair in the drawing room, trying to think what else he could do. Miss Fitzsimmons brought Augusta down for an hour or so of happy amusement, but after she had made her goodnight curtseys and gone back upstairs, Murray was at a loss.

'If I cannot find MacDougall,' he said, 'and I cannot find anyone who saw the dark-haired young man clearly, or can somehow identify him, then I cannot see how to make any progress at all, let alone before the King lands at Leith.'

'What shall we do tomorrow?' Isobel asked brightly. 'If the King does land, what are our plans? It's time you let your mind wander over something else for an hour or so, my dear, for at the moment your head is like a palette where someone has mixed lots of paints together, and instead of being a brilliant rainbow they are just a muddy mess. And I do like your brilliant rainbows, my love!'

He smiled at her.

'I'm sorry – I am not very good company at present. Pray go

on: what are your plans for tomorrow? Have you chosen a place from which to watch the procession this time?'

'I have a friend on Leith Walk who has offered us a place on his platform,' said Blair, already bouncing with excitement at the thought. 'I had a place opposite Oman's, but this is better. Smith has been to see the house and is sure he can carry me up the stairs, but if not, my friend has contrived a little sling with a board to sit on, and they will hoist me up! Is that not a fine thing?'

'Mrs. Helliwell and Augusta and Miss Fitzsimmons and I will all be accommodated, apparently,' said Isobel, 'and we are to wear our best finery and carry rose petals to scatter over the King's carriage. Had I not seen the pageant on Monday I should scarcely believe all this was happening, could you, Mrs. Helliwell?'

'Never in my lifetime,' agreed Mrs. Helliwell. 'I wonder if I might bring some sewing? I should say we will be waiting around for quite a while, and though the crowds themselves are almost spectacle enough, I cannot quite easily spend so much time with my hands still, can you?'

'I shall take my sketch book,' said Isobel. 'Or perhaps two. What about you, Charles? Do you know where you will be?'

'I wish I were going to be with you,' said Murray, 'but at present I am not sure.' He had a piece of paper in front of him, and had been writing on it, despite Isobel's painty metaphor.

'What have you written?' asked Blair at once.

'Just jottings. Just to take some of that paint out of my head,' he added, grinning apologetically at his wife.

'What is it, though?' asked Blair.

'I've written … well, places, first. New Assembly Close, Rose Street, Holyroodhouse, High Street, Leith Walk.'

'Good, good!' cried Blair. 'That is a sensible start!'

'Then,' said Murray, encouraged that Isobel had not objected so far, 'beside New Assembly Close I have written Maclean, Mrs. Duguid (and beside Mrs. Duguid a dark-haired young man, at her cottage at the Inch), and the Abernytes. With Rose Street I have Glengarry, John Ochill and the publishers, Hutcheon & Purvis. Beside Holyroodhouse I have Mrs. McGregor, Helen the maid, Glengarry, and a dark-haired young man, though of course there are many others down there, like Mr. Trotter and Lieutenant Colonel Stephenson and Mr. Mash. With High Street, then, I have Mr. Mash and Glengarry again, and young MacDougall, who, incidentally, may be young but is not dark-haired. And with Leith Walk … well, I don't know, yet. A dark-haired young man, perhaps, but where?'

'That is a good summary, I think, Charles,' said Blair. 'But what are you going to do with it?'

'As to that,' said Murray, 'I have almost no idea.'

Chapter Twenty-Six

THURSDAY, HOWEVER, DAWNED bright and fresh, and Murray knew that the best he could do today was to try to make sure that the King arrived safely at least as far as Holyroodhouse. What he, as one man, could do in a crowd of thousands, he was not sure, but at least he would be alert. He was carrying his sword, but also wearing his new plaid, and feeling a little odd.

There was much excitement, scurrying, brushing and folding and arranging, all through the household that morning, from first light and all through breakfast. Since they were really about ready by half past nine, Isobel and Mrs. Helliwell decided they might as well set off while the streets were not quite so busy, and meet Blair at the house on Leith Walk. Murray escorted the two ladies, along with Augusta and her governess, along Queen Street, where they found that half the city seemed to have had the same idea, and like yesterday everyone was heading in one direction, towards Leith.

'I'm not quite sure which number it is, but I know it's on the right hand side as we go down,' said Isobel. 'There will be a platform outside – not that that really helps,' she added, as they turned the corner into Leith Walk and saw it bedecked with wooden structures all the way down both sides. Then they heard a shout, and looked up. Blair, true to his word, was dangling one-legged from a rope and plank seat above their heads, being hauled even higher by Smith and two other men on the platform that hid the second floor windows.

'Papa!' cried Isobel, going pink, and hurried into the house. Murray and the others followed.

Up on the platform, the wind whipped the ladies' skirts as they stepped through the windows, and Miss Fitzsimmons reassured herself that the ribbons tied about Augusta's waist were also firmly around her own wrist. Blair was now on a chair with a cushion at his back, and there were others there behind a sturdy railing, so they and another party, probably Blair's friend and his household, could be seated in safety and security. Murray went closer to the edge as the others made themselves comfortable, and surveyed the street below with its rows of tenements.

The soldiers in the street were fairly easily spotted in their red coats, tall, sensible-looking men unexcited by the occasion, and therefore more likely to pay attention to the task in hand. There were plenty of them, too, enough to keep the spectators at street level under some control. And the spectators themselves seemed to be in high good humour: the day they had waited for so uncertainly, for so long, had finally arrived. The loyal citizens of Edinburgh were more than ready to welcome their King.

But Murray was still uneasy. Soldiers in the street, however numerous, would not prevent something being thrown from an upper window. They might act as a deterrent for those who did not want to be caught and punished afterwards, but for anyone who had a clear line of escape, or, worse, were determined or mad enough not to care about the consequences, could do anything. As for Murray, whether he stayed here on his perch or went back down to the street, he would be even more powerless than the soldiers, if anything untoward happened.

He looked down Leith Walk as far as he could see, then up again towards Picardy Place, with its fake gateway. Once the King had reached the junction, the open area was much broader, and it would have been hard for anyone, even a Grenadier Guard, to lob something injurious accurately from the nearby houses. The crowds at ground level, he had noted, were being corralled into the mouths of Leith Street, King Street and Katharine Street, so the soldiers who kept them back would be some distance from the King's carriage. If the warning had been about some random attacker, then Murray had no idea where the attack might come from. But if, as the note had been addressed to him, it really did bear some connexion with Mrs. Ochill's death and his investigation, then Picardy Place was where, instinctively, he thought the danger might lie. And since he now knew that one could get into the great elaborate gateway, and that one could climb up on to the canvas battlements, under which the

King would pass directly … harming the King right at the symbolic gates of the city. That would be a striking image of Scotland and her attitude to English rule.

'Isobel, I'm going back to Picardy Place. To the gateway,' he said softly in her ear. She turned and stared at him.

'But he's nearly here! You can hear the roars!'

They certainly could. It was hard to tell, though, whether they were roars of anticipation, set off by some minor incident, or whether the King had genuinely set foot on the stones of the harbour. But surely he could hardly put it off much longer.

'I have to go. I think I know where the attacker is going to be.'

'Charles!'

'I'll be careful. And you be careful too, my love. Watch for any wobbles in this platform, just in case. Stay near the wall.'

'Don't worry. Go and see what you can do.'

He squeezed her hand, patted Augusta's shoulder fondly, prayed this scaffolding would stay safe, and slipped off up the street.

It was slow going, as a mass of shifting people continued to arrive and press down the hill towards the harbour, more intent on the distant prospect than who they might be walking into as they went. Murray's size gave him some advantage as people moved round him to see better, rather than blundering into him, but it was still some time before he reached the broad junction of Picardy Place. Here the more patient spectators waited, and those with seats in windows could be seen fortifying themselves with cups of tea and glasses of something stronger, making an entertainment of the day.

Up to his right, the canvas still hanging visibly wet from the day before, stood the grand gateway with its temporary shrubbery to either side. The great wooden gate was now on its hinges and firmly closed, only to be opened to admit the King in state. A couple of elaborately liveried guards were chatting, arms folded, over a laurel bush, and another was giving a final polish to the gate metal with what looked like his handkerchief. None of them looked particularly useful, should a direct assault occur, but like the gateway they were very decorative. Murray decided not to bother them, and headed for one side of the gateway where there was still a substantial gap between canvas and nearby wall. Should the King choose to arrive in Edinburgh without benefit of the keys, he could easily leave his carriage and slip through.

At the back of the gateway, the canvas was now properly hung and the solid wooden frame was completely covered. It had not been painted with quite as much attention to detail as the front, perhaps in the hope that the King would not look longingly back once he was through, but it was still the mottled grey, black and cream of the buildings nearby, with sketchy mortar applied here and there and a couple of fanciful arrow slits painted on. The doorway at the foot of one side, which the nervous piper had told him about, was canvas, too, on a wooden frame, but painted to look like wood. Someone had had fun. Murray wondered if Isobel could possibly have had a hand in it.

The doorway was indeed tiny. Murray tried the little handle, and found that the door opened easily enough, with only a bit of scraping on the cobbles. Inside, the construction was complex and it took him a moment to work out how it fitted together, and where he could go. As he closed the door, the heavy canvas walls blotted out the worst of the noise from the streets, reducing it to a distant rumble. He stood in the shadows, looking about him as his eyes grew used to the dark.

Basically it seemed to be two separate towers inside, linked delicately by a very narrow walkway right at the top. The gateway was deep, forming, for the King, a tunnel of maybe twenty feet in length with the gate set into it by two or three feet from the Leith side. Though the tunnel had canvas walls, its roof was open to the rest of the construction, and it would be easy, Murray realised, to drop something directly on the King or into his carriage as he passed through – or even, though the angle was tricky, to shoot him.

As to the construction itself, Murray thought it had the air of something built in haste and with no great regard for expense: the original simple framework must have shown some weaknesses, and extra braces, struts and props had been added as they went along, nailed or tied in place, or on occasion just jammed in to stop something important from falling down. The whole thing was a cat's cradle of roughly sawn timber, its scent fighting against the smell of linseed from the canvas. It took Murray a little while to identify the precarious staircase up which the piper was to ascend. Murray, mindful of the size of the piper and assuming he had already made it safely to the top, began to climb.

Murray was not, as a rule, afraid of heights, but he had a healthy respect for the consequences of falling. Of course there was no handrail, and, bracing himself against the pain in his shoulder and side, he moved his grip with care from timber to timber, glad of his gloves – and indeed his hat – against ragged splinters. The planks beneath his feet dipped gracefully as he trod on them, and he noted that very few of them had actually been fixed in place. It was more like climbing a rotten tree than using a staircase.

Was there actually anyone here? He had assumed that the piper would already be at his post, clinging to the flagpole, but he had no recollection of hearing him – there were plenty of other pipes playing, so he could easily have missed it. But was anyone else guarding the place? Or hiding, as he feared, somewhere amongst all these props and planks? He stopped again, and listened carefully. A gust of wind caused the whole elaborate construction to creak for a moment, then eased into silence. He hoped that the piper was holding on tightly.

The last step was almost at his knee height, and he looked about him for something substantial to help him pull himself up. A flicker of movement caught his attention, somewhere at the other side, in the other 'tower'. He caught his balance and stared, then jumped at a flapping sound like falling playing cards. Pigeons, he realised with a smile. Trust pigeons to find themselves a ready roost. He hauled himself up on to the top step, pushed at some kind of trap door, and found himself out at last in the open air.

'Lord's sake!' came a cry from above him, and he turned unsteadily in the gap to stare at two thick calves, bristly with chequered hose. Looking up he discovered he was staring into the broad face of yesterday's acquaintance, the nervous piper. He was indeed clinging to the flagpole with one hand, the bag of his pipes tucked firmly under the other arm. 'I'd help you up, sir, but I'm that scared to let go!'

'It's all right,' said Murray, managing to find his feet beside the piper. It was all too easy to see over the surprisingly low battlements and gaze down at the serried heads below. 'I didn't mean to alarm you. Is all well?'

'Are you the inspector? I heard tell a gentleman would be coming round, sir. That there was to be an inspection at the last minute.'

'Isn't there always?' said Murray, with a vague smile. 'What have you seen? Is the King on his way?' He hoped the piper would not think he was a spectator desperate for a perch.

'Not yet, sir.'

'Has anyone else been up here? I noticed the pigeons are keeping you company.'

'Oh, aye, sir, they scared the life out of me on the way up. There was a crash over the other side, but I think it was just the birds, after all.'

'A heavy crash?'

The piper hesitated.

'Well …'

'It's only that if there's anything wrong with the structure, we'd need to know as soon as possible.'

'Oh, aye, of course. Aye, well, I thought it was the pigeons, but it did sound like – well, like a gey big pigeon, sir. Heavy, ken? Like you said, sir.'

'Hm. That walkway,' said Murray, pointing to the board that linked one side of the gateway to the other, 'it's a stupid question, I think, but is that the only way to get across to the other side?'

The piper stared at the plank, and stared at Murray. He was appalled.

'That's a way across? You're no going on that, sir, are you? I mean, it's your own business an' all, but I'd no do it myself. It'd be better to go down the steps again and across the other side that way.'

'At ground level? Is there a door on that side, too?'

'Aye, sir, did you no see it? Right enough, it's painted to look like a wee bit of the wall. I dinna ken what these painters were up to.'

A movement down on the street caught Murray's eye. A rider, not apparently connected with any of the soldiers, had come down Leith Street somehow, edging through the crowds. Murray wondered if he was lost or late, and should already be down at the harbour, lined up to greet the King. Then he recognised the horse, and then the flying plaid as the horse reached the open space in front of the gateway, and made a little speed.

It was Glengarry. What was he up to this time?

Chapter Twenty-Seven

'DAMN IT,' MURRAY muttered. Should he go down and talk to him? Where was he going? What was he planning to do to the King? 'I'll have to go. Carry on, you're doing a fine job.'

He lowered himself down through the trap door again, trying not to catch his plaid or his sword, searching for the top step with his feet, wary of knocking it so that it fell off its perch – in case he did the same. There came a crash, and for a moment he thought he had lost it. Then he felt it under his left foot, balanced warily, and tried to see where the crash had come from. Not the piper – he was still hugging the flag pole, his face white.

'What was that?' he cried. Murray scanned the battlements of the gateway, then ducked down to look inside the structure. Over at the other side in the darkness he could just about discern a figure, someone making their way, half climbing, half falling, down through the nest of criss-crossing props towards what must be the door in the other tower. Odd pieces of wood slipped and fell, but the person was making good progress. Murray did his best to manage a controlled fall in pursuit.

He heard the grunt of relief as the other person hit the ground upright. He was only a few feet off it himself, and took the risk of jumping the rest, landing fairly smoothly but jarring his ribs. He ran for the door. Footsteps a few yards away told him the other person was doing the same on his side. Murray hauled his door open, scraping the cobbles, but the other door must have rested on flatter ground and moved easily. It lay open, and the man, for now in the daylight Murray could see it was a man, was already running off round the corner of the gateway to lose himself in the crowds.

He was lost, yes, unless Murray were to be very lucky. But Glengarry, if he stayed on horseback, would be much easier to spot. Murray thought quickly as he ran on the trail of the other man. Unless he spotted the man at once, he would follow Glengarry.

But in any case, he thought, he was fairly sure he would recognise the man again, even after such a short glimpse. For he had seen the longish dark hair, the slim shoulders, and the green coat and good boots. He was fairly sure he knew exactly who the man was.

But for now, he had to focus on Glengarry – and there he was, slowed again as he tried to make his way on down Leith Walk. The centre of the road was relatively clear but people did keep drifting across it, despite the soldiers' best efforts, and Glengarry could not make a good constant speed. That he wanted to could be seen in the little spurts and dances of his horse on the clearer patches, the set of Glengarry's shoulders when he had to slow or stop once again. Murray almost felt he could catch up, but he, too, was subject to the same stopping and starting. The best he could do was to keep the distance about the same between them, and keep Glengarry well in sight. There was a chance that whatever he was up to, Murray might be able to stop him.

Down Leith Walk he pursued Glengarry and Glengarry's frisking horse, Glengarry's extravagant bonnet and Glengarry's flying plaid. He was aware that somewhere above him, at some point, Isobel, Blair and Augusta were probably already at a window, were perhaps watching him as he passed, were undoubtedly wondering what on earth he was doing. But he could pay no attention to that: though Glengarry was easy to see, negotiating the crowd grew more and more difficult as they neared the harbour, and he had no wish to crush a small child or trip over a dog, or just to slip on the greasy, gritty cobbles or any of the bits of rubbish dropped by the spectators in their careless excitement. Glengarry had slowed, too, as the route became less straightforward. Leith Walk had ended but they were still some distance from the harbour itself. There was some manoeuvring to be done in narrow spaces, and Murray wondered how on earth any carriage fit for the King was going to squeeze through when the time came. The fake gateway up the hill provided a more generous opening than these places.

They were almost there when a great cry went up from somewhere ahead of them. Cheers burst out, and the National Anthem could be heard, played and sung, from eight different directions and as many different times. Staggered shouts of 'God save the King!' echoed down the street, and the crowd, beside itself with excitement, shouted back. Glengarry paused, his way entirely blocked. Murray took a chance, and dived down a side alley that was slightly less congested than the main street, round the corner, and back towards the mouth of the street where Glengarry was trapped. He was between Glengarry and the King, at least.

Glengarry was still stuck, as far as Murray could see, though the crowd now was in motion, determined to make their presence felt. The noise was incredible, the press of the mob painful. It was only a matter of time until Glengarry and his horse would be free again – it would have to be, for the road had to be clear for the King. Murray turned to look in the other direction.

They were on The Shore, which might once have been where the gentle sea lapped the pebbly sand, but was now a grand stone harbour. Overlooking it was a lighthouse, and just as Murray turned, the Royal Standard broke from its flagpole. He strained to see over the heads and headgear of the people in front of him. Three pipers, looking frozen, stood near the water's edge, and all at once everyone around him seemed to produce a handkerchief, or some other cloth, to wave. Murray caught a glimpse of the water, and of what could only be the Royal barge rounding the head of the pier. He glanced back to see what Glengarry was doing, but instead could see only the buildings of the harbour laced with people everywhere, waving for all they were worth from doorways, windows, roofs and walls, cheering fit to drown out three separate bands trying to play the National Anthem. Murray suddenly found himself grinning and cheering with the rest. Good heavens, it was actually happening at last!

He peered forwards again, saw what must have been the blades of oars lifted like a protective railing as the barge neared the harbour wall. Then it was difficult to see anything at all for a little while: he hoped that the tricky moment between water and land was being managed with care, but he could just see a red carpet laid improbably on the cobbles for the King's royal feet. And then, slow as some stately galleon, the top of a cocked hat appeared, then a broad, amiable face, then gradually a great width of cloth of an Admiral's uniform and there was the King himself, actually the real King, on the ground of Leith. The crowd roared, and there was a smart 'three cheers' from somewhere, at which the King beamed.

Murray looked back towards where he had last seen Glengarry, but could not discern him. Where had he gone? He scanned the people around the King, mounted and not, as dignitary after dignitary was presented, smiled upon, and dismissed. A line of Royal Archers stood to attention, ready to defend the monarch, but Murray found them only slightly reassuring: they would barely have room to draw their bows in the mob. The King must have recognised one of them, and greeted him particularly. It was no one Murray knew. He wished they would finish all the welcoming and get the King safely away.

At last he was escorted, nodding and waving, to his open landau, where he was joined by some companions that Murray again did not know, clearly friends. Would he set off? The crowds, encouraged by the soldiers, began to part to let the carriage through. But the horses, eight splendid and obedient bays, did not move, and for a long moment it seemed that everyone was holding their breath. The King raised his hat once or twice, and smiled generally. Had Sir Walter planned something that for some reason had not arrived, or been forgotten?

The coachman, with a glance around, seemed inclined to gather up the horses and Murray thought his hands had already tightened on the reins when suddenly there was a clatter of hooves on the cobbles. Murray spun. Glengarry, plaid flying, was galloping towards the King, a grin splitting his face.

Murray shoved his way through the ranks of people before him. What could he do? He could try to stop the horse, but would he reach it in time?

He pushed free at last, and raised an arm.

'Glengarry!' he cried. Somehow, despite the noise and movement, Glengarry must have heard him. His face froze, just for an instant, meeting Murray's eye. But he did not stop.

He galloped straight up to the King's carriage, swung his horse around in an elegant curve, and swept off his bonnet, bowing his head.

'Your Majesty is welcome to Scotland!' he cried.

As if it had been the sign he was waiting for, the coachman started off, as the King waved to Glengarry. In a moment, Glengarry had again vanished, and Murray, now stuck behind the procession, decided the best he could do would be to follow it back into Edinburgh – if he were to be allowed through the ceremonial gate.

The gate – no, surely not? The man had left it, but he could have gone back. Or he could have left something there that could somehow fall on the King.

Cursing Glengarry with fervour, Murray reviewed his options and made quickly for an alternative route back up the hill to the city. Forcing his way through the various tails of the procession that waited in the side streets, he at last reached another road that would take him in the right direction.

The other road, though generally less used, was almost as busy today as Leith Walk, as people with the same idea as he had – skirting round the worst of the congestion to make for some further point in the procession – had all chosen it. The only benefit was that one did not have to negotiate the irregular legs of scaffolding and viewing platforms every five paces. But from what he could hear of the cheers from the parallel street, he was making better progress than the King and his escort. He took courage and sped on as best he could, trying to think what he might have to do when he reached the fake gateway.

When he turned the last corner and could see Picardy Place, full of people and carriages, he stopped short. On top of the gateway, the piper was bent over, struggling with something Murray could not see, and at least three other figures were up there with him. Murray kicked himself forward, and ran.

The little door to the piper's side of the gateway was open. Murray flung himself inside and stopped, catching his breath and staring upwards into the darkness to try to see what it was he would have to deal with. He closed the door softly behind him. There was no point in inviting even more spectators up here.

There were sounds from above, shouts and scuffles. A fight? He thought of the poor piper wrested from his flagpole, perhaps overbalancing, his worst fears realised. Murray made for the makeshift steps, and once again climbed up towards the canvas battlements.

The last step was such that it would not be possible for him to burst out of the trap door and take everyone by surprise – and in any case, he had no wish to frighten the piper any more than was necessary. Instead, he lifted the trap as quietly as possible, angled his head into the gap with his hat tucked into his plaid, and tried to see what was going on.

Ahead of him stood three University students, in their gowns, eagerly watching over the battlements to see the arrival of the King. Possibly due to the contents of the large flask they had with them, and the swigs they were taking, they seemed not to have a care in the world.

Murray turned slowly, holding up the trap door, looking for the piper. When he saw him, he pushed the trap back fully and hoisted himself up on to the unsteady floor of the battlements. The students cheered.

'Another one!' they cried.

'Are you all right?' Murray's attention was on the piper.

'The wind got up, sir, and betangled me with the flagpole, and now I canna get my arm about the bag for the plaid about my shoulders. And they lads are too fou' to do anything about it!'

The students laughed heartily, proving the piper's point. Murray made the man turn around and saw the knot he had made of himself. It took a few minutes to release him: he certainly could not have done it on his own.

'Have you seen anyone else up here since I left?' he asked, helping the piper to brush himself down and settle his pipes. 'Apart from those lads.'

'Not a one,' said the piper. 'They're all too busy down there.' He jerked an elbow at the crowds below, and settled his back firmly against the flagpole again. 'And that'd be himself coming now, would it no? Is yon the King?'

Murray looked towards the mouth of Leith Walk. The landau and its escort were just appearing through the ranks of scaffolding.

'That's himself, indeed,' he said. The students cheered, and the piper applied himself to his mouthpiece with determination. Murray glanced around, saw the battlements were clear, and ducked back down through the trap to survey the dark interior. There was definitely no one here. But had anything been left?

He worked his way across the irregular webbing of scaffolding inside the gateway. If anything was here, it would doubtless have been set somewhere near the passage through the gateway, where it was likely to do most damage. But Murray had no idea what he was looking for, if anything.

The going was hard with his plaid and his sword and his painful shoulder, and he was all too aware of the dim sound of horses' hooves outside at the top of the Walk, tapping closer and closer. He could see the cobbles below him where the landau and its escort would travel – in fact, now he could also see, gathering down behind the gate, the Lord Provost whom he had met in Sir Walter's carriage on Monday, and the magistrates and Town Council in all their civic robery. Murray almost laughed out loud. What would any of them do if they happened to look up and saw him hovering there like a stage fairy about to be lowered out of the scenery? This was patently ridiculous.

He went more slowly and carefully now, checking the timbers for anything that looked as if it shouldn't be there. There were ropes and nails all over the place, which made examination difficult. Down below, several of the town councillors, who had perhaps enjoyed a little too much hospitality nearby while they were waiting, began their own impromptu performance of the National Anthem, with a magistrate conducting emotionally. Murray took another tentative step forward, touched a rope, and felt a movement somewhere in the structure that he had not felt before.

He stopped, holding the rope so as not to lose it. With his eyes he followed its path down and across into the shadows above the councillors. One end was attached to a particularly large and shoogly block of wood perched at a precarious angle across a narrow plank. The other end, after leading up and down again just above Murray's head, was looped, in some way that Murray could not quite see, around part of the great gate. He traced it again, thinking hard. The hoofbeats were almost directly outside the gate now. If the gate were to be opened, the rope would pull this way, and the block would fall and swing …

He had just grasped the rope in both hands when there was a sudden hush outside, and three sharp raps came on the wood of the gate. And at once, it began to open.

Chapter Twenty-Eight

HE FELT THE tension increase as the rope shifted, and took a firmer grip with both hands. The gate eased open without unseemly haste, but to Murray the movement seemed to last forever as he used all his strength to counterbalance the great block of wood. He tried to see it more clearly. Was it heavier than he was? What would happen if it were? He glanced up at the plank above his head where the rope looped. Would he be hauled up there, his hands crushed or his head knocked in? Or would he fall untidily through the scaffolding and into the path of the procession? Neither outcome bore thinking about. He clenched his teeth, and did his best to hold everything steady.

Down below, the Lord Provost led the magistrates and councillors out into the sunlight, unaware of what was happening above them. Murray could hear distant voices, something about keys and city and love. Above him the piper, resolute on his perch, played on, wind-whipped. The same gust of wind caught one of the gates and threatened to slam it shut, but a quick magistrate jammed himself in the way. Murray, who had felt the movement right along the rope he was clutching, resolved that if he escaped from this with his life and his wits he would buy the man a case of claret.

And now, oh, Heavens, the eight bay horses were beginning to appear under him, their hoofbeats resounding up through the structure. There was the coachman. There were the companions, whoever they were – no doubt notable enough that if a large block of wood dropped on their heads it would make a stir. And there was the King, huge in his Admiral's uniform, smiling and waving to the last as he disappeared from public view and entered the tunnel of the gateway. Murray held his breath, and took another loop of the rope round his elbow to give himself a better grip. The block shifted half an inch, and Murray's heart thudded.

It took an age, but at last the King was through. But then another carriage followed, and another, and another. How long was this procession? The sunlight dazzled on it then dulled as each vehicle entered the tunnel and progressed through, not a one, in the open carriages at any rate, thinking to look up at what lay above them. The piper kept playing, but Murray was starting to lose all feeling in his hands. What would happen if they eventually shut the gate? He flexed his fingers on each hand in turn, wiggled his toes inside his boots, and eased his elbows just enough to brace them again. And still the procession came.

He could almost touch the block, he thought. Almost, but what would he do with it if he could? It was so delicately balanced he might well precipitate disaster. But there was a kind of palisade not very far behind it, where several of the thicker poles had been lined up almost side by side, perhaps to brace this side of the tunnel. If he could somehow drop the block behind those, it would certainly scare a few horses – the crash would be tremendous – but it just might get the block clear enough not to injure anyone. But could he in fact reach it? and if he could, could he direct its fall with enough impetus to get it beyond the palisade?

Below there was a very slight hiatus in the procession, a moment when someone or something must have delayed outside in Picardy Place – a world away from where Murray was almost dangling here, hauling on the rope to keep the block from falling. It was not clear what was happening, but then one of the soldiers who had been on sentry duty outside came into the tunnel. He must have thought that the pageant was over. He reached up to unlatch the door that was looped to the block, and tried to slam it shut.

Murray gasped. The sharp movement unbalanced him. Clinging to the rope, he slipped from his perch, and cried out as the coils of rope around his hands and arm snapped tight. He swung out into clear air as the block shifted. He twisted to face it, and kicked hard. He swung backwards, knocking his shoulders on another out-jutting post, but the block went the other way. It toppled, hesitated for a moment, it seemed, in midair, then fell, not quite cleanly but far enough, down behind the palisade. But in doing so it slipped from its rope. Murray felt the sudden release, the ease on his arms and hands even as he started to plummet down, bumped on this side and that but somehow still falling straight, feet first, towards the cobbles below. And just as the gate was firmly reopened, he landed, upright somehow, mostly undamaged, just in front of a smart pair of horses which very sensibly took exception to flying men, and shied.

For a moment it looked as if something somewhere was going to overturn or crash or break. Then the coachman, in an unusual if familiar livery, managed to gather the pair together with soothing words, and restore them to a more normal working position. And a familiar head stuck out from the carriage window, and cried,

'Mr. Murray! Where did you come from!'

It was Sir Walter Scott.

Sir Walter insisted on Murray once again joining him in his carriage, where his kindly friend David Stewart of Garth was already seated. Both men looked relieved, happy, and exhausted – though a little less happy when they had heard Murray's story.

'Do you think it was deliberate?' asked Sir Walter, deeply worried.

'I should say so, yes,' said Murray, picking apart the remains of his gloves and trying to test his knees. The fall had probably not been good for them. 'It looked a bit ramshackle, but so does all the structure inside. There are ropes and planks everywhere. It's just possible that it was set up as some mechanism for shutting the gate if it was left open by accident, but it seems highly unlikely.'

'And you have no idea who might have done such a thing?' asked Garth.

'None at all, sir. The thing is, I received a warning note about something that might happen during the procession, and I passed it on at once to Melville. I would have no idea about such things. I am only investigating the death of Mrs. Ochill at Holyroodhouse, not conspiracies against the King. But at the same time, as my wife pointed out, why was the note sent to me, unless it was connected in some way with one of the people I have been questioning about the death of Mrs. Ochill? Who else would know me, or if they knew me would know that I might have any connexion with Viscount Melville or, indeed, you, Sir Walter?'

'We should speak with Melville at once. Well, when we

reach Holyroodhouse,' said Sir Walter. 'He'll be there: he's waiting to be one of the party presenting the Honours to the King. Oh, it was all going so well!'

'Well, and nothing has happened yet, Sir Walter,' said Garth soothingly. 'Thanks to Mr. Murray here.'

'That's right, thanks to you, Mr. Murray,' said Sir Walter, laying a grateful hand on Murray's arm. He tried not to wince. 'But we'll have to talk to Melville.'

And so Murray, who really wanted to go home, was constrained to accompany Scott and Garth down to Holyroodhouse in the wake of the King, with the crowds once again waving enthusiastically at their carriage. At least, he thought, his plaid looked respectable. But his hat and gloves left quite a lot to be desired. He hoped he would be able to stay well in the background.

His wishes were granted. Even by the time Sir Walter's carriage had arrived at the Palace, the place was full, and even had he had some important role in the ceremonials he would have had to fight his way to the front. He gathered the King was in an audience chamber somewhere ahead, doubtless one painted and adorned by Mr. Trotter and his friend Mr. Stephenson: certainly the place looked well where one could see any of it through the crowd. He was glad to get his back against a dun-coloured wall, hoping it was not still wet, and do his best to avoid having his eye taken out by yet another eagle feather or clutch of foliage pinned to a passing bonnet. The damage done by hilts and knife handles that day in the way of accidental bruising and thumping was probably more than had been done by any of the weapons for nearly a century. Murray kept his sword as neatly by his side as he could, checked to see he still had Isobel's cairngorm brooch, and stood quietly reviewing his injuries while who knew what was happening somewhere else. He wondered if Isobel and Augusta were home yet.

There was constant movement in the passage where he waited, as, presumably, yet more of the procession tried to make their way in, though surely not all were entitled. He did not envy the sentries at the gate, but they must not have been able to resist one applicant, for to his surprise Murray saw Glengarry appear in the doorway, sweaty and unkempt, his boots filthy and still be-spurred, looking as if he had just left his horse after a long ride. He looked about him as if he expected the King to be standing waiting to greet him but all he saw was muttering and tutting gentlemen who clearly disapproved of his appearance. Glengarry frowned, and turned to leave. Murray slipped after him.

Glengarry seemed to know his way about the Palace, taking turnings and going through doorways that soon had Murray at a loss as to where he was. He wondered if Glengarry were trying to find a back way round to wherever the King was. Yet if he meant the King harm, why did he keep drawing attention to himself? Watching him now, it was clear he could move quietly and discreetly when he wanted to. Could he have set up the rope and block in the fake gateway? But if he had, what was the point in his gallop down to the harbour?

Passing a room with an open door, Murray caught a glimpse through a window, and saw that they were heading towards the back of the palace. Ahead, Glengarry had gone right into a narrow passageway that looked, at last, familiar. Murray followed, one hand on his sword hilt. At the end of the passageway was a new red velvet hanging, pulled back to reveal a freshly painted door. Glengarry pushed it open, and went inside.

Murray paused at the door, looking into the room that had been Mrs. Ochill's little parlour. The dusty furniture had all gone, replaced by several hard chairs and a small table. The room did not look as if it were in use, even redecorated. Glengarry stood at the window, looking out at Salisbury Crags.

'May I ask what your business is in this chamber, sir?' Murray said. Glengarry jumped, and turned to stare at him.

'Didn't I meet you yesterday?' he asked. 'I thought you were … Murray of Letho, wasn't that the name?'

'Indeed. And you are MacDonell of Glengarry. I saw you again down on the Shore earlier.'

'We have both been through the wars since then!' Glengarry said with a smile, taking in the state of Murray's gloves.

'What are you doing in here, though, sir?'

Glengarry looked about at the bland little room.

'I'm not sure now. This was not what I expected.'

'What did you expect?'

'I thought someone I knew lived here, but I see the place is empty.'

'The name of the person?'

'A Mrs. Ochill. Do you know her?'

'Only slightly,' said Murray evasively. 'All the tenants were asked to leave so that the place could be renovated for the King's visit.'

'He should be staying here,' said Glengarry. 'This is the proper place for the King.'

'How well do you know Mrs. Ochill?' asked Murray, careful with his tenses.

'I had not seen her for years,' said Glengarry. 'I did not know she lived here. I saw her by chance, a week or so ago.'

'Did you speak to her?'

'No … I saw her go into this chamber. I supposed she was one of the grace and favour tenants. I did not know that they had gone.'

'Can you remember more clearly when you saw her?'

'What does it matter?'

'I should be very much obliged, sir.'

Glengarry raised his eyebrows and considered.

'I have been in and out on a number of occasions since the renovation started. Let me see … it would have been Friday, I believe. Last Friday. I went to make sure that the fellow from the Lord Chamberlain's Office was not interfering again, the fool.'

'And did you speak with him? Mr. Mash, is it not?'

'I did, briefly. Can't stand him for longer than that.'

'And you saw Mrs. Ochill come in here. Can you remember what time that was?'

'I was just about to go home for dinner, so it would have been perhaps four o'clock? Or a little earlier.'

'Thank you. Was she alone?'

'Yes, she was. She must have left something here, I suppose, or thought she had. A shame that I missed her. Do you know where she went?'

'Somewhere on the Canongate, I believe,' said Murray, which was, he supposed, true now. Her funeral must have gone unnoted, in the midst of all the pomp and ceremony. She had slipped off quietly, just as she had done from New Assembly Close to Holyroodhouse eight years ago.

Chapter Twenty-Nine

HE HAD A time, now, up to which Mrs. Ochill had been alive and apparently alone. Had her attacker followed her, or was he already waiting for her? Though of course, all this assumed that Glengarry was telling the truth.

Glengarry had shifted away from the window towards the fireplace, a little nearer Murray and the door, his expression quizzical.

'What is happening here?' he said. 'I think it is my turn to ask the questions.'

'May I just ascertain one or two other things?' said Murray. 'It will help me to answer your questions in a more suitable manner.'

'Huh,' said Glengarry. But he nodded. 'Go on. This is becoming mildly interesting.'

'How do you know Mrs. Ochill? You said you had not seen her for years, but how well did you know her before?'

Glengarry hesitated.

'Let me think. I did not know her particularly well. I was acquainted with her husband, John Ochill. He was, at one stage, the tenant of a neighbour of mine.'

'Who was that?'

'Clark of Altbean. A good Highland gentleman, sadly too ill to attend this – this event. That was years ago, and then I caught sight of Ochill here in Edinburgh, oh, maybe ten years ago?'

'So your acquaintance really was very slight?'

'It was, yes.'

'Yet you came here today to look for her?'

'Well … you saw the crowds through there. I was about to leave, realising I could make no progress there, and then I remembered Mrs. Ochill and thought I would call to see if she was here.'

'You must have a remarkable memory, to recognise a woman you barely knew, ten years later, from behind in an ill-lit corridor.'

'I must, mustn't I?' Glengarry grinned. 'Now have you finished?'

'Mrs. Ochill is dead, I'm afraid,' said Murray. 'Murdered, probably last Friday. In the bed chamber, just through there.' He nodded at the door.

'Oh!' Glengarry seemed surprised. 'Oh, and let me see – was I the last person to see her alive? Apart from whoever killed her, of course.'

'It seems to be the case, yes.'

'Well.' Glengarry broke off, as if he had run out of words. He looked around the room, and stared for a long moment at the door of the bed chamber. 'Well.'

'You can see why I might be interested in that,' said Murray. 'Viscount Melville and the Duke of Atholl have asked me to investigate the mystery of her death. Particularly given that it happened here, in Holyroodhouse.'

'There would have been dozens of people here aside from me,' said Glengarry reasonably. 'Hundreds, perhaps.'

'No one that knew her, it seems. Apart from a servant or two, but they seem to have had no reason to kill her.'

'Nor had I,' came the quick reply. 'I had no reason whatsoever. One doesn't kill mere acquaintances.'

It was an odd way to put it, but Murray thought he knew what Glengarry meant.

'Did you know that John Ochill himself was dead?'

'I think I had heard as much. That was some years ago, too, was it not?'

'Eight years ago,' Murray acknowledged. Glengarry did not react. 'He was murdered, too. Coming back to Mrs. Ochill's death, though, did you see anyone else around that you thought perhaps should not be there, or was acting in any way suspiciously?'

'You mean apart from that fool Mash? I don't think he

should be anywhere near the place. I would pay for his passage back to London myself if I knew he would take it. No, I can't think of anyone.' But he was frowning, and Murray felt there was something at the back of his mind that he was searching for. Whatever it was, it seemed not to materialise. 'Have you a card, in case I think of something more?'

'Of course. I am in Queen Street.' Murray gave him a card. Glengarry turned it over between his fingers before pocketing it, as if there might have been some hidden message on the back.

'Tell me,' he said slowly, 'you are from Fife, are you not?'

'That's right, yes.'

'You have land? Tenants?'

'I do.'

'Are you improving your lands?'

'Well …'

'I suppose there is less call for it in the Lowlands,' Glengarry went on. He sounded for once unsure of himself. 'But in the Highlands, what are we supposed to do? The land is fit for sheep and barley, and the barley cannot support a man to pay his rent unless he malts it for whisky.'

He stopped.

'I suppose you are right,' said Murray at last.

'Of course I am,' said Glengarry, his usual arrogance back in a flash. 'Good day to you, Mr. Murray. If I think of anything helpful, I shall send word.'

And with a flourish too grand for the small room, he swept past Murray and down the passage, and was gone.

It took Murray a little while to find his way back to the gathering around the King, only to find that the King was already taking his leave, climbing into a closed carriage for the journey to Dalkeith where he was to stay during his visit. As the carriage drove off smartly, escorted by cavalry, there was a palpable sense of relief about the Palace, with a good number of the company disappearing at once in the hope of drink, food or the necessary. It had been a long day.

Sir Walter already had Viscount Melville by the elbow, and was talking earnestly to him when they both spotted Murray returning to the company.

'Come and tell me what has happened,' said Melville at once. 'There is a private room through here, and there is brandy – which I for one would like to taste.'

It took almost an hour for Murray, fortunately allowed to sit, to bring Melville up to date with everything that had happened. Several glasses of brandy were drunk, and some of the pain in Murray's shoulder eased very slightly. He had discarded his ruined gloves. When he had finished his account, there was a long pause while Melville and Scott took it all in.

'I had the note you sent,' said Melville eventually. 'You have no idea where it came from?'

'No, only that I assume it must have been from someone I had spoken to in the last few days. Otherwise why would anyone send such a warning to me? No one else would know I was in any way involved in the matter.'

'Indeed. Do you think it really did refer to the block and rope in the gateway?'

'As to that, I have no idea. No doubt there are several parties who would be willing to attack the King, particularly in such a way that they would not be named or apprehended. I don't think it was the students or the piper, for that reason.'

'Indeed,' said Melville again. 'We have the names of a number of individuals who might wish harm to the King or to the Union, and we are keeping a quiet watch over them. None of them was anywhere near the gateway.'

Murray cleared his throat.

'Now that his Majesty has arrived, my lord, do you want me to keep searching for Mrs. Ochill's killer? I believe you had hoped I would have found them before the King landed.'

'I did, but I know that was optimistic,' said Melville, with the ghost of a smile. 'The King will be here for another fortnight, and though he will probably spend much of that time safely in Dalkeith Palace, while the rest of us can breathe easily, there will be plenty of occasions still where someone could attack him. No, I should wish you to continue. You have several paths still to follow, have you not? For myself, if you can find a reason to have Glengarry arrested I should sleep more easily.'

'Oh no, my lord!' protested Sir Walter. 'Glengarry is a fine man, a fine Highlander! He is just a little impulsive.'

'He is in altogether too many places for my liking,' said Melville. 'The procession on the High Street, the Shore today, here now, and didn't you say he had run into you, too?'

'Yes, but I cannot see how that could have been deliberate or what advantage he might have thought it would have given him, my lord.'

'Nevertheless, he was there, again. Why will the fellow not stay at home and behave himself? He thinks there can be nothing of any consequence without his presence. No, Sir Walter, I know you have an affection for the man, but he is a lunatic, as far as I can see.'

Sir Walter, mouth open to protest, closed it again with a shrug.

'So, Mr. Murray, Glengarry, and your young dark-haired man, and surely you will find an answer somewhere between the two.' He sighed weightily. 'Ideally before the King's Levee on Saturday. That's the next time His Majesty will be here at Holyrood. Right?'

'Yes, my lord,' said Murray, and feeling himself dismissed, took his leave.

'The thing is,' said Murray, who was finding it hard to shift from the sopha after dinner, 'there was someone at the gateway. I mean the first time I was there, not the students that were drinking on the battlements the second time. I don't think the students would have stayed to see the effects if they had set up the block and ropes.'

He was feeling, to a certain extent, refreshed. He had bathed, and Isobel had once again rubbed salve into his bruises.

'I shall have to send for more from Letho,' she had told him. 'I had no idea you would use so much in such a short time. And I needed quite a bit for poor Mrs. Helliwell.'

Mrs. Helliwell, it appeared, had been pressed against a wall on the way back from Leith Walk, and in an effort not to be pushed through a window had twisted her arm quite badly. She was now seated rather tenderly in a soft chair, after the humiliation of having her food cut up for her at dinner. Murray had felt for her.

'I suppose there was someone there,' said Isobel. 'But was it anyone with any harmful intentions?'

'As to that, I don't know,' Murray admitted. 'The piper was there – remember, the one I told you about who was so reluctant to climb up inside the gate? He was right there, as it happens. The place was still a building site.'

'But he meant no harm, surely?' asked Blair. 'The piper, I mean.'

'I don't believe so, no. He was clinging to the flagpole as if he feared someone might throw him to the ground. And he told me that he had been told an inspector would come round at some point – I don't know to what end, for there would have been no time to render the place remotely safe for anyone who had to climb it. He thought I was the inspector, and I did not disabuse him of the idea.'

'No, you wouldn't want to be taken for some spectator desperate for a perch,' Isobel agreed. 'Half the town would have been up there after you.'

'Exactly. But there was one other person up there, another man. It was hard to see him, for he did not come out into the clear light of day. He was inside the structure, which was quite dark. But I followed him down and outside, and he ran off.'

'Not what you would expect from an inspector,' said Blair thoughtfully.

'No, indeed. Not unless he were in a great hurry to the next thing he was to inspect, which I suppose – just at the moment in Edinburgh – might just be the case. I might be inclined to think it is.'

'Why so?' asked Isobel. 'Clearly there is something you found suspicious about the man.'

'Yes …' said Murray, 'I did. I thought he was furtive. And he did not even call out a greeting, or tell the piper he was there, or challenge me for being there, which I thought was strange.'

'So what makes you think he was innocent?' asked Mrs. Helliwell, rubbing her bruised arm gently.

'The fact that I had met him before,' said Murray. 'He is staying in this house. It was Willie Jack's acquaintance, Hepburn.'

Chapter Thirty

'WELL,' SAID ISOBEL, after a moment. 'I suppose he must have been sent there by his revered Mr. Mash of the Lord Chamberlain's Office, to make sure we Scots were constructing a fake gateway in the approved London manner.'

'It is possible,' said Murray.

'Is he back yet?' asked Blair.

'No, sir, he is not yet back,' said Robbins at once. 'He is later than he had advised us, but of course times are unpredictable at present, sir.'

'Of course. Nothing suspicious in his being late,' said Murray. 'But I do wonder if I should pop along and make a call on Willie Jack before I meet Hepburn again – just in case there's something he has not told me about his acquaintance. He may well have recognised me, lumbering down the gateway behind him, but there is no reason he should think any of you knows he was there, so if he was up to no good there should be no danger.'

'Danger!' said Mrs. Helliwell, who had clearly had enough for one day.

'Not if we don't say anything,' said Isobel. 'And there will be plenty to talk about without mentioning gateways or potential attacks on the King. Though, Mrs. Helliwell, you might want to take supper in your room and lie down for a little? You've not had the best of mornings, have you?'

'Do you know, I think I shall, Mrs. Murray?' said Mrs. Helliwell, always sensible even if she did not like to look like a difficult guest. 'I find I am more tired than I thought I was.'

'I'll fetch my maid to help you,' said Isobel, rising and walking with her to the parlour door. 'No doubt you'll have stiffened while you were resting.' The two disappeared into the hall. Murray and Blair looked at each other. Robbins awaited instructions, quietly tidying the tea things.

'Do you really suspect him, Charles?' asked Blair.

'I don't know. We don't know much about him, and he had a good enough reason to be there. But he did act oddly.' He tapped his fingers on the arm of the sopha, staring at the window, at the bright sky that illuminated the King's first afternoon in Edinburgh. He hoped his Majesty was quite comfortable, while the world galloped around him. 'And he matches the description, the only description, we have of any kind of suspect. But then there's Glengarry. And what his plans were today I have no idea. Nothing the man does makes any sense to me.'

'It seems to me, Charles, that you will need something more before you can confront Glengarry again. He does not strike me as the kind of level-headed man who might take such an accusation well or reasonably.'

'You're right, of course. I shall have to leave him for now. I'll tackle Hepburn first. Robbins,' he sighed, 'could I have my hat again, please?'

Willie Jack Dundas was one of Murray's oldest, if not necessarily closest, friends – the kind who is always somewhere in the background. It had been some years since Murray's first encounter with Willie Jack's new wife, a woman whose charms were not always reserved for poor Willie Jack alone, and although Willie Jack and Murray had met on neutral territory several times since, Murray had carefully avoided any prolonged visits to Willie Jack's flat at the west end of Prince's Street. It seemed that in the current circumstances about fifty friends and acquaintances had not been so careful. The flat was full to the brim.

'We could go for a walk,' Willie Jack suggested rather desperately, as three children swung in turn around his legs and disappeared under the dining table. There was a peal of slightly inebriated laughter from the parlour, and the harsh sound of furniture being shoved when it should have been lifted. A dog barked, and was joined by another.

'We could,' Murray agreed at once. He had not seen Willie Jack's wife on this occasion, and had no wish to. Willie Jack found a hat that might or might not have been his own, and followed Murray back to the door, edging past a pile of luggage, down and out into the street. His shoulders sagged at once in relief.

'Thank you so much for taking on young Hepburn at such short notice,' he said when they were clear. 'You can see that the poor fellow would have had no peace here, and he, for one, is actually in Edinburgh to work. Letitia's family seems to increase every day …'

'But she is well?' Murray asked dutifully, as they crossed Prince's Street out of the worst of the press of people.

'Oh, indeed! Indeed,' said Willie Jack, with a sideways look at Murray. Willie Jack had no illusions about his wife. 'Anyway, how can I help you? Please do not ask me to take Hepburn back! There are three people in his bed already!'

'No, not at all,' said Murray, thinking that if Hepburn had done what they suspected him of doing, he would certainly not be going back to Willie Jack's. He steered them along the footpath towards the east end of the street, strolling slowly, with no particular destination in mind. 'No, I just wanted to know a little more about him. You said, I think, that he had once worked for your brother Harry?'

'That's right. You know Harry is in London now, and he sent a letter with Hepburn. What is the lad's Christian name? Andrew, I think.'

'What did he do for your brother?'

'I believe he was a clerk in Harry's law practice. He's a Scot himself, obviously – or perhaps it's obvious only in his name, for he has been south since he was a boy, I think. And he was promising enough, and ambitious, though a little awkward, as no doubt you have seen. I liked what I saw of him, but we could not keep him at our flat. I hope,' he added belatedly, 'I hope he has not caused any trouble with you? He did not seem the type to steal the spoons, or seduce the kitchenmaid.'

'He has barely had time,' said Murray, non-committally. 'No, I wanted to know more of his background, and he is hardly around to ask. You say he is Scottish, but from where?'

But Willie Jack had spotted a friend.

'Armstrong! Hello, over here!'

A thin, tall man of their own age peered round for a moment, then saw them and came over. Patrick Armstrong had been another friend of their childhood, now comfortably established in a law practice of his own.

'Good day to you, Willie Jack. Good day to you, Charles – I had no idea you were in town.'

'Yes, sorry, Patrick,' said Murray. 'I have been caught up with business ever since I arrived.'

'Indeed it is a busy time.' Patrick Armstrong's usually solemn face took on a hint of satisfaction. 'Good business, for many people. Including lawyers,' he added.

'You're involved in the visit? How?' asked Willie Jack, baffled.

'Oh, it's Holyroodhouse,' Armstrong explained. 'All that making people leave their apartments to make way for the King. It's all been very badly handled, you know? And when matters are badly handled, lawyers make money. We all know that.'

Murray frowned.

'You weren't acting for a Mrs. Ochill, by any chance, were you?'

'Ochill? No – that's not one of ours. Is she discontent? Does she need a lawyer?'

'Not any more,' said Murray.

'Then I'm afraid I must hurry on,' said Armstrong. 'So many papers to examine! But you must call, Charles. And you, Willie Jack – do call.'

Armstrong marched off towards the Old Town, leaving Willie Jack confused in his wake.

'I didn't understand half of that conversation,' he said sadly, 'but no doubt I shall call and – and still not understand. Now, what were we talking about, Charles?'

'I was asking where your acquaintance Hepburn was from in Scotland,' said Murray, smiling.

'Now then, let me see. Do I know? Did Harry ever say? I'm not sure.' He lapsed into silence, allowing Murray to guide him round a piper and his small audience, and back on to the pavement to avoid two men jogging along with a chair between them. 'His family went down to London when he and his brother were small. But before that they lived in … was it Appin? Or somewhere up in that direction? His mother was a Grant, if that helps.'

'A Grant?' Murray managed not to misstep. It could be a coincidence, for there were plenty of Grants in the world. But Mrs. Ochill's maiden name was Grant. Mrs. Grant had written to her of her family. 'He would not have been from Drumnadrochit direction, would he?'

Willie Jack slapped his own thigh.

'That's the place, yes! How on earth did you know? But then you always know things, don't you? And it is most amusing, for he has no interest now in the Highland clans at all. He is – and I'm sure he cannot have been two nights in your household without you realising this – he is a ferocious devotee of the Lord Chamberlain's Office, and will never hear a word said against it.'

'I had noticed, yes,' said Murray with a smile. Willie Jack turned to look at him.

'Oh, go on, Charles. What is it this time? For I know you have quite a reputation now for solving all kinds of mysteries, and I think that if it is my brother's old clerk who interests you, I have a right to know why!'

'Hm, well, let us just say that it is your kinsman, Viscount Melville, who has involved me.'

Willie Jack's eyes opened wide, and he sneezed.

'What, the way his father did that time … you know …' He distracted himself with a scrabble for his handkerchief. Murray cast his mind back some ten years, to when the first Viscount Melville had drawn Murray into solving a family problem. The effects, for Willie Jack, had been drastic. Fortunately he had never held Murray directly responsible, or not for any length of time.

'Did he mention any relatives he might have hoped to see while he was here?'

'I don't think so … He did say something about an elderly lady he would have to call on, would that be it?'

Murray did not think that Mrs. Ochill would have relished being called 'elderly'.

'It might well be. Did he say anything about her?'

'Only that she lived in the Old Town – somewhere about the High Street, I think. It wasn't that he told me specifically, but he had said that Mr. Mash was to meet him on the High Street and that that would be very convenient. But you'd better ask him, Charles: I could be telling you all sorts of nonsense, for you know I don't always take things in when people are talking.'

'Don't worry, Willie Jack: I'll be speaking to him as soon as I can. But he's a busy man, isn't he?'

'He certainly is! Mr. Mash must value him highly.'

'Perhaps I should speak to Mr. Mash.'

'What on earth for?' asked Willie Jack. 'Mr. Mash won't know anything about the lad, or his elderly friend, I shouldn't have thought. And he won't have time to talk to you, whatever it is you want.'

To find out whether or not Mr. Mash had sent his young assistant to inspect a fake gateway, Murray thought. And if he had, whether he knew anything about a block of wood and a length of cleverly tied rope.

But he had no idea where Mr. Mash was staying, and though, when he returned home, he sent a note to Sir Walter asking him if he knew the Lord Chamberlain's representative's whereabouts, he did not expect to receive a reply that evening. Sir Walter would be exhausted.

Young Andrew Hepburn had still not returned from whatever tasks Mr. Mash had sent him on. Could the elderly lady he had gone to visit be Mrs. Ochill? He could have had her old address, if it were some family matter, and not know that she had moved to Holyroodhouse. But then no one at New Assembly Close knew she had moved there, only that she had left. The same question arose as before: if there were some family rift that had driven Hepburn to murder his kinswoman, why wait eight years to do it? And more puzzlingly, if he had killed Mrs. Ochill for some family reason, why did he also wish harm to the King?

Murray sat in his book room for a solitary hour before supper, allowing his mind to wander, trying pieces together to see how they looked. What if, for example, Andrew Hepburn was a paid killer who had been sent to Edinburgh to kill the King and had decided to deal with a family matter at the same time, for convenience's sake? He laughed out loud at that one. What if Glengarry had known Mrs. Ochill much better than he had admitted, and had perhaps killed her husband as a rival for her affections? Then she had spurned him and fled, and he had taken his revenge? That made him smile. What, though, if there were more than one young man with slim shoulders and dark hair worn a little too long? Well, obviously there would be many young men who fitted that description, but what if one were Hepburn, possibly related to Mrs. Ochill and looking for her when his work allowed, and another one who was not Hepburn but had, for some reason, murdered Mrs. Ochill? He shook his head. He would not go inventing other suspects until he had found out more about the two he had – until he had found out more from the naval officer MacDougall about what he had said to Glengarry, and until he had talked to Hepburn himself.

Chapter Thirty-One

FOR THE PEOPLE of Edinburgh, Friday morning dawned dull in more ways than one. The great arrival had occurred, and now the King was tucked away at Dalkeith, out of sight, not even in the city itself, and no appearances were planned today. For most, it was a chance to catch up on ordinary life, brush out the Sunday skirts and coats, tidy the streets, meet on street corners and compare experiences of the day before. For Mrs. Helliwell it was a day to take things easily, and await the arrival of Murray's Edinburgh physician to see that her arm was not badly damaged. For Isobel it was a day to visit her father in his own house and greet his many guests. The Balfours, exhausted by their rounds of social engagements (partly undertaken, Murray suspected, in order not to depend on the hospitality of the Murray household too much), were also to spend the day quietly. Murray himself took a morning walk in the direction of Calton Hill, saw it was still covered in tents and the remains of bonfires, walked back along a Prince's Street of almost Sabbath quietude, and returned home to see if young Andrew Hepburn had put in an appearance.

'He has, sir, some twenty minutes ago,' said Robbins. 'He asked for hot water, but nothing else, so I suppose he must have breakfasted elsewhere.'

'Did he say anything about going out again?'

'No, sir.'

'Then please tell him I shall be delighted to see him in my book room at his earliest convenience.'

'Yes, sir.'

'And we'll see what he has to say,' said Murray. He had walked off some of his stiffness, but hoped that Hepburn did not keep him waiting too long or he would turn to wood again, like some awkward assembly of parts of the fake gateway. It would make him much less even-tempered for the interview to come.

Hepburn must not have liked waiting, either, for within half an hour there was a sound at the bookroom door.

'Mr. Hepburn, sir,' Robbins announced.

Hepburn came in, looking … what could one say? Defensive? Hunted? Or simply anxious for an unexpected interview to be over so that he could get on with whatever duty his revered Mr. Mash had sent him on next?

'Please take a seat, Mr. Hepburn,' said Murray, turning at his desk to face him. 'I hope I am not keeping you from your duties?'

'Not at all, sir, or not for the moment. Mr. Mash requires me to attend him later in the day at Holyroodhouse, sir.' He sat, but not quite straight in the chair, and had to re-adjust himself.

'He has been keeping you very busy, has he not?'

'Oh, indeed, sir. I spent the night in the dressing room of his hotel place, sir, for we had worked very late after all yesterday's activities, but we were breakfasted most handsomely this morning, sir.'

'I'm glad to hear it. No one works well on an empty stomach, do they?'

His smile seemed to do little to put Hepburn at ease. Had Hepburn recognised him at the gate yesterday or not? Murray was not sure.

'I asked you here for this little chat really because I feel I have hardly been any kind of host since your arrival. Everything seems to be so busy. William Dundas who arranged your stay has only told me a little of your background. I gather you worked for his brother, Mr. Henry Dundas, in London?'

'I did, sir, yes. He was a very good master.'

'I'm delighted to hear it. And then you took up your post with the Lord Chamberlain's Office.' He went on quickly, before Hepburn could extol its virtues once again. 'Yet I understand you are from a Scottish family?'

Hepburn's face, which had brightened briefly, now turned less enthusiastic again. He drew out his handkerchief, then seemed to wonder what to do with it and fidgeted with its hem.

'I'm not sure … I live in London, sir, have done for years.'

'But perhaps you still have family in Scotland? Come, Mr. Hepburn, it is surely not a crime!'

'Mr. Mash of the Lord Chamberlain's Office does not look with favour on the Scots, sir.'

'That is most unfortunate. He must be having a very uncomfortable time just now.'

'He is, sir!' Hepburn exclaimed, then subsided. 'He's not enjoying himself at all. And then he grows quite cross.'

'And so, if you chose perhaps to try to seek some of your relatives while you were here – to visit one of them, perhaps – he would not look on that with favour, either?'

'Not at all, sir.' Hepburn had developed a wary expression. There was a slight tearing sound, and a hole appeared in his handkerchief. He looked down at it in dismay. 'Oh, dear.'

Murray stayed silent for a moment, perhaps as a mark of respect for the handkerchief, or perhaps to let Hepburn think himself out of immediate danger. He did, however, note a slim gold ring on Hepburn's little finger.

'Do you know a Mrs. Ochill, Mr. Hepburn?'

Hepburn jumped, and the handkerchief ripped across. He looked up at Murray with his mouth agape.

'How did you know …?'

'She's a kinswoman of yours, isn't she?' said Murray. 'Perhaps your aunt?'

'My mother's cousin,' said Hepburn faintly. 'Her father and my mother's father were brothers.' He stared at Murray as if he thought he had suddenly encountered the Recording Angel.

'Grants, yes?'

'I – yes, sir.'

'I believe – correct me if I am wrong – that there was some kind of rift between the two brothers?'

'There was – a matter of some land, long before I was born – sir, how do you know all this?'

He was on the edge of his seat now, the handkerchief forgotten on the floor.

'Don't worry about that,' said Murray, waving him back. 'I just need to know what you've been doing while you have been in Edinburgh – the bits that Mr. Mash does not know about. Nor need to know about.'

There was a hint of relief on Hepburn's face as he tentatively took in that last bit. If Mr. Mash was not to know, then perhaps he was safe – for now.

'I … um. My parents are dead, sir, and apart from a younger brother, who has gone as a clerk to India, I am alone in the world, or so I believed until the time of my mother's death, which happened three years ago. Then I found she had a cousin, this Mrs. Ochill, to whom she had written in Edinburgh. There was a book of poetry, you see, that Mrs. Ochill had written, and I think that helped my mother to find her after many years of … well, when the brothers did not speak, nor did their families. But my mother was never one to bear a grudge and she had taken a note of the publishers' address, here in Edinburgh, and told me she had sent a letter to Mrs. Ochill. Anna Grant, as she had been. My mother was Mary Grant.'

'Did she receive a reply from Mrs. Ochill?'

'I think she must have, because she had a proper address for her, not just care of the publisher. A place off the High Street, called New Assembly Close. So, since my mother had asked me to try to seek her out if I could, I went there to find her.'

'Recently?'

'Yes, sir. I had no chance to visit Edinburgh before this.'

'And what did you find at New Assembly Close?'

'Someone there told me she had left nearly ten years ago, after her husband had died. But they didn't know where she had gone. I asked all the neighbours, but not that many of them were the same as the ones from when my kinswoman was there, and I thought I would never get any further. Then someone remembered that Mrs. Ochill's maid had not gone with her to her new home, but had instead married a man who worked at the Inch, at Inch House. It was a few days before I was able to go there to find out more, and when I did – well, it was difficult.'

He flushed deep red, the embarrassment of the very young making a fool of themselves.

'What was difficult about it?' Murray asked innocently.

'Um … I found out where the maid lived, and I was going to ask her if she knew where Mrs. Ochill was. And then someone told me that a woman had recently moved in with the maid, too, and I wondered if she might actually be Mrs. Ochill. It was the lodge of the estate, you see, sir.'

'So you called on the maid, or the former maid?'

'I tried to, sir. Twice.' He was squirming now.

'But she was not in, perhaps?'

'I don't really know, sir.'

Murray took pity.

'Was there, perhaps, a dog in the case?'

'A dog, sir!' Hepburn turned white. 'A dog? I thought it was the very devil, sir! And now I begin to wonder if you are in league with it, to know all this!'

'So, did you find Mrs. Ochill in the end?'

'No, sir, I have not found her. I don't know where she is. If you do, sir, perhaps you'll be kind enough to tell me? Maybe you have some way of knowing all about her as you seem to know all about me!'

Murray made a face.

'I know a little about her. I need to know more, though. And I have some bad news for you, Mr. Hepburn – Mrs. Ochill is dead.'

'Oh. I feared she might be. When did she die? Not long after her husband, I suppose.'

'They were not elderly. No, Mrs. Ochill died last Friday.'

'What? But I was already in Edinburgh then!'

'I know.'

But Hepburn did not appear to take this in.

'To have missed her by so little! That is so very sad.' He took a moment to reflect. 'Where is she buried? I should visit her grave, at least.'

'She is in the Canongate kirkyard, I believe. She died at Holyroodhouse.'

That shocked Hepburn much more than the news of his cousin's death.

'In the Palace? In Holyrood?' Then he thought about it. 'Last Friday? But it was being painted. Did she work there?'

'She had lived there. It seems she went back, perhaps to meet someone, in her old apartments there.'

Hepburn frowned. He was starting to realise there was more to the story.

'"Perhaps to meet someone" – don't you know? Who was the someone?'

'There is more bad news, I'm afraid. Whoever she met killed

her, and we do not know who or why.'

'Killed her? Killed her? Dammit – forgive me, sir, but killed my mother's cousin? I must know who!' Hepburn's face flushed again, this time with outrage.

'And as I say I cannot tell you. But I am trying to find out.'

'Then if I can help you in any way, Mr. Murray, you have only to ask. I never met her, but my mother was fond of her. Tell me what to do.'

'Well, firstly,' said Murray, not particularly optimistic, 'tell me all you know of her, for she has been a very elusive woman.'

'Oh,' said Hepburn. 'I'm not sure how much I know. My mother spoke only a little about her, at the end, for I don't think she knew much, either. They had lost touch, and my mother regretted it deeply.'

'Whatever you do know might help,' Murray encouraged him. Hepburn frowned, staring back into the past.

'Well, she would have been born in Drumnadrochit, the same as my mother, for they knew one another as children and the brothers lived near each other.'

'Which was the elder?'

'I should have said, from the way my mother spoke of her, that they were about the same age.'

'Who moved away first?'

'They didn't move at all, at first,' said Hepburn. 'Both brothers wanted the land and neither would give up, that's what my mother said. But then someone died – maybe it was the other brother – and then his family moved away. I mean Mrs. Ochill and her mother, anyway. I'm sorry, I wasn't taking notes. My mother was ill, and wanted to talk about the past, and I listened.'

'I understand.'

'They went south somewhere. My mother did say the name, but I'm not sure …'

'Aberchalder?' Murray remembered the name from the marriage lines.

'That was it, yes.'

'So they moved straight from Drumnadrochit to Aberchalder, presumably – the whole family, and then Anna Grant met John Ochill and married him.'

'As to that, I have no idea,' said Hepburn. 'Though there

must have been some communication, for my mother knew when she saw the book of poetry – Anna Grant Ochill, it said on the front, and she knew it would be her cousin. So she must have known that her husband's name was Ochill. She said she was that pleased when she saw it, and guessed she could find Anna, that she cried for an hour.'

A hint of Scots crept back into Hepburn's voice with the words, and a smile touched his eyes. He had been fond of his mother, clearly. And Murray was almost convinced by his concern at the news of Anna Ochill's death. But what if his mother's intentions towards her cousin had not been so loving? What if, after all these years, old Mary Grant or Hepburn had asked her son, on her deathbed, to heal the old family rift with murder?

Chapter Thirty-Two

THEY WERE DISTRACTED for a moment by the sound of the front door opening and voices in the hall. One was Isobel's, but the other was not familiar. Murray nodded to Hepburn.

'Thank you for your help,' he said. 'If I find out more about Mrs. Ochill's death, I shall let you know.'

'Thank you, sir.' Hepburn had the sense to know he was dismissed, and was already heading back into the hall when Isobel appeared in the doorway.

'Have you a moment, my dear?' she asked. Murray grinned.

'Of course.'

She closed the book room door behind her, and they embraced briefly. She was in a hurry with her news.

'I have a visitor for you, upstairs in the parlour. Guess who?'

'I didn't know the voice.'

'Mr. Macdougall! The one you were looking for.'

'Good heavens! How?'

She rolled her eyes, but she was smiling.

'Papa, of course. You know he knows everyone. He sent a message or two, and lo and behold the man himself turned up. So I brought him here.'

'Then I must see him. What is he like? He seemed an assured, smart young man.'

Isobel wrinkled her nose.

'A touch too assured, I should have said. And not inclined to consider a woman worth talking to in any serious way. Not that I would have interrogated him, of course, but it's a dull walk with a companion who will not confide at all.'

Murray knew well that Isobel, very reasonably, preferred

being treated as someone with a mind of her own. He stroked her hand.

'I daresay that didn't stop you discovering something about him, apart from his assurance. What did he talk about?'

'Apart from all the pretty decorations for the royal visit?' She was still bristling a little. 'Well, he knew from Papa that he was to be asked about Glengarry, and from something he said – he said that it was a strange duty to perform but beggars could not be choosers, and then he fell silent on the subject – from that I concluded that someone was perhaps paying him to keep an eye on Glengarry. For the duration of the royal visit, at least.'

'Keeping an eye on him? That's odd, but I suppose it might make sense. Could it be Scott, I wonder? He doesn't want to exclude Glengarry from the festivities, but at the same time Glengarry is unpredictable when Sir Walter wants everything to go according to plan. And he knows the Macdougall boys, or so it seemed …' He thought about it.

'Keeping an eye is one thing, though,' said Isobel. 'But if that's the case, he doesn't seem to be stopping Glengarry from doing odd things, does he?'

'He seemed to know enough to rein him in on the High Street,' said Murray. 'Whatever that was. But no, Glengarry has disrupted things twice, and turned up at Holyroodhouse when he was not expected. Perhaps whoever is paying Macdougall –'

'If I'm right,' put in Isobel.

'If you're right, perhaps they have in mind the prevention of something worse than just a ridiculous interruption. Well. He's in the parlour, you say? I'll go up.'

At Murray's arrival in the parlour, young Macdougall turned smartly from gazing out of the window and bowed.

'Ewan Macdougall, at your service, sir.'

'Charles Murray of Letho. I believe my father-in-law, Alester Blair, arranged this meeting? Thank you for agreeing to it.'

'I understand it is a matter of a possible threat to the King's Majesty, sir, so of course I am at your disposal.'

'Please take a seat.'

Macdougall without hesitation disposed himself in the centre of a sopha. Murray took an armchair opposite, and poured two glasses of wine from a decanter Robbins must have brought when Macdougall arrived. He offered one to Macdougall, and sat back for a moment.

His initial impression, from the incident on the High Street, was confirmed – Macdougall was a handsome youth, afflicted by nothing very obvious in the way of self-doubt. The confident hand that had reached out to grasp Glengarry's stirrup now lay casually across a cushion, and the long, elegant legs were comfortably crossed. He watched Murray expectantly, but without impatience. Murray noted that Macdougall's hair could not be called darker than dark blond, and was kept neatly trimmed. He decided to make a bold start.

'I am interested in information concerning Alasdair MacDonell of Glengarry. I understand that you have some duties concerning him.'

'I have, sir. I have been asked to ensure that he does nothing to bring disgrace on the city in the course of the King's visit.'

'Disgrace? That is a strong word. Have you, or has your employer, something specific in mind?'

Macdougall hesitated slightly. Murray almost missed it. At a guess, Macdougall was not as fully in the confidence of his employer as he would like to be.

'We are prepared for most eventualities,' said Macdougall, clearly pleased with his own reply. 'A good warrior keeps an open mind.'

'Indeed,' said Murray, none the wiser. 'Are you able to tell me who has asked you to look out for Glengarry?'

'I should rather not say, sir. You'll understand.'

Not really, no, but Murray was not surprised.

'You were present when Glengarry stopped the procession going up to the Castle for the Regalia.'

'I was, sir.'

'And when he galloped along The Shore to greet the King?'

'Indeed.' Macdougall almost purred.

'For how long have you been watching him?'

'How long?' Macdougall looked slightly confused. Murray wondered who was watching Glengarry just now, or if Macdougall had the day off while the King rested at Dalkeith.

'I mean when did this duty begin? Just when the ceremonials

began on Monday, or before?'

'Oh, I see what you mean, sir!' said Macdougall. 'No, I started – or we started – before that. I have been watching him for rather over a week.'

'Just you? You are not, perhaps, taking turns with someone else?'

'I have been solely entrusted with this charge, sir,' said Macdougall proudly. Murray thought that might have been a mistake, but let it go, hoping for the best.

'Then you would have been watching him last Friday?'

'Of course.'

'Tell me what he did and where he went, if you please.'

'Of course,' said Macdougall again. 'I have an excellent memory, and will be able to give you a full account.' He paused, no doubt consulting his excellent memory. 'He left his house in the New Town in the late morning, and rode down to Leith Sands where he spent some time exercising his horse. Then he returned to the town, and went to a coffee house on the Lawnmarket to read a newspaper. After that, I followed him to Holyroodhouse where he went in and talked to a number of the workmen – it is easy to follow him in there as there are so many corners,' Macdougall added helpfully.

'But could you see him the whole time he was there?' asked Murray dubiously.

'When I could not see him, I could hear him,' said Macdougall.

'Did he speak with any women?'

Macdougall raised his eyebrows and a small smile played around his lips.

'No, not at all. I must say that there has been nothing of that kind. Mrs. MacDonell, I am told, is something of a character.'

For an awful moment Murray thought Macdougall was about to wink at him, but mercifully the young man thought better of it.

'What time did he leave Holyroodhouse?'

'Around half past three, sir. He returned home, I suppose for dinner, and did not leave for the rest of the evening – several visitors called on him around supper time, and left much later, with evidence of a good deal of drinking.'

That all accorded with what Glengarry himself had told him

about his movements in Holyroodhouse that Friday. It seemed he would have had little chance to murder Mrs. Ochill then.

'What about Saturday?' Though he was sure, as the doctor had been, that Mrs. Ochill had been dead before Saturday.

'He and Mrs. MacDonell visited friends in Cramond for the day,' said Macdougall, without hesitation. 'They left early and returned late.'

'Very good. Now,' said Murray, 'back to the day of the procession to the Castle, Monday. Glengarry stopped the procession and claimed his right to lead it. There was some altercation with the crowd –'

'The little man from the Lord Chamberlain's Office,' Macdougall interrupted with a sneer.

'Indeed. Then you seized Glengarry's stirrup, and said something to him. Something about a secret in his past? If something were known, I think you suggested, he would not be considered such a gentleman?'

Macdougall frowned slightly, but it seemed to be another consultation with his memory. Then he smiled.

'He challenged me to a duel, didn't he? That came to nothing: I haven't heard anything of it since. I was warned he might do that.'

'Do you know where he went after that?'

'Yes, I followed him. He went home.'

'Were you following him yesterday? The day of the King's arrival?'

'Of course. He rode from his house down to The Shore, then round to Holyroodhouse.'

'Do you know the fake gateway in Picardy Place?'

'Yes, indeed.' A slight sneer on Macdougall's face again.

'Did you see Glengarry approach it, at all? Perhaps even go inside it?'

'Inside? I had no idea you could. No, he paid it no attention, that I could see.'

Murray paused, retracing his mental steps.

'But as to what you said to Glengarry on Monday, as you held his stirrup – did you know something to his discredit?'

'It's just a story,' said Macdougall, suddenly a little uncomfortable.

'It must have been more than a story. It stopped Glengarry in his tracks.'

'It did, didn't it?' The frown this time was much more concerned. 'I don't know. I heard it long ago. You know these Highland gentlemen are intent, most of them, in clearing their lands for improvements? For breeding sheep, mostly.'

'Yes, of course. But has Glengarry done such a thing? He talks a great deal about supporting the Highlanders on his lands.'

'Ah, well, a man may say one thing and do another, Mr. Murray,' said Macdougall, as if imparting advice that would be new to Murray. 'Glengarry has cleared hundreds off his lands.'

'Yet,' said Murray, 'presumably that is no secret.'

'Not really, no. But there was one incident – you'll understand that in general it is the laird's factor who organises the actual evictions? The lairds, on the whole, are not directly involved.'

'So I understand.'

'Glengarry thought he would lend his factor a hand, one day. A cottage on the borders of his estate, where, as the factor reported, a young couple were determined not to move. Glengarry helped with, shall I say, enthusiasm? And it may well be that he had not been told that the young woman was near her time. The eviction, and the wildness of Glengarry's actions, resulted in the death of both babe and woman. That, I think, does not accord with his image as the Highland gentleman.'

Murray could picture it, no doubt, having seen Glengarry's mad gallop and brandished sword. It was credible. Many rumours of brutality were reaching Edinburgh from the Highlands. But would Glengarry really be so concerned about it?

'How did you hear about this incident?' he asked at last.

'My father knew tenants on the neighbouring estate – I said that the cottage was close to the border of the estate. They saw it all, but were powerless to help. The man, Ochill, his name was, told my father that it all happened too quickly.'

Murray paused, making himself breath out and in.

'Ochill? I wonder where he is now?'

'Who knows? My father is dead.'

'Of course. Neither Ochill nor your father could have told many people,' said Murray. 'It does not seem to be a story generally known, does it?'

'I think not. My father was already ill at the time, and the impression I have of Ochill is that he was not a gossip. Perhaps he feared retribution. Glengarry is really quite wild. Can I be of any further assistance, Mr. Murray?' he asked. 'For I should be returning to my duties soon.'

As soon as Macdougall had taken his leave, Isobel appeared in the parlour, the sketchbook in her hand just an excuse.

'Well?'

'Well, it seems to me that the chief problem at present is that every man and woman in the Highlands is intent on bringing their problems to Edinburgh.'

'Who is paying him to watch Glengarry?'

'He wouldn't say. But he did have an interesting story about Glengarry himself – and it involves the Ochills.' He told her all that Macdougall had said, while Isobel sat on the arm of his chair – on the left, to avoid his sore arm.

'What do you think?' he finished.

'Hm,' said Isobel. 'To me that does not sound enough. Sad to say, it seems not to be out of the ordinary in the Highlands just now. One reads terrible things in the newspaper. Only … Ochill? Really, the same Ochill?'

'It seems more than likely,' said Murray. 'For one thing, it is not so common a surname. For another, Glengarry himself said that the Ochills were tenants of his neighbour. But you're right: would he have killed both of them, just to keep them quiet? And could he actually have killed Mrs. Ochill at all?'

Chapter Thirty-Three

'WHAT ABOUT HIS tail? His followers?' asked Isobel. 'Would he ask one of those to do such a thing?'

'It would need to be someone he really trusted,' said Murray. 'Someone to whom he could admit that level of dishonour. I'm struggling to see it, myself. After all, surely there would have been others there who could have told the story? The factor? The husband of the dead woman? Other neighbours? And Ochill had already had the chance to tell Macdougall's father before they both died, and how many other people might he have told, or might Mrs. Ochill have told?'

'You're right,' said Isobel, 'it makes barely any sense. The story must be quite well known by now, surely, and if it is not then killing one woman is not going to make much difference.'

'And he did not enter the fake gateway, nor did he have anything to do with the viewing platform collapsing on the Lawnmarket. I don't know what the man is up to, but it's becoming increasingly clear that he had no reason or opportunity to kill Mrs. Ochill, to bring down the platform and kill Mrs. McGregor, or to set up the block and rope in the gateway. I need to find this dark-haired young man. And it's not Hepburn,' he added, as Isobel opened her mouth to query this. 'Or it doesn't look like it. But he does have a connexion. Mrs. Ochill was his mother's cousin, and he had been looking for her.'

'But did not find her?'

'According to him, he had the address in New Assembly Close and went there, and was told that no one knew where she had gone but that her previous maid had moved to the Inch. So he went there, and was frightened off by the dog – twice, I should say. He seemed quite upset at the news of her death – if he had only been a little earlier he might have found her. He has only a brother left now, and he is in India. Yet I don't think he was keen to let Mr. Mash know he had any connexion with the Highlands, all the same.'

Isobel, still leaning against him, stroked his shoulder thoughtfully.

'I had hoped that Mr. Macdougall might be of more use,' she said.

'He was very useful. No point in wasting time chasing Glengarry if we have good reason to think him innocent.'

'It was a moment of excitement, anyway, when Papa said he had found him. The town is very dull today. I think everyone thought it would be endless delirium from the moment the King arrived, but it feels like an anticlimax.'

'Is there nothing at all planned for today? Even if the King himself does not appear?'

'It looks as if people are putting illuminations up, in their windows and across the tops of buildings. It might be nice to go out tonight and see if there are any striking ones.'

'They would need to be striking, or we'll hardly see them at this time of year. It grows dark far too late, still.' He sensed a slight disappointment, and remembered that she and Mrs. Helliwell had been cutting paper to put in their own windows. 'Though it would certainly be worth going out to see. Perhaps Augusta might be allowed to stay up late.'

Isobel smiled.

'I think she would like that very much.'

'Aside from that, is everything as normal in the town? Businesses open, and so on?'

'Yes, so far as I saw.'

'Then why don't we walk along to that publisher in Rose Street, and see what he says about your drawings? Even if it were only a question of having a dozen or two copies printed for the family, would it not be a fine souvenir of all these events?'

'Oh, Charles! That would be fun! And of course you want to know more about his connexion with Ochill,' she added astutely.

'Then let us go and see Mr. Hutcheon.'

Mr. Hutcheon's offices were indeed open, and in fact the

New Town seemed quite busy with people hurrying around for last minute gloves and bonnets or perhaps gifts for friends who had not been able to come to Edinburgh. Mr. Hutcheon himself was talking to his clerk with another customer as they entered the premises, but the clerk gave a little cry of alarm when he saw Murray. Mr. Hutcheon scowled ferociously, so that his ginger whiskers seemed to grow out sideways. But he advanced towards Murray courteously enough, and bowed. Murray, sensing Isobel beside him wanting to giggle, bowed back.

'Mr. Murray, I'm afraid my clerk took up far too much of your man's time the last time you were here! Gossip has always been one of his worst faults.' He made it sound as if the clerk was made up only of faults, of varying degrees. Murray glanced at the bespectacled young man cowering behind the desk, and thought it was probably not so. The fact that the clerk had dark hair was really no sign of criminal intent.

'Not at all,' said Murray smoothly. 'But it must have been a dreadful shock for you to discover that a man had lain dead outside your door all night – and a man of your acquaintance, too.'

'It certainly was, Mr. Murray,' said Hutcheon with an elaborate shiver. 'When I reflected that I must have walked past him, as unaware of his cold body as –' He looked suddenly at Isobel, and cleared his throat. Murray wondered what strange simile he had been going to use. Hutcheon half-turned back to the clerk. 'Carr, go and tidy the yard.'

The clerk blinked at him, looked at the Murrays, and slid resignedly off his stool.

'Yes, sir.'

Murray waited until he had gone, as that seemed to be what Hutcheon wanted.

'Yet he could hardly have been cold, from all I heard,' he said. 'For the struggle had occurred only a few moments before you returned home. How tragic, that you might, with the difference of only a moment or two, have been able to save his life!'

'Oh, I doubt it, I doubt it,' said Hutcheon. 'Of course I have taxed myself with that, over the years, in the darkness of night when all such unfounded guilts assault a man. But it seems to me that if I had arrived any earlier, the violent incident would simply have occurred in another place – perhaps the next lane.'

'But perhaps, in those very nights of reflection, you remembered something you saw? Someone, perhaps, running from the scene?'

Mr. Hutcheon eyed Murray with an odd, sideways look, like a hen eyeing a promising insect. He hesitated, then bit his lip.

'Do you know, it has come to me over time that I did remember someone?'

'How very interesting!' Murray said, encouragingly.

'Isn't it? Of course, at the time I thought nothing of it – a shadow, slipping away along the street. Nothing more to be seen than that.'

'Nothing at all? Height? Build? Male or female?'

'Oh, male, no doubt,' said Hutcheon at once. 'But as to the rest – not heavy and not light, not short and not tall. A shadow, fading into other shadows. There, and then gone.' He heaved a sigh that lifted his shoulders in a great, hopeless shrug. 'What more can I say?'

Murray was not wholly convinced that Hutcheon was telling the truth, but then a memory that develops over time is hardly reliable anyway. He had not hoped for much here today and it seemed that he had been right.

'Well, we are not here to talk about such unhappy events today, anyway. But I have interrupted your business.' He turned for the first time to look properly at the other customer, who was smiling and bowing to him. 'Mr. Abernyte! Good day to you.'

'Good day to you, Mr. Murray!'

'I hope all is well with you, and that you have had a chance to see something of the excitements of yesterday?'

'A little, sir, yes, thank you. It has indeed been most exciting. My employer, Mr. Armstrong, allowed us to go down to Holyrood and see His Majesty's arrival there. Quite a spectacle!'

'Well, I am sorry to have interrupted your business here today – no doubt you will have to hurry back to Mr. Armstrong's office.'

'I think I must, sir. Mr. Hutcheon, I will have to postpone our discussions until another day, if I may.'

'Of course, Mr. Abernyte.'

Robert Abernyte bowed to everyone in turn, and left the office, presumably to scurry back to Mr. Armstrong's service. There were plenty of Mr. Armstrongs in the world – Murray wondered distantly if his friend Armstrong the lawyer might be Abernyte's master. He thought quickly.

'He was here on his own account, then? I believe I am acquainted with his master, Mr. Armstrong.'

'I am not, sir,' said Hutcheon. 'Mr. Abernyte was indeed here on his own account.'

'Not another poet?' asked Murray with a smile, but Hutcheon shook his head.

'I don't know yet,' he said. 'Negotiations are at an early stage. It is all very mysterious. But then, many writers are disinclined to trust anyone with a view of their work. They seem to fear that anyone who might gain access to it – even a reputable publisher like Hutcheon & Purvis – might run away with their precious manuscript and make a fortune from it. Whereas I'm afraid … well, very few manuscripts will make any kind of a fortune for anyone.'

'Well, we are not seeking our fortune today, are we, my dear?'

Isobel, who had remained quiet throughout the preceding conversation but was no doubt observing closely, shook her head.

'Mr. Hutcheon, my wife Mrs. Murray,' said Murray. It still gave him a little thrill to say the words. His previous wife had not been Mrs. Murray, of course. Nor had anything about her given him a thrill.

'Perhaps another poetess?' asked Mr. Hutcheon politely, as if he had never said anything about wary authors and unpromising manuscripts.

'No,' said Isobel, 'a sketcher of interesting events.'

'I see,' said Mr. Hutcheon.

'It would be a matter of a dozen or two copies for friends,' Murray explained, as Isobel brought one of her smaller sketchbooks out of her reticule. 'And of course, the work is not yet finished.'

'Sketches of the King's visit?' asked Hutcheon warily. 'Did you get a good view of His Majesty, madam?'

'I barely glimpsed him,' said Isobel. 'No, these are characters amongst the crowds, mostly. The Celtic Society in training. A Highland piper. The spectators on Leith Walk.'

Hutcheon took the sketchbook and flicked through it, then

stopped and turned more slowly from drawing to drawing.

'These are remarkably well-observed, sir. And, if I might make the comment – well, very witty, too. Ha!' He laughed out loud at a picture, and Murray tried to see, upside down, which one it was. Hutcheon finished a more thorough perusal, then handed the book back, reluctantly, to Isobel.

'Is this the only sketchbook?' he asked.

Isobel and Murray both laughed.

'Not at all. There may be fifteen, so far. And of course, as I said, there should be more.'

'They would sell …' said Hutcheon thoughtfully. 'Not the whole collection, but a carefully edited selection. With captions. Had you thought of a colour wash?'

'No, I chose not to,' said Isobel firmly.

'Well … that would certainly keep the costs down …'

'But printing them is something you would be prepared to do?' Murray asked, making sure.

'Oh, yes, sir, yes. Please do me the honour of letting me see them again when the collection is complete. And sir, I would entreat you to consider seriously a proper publication of these, not just a private issue. I believe it would make your name, and be a very profitable exercise for all concerned.'

Murray looked at Isobel. She had turned rather pink, and he was not sure whether she was pleased or not. This might take some discussion, but in the end it would be her decision.

'Well, we shall see, when they are finished,' he said at last. 'Thank you for your help, Mr. Hutcheon.'

'Well, what did you think of that?' Murray asked Isobel, when they were clear of the publishers.

'I'm not sure how I feel about strangers poring over sketches I did for my own amusement,' Isobel said. 'I shall have to think about it.'

'There are other publishers, of course,' said Murray. 'You could always have a second opinion from one of them.'

'I think I should like to do that,' said Isobel. 'Just to be sure. I didn't really take to Mr. Hutcheon.'

'No, I prefer his clerk,' said Murray. The memory of the poor clerk, Carr, shuffling away to 'tidy the yard' slipped out of his mind, nevertheless, as they walked home. He and Isobel discussed the ins and outs of publication, and if someone had happened to follow them through the broad streets of the New Town, they were too occupied to notice.

Chapter Thirty-Four

'IT'S FAR TOO light just yet for any illuminations,' said Isobel after dinner. She was toying with the papers she and Mrs. Helliwell had cut, which now adorned the panes of every window that looked towards the street. 'There's no point in lighting anything, or cutting any more.'

'I don't think I could cut any more, in any case, Mrs. Murray,' said Mrs. Helliwell with a wry smile. Robbins had had to cut up her meat for her again at dinner, and she was still rather embarrassed.

'No, indeed, you have done all you can, and must rest. What will Mr. Helliwell say to us if we return you to him worse than when you left?'

Mrs. Helliwell grinned.

'Well, he will have to help with the garden, for once, and leave his books be for a morning or two. But I don't think I can come with you this evening, Mrs. Murray. The very thought of more crowds makes my ribs ache. I thought perhaps, though, I might make myself useful by watching out for fires – no doubt you had thought to leave a servant to do that, but perhaps I can replace them and let them go to see the fun?'

Isobel looked at Murray. Robbins had indeed mentioned staying at home to deal with any conflagrations. Murray nodded.

'It's a generous offer, if you are sure, Mrs. Helliwell. But there will be a servant to stay, too: there is no sense in one person running up and down the stairs if two can watch separately.'

'And until then,' said Isobel, 'shall we have someone read something? Do you still have that poor woman's book of poetry, Charles? Is it any good?'

'You shall be the judges,' said Murray. 'I've barely glanced through it, myself.'

He went downstairs to fetch *A Gaelic Garland* from the book room, and returned to settle in his favourite chair. Mrs. Helliwell relaxed, her arm and ribs gently cushioned, and Isobel busied herself with pens and paper at the table. He was sure the King himself could be no more comfortable.

'I shan't trouble you with the Gaelic poems,' he said.

'What a shame!' said Mrs. Helliwell mischievously. 'I'm sure I should understand every word!'

'Well, he does,' said Isobel, 'but he says his pronunciation is poor.'

'Awful,' Murray agreed. He loved languages, but had not been able to find anyone who could reliably coach him in this one. 'So let me see … There are about thirty poems, none of them very long. Shall I just begin at the beginning and go on until we've had enough?'

The first poem was a kind of ode to Gaelic poetry, and though over-flowery for Murray's taste was well worked with a nice use of language. The second described a garden, and had Mrs. Helliwell, keen gardener, nodding along in appreciation.

'They feel very youthful,' said Isobel. 'I suppose she must have been writing them for a while, then collected them together.'

'Yes, I hear what you mean,' said Mrs. Helliwell. 'There's a brightness to them.'

'Less so with the next one,' Murray warned them, reading ahead. This time it was poem full of wistful longing for home, for curlews crying, for the way the mountains swept down to the rustling shore of the sea. He could almost smell the wrack and feel the wind on his face. When he finished reading, there was a pensive silence. Mrs. Helliwell at last wiped the corner of her eye, and said,

'That was a bit of a shock after the first two! Dear me – she must really have missed her home. Where was it you said she came from?'

'From Drumnadrochit,' said Murray. 'And then latterly she lived with her husband on the Altbean estate, near Aberchalder.'

'Well, she must have lived near the sea at some point,' said Isobel, clearing her throat. 'Hearing that I feel as if I am there myself. You can see why she was so popular, when the book first appeared.'

'Though if she were reading that to them,' said Mrs. Helliwell, 'all the Highlanders in Edinburgh would pack up their plaids and go home. Dear me!' she said again, and blew her nose.

'Shall I go on?' asked Murray, now he had recovered his composure.

'Please do, Charles. That was quite lovely.'

Several poems followed describing life on Mrs. Ochill's Highland shore, the steel-grey waves, the fishing boats, the mist and rain, the hard work, the music and laughter, and the low dark cottages where they lived. It was not, Murray thought, a wholly romantic view, not a scene that Sir Walter would necessarily include in one of his own works, yet it was so skilfully drawn that once again he thought he could see it himself. Isobel had sat back in her chair, leaving her papers undisturbed, and Mrs. Helliwell hung on every word. Murray had to admit he was surprised. He had assumed, for no good reason, that the poems would be sentimental silliness.

'These are far from that,' said Isobel, when he confessed this. 'And you say she wrote no more?'

'The publisher, Hutcheon, told me she wrote to him when her husband died, saying she would publish no more, and there was nothing in her papers. Not even the manuscript drafts of these poems.'

'Ha! Perhaps it was her husband who wrote them, but he thought it might look better if they came from a woman's hand?' suggested Isobel. 'Then he died, and so of course he could write no more, but she could not, either.'

Murray grinned.

'I must say that from all I have heard of him, he seems even less likely to have penned these sensitive lines than she does. But who knows? It would certainly explain why this was the only volume. I wonder how we could ever find out? And if it were the case, could it have something to do with his death? Or hers?'

'Ah,' said Isobel, 'it seems impossible. But didn't Sir Walter Scott go to her soirees? Would he have realised if the poems had been Mr. Ochill's instead of his wife's?'

'I could ask him,' said Murray. 'If we go out later, we could call.'

But before that, he went down to his book room, and drew a

large, flat volume off a low shelf. A thought had struck him, and he wanted to see if it could possibly be true.

In the servants' hall downstairs there was markedly more enthusiasm for the evening's entertainment than there was in the drawing room. Robbins listened to the various pleas for permission to be out in the streets, which came from everyone from the cook to the scullery maid. The only one who did not seem keen to go out was young Matthew: Robbins took this as a sign of his general resignation that as the youngest male servant, the duty of staying at home and watching for fires would almost inevitably fall on him. When, therefore, Robbins told them that all but Matthew were free to go out, there was no hint of disappointment on his face.

'I shall stay at home, with Mrs. Helliwell upstairs,' Robbins explained. 'So I shall know at once if any of you is back even a minute late. Matthew, you'll attend the master, and Miss Fitzsimmons will be looking after young Miss Murray. The streets will be crowded, and we don't want any trouble.'

'Sir,' said Matthew. Robbins examined his face. To tell the truth, he did not look much different from when he thought he would not be going out at all.

Around nine o'clock, with Augusta roused and dressed in great excitement, Miss Fitzsimmons and Matthew in attendance, and everyone in warm shawls, the Murray party departed the Queen Street house to see if there were any illuminations worth seeing, and failing that to call on Sir Walter Scott. Almost at once it was clear there was a frisson about the town again. The lacklustre passersby of the morning had turned into good-humoured little gatherings of people, pointing and smiling. Turning, they saw that every house in the terrace had its windows lit, many of them behind cut paper decorations like the ones Isobel and Mrs. Helliwell had made – though Murray thought at once that Isobel's were far superior to every other household's. Some had used coloured paper to great effect, or painted scenes on, or cut out loyal slogans. It was a remarkably fine sight, and at first they thought that all they would have to do would be to promenade the length of the street, admiring all the different ideas.

But when they climbed Castle Street to see if Sir Walter was at home, they realised that there was much more to the whole spectacle. Every business or office had some illumination done by gas light, whether the Royal Arms, or a thistle and a crown, or ships, or castles, or even, in one ambitious display, a Highland piper in his kilt. Emerging on to Prince's Street without even thinking of stopping at Sir Walter's, they saw that there were lanterns along the battlements of the Castle, and Calton Hill's bonfires flared up into the night, and as ten o'clock struck there was the firing of small cannon and other firearms, blanketing the valley in a layer of smoke and making Augusta shriek and cover her ears, laughing.

And despite Robbins' fears, the crowds were quiet and respectful, awed by the scenes around them. Matthew seemed perhaps the least impressed: he observed the crowds rather than the illuminations, keeping an eye on his charges, and watching intently as they met and greeted acquaintances. Willie Jack with the extensive party of his wife's relations swept along, waving, children and dogs in their wake. Armstrong the lawyer smiled and his wife and Isobel curtseyed to each other amicably, remarking on the beauty of the night. They met by chance the Duke of Atholl, who bowed in recognition.

'You could let a five year old child run about here without fear,' he remarked, evidently impressed by all he saw. 'I could wish every Friday night in Edinburgh as peaceful as this. I don't suppose you have found the murderer? Though this evening it almost feels as if it could not possibly matter.'

Murray had been thinking, since his visit to his book room.

'You know, your Grace, I have the sense that I might have at least part of the solution – no proof, as yet, but perhaps a motive, at the very least?'

'You have? Tell me.'

'I'm not sure that this is the place, your Grace. Will you and Lord Melville be at Holyroodhouse tomorrow?'

'We shall,' sighed the Duke. 'We must be there for the King's Levee. Are you attending?'

'No, your Grace, but –'

'I shall see you are admitted, of course. You'll need to be there early, I should think. They plan to see some thousand gentlemen through the doors for a royal greeting, and the King is to be there for about five minutes, or something ridiculous like that.

Come early, and I shall ensure Melville and I are at your disposal.'

'I shall try my best to make it worth your while, your Grace,' said Murray, alarmed at this level of attention. He was not at all sure of his ideas yet. There was more he could find out, if people were prepared to be truthful. But would he find out in time?

A party of ladies passed and several called out to the Duke. He bowed again, and went to join them. Murray continued with his own party, trying to think how he could obtain the information he needed. New Assembly Close was one possibility. It was too late to call now, though: while most people might be out looking at the illuminations, he suspected the person he wanted would not be out at all, and would therefore very likely have retired for the night – and it would be better if he were co-operative. How early could Murray hope to call in the morning?

'Well, that has been wonderful,' said Isobel at last. 'I'm so sorry Mrs. Helliwell had to miss it.'

Murray looked about him. The illuminations were going out, one by one or in little batches as if a group of neighbours had decided on a time together. Lamp boys were everywhere, ready to help people home along the now darkened streets. Augusta was beginning to sag, heavy in Miss Fitzsimmons' arms. Murray took her, feeling her tired arms looping around his neck, and gestured to Matthew.

'Find us a link boy and let us go home,' he said. 'We can share with some other party going to Queen Street, if need be.'

But there were plenty of boys, and Matthew found one at once. They had not strayed too far in the end, only a little way up the High Street, and though it now felt like four in the morning instead of midnight, it did not take them too long to walk home. They met the Balfours on the way and talked quietly of the evening, while Murray continued to wonder about the next morning. What would Melville think of his idea?

But back at the Queen Street house, he was not to be left alone with his thoughts. Robbins opened the door at once with a look on his face that told Murray there was something wrong, and while the maids, home promptly half an hour before, helped Isobel and Miss Fitzsimmons and Augusta, Murray went with Robbins into the dining room. And there was Hepburn, collapsed across the table.

Chapter Thirty-Five

'WHAT HAPPENED?' MURRAY was beside Hepburn in two long strides. Robbins stepped smartly after him. Hepburn was breathing, at least – with his head to one side, and snuffling noises, and a thin cord of spittle fastening his slack lips to the table.

'Drunk, sir. He arrived on the doorstep almost incapable.'

'And passed out here?'

'I tried to encourage him to go to his bed, sir, but there was a great deal he wanted to say. So I guided him in here, thinking at least he would be out of the way when Mrs. Murray returned, but before I could get him into a chair he just collapsed, as you see. I doubt I'll need to give the table a bit of a polish again in the morning,' he added, his pale face creased in a frown.

'So what was it he wanted to say? Or was he coherent?'

'Something of what he said made some sense, sir. He's very angry with a Mr. Mash – the gentleman from the Lord Chamberlain's Office, I believe?'

'It's not a common name, certainly. He was angry with Mash? I thought he was Mash's devoted servant?'

'Not just now, sir. Not happy at all with Mr. Mash. He was saying, as far as I could judge, that he had done everything Mr. Mash had asked, done his best, gone beyond what he had been asked, and Mr. Mash, it seems, did not appreciate this level of service.'

'So he took to drink, I suppose.'

'I wondered if he had taken to the drink first, sir, then gone to report for duty and been told that his inebriated state was not acceptable.'

'Of course. That's possible. I wonder if this is something he does habitually? Perhaps Willie Jack Dundas would know. And I wonder if he has, in fact, lost his position. Still, I daresay we'll know nothing more till the morning – late morning, perhaps. Will you be able to get him upstairs? All the way up to the nursery floor?'

Robbins looked as if he had been trying to work that out for some time.

'It's going to be difficult, sir.'

'I could help,' said Murray, well aware that he was at least taller than Robbins.

'Aye, I thought you'd say that, sir, but then the last staircase is narrow. Would we all fit?'

'Good point. Any other ideas?'

'Leave him here for the night, sir, and serve breakfast in the parlour upstairs. I'll bring a blanket or two to put over him: he should be warm enough.'

'Well, if you're happy about the consequences for the table …'

'We'll see how bad it is afterwards. I doubt him spending the night on it will make it much worse than him falling across it in the first place, sir.'

'It probably won't do much for him, but then much of his pain will be self-inflicted. I wonder where he was drinking?'

'No idea, sir, but I think it was brandy, from the smell.' Robbins' fastidious nostrils flared. 'I'll maybe have a bucket handy, too, sir.'

'Maybe for the best, yes. Anything else? No fires or alarums? The streets were crowded but remarkably quiet.'

'All very peaceful here, too, sir. Mrs. Helliwell was very content when I took her up some tea about an hour ago. She was enjoying the views from the window.'

'It was much better than I had expected. I'm glad she was able to see at least some of it. I suppose Mrs. Murray has gone up to join her, so I shall, too, if you could arrange some more tea.'

'Sir.'

In the hallway the boy Matthew was waiting.

'Fetch a couple of blankets from the press on the landing, Matthew, and take them into the dining room and lay them over Mr. Hepburn,' said Robbins.

'Sir,' said Matthew, but cast a look at Murray rather than darting off at once. Robbins was quick.

'Something you need to tell the master?'

'Yes, sir.'

'Go on, then,' said Murray.

'Sir,' said Matthew, 'this may sound odd, but as we came home just now …'

'Yes?'

'I believe we were followed, sir.'

'Followed?' Murray echoed.

'Yes, sir. A young man with dark hair, sir. Came all the way along Queen Street behind us, and as we went inside he was standing across the road, watching. And I believe, sir, I saw him near us on Prince's Street, too.' He stood straight, clearly ready to be disbelieved.

'Is he still there now?' asked Murray. Robbins made a move towards the dining room. 'No, upstairs. You make sure the front door is locked, and I'll go and look.'

But though he peered carefully out across the street from the drawing room window, under pretence of catching the last of the illuminations, he could see no one lurking in the darkness of the parkland across the street. Oh for a platoon of armed members of the Celtic Society just now! he thought.

'What's the matter, Charles?' Isobel asked, not convinced by his pretence, of course.

'It was bonny out there an hour or so ago,' added Mrs. Helliwell, 'but most of the lights have gone out now. The gardens were all lit up!'

There was no sense in hiding it: they were both sensible women.

'Matthew saw someone following us from Prince's Street. A young man with dark hair, apparently.'

'And not, I suppose, Mr. Hepburn?' asked Isobel at once.

'No, for one thing Hepburn is blind drunk and sleeping on our dining table,' said Murray. Isobel raised her eyebrows.

'We'd better not tell Miss Fitzsimmons. I doubt she would like the thought of having given up her comfortable room only for it to be spurned in favour of a wooden table.'

'Will he be all right?' asked Mrs. Helliwell, more charitable than Isobel.

'Robbins is seeing to it that he is looked after,' said Murray.

'Apparently he has had a falling out with his beloved patron, Mr. Mash. Whether the drink was a reaction or a contribution is not yet clear.'

'Well,' said Isobel. 'about the other man, then. Who is he?'

'That is the question. And I'm wondering how long he was following us, and what he might have overheard? Was he there, for example, when I was speaking with the Duke of Atholl?'

'My, but Edinburgh society is grand!' murmured Mrs. Helliwell. 'Just to have a claik on the street with the highest in the land!'

'Yes, they can catch you anywhere!' Murray agreed. 'And make sure you are doing all that is expected of you. Now, what did I say to the Duke?'

'You said you thought you knew who was responsible, I think,' said Isobel, 'for I thought at the time it was a brave thing to say. Raising expectations.'

'You could be right, my dear. But at the same time, if the young man with the dark hair happened to hear that …'

Isobel's eyes widened. He could see that she was running through her memory to pinpoint what else he had said.

'But you told him you would talk to Viscount Melville tomorrow morning, didn't you?'

'That's right, yes. I think I actually said that I knew why the murder had occurred, not that I knew who had done it.'

'I don't think that matters,' said Isobel quickly. 'I don't think that young man will be mincing words at this stage, do you? You said you knew something, and that you hadn't told Viscount Melville yet. And you didn't tell the Duke. So he's going to think that all he needs to do to prevent his identification is –'

'He won't, my dear.'

'You don't know that!'

'I'm sure he won't. What could he do? We are securely locked in our house.'

'He could burn it down! He'll think he has only to destroy you to preserve himself!'

The thought had occurred to Murray. There had been a fire in the Queen Street house before, a long time ago, lit by a misguided and unhappy person. But they had had the benefit of the element of surprise. If this young man had laid the block and ropes in the fake gateway, then he was clever, and patient. Would a man who was clever and patient carry out an attack on a large and secure house, full of servants, with the strong possibility of not achieving his goal of killing one person, if he could wait and deal with the matter some other way? He did not seem like the man for a blunt assault. But Murray would be very careful next day as he went about the town.

Nevertheless, he and Robbins sat up that night, taking it in turns to patrol up and down, front and back, and told the stable lads to do the same in the mews. Stables were always vulnerable. There was no sign of any trouble, or indeed anyone around at all. It was as if the beautiful illuminations had lulled the town to sleep, and the only people awake were Robbins and Murray, padding about the house.

Towards morning, Murray heard a sound from the dining room and knocked gently on the door. A groan issued forth from inside, and a feeble 'Come in.'

The room reeked: thank heavens Robbins had planned to serve breakfast in the parlour. Hepburn was still lying on the table, now with his knees on one of the dining chairs. Someone must have removed his boots at some point, for they stood, sentry-like, by the door, waiting for him. He stared sideways at Murray for a moment, then, with a visible effort at recollection, scowled and pulled himself into a semi-upright position, bracing his arms on the table as if afraid it might capsize. His colour was not a healthy one.

'Good morning, Mr. Hepburn,' said Murray. 'How are you this morning?'

'*Where* am I this morning?' Hepburn retorted, squinting as he scanned the room. 'Oh … is this your dining room, sir?'

'It is,' said Murray easily. 'It would have been difficult to carry you upstairs, and you seemed unlikely to undertake the venture yourself. I hope you have had a comfortable night.'

Hepburn's face scalded red. It made a change from his previous appearance.

'I suppose I must have, sir. Please forgive me for not standing. I'm not very sure how to.'

'That's all right,' said Murray. 'I gather you've had a falling out with Mr. Mash of the Lord Chamberlain's Office?'

'I … Who told you that, sir?'

'You gave some account of it to Robbins last night when you arrived.'

'Did I? Oh.' Hepburn tried to wipe his face on his upper arm, still not removing his hands from the table. It was not successful.

Murray crossed to the nearest window, opened the shutters and then lifted the sash, not before checking the street outside for young men with dark hair.

'A little fresh air often helps, does it not? Would you like to tell me about Mr. Mash?'

'No,' said Hepburn, after a moment. Murray waited, enjoying the morning chill. 'I did all I could for him.' Silence again. 'And in the end he didn't appreciate it at all. Didn't understand. All I've done for him! And I thought I would be there for the rest of my days, in the Lord Chamberlain's Office. Now what? Where am I to go? That was where I was going to be.' Hepburn swallowed hard, twice. He was gulping back tears. Murray saw that Robbins had left a jug of water and a glass for Hepburn, and handed a full glass to the young man. Hepburn cautiously lifted one hand from the table, and took it.

'What did you do wrong?' Murray asked gently. Sipping the water seemed to have suppressed the tears a bit, and Hepburn took a few deep breaths. He shook his head, then apparently regretted the sharp movement. 'Was it the drink?'

'No, not at all. I was sober when I saw him. It was only afterwards … He would be so ashamed of me. Again.' He sniffed copiously, and dug in a pocket to produce a much-used handkerchief. Murray waited again, as Hepburn shoved the dirty cloth away again, and eased himself backwards off the table to stand beside the chair that had supported his legs. He still clutched the table with one hand, but he was a little less deathly in appearance. He took another breath. 'I must apologise for my behaviour, sir. No doubt you are anxious for me to take my departure. Please be assured I shall be away by … oh, what time is it?'

'Not yet seven.'

'Oh! It's the Levee today, isn't it? I should be … perhaps if I turn up and do my duty as usual, perhaps he will forgive me?'

'But what did you do?'

'May I at least take advantage of your hospitality, sir, to wash and change my linen?'

'Of course you may,' said Murray. 'In fact, you are welcome to stay on. I don't know where you would find somewhere else to stay just now anyway.'

'To stay on?' Hepburn gaped. 'After this?'

'I hesitate to admit it, but I don't think you are the worst this house has ever seen,' said Murray, remembering one or two evenings in that very dining room with his brother George. He smiled. 'Go and wash and change – perhaps wait an hour before calling for hot water, though. Robbins has done enough for you in the last little while. Then, if you think it wise to report to Mr. Mash for duty, please do so. And later you can tell me the whole story,' he added, as a note that perhaps Hepburn at least owed him a good tale after dinner.

'Sir,' said Hepburn, steadied himself once more, and lurched, mostly successfully, from the dining room. Murray hoped he would find his way to his room.

Chapter Thirty-Six

SOME TIME LATER that morning, but as early as he could possibly persuade himself that it was acceptable, Murray strode along Queen Street to Castle Street, to assess whether or not Sir Walter Scott was receiving callers. There had been a lively discussion with Isobel, and then with Robbins, about the wisdom of Murray going out alone and the dangers of leaving the house unattended by the full staff, and in the end Murray had agreed to take Matthew with him, leaving Robbins in charge. Matthew was certainly no drawback, quieter than most servants Murray had known, and endowed, so far in his career anyway, with good sense. Still, Murray would have liked to have left him at home to help Robbins if anything happened.

By the constant shifting of various people back and forth around the doorway of Sir Walter Scott's house, Murray decided that the household was up, and went to join the small queue of visitors on the steps. The footman in pale blue tartan took his card and passed it back at once to someone inside, and in a moment Murray was ushered in. Matthew remained politely outside: it looked as if the house could hold no more.

Being inside did not, though, mean that Murray had Sir Walter's full attention. He was not, of course, the only caller, and both Sir Walter and Stewart of Garth were busy with all kinds of papers, letters, notes, reports and daybooks, presumably keeping some track of who was doing what, where, and dressed in what manner.

'The King's Levee today!' Sir Walter cried when he saw Murray. 'My dear Murray, I hope with all my heart that you are not seeking an entrée to the Levee. Even as it stands, I don't expect that His Majesty will have more than – what did we say, Garth?'

Stewart of Garth consulted a paper pinned to the wall in front of him.

'One hundred and thirty eight seconds, Sir Walter,' he pronounced.

'That. That's all the King will have with each gentleman. Garth does the arithmetic, so don't even think to ask me what difference one more would make.'

'Please believe I have no wish to attend the Levee!' said Murray, hoping that Sir Walter would not be offended, and even more that he should not succeed in squeezing Murray in at the last minute. 'I should not aspire to such heights. No, I'm afraid I come with another question about Mrs. Ochill.'

'Good gracious!' Sir Walter's face fell. 'I confess that I have scarcely thought about her. Poor woman,' he added, abstractedly. 'But what is your question? For as I said before, I did not know her well at all.'

'No, but you went to some of her soirees, did you not?' Scott had had an entrée to the soiree and the Levee. Murray tried not to laugh.

'I did, I did. She had quite a year of it, or a season, at any rate, until her husband died.'

'What was she like at the soirees?'

'Like? Like a woman of middle age who has written some poetry, I suppose. She would read some of it out, and then the guests would applaud and sometimes they would bring some of their own poems for her to comment on – a painful business, for an author – and sometimes they would ask her questions – you know the kind of thing. Where do you find your ideas, what time of the day do you write, what kind of ink do you use.'

'And how did she handle such questions?'

Sir Walter, about to answer, shut his mouth and frowned, thinking back.

'She wasn't very good at it, as I remember,' he admitted at last. 'She mumbled a good deal over that kind of thing, though she read the poems out very nicely. I suppose she could practise that, but the questions, for her at least, were unexpected ones. She was a little awkward over it. Strange, I had forgotten that. It can often happen, though, that the work of a person, be it man or woman, is more impressive than the person themselves. And vice versa, I suppose.' He lapsed for a moment into thought, and Murray wondered if Sir Walter were wondering about the impression he himself made, and how it compared with his work.

'And did you ever hear her asked what had inspired her poetry?'

'Oh, I can't remember.' Sir Walter's gaze had returned to his desk and the papers on it. Murray realised he had run out of time. 'Whatever she said, it cannot have been very impressive. Now, I'm so sorry, Murray, but …'

'I understand, Sir Walter. Thank you for seeing me, and I hope the Levee is a success.'

Murray bowed and left, not wanting to take up time or space any more than was necessary.

Collecting Matthew, he walked briskly to Holyroodhouse. It was too early to catch Viscount Melville there as the Duke of Atholl had instructed him, but it was not Melville he had come to see. Feeling that he was beginning to find his way about the place, he headed for the kitchens to see if he could find the maid Helen he had spoken with before.

The kitchens were busy, but not as frantic as he had feared they might be.

'We're only feeding His Majesty and a few others,' said Helen, when he found her scrubbing carrots. Her hands were red and raw. 'Mind, they'll still want more than their fair share laid out … sorry, sir. It's not my place to comment.'

'I shan't tell,' he said. No doubt the servants here would eat well on the leftovers from this grand occasion, nevertheless.

'What can I do for you, sir?' she asked. 'Is it about Mrs. Ochill?'

'This time it's about a gentleman who was seen around the Palace,' he said. 'Alasdair MacDonell of Glengarry. Do you know who I mean?'

'Oh, aye, him,' she said. 'He's been around a fair bit, right enough.'

'Can you remember if you saw him here last Friday or Thursday?' Not that Thursday mattered, but he did not wish to sound too fixed on Friday.

She flicked the carrot she had just finished into a bucket, and paused, hands dripping, before plucking up the next one.

'He was here near every day last week. Thursday I didna see him, for I had messages to get, things that had been forgotten, ken? There's always something. Friday, though … he was here, indeed, late on in the day. Well, no affa late: I should think he was away home for his dinner, right enough. It was a busy day, for the decorators were starting to think they'd never be done and that Mr. Trotter was going mad running round, and Mr. Mash, the wee nyaff – sorry, sir, I ken I shouldna say sik things – Mr. Mash was running after him telling him what to do, and then a couple of the tenants came back for stuff they'd forgotten – there's always something, aye. It was madness in here on Friday, and all the time till Monday, if it comes to that.'

'But you saw Glengarry leave before dinner time?'

'I did – as it happens I even saw him ride off, for I was outside getting more water.'

He was glad he had discovered Helen. Her knack for being round and about the place was valuable. Then he reflected on what she had said.

'Did you say a couple of the tenants had come back for things?'

'That's right. I saw one fellow up on the top floor looking for a bonnet. The poor old fellow was wearing it on his head. They should never have gone putting old folks like that out. It only makes them worse. And the other one was Mrs. McGregor – ken, I think I tellt you about her afore, did I no? She was the closest Mrs. Ochill had to a friend in here, or a neighbour anyway. And I tellt you she was away to live with her nephew, or her grand nephew, did I no?'

'Yes, you did.'

'Aye, I thought I had. So let me see … I saw her near her old room. What's this she said she was after? I think it was a needle case she'd dropped – ken she was a seamstress, so I doubt she had only the one. I thought myself at the time she was only there to gawk. So I let her be, for I was cleaning this and that but I was nearby for I thought Mr. Trotter wouldna want her lingering. And she came out fast enough with a wee smile on her face, for I doubt she maybe thinks that's her apartment all done up now and when she comes back it'll be all fine, ken?'

Murray hesitated. Helen did not seem to have heard of Mrs. McGregor's death. He left it for now.

'Well, it has certainly all been smartened up,' he said.

'All yon donkey brown,' said Helen dismissively. 'Then she stopped to talk to someone, so I just carried on cleaning. There's aye cleaning,' she added philosophically, as profound as if she had said 'The poor are always with us'.

'Who was she talking to? The old man from upstairs?'

'No, not a bit of it. It was a young fellow that's been around a fair bit recently – I've seen him a few times myself. Dark-haired, slim. I dinna ken his name. He seemed to know her, or she knew who he was, something like that. He's always got a pile of papers with him, so I dinna ken if they're designs and he works for Mr. Trotter, or if they're instructions and he works for yon fellow Mash, or if he's something else altogether.'

Working for Mr. Mash … could it have been Hepburn, after all?

'Have you seen his face? Would you recognise him again?'

She shook her head.

'He's ordinary looking. And my eyesight's no so good any more.'

'Was there anything distinctive about him?'

'Not really, so far as I could see. Only …'

And here Murray was surprised to see a smile creep across Helen's worn face, a smile that was – what could he say? – as dreamy as a lass thinking of her love. Wondering what on earth the answer was going to be, he prompted her gently.

'Only what?'

Helen grinned.

'Only his voice, see. He has that lovely voice – oh, it's like angels singing!'

'What kind of voice?'

'He'll be from the west coast, or maybe the Western Isles. Ken? That lovely musical voice. Doesna matter to me what he looks like: that voice would do it for me!'

Murray knew what she meant. His own maid, now Robbins' wife, Mary, had that same lilting, liquid voice. He remembered clearly the first time he had heard it, the first time he had met her. But that was a long time ago. On a practical level, he wondered if perhaps they should have brought Mary with them to Edinburgh after all, for she might have some insights that would help just now.

It was probably too late for anything to be useful.

Yet he had a feeling he knew who this man was – and it was not Hepburn. As far as he remembered, the man in question had claimed to have been working both when Mrs. Ochill was murdered and when Mrs. McGregor was killed under the scaffolding – and for all Murray knew, he might also have some kind of alibi for the time when the block and ropes had been set up inside the fake gateway, though when that might have happened was a little more obscure. But there was someone else who would know whether or not the man had been working at those times, and Murray was going to go and find him.

'Oh, heavens!' exclaimed Helen, breaking through his thoughts. 'There he goes again!'

She was staring past him at the kitchen doorway. Murray saw no one. She shook peelings off her hands.

'That wee man Musgrave from the top floor – he's supposed to be staying up the Canongate but he keeps getting out and coming back! I'd better go after him,' she said, with a despairing look at the carrots.

'Let me go,' said Murray. 'I've seen him before – I know what he looks like. Wait here, Matthew.'

'He'll be away up the back stairs,' said Helen, gratefully. 'And he's quick – quicker than he looks! Watch him.'

Murray strode back to the door just in time to glimpse the old man disappearing around a corner at the end of the passage. He ran after him, but by the time he reached the corner, Musgrave could be heard trotting up the winding stone staircase. Murray tried to take the stairs two at a time, then hit his head on the steps above and had to slow down. The staircase passed an open door into a small, dark, panelled room, but he could still hear footsteps above him, and carried on upwards. At the top, a narrow passage led along one wing of the palace, and Musgrave was just opening a door on the left hand side, allowing a little dim light through. Murray hunched over, and hurried after him.

The room was tiny, and panelled just like the one downstairs. Musgrave, wide blue eyes staring through Murray, stood by the little window. Murray reached out a hand, trying to calm him.

'Mr. Musgrave, we'll need to go back downstairs now. I don't think you left anything here, did you?'

'My bunnet,' said the old man. 'Where's my bunnet?'

'You're wearing your bonnet,' said Murray, gently. It was a generously-sized pale blue one, slumped over the old man's white hair. Musgrave looked at him suspiciously, then raised a hand to his head. He felt the cloth.

'That's no my bunnet. That's my … my …'

'Well, anyway,' said Murray, remembering similar conversations with his old housekeeper, 'I can't see your bonnet here. It must be downstairs, I think. Will you come and help me look?'

'I'll no,' said the old man, suspicion turning to alarm. 'I'll no go downstairs with you! Downstairs to the dungeons! I'll no! I'll no!'

'All right, then,' said Murray. 'We'll wait here for a bit, shall we?'

He glanced around the little room. Mr. Trotter's efforts had extended even up here, and the panelling was coated with the same dun paint as the apartments downstairs. It even looked as though he had had a cupboard painted over, for there was a small keyhole in the wall just behind Musgrave, half-filled with paint. Maybe there was another bonnet in there, or something else with which he could placate the old man. He stepped across, approaching carefully.

'Let me just see this, Mr. Musgrave. Have you the key of this door?'

'A key? No! I have no key. I ken nothing whatever about that cupboard. There's no cupboard there, not that I know about. If they ask me, that's what I have to tell them.'

'If who asks you, Mr. Musgrave?' Murray paused, with his hand at the keyhole. The old man had turned stubborn.

'Anybody,' he said firmly. 'Anybody at all.'

'And, um, who told you not to tell anybody?'

'Och, wee Anthony, that's who. He kens everything, see? He'll ken where my bunnet is, an' all.' He smiled. Murray tried not to frown. He thought he had been told that the old man had no known relations, and was living in the flat of one of the Palace servants on the Canongate. So who was Anthony?

The cupboard door was stuck, but he thought the lock might be simple enough, if he could slide something down between door and jamb. He took out his knife, keeping it well away from Mr.

Musgrave, just in case. Breaking the seal of the paint, still soft, he slipped the blade into the crack, manipulated it a little, and levered the door open with a sticky creak.

Inside, on a shelf, was a stack of printed handbills. He could read them from here.

'Death to the Fat Hanoverian! Give us Reform!'

He handed Musgrave over to the kitchen staff and acknowledged Helen's grateful smile, but said nothing to anyone about the cupboard he had once again jammed shut. If Musgrave was one of Patrick Armstrong's clients, it should be easy enough to find out who Anthony was without arousing more suspicion at the Palace, and if he were not it might still be safer to enquire externally. Musgrave himself had seemed entirely unbothered by the cupboard once it was opened, and instead had marvelled at the discovery of his bonnet, which had been on his head all along! A miracle.

'I feel,' Murray said to Matthew, 'like a man who has been told that this is the only doorway, and just as he's about to go through it, it turns out that there's another one just beside it. Not the most memorable of metaphors, but there we are.'

'Yes, sir,' said Matthew dutifully.

They had worked their way through the maze of the palace's ground floor, now without a decorator to be seen but full of flower arrangers and cleaners, and were about to leave by the main door when Murray heard a very pointed cough behind him.

'Mr. Murray, leaving so soon?'

He turned. The chunky London accent had given him away at once, so it was no surprise to see the flaxen wig and taut red waistcoat of John Townsend, Bow Street Runner extraordinaire.

'Mr. Townsend. Still on duty, I see?'

'Always, Mr. Murray, always. To be on duty, as I have told you, is to observe, constantly. To observe means that one sees all kinds of things the ordinary man might miss. To see such things,' he raised one hand as if to stall an interruption, 'causes questions to arise, questions that require one to assemble all the facts at one's disposal, questions that would not necessarily occur to the ordinary man. And such questions, of course, require answers.'

He nodded solemnly. Murray suppressed a sigh. Time was short.

'Well, I hope your questions are quick ones,' he said, 'if you are planning to address any of them to me.'

'They may be, they may not,' said Townsend weightily. 'For I have of course observed that a Scotch gentleman whose name is not on the list of attendees for His Majesty's Levee this afternoon – for which event of course I have been charged with ensuring the complete security – is currently on the premises, too early for admission and, if I may say so, having observed it, not appropriately dressed for a Royal Levee, not in my experience.' He made his experience of Royal events sound extensive, though Murray suspected it was not at all. And as he had heard it, Townsend's responsibilities began and ended with teaching the Edinburgh police how to apprehend pickpockets. This time he did sigh.

'I am not here for the Levee, and have no intention of being so, except to take the opportunity later to report to the Duke of Atholl and Viscount Melville, to whom I am answerable for my present actions.' To tell them, particularly, about a cupboard full of seditious handbills in the royal palace itself. 'Good day to you, Mr. Townsend.'

Then a question occurred to him, and he paused.

'If you are responsible for the security of the Royal events,' he said, 'presumably the safety of that ceremonial gateway at Picardy Place falls within your remit?'

Townsend shifted slightly.

'The gateway? Of course. I inspected it personally on Thursday morning.'

'You have some expertise in engineering? Or do you mean you checked to see that no one had, perhaps, added anything to the structure?'

Townsend thought for a moment.

'The latter,' he said.

'How long did you spend looking over it? For you must have had numerous duties that morning.'

There was a little more shifting from foot to foot.

'Ten minutes, I should think,' said Townsend after a moment. 'A trained observer, such as myself, can see things in ten minutes that the ordinary man would almost always miss.'

'Of course,' said Murray. 'So you're clear there was nothing added on Thursday morning.'

'Yes …' said Townsend, but a flicker of worry passed across his face. 'And of course there was nothing. His Majesty passed through the gate safely, did he not?'

'He did,' said Murray, his arms aching briefly in recollection. 'Good work, Mr. Townsend. And now I really must go, for like you I have too many duties to allow myself the pleasure of chatting in doorways. Good day to you,' he said again, and this time managed to leave.

Chapter Thirty-Seven

MINDFUL OF THE time, Murray and Matthew hurried away from the palace and up towards Newington. The Armstrongs lived in St. Patrick's Square in a modest terrace, and Patrick Armstrong, whom he had met when he was walking with Willie Jack on Thursday, had inherited his father's practice as advocate as well as building up a small business just off South Clerk Street, where his staff were able to provide various legal services. Armstrong was an unusual man who preferred mathematics to people, but his unexpected business acumen at least allowed his mother to enjoy a greater degree of prosperity in her old age than she had earlier in her life. Also unexpectedly, Armstrong had married and fathered two sons, both of whom, when Murray had occasionally met them, had indicated solemnly their intention of following their father into his business, when they came of age. Armstrong's wife was a quiet, kindly sort that positively encouraged a husband to stay at home, and so Murray was not sure if he would find Armstrong there or in his office. The office was closer, but he decided to try the house first. The questions he wanted to ask were probably better asked in private.

'Charles! How lovely to see you!' Old Mrs. Armstrong rose and curtseyed like a girl, just as clever and attractive as ever Murray remembered from his boyhood. 'Come in and sit down. I had no idea you were in town – though of course half the world is here! Isn't it fascinating?'

'I'm sorry I haven't called,' said Murray. 'It has been a little busy, and I have been remiss with all my friends.'

'Don't tell me you are caught up in all these preparations? I know dear Mr. Blair knows most of the – what shall we call them? Instigators?' She chuckled with him. 'But to involve you as well!'

'No, Blair did not involve me. Though you can imagine how much he loves all this.'

'How is dear Isobel? And little Augusta? You must bring them here. Tell Isobel to call as soon as she may, and never mind the hour.'

'I'm sure she will – she'll be delighted. They are both very well, I'm pleased to say.'

'But I daresay it's Patrick you want to see,' said Mrs. Armstrong, after some more exchange of news and experiences of the Royal visit so far. Murray thought the subject would keep Edinburgh people in conversation for years to come. 'He is at home, I believe, though he is in his book room. Once his work at Holyroodhouse was done he closed his office for the duration of the visit. He has absolutely given up on his clerks concentrating on anything, and they were coming to work in the most outrageous outfits, too: tartans and bonnets and all kinds of feathers and foliage. Can you imagine?'

'I think I can!' he said. 'The sights on the streets are quite extraordinary. I don't see why an office in Newington should be spared.'

'I'll have Patrick fetched. And of course you'll take some refreshment?'

In a few moments both Patrick and a tray of tea things had arrived, and once she had poured out two cups Mrs. Armstrong discreetly excused herself, sensing that Murray was there on business rather than pleasure. Patrick himself was slower to grasp that, but happy at last to turn to more serious matters. He was not a frivolous man.

'Yes, Mamma is quite right,' he said. 'I closed the office over a week ago. No work was being done at all. My senior clerk took some papers home with him to go over – he's a sensible man, not given to all this daftness – but the rest of them were of no use at all.'

'You employ a Robert Abernyte, do you not?'

'I do. How did you know that?'

'He told me himself that he worked for a Mr. Armstrong in Newington, and I guessed it must be you. Is he a good worker?'

'He is, for the most part – no one is perfect, of course.' Armstrong always had high standards, and was puzzled at anyone preferring entertainment to work.

'Has he also been caught up in this excitement?'

'Oh, yes. They all are. None of them is behaving as they usually do. And there is so much work to be done just now: I think I told you we have had a job of it at Holyroodhouse with the grace and favour tenants. It was all very badly handled, of course. One poor man had been there for years, had no idea what was happening or where he was to go. Fortunately one of the servants who lives at the bottom of the Mile took him in, but I think she's had a time of it, for the poor man wanders and keeps going back to the Palace. Very badly handled indeed.'

Murray hesitated.

'That would not be a Mr. Musgrave, would it?'

'That's the poor man, yes. Have you met him?'

'Just now, in fact. Do you know anything of his history? Why was he living in the Palace?'

'Forty years of loyal service to the Royal Household, so they said at Holyrood. It's hard to imagine now, but he was a senior clerk of some kind, apparently.'

'There was no hint at all of any suspicion against him?'

Armstrong looked at him oddly, as he reflected back on any information he might have received about Mr. Musgrave.

'No, nothing,' he said at last. 'You must understand that from my point of view, we suddenly had a gathering of new clients about whom we previously knew nothing. But it is an odd question. Why do you ask?'

'Has Mr. Musgrave no family to go to?' Murray persisted, holding up a hand to plead for Armstrong's patience. Again, Armstrong carried out a mental review before replying.

'I could check the papers, but my senior clerk has them, and I'm sure I remember correctly. There was a grandson, but he could not be found, even though some of the staff remembered that he had visited his grandfather on several occasions. No one seemed to know his name. The whole business was very badly organised from the start, never mind when they began telling people to leave.'

Murray quickly went over in his mind whether or not there was anything more here he could learn about Musgrave, then turned back to his original reason for visiting Patrick Armstrong.

'You say you shut the office a week ago. Just to be sure, does that mean that none of your clerks was working last Friday?'

'Apart from the senior clerk, I should think not, no. Charles, is this one of your mysteries again? I know you were involved in something for the late Lord Melville, were you not? My father told me you had come to him for some legal advice – this was years ago, though. But haven't you found yourself in some unfortunate circumstances since then?'

'I try not to,' said Murray, 'but things happen.'

'I daresay it's Mr. Blair,' said Armstrong bleakly. 'He's always been a most extraordinary man.'

'He hasn't often started matters,' said Murray, being fair. 'And he has often helped me out of them.'

'Of course you married his daughter,' said Armstrong, as if that must be Murray's reason to defend him. 'So is this one of your mysteries?'

Murray sighed.

'It is, I'm afraid. And it was the current Lord Melville, and the Duke of Atholl, that brought me in. A woman was found dead in Holyroodhouse last Sunday, and they were concerned that there might be some link with a threat to the King.'

'And is there?'

'So far, it seems unlikely,' Murray admitted. Or it had done until he had found subversive handbills in the Palace attic. 'But your clerk Abernyte was acquainted with the woman – they had been neighbours in a stair in New Assembly Close before she moved to the Palace – and I think he may have visited her. He certainly seems to have been in Holyroodhouse last Friday.'

'Then he wasn't there on my account,' said Armstrong firmly. 'As far as I knew, no one was left there to question anyway. What was he doing, admiring the new decorations?'

'Talking to a neighbour of the dead woman, anyway. A Mrs. McGregor.'

'Seamstress?'

'That's right.'

'Yes, she's one of ours. Her nephew – or is it her grand nephew? He wanted compensation for the inconvenience of having to put her up during the visit. And he wanted to know what was going to happen after the visit, for there's nothing clear yet about whether these people are going to be able to move back in. It's all been handled very badly.'

'So Mrs. McGregor would have known Abernyte when she met him?'

'Oh, I should think so. He would have spoken to her several times, at her nephew's. A man named Boot, I think. Offered me a space on his viewing platform on the Lawnmarket for the processions. Couldn't understand why.'

'Did you know Mrs. McGregor is dead?' asked Murray.

'No! Really? When?'

'On Monday. It looked as if the scaffolding for the viewing platform fell on her.'

'Oh? Oh, that viewing platform? Looks as if I had a narrow escape, then. Stupid idea. But very sad. Wait,' he said, for he had never been a dim man, 'you said "it looked as if the scaffolding fell on her". What did you mean by that?'

'I believe she was murdered, and left under the platform.'

Armstrong studied Murray closely for a long, silent moment.

'You believe Abernyte killed her, don't you?'

'I think it's a possibility, yes.'

'Why?'

'I'm trying to make sure of that. I suppose there is no chance that Mr. Musgrave is Robert Abernyte's grandfather?'

'Good heavens! But no, I don't believe so. Abernyte is from the West Coast through and through, and very proud of telling us so. All his family were about Gairloch or Ullapool. Mr. Musgrave is, I believe, from Lanark or thereabouts, and therefore in Abernyte's eyes a thorough-going Lallander. But in any case, why would he kill Mrs. Magregor? Mr. Boot seemed to me a much more objectionable person, should he have wished to kill anyone.'

'Well, in her case,' said Murray, trying to sort information in his head as he went along, 'I think it was only because she recognised him, and could give witness that he was there in Holyroodhouse last Friday afternoon. The afternoon that the other woman was murdered.'

Armstrong paused for another minute, then shook himself like a dog.

'It's all peculiar. The whole town has gone mad.'

'That's possibly true,' said Murray. 'But just to let you know, I'll be speaking to Robert Abernyte.'

'When?'

'Soon. After I've reported to Viscount Melville, and made sure that he is happy with my conclusions.' Though what were his conclusions now? Had Robert Abernyte stored seditious material in Mr. Musgrave's cupboard?

'I would not do what you do for a fortune, Charles.'

'I did not wish for it myself,' said Murray. But to solve a puzzle, and see justice done – even if he did not go out seeking for such things, it was hard to resist them when they presented themselves.

'What time is it?' Murray asked when he and Matthew were back on South Clerk Street. He drew out his watch to answer his own question. 'Ten o'clock. Early yet: the Levee does not start until two o'clock, I believe. Let us go back to Holyroodhouse and see if Viscount Melville is available – he was supposed to be going there early.'

Matthew followed him at exactly the correct distance, down South Bridge and over the Cowgate, up to the High Street at the Tron and down again to the left, towards Holyroodhouse.

'It's busy today,' Murray remarked, then took a closer look at the carriages already starting to line the street down the hill. 'Good heavens: they're queuing already!'

It was true: the traffic in the narrow cobbled street with its dogleg was jammed with heraldry and livery, the servants in their very best uniforms, the passengers in tartans and velvets, many holding their large bonnets on their laps for fear of crushing feathers or herbage. There was a kind of excited resignation about the whole thing.

'Yes, they're going to meet the King,' Murray murmured to Matthew, 'but oh! what a long time they are going to have to wait, struggling to stay looking perfect! I am heartily glad that we shall be well clear of the palace before all that ceremonial starts. If I can find Viscount Melville.'

A few people already lined the street, clogging up the edges, watching the great and the good process past. Murray had half an eye open for Blair, but instead saw a different familiar face. The man looked for a moment as though he did not wish to attract Murray's attention, then realised he had been recognised and gave a half smile.

'Good day to you, Mr. Murray. Have you found your murderer yet?'

It was Mr. McLean, the man from the top flat at New Assembly Close who had given him information about the Ochills. He was seated on a folding campaign chair, with his manservant standing by protectively.

'Not quite, sir.'

McLean's smile spread.

'You'll have found it a difficult task, no doubt. I trust you have not met with any danger, yet?'

'Not yet, no.' Murray remembered Maclean's warning when they had last met. He had not been encouraging. And yet, had his warnings been unfounded, when Murray had spent last night watching to see that no one attacked his house? And there had been those unhappy moments in the fake gateway, with the block and ropes. He would not have been there at all if it had not been for the note that had been sent, warning him of a planned assault on the King on his way from Leith to that fake gateway. Who had sent it?

He pulled himself back to the present, and found that Maclean was watching him closely.

'You look weary,' said Maclean. 'No doubt you have been very busy, running here and there. No wonder you haven't found the killer yet. These high heidyins all have great expectations, but when it comes down to it they ask too much, don't they?'

'How did you know about the device in the gateway, sir?' Murray asked.

Maclean blinked in surprise, but there was more to it.

'A device? I heard nothing of a device.'

'A block, on ropes, intended to strike at the King's carriage as he came through the grand gateway. You sent the note, didn't you, warning me?'

Maclean turned to his manservant.

'William, where is that flask? I need some wine.' He waited impatiently while William poured some into a small cup. 'I know nothing of any device in a gateway. It took me an hour to reach this point today, a walk that would take you five minutes. Do you think I have the strength to go clambering around in gateways?'

'You did send the note, though, didn't you?' Of all the people Murray had spoken to in his capacity as Viscount Melville's agent, Maclean was undoubtedly the most likely. He should have thought of that before. Maclean shook his head a little, then said,

'Yes, I sent the note. I thought some distraction would do you good. For your own safety, if nothing else.'

'And the gateway?'

'I don't know what was in the gateway. I have never even seen the gateway – it sounds horrendous. I only thought that that route from Leith was as likely as anywhere else for any attempt on the King to take place. And it would keep you well away from … from danger.'

'What danger? What do you know, sir?'

'Know? Barely anything. Barely anything. Just be careful, eh? Someone who waits eight years to murder will not let anyone get in their way, when it comes to the bit. I've told you that before.'

'The Abernyte children, in the flat opposite the Ochills. What was their mother's maiden name?'

'How should I know or remember that?'

'They didn't go abroad, did they? And they weren't strictly children, either.'

Maclean eyed him with those bright, sharp eyes.

'Ah, you're closer than I thought. Take care, Mr. Murray.'

Then he shut his mouth decisively, and would say no more.

Chapter Thirty-Eight

'THE QUESTION IS,' said Murray to Matthew as they made their way on down the Canongate, the last and lowest part of the Royal Mile, 'if it's so crowded here already, with a queue this long, will they even let me in to see Viscount Melville? Even with the Duke's word?'

This part of the Mile was a guddle of old and new buildings, and some made to look new with freshly painted render, and the grand and the humble, from large villas set back from the street, built by the nobility in the days when royal activity centred on Holyroodhouse, to rambling little tenements and shops tucked into hidden courtyards. The Canongate Kirk, where they had so recently buried Mrs. Ochill, sat back with its ogee gable end on the left-hand side. Murray and Matthew edged past, as the crowds of spectators thickened like cream turning to butter.

The familiar gates ahead at last were not yet opened to the queuing guests, and Murray avoided them. Further on, he led Matthew round a small stone building towards a side gate where a lone soldier stood sentry. Murray straightened his shoulders and his hat, and approached.

'Charles Murray of Letho, to see His Grace the Duke of Atholl and Viscount Melville,' he said, at an unnecessary volume. The soldier snapped upright, though he had not been slumping before.

'Sir!' he said smartly, and opened the gate to let Murray in. Murray hoped that nothing he did on his visit would result in trouble for the poor sentry, though he probably did need a lesson in security. Murray could really have been anyone.

He was not the only person crossing the broad gravel sweep

in front of the Palace, fortunately, though he was one of the few dressed plainly. Royal Archers in their green uniforms, and members of the Celtic Society in their manifold tartans, marched purposefully back and forth, though Murray could see little in the way of their purpose other than to show they were there, and important. They were clearly conscious of the members of the public watching them through the main gates, and performed to the best of their ability. Around the edges scurried gardeners making last minute adjustments to the floral displays, clipping the low hedge around the central flowerbed, raking spots where excessive marching had disturbed the gravel. Without drawing the attention of any of them, Murray managed to reach the main entrance once again, and with Matthew behind him he strode inside and, unchallenged, reached the courtyard beyond.

'Can you remember how to find the kitchens?' he asked Matthew.

'I think so, sir.'

'Good. Go there, and see if you can find anyone who knows the name, or the address, or both, of Mr. Musgrave's grandson, the one who used to visit him. Then … well, if you can make yourself useful, or find a spot where you aren't in the way, then it's probably best that you wait there until I call for you or need the information.'

'Yes, sir.' Matthew bowed and trotted off in what Murray was sure was the right direction. How pleasant, he thought, to have such an uncomplicated and intelligent servant – a fine assistant for Robbins. If only the lad sometimes looked a little happier, it would help.

Still, now that Murray was in the Palace, it was time to find someone who could help him. He stopped a smartly dressed manservant.

'Can you take me, please, to Viscount Melville?'

The servant bowed.

'I'm sorry, sir, but Viscount Melville has not yet arrived. He is expected imminently.'

'What about His Grace the Duke of Atholl?'

'Alas, sir, His Grace is not yet arrived either. If you wish me, sir, to take you to a chamber where you could await His Grace or His Lordship, I can ensure that as soon as they arrive your presence can be made known to them, sir.'

'Yes … yes, thank you, that would be good.'

'If you'll be so good as to follow me, sir,' said the servant, and led the way to the right, towards the main stairs. Murray expected him to go up, but instead he led Murray into a small chamber off to the left, with a window looking out on the central courtyard. It had two hard seats and a small gateleg table with a used cup and saucer on it. 'I'm sorry it doesn't seem much, sir, but you see all the next floor is taken up with the route the guests will follow to be presented to His Majesty, and once they are let in, sir, I would not like to think how crowded it might become. May I bring you some refreshment, sir?'

Murray looked at the cup and saucer, and realised how long it was since he had taken any refreshment – well, at Patrick Armstrong's house, but it seemed an age ago.

'Yes, please. Some tea would be very acceptable.'

'Sir,' said the servant, took the dirty cup and saucer, and bowed his way out. Murray wondered if he would be back. Everything seemed so busy that one random minor lowland laird could easily be forgotten. But no: in five minutes the servant was back with a cup of tea, milk already added, no sugar, and no pot.

'It's a little stewed, I fear, sir,' said the man, but it was clear he had done his best. Left alone, Murray sipped the reviving tea and sat at his little table, listening to the silence in the room and the bustle of the Palace beyond. It felt like the calm in the centre of the storm.

He rested for a little, going over in his mind all he intended to tell Melville. He had been nine-tenths sure he had well-founded suspicions of Robert Abernyte, but now he wondered if he were right. After all, what would Abernyte's motive have been? Why would he, as a young man, have killed his neighbour, Ochill, and then gone on to kill his widow? Murray had liked the Abernytes when he had met them in their flat. He would have asked Patrick Armstrong what he thought of young Robert, but Patrick was never very good at assessing characters beyond their efficiency and capability at work, and their general intelligence. He would leave questions such as amiability, trustworthiness, and decency, to his mother or his senior clerk, depending on the context. Who else knew the Abernytes? Mr. Mclean, who had lived above them in New Assembly Close. He had given Murray the impression that the

Abernytes had left there as children, not young adults. He had then distracted Murray with the anonymous note. Was he trying to protect the Abernytes? If so, why? And despite what Patrick had said of Robert Abernyte's West Coast heritage, was there a possibility that Abernyte was in fact Mr. Musgrave's grandson, and the author of those seditious handbills?

But then, Mr. Musgrave had told him that 'wee Anthony' had warned him against telling anyone about the cupboard and its contents. So was wee Anthony his grandson, and there was no connexion with Abernyte? In that case, he was back again with his first question. Robert Abernyte had the opportunity to kill both women, Mrs. Ochill and Mrs. McGregor. He had behaved suspiciously last night, after the illuminations, and had apparently been watching Murray's house in Queen Street. But if he had killed the Ochills, what had been his reason? Even a young man who kills impulsively at – what age had he been? Let's say seventeen or eighteen, and sometimes it did happen, before a man learned to control his temper – even a young man who had done that would hardly turn up eight years later to kill again, would he? Or had Mrs. Ochill known more than she had ever told anyone, particularly the government men investigating her husband's death? But why would she hide it? Why would she protect Robert Abernyte then, and threaten him now? Murray had the infuriating feeling that he almost had the answer, almost. Almost. But if he had, then what was it?

He stood abruptly from the table, and paced the little white-washed room. It was chilly in here compared with the August warmth outside: the walls were thick, and the light that came in through the window was thinned out and cool. He leaned his elbows on the sill, staring out at the courtyard and the other wing of the building opposite. The architects had been playing with their classical orders, he noticed: this ground floor had its columns in the Doric order, the first floor in the Ionic, and the second floor Corinthian, neat and measured. Like some of the Canongate houses, on that side of the courtyard the order hid much of the original mediaeval palace with its more assorted staircases and misshapen chambers, windows where they were needed, not where the dimensions said they should go. Brought up in similar mixtures of classical and older, Murray was not sure which he preferred: the old-fashioned rooms were often cosier, but as a tall man he was vulnerable to low doorways and ceilings. His mind was wandering.

It was brought back suddenly to the present. There, on the first floor across the courtyard, standing half sideways to a window, was Robert Abernyte, staring down at the busy courtyard below.

Murray let out a yelp of surprise, and made for the door. He was already at the foot of the grand staircase when he stopped to think. He needed to go upstairs, then north, if he could, then turn right. But what would happen if Abernyte had moved on before he reached there, whatever there was? He had no idea. He ran up the grand stone staircase, pushing past Royal Archers taking their places, and in a moment reached the top and turned left, north. But the doors there were closed against him, and a crowd of gathered Celtic Society members had adopted the landing as their own and were adjusting sporrans and sgianan dubha in an impenetrable knot of plaid and velvet. Murray turned and ran back down the staircase and out into the courtyard.

Halfway along the north side was the entranceway by which he had come in. The cloister that ran right round the courtyard was empty, then suddenly it was full. The gates had been opened and the guests for the Levee were beginning to surge into the Palace. Murray darted in and out of the cloister, trying to get round them, but the crowd was intent on a slow and dignified progress across the courtyard.

'No, not the Grand Staircase,' Murray heard one of the Archers tell a guest. 'There's another staircase. Don't worry, it's not the servants' stairs. It's just over there. It goes up to the Long Gallery, just up there. No, not the Grand Staircase,' he repeated to the next party. 'There's another staircase. Just over there. No, not the servants' stairs. No, not the Grand Staircase …'

The Long Gallery, thought Murray. The Archer had nodded up to the north side of the courtyard. That was where he had seen Abernyte. He wondered if there were a less crowded route, but he was not sure enough of it, and followed the procession of guests. But when he glanced back up at the window where he had seen Abernyte, the man had gone.

But in a few minutes he was up at the door of the Long Gallery himself. And to his dismay, the Bow Street Runner, John Townsend, was firmly established in the doorway, checking the guests.

'I don't remember your name on the guest list, Mr. Murray,' he said, rocking confidently back on his heels with his hands behind his back. The fact that he had to look up into Murray's face did not disconcert him in the least.

'I think you have a more dangerous intruder, Mr. Townsend,' said Murray in a low voice. He had no wish to cause a panic, and besides, how dangerous would Abernyte be to the guests? He still had no idea of Abernyte's motives.

'A dangerous intruder?' For a moment Townsend looked as though he would bar the door to Murray anyway. Then he seemed to reconsider, a look of uncertainty in his broad face. 'Well, I know who you are, anyway, Mr. Murray. I'll have my eye on you. And if there is someone dangerous in yonder, then best you deal with him and get it over with, eh? I have better things to do here.'

'Very wise, Mr. Townsend. Delegation is sensible,' Murray muttered. Townsend, after all, had only been brought from London to advise on apprehending pickpockets. A Scottish troublemaker was not his field of expertise. Murray squeezed through the doorway past a man with five grown sons in Highland garb all collectively overawed by their surroundings, and plunged into the Gallery.

It was filling fast, though it was a splendid room. Windows lined one wall – one of them was where he had seen Abernyte – and on both long walls were dark portraits of curiously similar faces, the Scottish monarchs of the past. Some of the names, as Murray glimpsed them, were far from familiar. There were several doors on the side with no windows, and further doors at the far end. But where was Abernyte?

Then Murray caught sight of a slim, dark-coated back at the far end of the room, dark hair worn a little long. The man reached one of the doorways in the far wall, and put out a hand to the handle. Murray took a breath, and began to work his way down the gallery towards him.

Chapter Thirty-Nine

MEN STOOD IN family groups or society clutches, and a queue had already formed at two doorways presumably to closets, with men mindful of the long coach journey behind them and an even longer wait to come. It was impossible to strike a straight line down the gallery, but Murray did the best he could, keeping to the centre. By the time he reached the far end, the figure he was following had vanished. Murray made for the same door. This would be the oldest part of the palace, he thought to himself: Mrs. Ochill's chamber was somewhere below this, but the other end. He passed through one or two rooms where other men waited, either too grand or too functional to join the crowd in the gallery. He stopped another servant, reckoning the staff were less likely to be concentrating on being seen and more likely to see.

'A youngish man, slim, dark hair – and not in Highland dress. Did he pass through here?'

'Oh, aye, sir. He went down the stair there.'

In the corner of the room was another narrow spiral staircase. Ducking by instinct, Murray just missed hitting his head and slid down the stairs more by dint of centrifugal force than anything else. At the bottom he found himself once again at the corner of the courtyard, not far from the main entrance. The line of dignitaries was a thick, slow-moving chain, half a dozen men deep, across the centre of the courtyard. But the figure was hurrying now, back towards the main staircase from which the guests had been redirected. He managed to slip across the queue with remarkable ease, and Murray felt that he blundered after him, knocking a bonnet or two and treading on a smartly-booted toe. Flinging apologies to left and right, he reached the doorway on the other side, just by the little chamber in which he had drunk his tea. Round and round, he thought. But where had the young man gone?

The Royal Archers were still lining the staircase, so presumably the King was going to come up this way when he arrived. Murray wondered what time it was now.

'Young man, slim, dark hair – did he come this way?' he asked the nearest Archer.

'Yes, and he'd better be well clear before His Majesty arrives,' snapped the Archer, unwilling to have his moment of glory marred. 'And you too, sir. He went away on up.'

'On up?'

'There's a door at the top – takes you on to a smaller staircase to go on up to the second floor and the attics.' He sighed. 'There's already some gentlemen up there getting changed into their tartans at their leisure, as if they owned the place. I saw their servants taking up their kists and a few bottles of brandy.' Murray was not sure if the man was disapproving or envious. 'Aye, well. On you go, sir, and remember to stay well out of the way.'

'Thank you.' Once again, Murray bounded up the broad, low stairs, and asked the Archer at the top for directions for the next flight. Through the door and up again, and no sign of anyone ahead of him. But when he reached the top, he found himself at the end of a long corridor – very much like the corridor outside Mr. Musgrave's rooms, but this time on the south side of the palace. Ahead of him was the man he was following. He burst into a run.

'Abernyte!' he called. 'Wait!'

The man turned, revealing a pale, bespectacled face. It was not Abernyte.

'Mr. Murray, isn't it?'

'Oh!' Murray struggled briefly. 'Oh, you're … from the publishers. From Hutcheon & Purvis, aren't you?'

'That's right, sir.' The man bowed. 'Did you need me for something?'

'No, I was looking for – I thought you were – oh, but you know the man, I believe. Robert Abernyte? I think he's a customer of Hutcheon & Purvis, isn't he?'

'I have seen him there, sir, but I have no idea if any contract has been drawn up,' said the man discreetly.

'Carr, isn't it?' Murray suddenly remembered hearing

Hutcheon address him.

'That's right, sir!' This time Carr was surprised, and, it seemed, not too happy.

'Well, have you seen Abernyte here? I'm sure I saw him earlier, in the Long Gallery.'

'I should think all of Edinburgh is in the Long Gallery by now, sir, wouldn't you? But I'm afraid I haven't seen Mr. Abernyte today, or not to remember, anyway. I'm afraid I don't know him well, and of course my eyesight is not what it could be.'

He pushed his glasses up his nose, and gave a small smile.

'If that is all, sir, I do have … things to attend to.'

'Are you a guest at the Levee?' asked Murray. Even from here, the general noise from downstairs seemed to be intensifying. He moved to the window, and looked down at the courtyard with its slow multicoloured snake of dignitaries shifting across it, then over to the windows of the Long Gallery. It seemed packed already. 'I'm not sure they will all fit in the Gallery, you know. Where will they put them all?'

He turned with a smile, only to find that Carr had vanished. And that was not the action of an innocent man. Murray darted round the corner to find himself, as he had suspected, in the corridor along the east side where Musgrave's room was. He was about to go there when a door burst open beside him, and three Highland gentlemen emerged, one of them, to the probable dismay of any Royal Archers, clutching a brandy bottle.

'Come, come, come!' said the first man, his tartan mostly red. 'We mustn't be late! We mustn't miss it!'

'Ssh,' said the second. 'That's a lot of noise. We mustn't disturb the King!'

'The King!' cried the third, raising the brandy bottle enthusiastically. 'God save the King!'

'God save our gracious King! Long live our noble King,' began the other two, the opening words of the National Anthem slightly slurred. 'God save the King. Send him to Edinburgh so we can all meet ye …'

'How does it go on?' asked the second man, the one in green tartan, as the other two wobbled to a halt.

'And we can drink your hea-ealth too, God save the King!' sang the first man triumphantly, emptying the glass in his hand. The three men entirely blocked the narrow corridor, but in any case Murray thought he might as well go back downstairs to try again to find the right dark-haired man. He tried to turn, but the man in red tartan caught his arm.

'Where you from?' he demanded. 'Are you a Highlander? I am. I'm a Highlander!' He burst out laughing, and the other two joined in. 'We're all Highlanders today! We're all Highlanders to meet the King!'

'God save the King!' cried the one with the brandy bottle, and once again thrust it high. Unfortunately, this time he was standing directly by the door. Hand and bottle hit the low lintel and the bottle fell, smashing on the floor. There was a moment of awful silence as they all gazed down at the casualty. Murray took advantage of the distraction to leave, hoping the man's hand was undamaged, though he would hardly feel it till tomorrow, anyway.

What time was it? He had meant to look at his watch before running upstairs, but now he took it out as he strode back towards the staircase. There was no second floor on the west side of the palace, so he would have to go back down. And it was a quarter to two. The Levee was to start at two.

He reached the stairs and, suddenly aware of movement below, tiptoed down them as quietly as he could, stopping before the door at the bottom. Low voices and slow steps, that seemed to be what was happening beyond. He noticed a little crack between door and post, and put his eye to it.

What seemed to be passing, only a foot or two away from the doorway, was a mighty mountain of red tartan, adorned with a variety of jewels on the hilts of dagger and sgian dhu. A plaid jacket sleeve, a large sporran thick with fur, a swinging kilt, and cross-checked hose – and some strange pink silk undergarments, clearly visible. Who on earth had devised this Highland costume? And who had the audacity to be wearing it?

Another followed in the same tartan, then further figures, all moving at the same solemn pace. The Royal Archer Murray could see opposite was standing rigidly to attention.

'Oh, my word.' Murray mouthed the phrase silently to himself. 'Oh, my word. That was the King. Wait till I tell Isobel.'

There was Viscount Melville, he realised. And there was the Duke of Atholl. Well, all he could do now then was to try to find

Robert Abernyte. When the small procession had passed, a mere two dozen or so men compared with the hosts waiting in the Long Gallery to greet them, Murray leaned heavily against the wall beside him. He was not sure if he were more overcome by the proximity of the King or the fact that he himself had so nearly walked out in front of him. He waited until his heart had calmed a little, before edging the door open, watching the Royal Archer opposite for any signs of warning. But the Archer grinned.

'You just missed him!'

'I know,' said Murray, grinning back with relief. 'Now I think I need to get back to the Long Gallery. Can I go across on this level, or must I again go down?'

'You're better going down,' said the Archer confidently. 'The best way on this level is that way, and you'd have to go past the King which wouldna be just the thing.'

'No, indeed.'

'Mind, you'd know him if you saw him,' the Archer continued, dropping his voice. 'You never saw such an outfit in your life. You can see why it cost what it did. There must have been twa mile of tartan in the kilt alone!' He nodded, and stepped back discreetly to his post, his feelings relieved. His neighbour on guard duty, a short member of the Celtic Society pink with excitement, scowled at this disloyalty.

Murray went back down the Grand Staircase again, almost feeling by now that he was on speaking terms with the huge angels in the plasterwork ceiling. Outside in the courtyard the queue had come to a standstill, and some of the guests already looked weary. Murray glanced up again at the Long Gallery windows, as if he might catch another glimpse of Abernyte. What was he doing here, anyway? Surely he could not have an invitation to the Levee. And what about Carr, the publisher's clerk? And neither of them had been dressed for the occasion, any more than Murray himself was. He wondered how long the Levee was supposed to last – what had Stewart of Garth said? An hour and a half? An hour and a quarter? How was the King to greet even half these men in that time? And even then, he thought, going back to his own concerns, Melville and Atholl might well not be free for who knew how long, if the King wished to talk with them. If he did find Abernyte, what would he do with him? Lock him in a cellar?

He found a stone bench in the cloisters, a little distance from the long-suffering queue and the various Archers, footmen and Celtic Society attendants, and sat for a moment, trying to collect his thoughts. He was no further on than he had been when he and Matthew had arrived at the Palace this afternoon. He was still not totally sure of Robert Abernyte's guilt, or why he might have murdered three people. He wondered what progress Matthew might have made in the kitchens, and hoped he was not making a nuisance of himself. It seemed unlikely.

Well, he thought, scanning the courtyard in front of him again, he could not really carry out a systematic search of the whole Palace, not on his own. He was not sure why Abernyte was here. But it seemed to make sense to look not everywhere, not room by room, but in the places he was most likely to be. If Melville was right, and Abernyte threatened the King (and if he were the printer of the seditious handbills then that fitted nicely), then the most likely thing he would do would be to join the queue for the Levee and hope to be missed in the crowds. Likely enough that was why he had been up in the Long Gallery earlier, and perhaps Murray had just missed him, in his belief that Carr was his target. But where was he now? In the Gallery or still in the queue? Murray pushed himself to his feet, and made for the queue. He scanned it from end to end, walking along each side of it in turn – his lack of Highland costume seemed to make him invisible to the dignitaries. But there was no sign of Abernyte. So it was back to the Long Gallery, Murray thought, and made his weary, anxious way back to the stairs.

Chapter Forty

'YOU AGAIN, SIR?' Townsend's nasal tones greeted him as he tried once more to edge past the stationary queue at the door of the Long Gallery. 'Not found him yet? Off raising a rabble, maybe, is he?'

'Maybe,' said Murray. 'But I think he might be somewhere in there.'

Townsend raised a cynical eyebrow as he turned to look back at the Long Gallery. If it had been crowded before, it was packed to absolute capacity now. Murray fleetingly hoped the floor would hold.

'You're welcome to look – that is, if you're any good at walking along the ceiling and looking down from there.'

'Mr. Murray!' came a familiar voice, not far inside the Gallery. Murray saw it was Glengarry again, standing in a little knot of his loyal followers – or men in the same tartan, anyway – in a good position near the door. Glengarry seemed to be in fine humour despite the circumstances. 'I'm glad to see you again, Mr. Murray, and more glad still to find you keep to your Lowland fashions.'

'I am a Lowlander, sir,' Murray acknowledged.

'And attired modestly and decently as becomes one – not flaunting fake finery, like certain noted members of the Celtic Society!' His eyes gleamed with outraged mockery. 'There are some of them who would be hard put to speak English, let alone Scots or Gaelic!'

'All right, all right, sir, we've had enough of that,' said Townsend, with more courage than Murray would have given him credit for, though perhaps his successes against the underworld of London had made him immune to any threat of danger.

'Nonsense, man! You found one of them yourself, did you

not? Not ten minutes since. I tell you, Mr. Murray, this is a man to be reckoned with. There is the fellow, climbing the stairs just here, kilted and adorned with every kind of jewelled and glinting weaponry, bonnet draped just so, plaid swinging over his shoulder as if Stewart of Garth himself had arranged it – which he probably had – and this eminent gentleman of Bow Street here stops him with a look.

'"Sir, do you call yourself a Highlander?" says he.

'"Yes, certainly, you don't mean to offend me, sir?" answers the bonny fellow.' Glengarry mimicked a thin-lipped English accent – which, as Murray understood, he would be well able to do, having gone to an Oxford college himself.

'"If I mistake not, sir," says this fellow, "I have seen you some twenty years ago, a singing boy in the choir of Hereford in England." Can you imagine, Mr. Murray? The blushes, the mutterings, the excuses – the poor pretender was disconsolate! And he is not the least of the Celtic Society's fakeries, is he?'

'I'm looking for another Lowlander,' said Murray, trying to focus on the problem at hand, 'or at least, a man not dressed in plaid today. A young man, with dark hair cut a little long, wearing a blue coat.'

'What, in here?' asked Glengarry, already scanning the room.

'I believe so, yes.'

'Good heavens, man, you have no chance! I hope you are not in any kind of a hurry to find him.'

'Well …' said Murray.

But at that moment, he heard clocks in the Palace and nearby strike two, and the Royal Archers by the door of the Long Gallery stood straight, their bows upright. A small, self-important figure dressed all in black bustled towards them. It was Mr. Mash of the Lord Chamberlain's Office.

'Now,' he said smartly to the Archers. 'Make a start, but not too fast. His Majesty is ready.'

There was a collective gasp among those near enough to hear. The doors of the Long Gallery were opened fully. Townsend presented his broad back to those in the queue who had not yet been admitted to it, and the Royal Archers ushered those who had been waiting inside, in a narrow line, into the next room along the south side of the Palace. Mr. Mash led them, setting a solemn pace which did not accord with all the flutterings and last minute adjustments among the guests behind him.

'Is His Majesty just in there?' asked Murray in surprise.

'No, he's three or four rooms away,' said Townsend. 'Far corner of the Palace.'

Murray watched for a moment, feeling the sighs of relief as the Long Gallery's crowds eased, only for any space made to be taken up by the tail of the queue gradually allowed into it by Townsend. The Gallery now accommodated a great loop in the line but at least it was moving, shuffling slowly along. Murray watched carefully, and though he might not have admitted it, he was sure that Townsend was watching, too.

Conversation, which had been growing louder in the sweaty, impatient Gallery, now hushed to a low murmur, as if the King could hear them. Any remarks Murray could catch were only admiring of the room and the decoration and the view from the windows to the back of the Palace, or warning of twisted hose or crooked belts. There were indeed a number of men not dressed in Highland gear. Many were in uniform, for example, of the army, navy, or other bodies: Murray prayed for their sakes that the uniforms were authentic and reasonable, for the King was reputed to have great expertise in this matter, and a tendency to mark people out if they had made a mistake. Almost all of them looked smart, at least. Some, perhaps summoned and honoured by the summons but unwilling to pretend to be anything other than they were wore formal Court dress, and among these, to Murray's surprise, was Blair, being pushed along in his wheeled chair by a grim-looking Smith. Blair waved excitedly.

'Charles, my boy! Isn't this splendid?'

'How did you come to be here?' Murray asked, going closer to speak more confidentially. He felt he should not have been surprised at all: Blair knew everyone, and probably called on the King whenever he was in Sussex.

'Sir Walter, at the last minute,' said Blair happily. 'I don't think Smith is too pleased, though,' he muttered. 'He had no time to buy a new coat. But look at all this! So many people, all looking so fine! Are you to be presented, too?'

'I pray not,' said Murray. 'I hope instead to be apprehending

... well, I thought I knew who, but things have taken a turn. You haven't seen a young, dark-haired man in a blue coat, have you?'

'Oh, yes,' said Blair, eagerly. Then his mobile face fell. 'Several.'

'Ah, well. As long as he doesn't get to the King –'

But at that moment, the crowd thinned and Murray suddenly saw once again a dark-haired, slim figure at the far end of the gallery. And this time, he was sure it was Abernyte.

'Excuse me,' he said, and darted off to try to make his way through the queue while not attracting Abernyte's attention.

If he did not attract Abernyte's attention, he certainly attracted everyone else's.

'Hi!' cried several. 'Where are you going?'

Patience was wearing thin at this end of the queue.

'Has he stolen something?' someone demanded.

'Maybe he knows a short cut to the King!' cried someone else, and for a moment everyone turned to stare at him. A few people took steps in his direction, before an Archer or two guided them back to the paths of righteousness, allowing Murray to blunder on beyond them. But Abernyte had already passed through the doorway, the same one that Carr had taken earlier. Feeling as if time were spinning round in circles, Murray abandoned the Gallery once again, and headed into the old apartments in this corner of the Palace. Fortunately this must be as far as possible from where the King was bracing himself to receive the long line of loyal visitors.

Once again, Murray found himself squeezing up the awkward spiral staircase, never built for a man of his height. Once again, he emerged on the corridor that ran above the Long Gallery, and saw Abernyte disappear around the corner at the other end. Once again, despite the sloping walls and narrow passageway, Murray sped as best he could towards his quarry. If Abernyte knew of another staircase, perhaps at the south east corner of the Palace where the King must be, then he could be there before Murray could ever reach him, and do whatever damage he wanted to do.

Murray turned the corner. The next corridor, the one on the south side, was empty. But several doors were open on to it. He slowed, stepping more quietly, and approached the first one.

The room beyond, much like Mr. Musgrave's room that he had seen earlier but a little larger, was empty. Murray breathed, checked quickly behind the door, and moved on to the next one. It was empty, too, a mere cupboard in the wall.

The third, though, was in fact Mr. Musgrave's room, and inside was Carr, the clerk from the publishers. He had the cupboard open, and his hands full of handbills.

'What are you doing?' asked Murray.

'Doing?' squeaked Carr. 'Nothing!' He dropped a bundle of papers, and crouched at once to gather them, crumpled, into his hands.

'Why are you here? What are you doing with those handbills?' Murray repeated. He saw that the little fireplace in the room, which had been empty before, was full of papers.

'Are these yours?' he asked. 'Wait – are you Anthony?'

'What?'

'Are you Mr. Musgrave's grandson?'

'You mustn't pay any attention to him,' said Carr quickly. 'He's very confused. He keeps saying I put these papers in his cupboard, but really, I have no idea how they got here. I'm just clearing them out for him, making the place tidy for him if he comes back.'

He thrust his armful of papers into the fireplace with the others, and took a candle from the mantelpiece. Murray had not noticed it before, but it was lit. Carr knelt by the hearth, and touched the candle to the papers.

'These are yours, aren't they?' said Murray. 'You're "A.C.".' He snatched up one of the handbills, and pointed to the initials.

'Of course not,' said Carr, but his teeth were chattering as he held the candle flame to the tottering heap of crumpled papers. 'Why would I put my own initials on it?'

'Because you didn't think, did you?' asked Murray. 'Any more than you thought what might happen if you hid seditious papers in a royal palace when the King was threatening to visit. All turned upside down, and who knows who found out about your little store of handbills? Mrs. Ochill, perhaps? Is that what happened? Because she would have known who you were, wouldn't she? She recognised you, and so once she was gone, and Mrs. McGregor was gone, you had to come back to retrieve all this, hidden in your grandfather's cupboard.'

Carr would not look at him, concentrating on the fire.

'Well, I couldn't – I mean, maybe whoever owns them, maybe they couldn't keep them at their work? I mean, who could?'

'Oh,' said Murray suddenly. 'But you used to keep them at work, didn't you? You had them hidden at Hutcheon & Purvis – presumably working there enabled you to meet a sympathetic printer or two – but then someone came investigating, didn't they? A government agent, looking for anyone working against the government, and he actually comes in to have his wife's book of poetry published. That must have been quite a shock for you!'

'I don't know what you're talking about,' said Carr stubbornly.

'You admitted to my manservant that you were there, in the shop, the night that Ochill was killed just outside. But you weren't inside at that point, were you? You were outside in the lane, stabbing Ochill.'

'What?' Carr spun from the hearth, alarmed. 'I never stabbed anybody!' He struggled to his feet, staggered over to the cupboard and snatched up another handful of papers. 'Never in my life!'

He threw them with emphasis on to the fire. The whole blazing edifice hissed, toppled, and sprawled, flaring, across the floor and against the freshly-painted wooden panelling. There was a sudden stink of oil and aniseed, and the wall began to burn.

Chapter Forty-One

WITH SOME PART of his mind struck by the fact that his day was growing steadily worse, Murray looked about for something to smother the flames. There was nothing: no curtain, no rug, no stray plaid. He hauled off his coat and tried with that.

'Come on,' he shouted at Carr, 'this is your fault. Use your own coat!'

'I want the papers destroyed!' Carr shouted back.

'But not the whole Palace, you fool!' cried Murray, hauling at Carr's coat with one hand while trying to crush the flames into submission with his other. Carr pulled away and ran to the door, but after a moment turned and tugged at his own sleeves.

'All right, then,' he said sulkily. Fortunately he was just in time: the two coats, though adding the fragrance of burning wool to the ensemble, did indeed stifle the flames, and in a moment or two Murray felt able to step back and survey the damage. In the fireplace a small fragment of the conflagration still burned. Carr went back to the cupboard, took up the next pile of handbills, and added them, with considerably more care this time, to the fire.

'Why didn't you just run?' asked Murray. His coat was now unwearable, with one sleeve burned through, and he was struggling to find something good about Carr who had been prepared to let his confused grandfather take the blame if the handbills had ever been discovered. But at least Carr had stayed to fight the fire.

'Door's locked,' said Carr, unwittingly destroying Murray's hopes for his redemption. It took a moment, then Murray stepped across to the door and tried it for himself. Carr was right. The door was firmly locked. Murray took a deep breath, and for want of anything else to do with it, put what was left of his coat back on. At least he had the pockets. He propped himself against the wall beside the cupboard, and looked down at Carr tending the fire.

'So, let's get to the truth here,' he said, after a long, thoughtful moment. 'These are your handbills, with your initials on them. Mr. Musgrave is your grandfather.'

'I never said that,' said Carr, obstinately.

'Just at the moment, I don't care. We'll find evidence later,' said Murray, thinking of Matthew down in the kitchens. Carr was an unconvincing liar, anyway.

'Well …' he said.

'Be quiet until I ask you a question.' Murray's patience was wearing thin, and just to spite him, his shoulder had begun to ache again. He wondered if Blair had met the King yet, in some distant, different realm one floor down. He wondered what the King had thought of him.

'You hid your seditious materials in your grandfather's cupboard because you couldn't hide them at work, which is also where you live. Presumably, then, your employer is unaware of your political activities.' Carr turned to look at him, but said nothing. 'Ochill found out what you were doing, eight years ago – either he came to the office to investigate, that night, or you somehow lured him there and killed him. Then,' he went on, cutting across Carr's intake of breath, 'last week, presumably when you returned here to rescue your stock, you met Mrs. Ochill and decided she was also a danger to you. In the process of this, her neighbour, Mrs. McGregor, saw you, so she also had to be disposed of. And then you return today to destroy what is left, with the King in the very building.'

Carr shoved the final stack of papers into the fire, watched for a moment to see that they were not going to fall out, and scrambled to his feet, surly-faced.

'All right,' he said. 'Yes, I had these handbills printed. I had loads of them done, a couple of years ago when it looked as if we might be getting somewhere, politically. And then all that came to an end, and there were hangings …' He shivered. 'I'd only printed these, that's all I did, but then I wasn't very sure what to do with them. I should have known better: we get authors in all the time wanting hundreds more copies than they'll ever sell, and then coming back wondering what to do with all the extra stock. Yes, Thomas Musgrave is my grandfather. He's a nice old fellow, but he's a real Royalist – or he was when his memory was working properly. He was happy enough to store stuff for me but he had no idea what it was. It gave me a laugh to think of it here, in his cupboard. I had the only key. I never thought he would get into the cupboard, or get into any trouble over it.'

'Fortunately, so far that is still the case.'

'Well, there you are, then,' said Carr.

'And the Ochills?'

'Listen, sir,' said Carr, gritting his teeth, 'I have never killed anyone. I have never even tried to, or plotted to, or hoped to. I know Mr. Hutcheon didn't like Ochill – I think he was a little afraid of him, even – but I don't suppose Ochill ever even noticed I was there, and in any case,' he drew breath, 'eight years ago I had never even thought about printing handbills like – like those.' He gestured to the hearth, where the last of the papers was flaking quickly away into ash. 'So why would he have been a threat to me, or I to him?'

'Ah,' said Murray. 'And Mrs. Ochill?'

'Where was I supposed to have met her? I haven't seen her since she last came into our office about her book of poetry. Mr. Hutcheon mentioned that she wouldn't be producing any more, and that's all I know about her. She could have gone to the West Indies, for all I know.'

'She had one of your handbills. She was living downstairs. She had been for the last eight years, since her husband died.'

'Well, I had no idea. Here? Really? I never saw her.' He stopped, clearly reflecting on his visits to his grandfather over the years. 'Grandfather never mentioned anyone of that name, I'm sure. How strange that she should be here!'

Murray watched him for another moment, and sighed. He was almost convincing. And Mrs. Ochill had, by all accounts, kept herself to herself here.

'Right, well, say I believe you – for now, anyway.'

'Oh, what now, sir?' Carr snapped.

'Only that we're locked in,' Murray reminded him. 'You might squeeze out through that window, but I certainly won't be able to. And there's the small question of why we have been locked in, and by whom. Any ideas?'

Carr cast a look at Murray that suggested he could think of several reasons why someone would want to lock Murray away, anyway. Murray nodded.

'Yes, you're right, it could be directed at me. In which case I apologise – though in fact I was only in this room because of you and what you were up to. But is there any reason why someone might have wanted to lock you in? Is there anyone here that you know, today in particular?'

'Not that I can think of,' said Carr. 'My social connexions are probably not much represented on His Majesty's list of guests. Or Sir Walter Scott's.'

'Robert Abernyte was here.'

'You mentioned him earlier, sir. I haven't seen him. And I can't think why he would be here, or why, having found himself here, he would go out of his way to lock me in an attic. But perhaps you know more about it than I do, sir.'

'Perhaps I do. If you did not kill the Ochills, then I'm afraid Robert Abernyte is the next most convincing suspect. And yet I cannot think why he would have done it.'

'Why do you suspect him, sir?' For the first time, Carr started to sound interested.

'It's all very circumstantial,' said Murray, irritably. 'He knew the Ochills and was their neighbour when Mr. Ochill was killed. He was seen in the Palace on the day of Mrs. Ochill's murder, and he lied about why he was there. He was seen talking with Mrs. McGregor –'

'I don't even know who she is, sir,' said Carr.

'A retired royal seamstress, who also lived downstairs. She was killed when that viewing platform collapsed on Monday on the High Street.'

'I heard about that. But that was an accident, wasn't it?'

'The collapse probably was. The death, perhaps not. Anyway, Abernyte also lied about his opportunity to be there. But …' he shrugged, 'I have no idea why he would have killed either of them.'

Carr frowned.

'Does Abernyte know you suspect him?'

'He might do. He may have overheard a conversation I had last night, during the illuminations. And then he followed my family and me home.'

Carr licked his lips, nervous now.

'And does he know you're here?'

'He may have seen me earlier, on either of the occasions when I caught a glimpse of him.'

'So he may, in fact, have locked us in here?'

'He might have, yes.'

'And if he thinks you suspect him of murder,' Carr licked dry lips again, 'what are the chances that he will just leave us here? And if he does, who is going to find us? As you say, sir, that window is small.'

'It is, yes. I believe some gentlemen came up here to change for the Levee, so there may be people around later.' Clearing up broken brandy bottles, for example, he thought.

'But we could be here for a while?'

Murray made a face.

'We certainly don't have to be, now …' Now that I'm convinced of your innocence, with regard to the murders, anyway, he added to himself, and felt in the pocket of his ruined coat. 'Let's see if this works: it opened your cupboard, anyway.'

He brought out his knife, slid it between door and jamb in the approved fashion, and manipulated it. The lock clicked open. Carr leapt for the door, not taking any further risks, but Murray insisted on opening the door carefully, in case anything unpleasant was waiting for them outside. But the corridor was empty. Carr headed at once for corner, but Murray called him back.

'Abernyte was at Hutcheon & Purvis yesterday,' he said. 'Has he been there much before?'

Carr glanced back over his shoulder, sighed, and stopped, letting Murray catch up with him.

'He's been there a few times,' he said, 'and no, I haven't paid him to kill anyone either, or connived with him. I hardly know him.'

'But why was he there?'

'Oh,' said Carr, rolling his eyes, 'another poetry book.'

'His own?'

'No, his sister's. She's pretty much housebound, apparently, so he's negotiating on her behalf.'

'Just like the Ochills,' said Murray slowly.

'It's common enough. Talented woman, sends man in to represent her and do the business side.'

'Of course. Are the poems good?'

'No idea,' said Carr. 'I'm not paid to read the manuscripts. I just write out the letters of acceptance – or rejection.'

'And are Miss Abernyte's poems to be accepted?'

'I think so,' said Carr. 'Now I come to think of it, Mr. Hutcheon was pleased with them. I don't know that his Gaelic is much good, but he likes the English bits.'

'And you? Do you read Gaelic?'

Carr shrugged.

'Too many vowels for me,' he said. 'I like a few consonants in my words. Now, if you don't mind, Mr. Murray, I'd really like to be getting back to my desk, before Mr. Hutcheon realises I'm taking a gey long time to deliver three assorted letters round the town. If you need me, sir, that's where I'll be. Good day to you, sir.'

'Good day, Carr. Thank you.'

He moved across to stand looking down at the courtyard again, the sun casting angular shadows across it. The guests were already marching off, appearing from the direction of the grand staircase and vanishing through the main entrance to the forecourt and gates beyond, gossiping and laughing as they went. How long had each had with the King? Not long, to judge by the numbers going through and their speed.

Someone shouted,

'Dammit! Where's my pistol?'

'Never mind that,' said another voice, 'my plaid's been ripped – look!'

Murray watched as Townsend, the embodiment of London law and order, appeared to deal with the complainers, waving two great soothing hands to calm things down.

Abernyte's sister had produced a book of Gaelic and English poetry, just like Mrs. Ochill.

Abernyte had approached Hutcheon & Purvis to publish it, just as Ochill had.

Murray thought of the poems he had read aloud, only last night. The lyrical language, the evocative imagery, telling the story of life by the sea, on the West Coast. Where Mrs. Ochill had never, to the best of his knowledge, lived – but where the Abernytes had, until they came to Edinburgh.

He frowned.

Abernyte was no danger to the King, was he? All he was

trying to do here in Holyroodhouse was to stop Murray reporting all he had found, and all Abernyte thought he had found, to Viscount Melville, who would, presumably, have Abernyte arrested for murder. He had locked Murray in Mr. Musgrave's room. Did he think Murray would stay there? Or had he other plans to stop him?

And, he thought suddenly, had that missing pistol anything to do with it?

Chapter Forty-Two

MURRAY MOVED BACK from the window, and looked about him. The corridor was empty still, and by the sound of it so were all the rooms off it. All palace activity was focussed on the floors below.

What did Abernyte want to do? He could flee Edinburgh – but if he had wanted to do that, why was he wasting time at Holyroodhouse? Why had he not just gone? That, Murray thought, was straightforward: his sister depended on him, and would presumably be destitute without him. Murray thought back to that comfortable little parlour, and how much he had liked the brother and sister that day. Robert would not have liked to let her down.

So if Abernyte did not want to flee, then it would be of no use to him to lock Murray in a room in the Palace and forget about him. Someone would find him, sooner or later. While he was locking the door, Abernyte must have been aware of the fire inside – in fact, that was what had given him the chance to lock the door without either Murray or Carr seeing him. He had presumably been quick to take a similar opportunity when the viewing platform collapsed and he was able to conceal Mrs. McGregor's body under it. Had he hoped that Carr and Murray would suffocate in the smoke, or be burned to death? But someone would realise they were there, at some point. The Palace had not burned down. There must be patrols of some kind around the Palace, whether it was Townsend and his colleagues, or some of the English soldiers, or the Royal Archers – or even the Celtic Society. They would find a burnt-out room if there was one, and even more easily find two rather cross, imprisoned men and a long-extinguished fire.

He must know, Murray thought, that Murray had not been

alone in the room, so if he came back to try to deal with Murray there would be another man there, too. In the case of Ochill, he had presumably been able to take the man by surprise. With the two women, Mrs. McGregor and Mrs. Ochill, he would undoubtedly have been the more powerful. But he would know that Murray was taller and heavier, and more importantly would be expecting him. So what would he do?

With a jerk of alarm, he thought again of the conversation he had overheard from the courtyard. Someone had lost his pistol in the crush. Could Abernyte have done that? And if he had done so, could he have loaded it?

Murray felt his heart beat faster. He had a brace of pistols – at home, in their box, all neat and polished. He only really carried them when he was travelling. Carr had gone – probably just as well, as he would have had no pistols and might not have been any use. So the only thing Murray could see in his favour was that Abernyte would expect the two of them still to be locked in Mr. Musgrave's room. Unless he had seen and recognised Carr downstairs, or seen Murray standing at the window just now … no. Murray would have to hope that neither of those things had happened, and that Abernyte was awaiting his opportunity, somewhere in the Palace, to sneak back up the stairs and finish off Murray and Carr.

The door of the room beside Musgrave's was ajar. Murray listened at it for a moment, then pushed it open and slipped inside, shutting it almost completely again. Then he settled back, leaning against the wall, to wait, praying this room would not be another trap. If someone had told him he was entirely alone in Holyroodhouse, at that moment he would have believed them.

Downstairs, however, the well-marshalled line of visitors queuing to see the King was now almost completely through and clear and milling about the forecourt gossiping, despite the soldiers' best attempts to get them all tidied up and out through the gates and away. To one side of the main entrance a red-faced gentleman official, clad in scarlet and gold and high boots and with a rich cap of black velvet draped over his head, was arguing with a number of individuals with notebooks, who appeared to represent the Press.

'I tell you, it will take me weeks to list every gentleman who was in there! Weeks! I don't care when your paper must be out – it must be out without the list!'

Blair had directed Smith to push his chair, quite a job across the gravel, to the central flowerbed from which he could see all kinds of fascinating people. One he could not see, however, was his friend Murray.

'Surely he should be out by now?' asked Blair peevishly. 'Unless Lord Melville has detained him, of course. Of course, that will be it. But where is he, though?'

'Didn't he come out with young Matthew?' asked Smith, who remembered the lad from his time in Blair's household. 'You mentioned that Mrs. Murray had said so.'

'You're quite right, Smith: yes. He had Matthew with him. But Matthew wasn't with him, of course, when we saw him in the Long Gallery. He must have lost him somewhere along the way.' Blair spoke as if Matthew were a pocket handkerchief, though in truth he valued his servants much more than most people, and knew that Murray did, too.

'I'll try the kitchens, shall I, sir?'

'Yes, yes,' said Blair, bouncing with eagerness. 'I would try them myself, you know, but you will be much quicker on your own.'

Smith strode smartly away across the forecourt, leaving Blair alone. Not for long, of course, for a series of acquaintances spotted him and came over to share their experiences of meeting the King – an average, one of them reckoned, of three seconds per visitor.

'Three seconds well spent, then!' said Blair with enthusiasm. 'What a spectacle!'

Smith, back and hovering, waited until Blair was free before approaching. He had Matthew with him.

'Ah, Matthew, where is your master?'

'I don't know, sir. He said he would summon me when he needed me, but I have not heard from him.'

'What did he send you to do?'

Matthew hesitated only briefly. As far as he was concerned, the Blair and Murray households were pretty much the same thing, so he was not telling tales.

'He asked me to find out about Mr. Musgrave, sir, and his grandson.'

'And who is Mr. Musgrave?'

'He's an old gentleman, sir, who lived in the attics here until – until everyone was asked to leave.' Blair suspected that the kitchen staff were not phrasing the eviction of their previous tenants in quite these words. 'He has a grandson, sir, who used to visit him, but when Mr. Musgrave had to leave the grandson could not be found. Mr. Murray wanted to know the grandson's name, sir.'

'And did you find out?'

'Yes, sir. He is Anthony Carr, of Hutcheon & Purvis, Publishers.'

'Weren't they the publishers who dealt with poor Mrs. Ochill?' asked Blair, but as neither of the men with him were privy to that information, they both shrugged. But Blair was fairly sure he was right.

'So there is a connexion between Mrs. Ochill and someone else who lived here,' said Blair. 'I mean to say, that must be obvious, because she lived here, and although she seems not to have gone out much there must have been some communication between her and others here. But …' he frowned, trying to follow his own train of thought. 'But there was a connexion between someone here, Mr. Musgrave, and Mrs. Ochill's former life. Is that what I'm trying to say?' He looked up at them with watery eyes. Smith nodded.

'Yes, sir, I think so.'

'Good. So … so what next? Whoever this Mr. Carr is – the grandson of Mr. Musgrave and something to do with Mrs. Ochill's publishers – Charles, Mr. Murray, seems to be interested in him.'

'Yes, sir,' said Smith, encouragingly.

'Do we know what Carr looks like?'

'Sir,' said Matthew, 'I asked in the kitchens, just in case, though I believe Mr. Murray does know him to see. He is a young man, slim of build, with dark hair.'

'Another one!' exclaimed Blair.

'And wearing spectacles, sir.'

'Well, that's something, I suppose.'

'But I don't know where Mr. Murray is, sir.'

'I thought he might be meeting Viscount Melville,' said Blair.

'From what I heard in the kitchens, sir, Viscount Melville and some others are in conference with His Majesty. They were taking up brandy and cake, sir.'

'Oh. Perhaps he is waiting somewhere? Perhaps he has already apprehended this man Carr, and is securing him somewhere?'

Once again, Smith and Matthew were unable to help him. Blair wriggled in his chair, frustrated, wishing he could go and look for himself. Was Charles safe? Was he touring the Palace, seeking this Anthony Carr? Or had he given up and left to hunt for Robert Abernyte, his previous suspect? Whatever he was doing, what would be the best way of helping him? Blair considered every option he could think of, unconsciously making the most extraordinary faces as he did so. Smith and Matthew remained still, awaiting instructions.

At last, Blair heaved a great sigh.

'I want the two of you to go back in. See if you can find Mr. Murray, and if you can, come back and let me know what he is doing. But if, along the way, you should see this Anthony Carr, then … then if you can without danger to yourselves, apprehend him and, um, bring him … yes, bring him out here so that I can talk to him. If you can't take him without danger, then run away fast and come and tell me. And – oh! I wish I could go, too!'

'I could push you, sir,' said Smith.

'I would only slow you down. And besides,' said Blair, resigned to his fate, 'if any of them does come out this way, at least I shall see them and will be able to tell Mr. Murray later. Unless it's him, of course. In which case I can stop him, and find out everything.' He brightened a little at this thought, and shooed them away on their somewhat complicated quest.

Then he settled in his chair, looked about him for anything of interest, and tried to work up his patience for a long wait.

'The thing is,' said Isobel, after what had been a long silence.

'I know,' said Mrs. Helliwell.

They had written their morning letters, and made their morning visits, and were at that perilous point for intelligent females, the loose end. Isobel caught Mrs. Helliwell's eye as they walked through Newington.

'If it is Robert Abernyte – and why would he have been watching the house last night if he were not guilty? – then what about his poor sister?'

'Exactly,' said Mrs. Helliwell. 'If Mr. Murray is this close to apprehending him, then either he will flee and she will be abandoned, or he will be caught, and it will be so much worse.'

'Exactly,' echoed Isobel. 'And she may not even know what he has done – if he has done it. Or why.'

'Well, we don't know why,' Mrs. Helliwell reminded her.

'That's true. What could it be? It's a strange dispute amongst neighbours that carries on eight years after they all move away.'

'Some are better than others at bearing grudges,' said Mrs. Helliwell, with feeling. Isobel thought that possibly Mr. Helliwell, minister or not, fell into that category.

'So do you think, since we are this direction anyway, that we should call on her?' she asked. 'Or we could go and rest a little at my father's before walking home, if you would prefer.'

'No, let us go and call on her,' said Mrs. Helliwell, as Isobel had known she would. 'I think we shall not benefit from a rest until we have at least done our duty.'

They adjusted their course very slightly, and headed for the Pleasance and the Abernyte flat.

Chapter Forty-Three

UP ON THE attic floor of the Palace, Murray waited.

He could still hear the remote murmurings of the guests, trailing their way out of the Palace by way of the courtyard, the occasional spike of laughter escaping as they relaxed. Surely they must all be through now? And then what? The King would no doubt return to Dalkeith to rest after his exertions, sitting having his hand kissed for an hour, though come to think of it Murray himself would have liked some respite after that kind of experience. His Majesty's closest companions would go with him, and Viscount Melville and the Duke of Atholl would be free to meet Murray. And that was what Robert Abernyte would try to prevent, but then he did think that Murray was safely locked in. Murray hoped he would come soon. He wanted to get this over with, whatever way it turned out.

He had started counting the panels in the walls of the room where he was hiding when he heard a soft step, somewhere in the passage outside. The kind of step someone takes when they hope not to be heard. Murray moved silently to the door of his hiding place, made sure it was still open just a chink, and stood where he would have the best view of anyone passing – assuming they would come from the right direction.

And they did. In a moment or two, a slim figure passed the door, with dark hair cut a little long, and in the hand that Murray could see, a pistol. The footsteps stopped three seconds later, just outside the door of Mr. Musgrave's room. Murray had left the door closed. There was a clunk of metal, and he could picture Abernyte trying to open the door while holding a pistol in each hand. The door opened with a faint creak, and Murray heard a gasp. It was time to move.

He plunged out into the passage, but at the last minute his burned sleeve caught on the door catch and he was spun off balance. In the instant it took him to right himself, Abernyte had turned to face him – with both pistols pointed at his chest. Murray froze.

'How – how did you get out?' asked Abernyte, his voice a good bit higher than Murray remembered.

'You expected two of us, didn't you?' Murray nodded at the pistols. 'Not yours, I assume.' He tried to keep his own voice calm, but it was not easy. The tremor in Abernyte's hands was distinct.

'Not mine, no,' said Abernyte. 'But I thought it was the only way I could manage both of you. Carr knows me, of course. What was he doing here, though? Is he working for you?'

'No, but he'll know what you've done, of course,' said Murray. 'It might be best to end this here, don't you think? Otherwise you just have to go on and on – Mrs. Ochill, and then Mrs. McGregor, and then me, and then Carr – and of course, most of my household saw you outside last night. Some of them are here now, downstairs. They'll know what has happened, and who did it.' Well, one of them, he thought. But Matthew was a bright lad, and he would tell Robbins and Isobel, and they would work it out. If Robert Abernyte killed him, that is.

'But if I killed you, I could get away,' said Abernyte, though he did not sound wholly convinced.

'You wouldn't want to abandon your sister, would you?'

'I'd be abandoning her either way,' said Abernyte, realistically. 'Is it worse for her to have a brother who has fled, or a brother who is tried and – and hanged?'

'That's a hard choice,' said Murray, 'though at the moment I'm quite interested in the disadvantages to me of you killing me. I have a young wife and daughter,' he added, trying to sound businesslike, and not, not to think of Isobel and Augusta.

Abernyte was not concerned, however, with Murray's problems.

'I think if I ran away, you see – perhaps went down to Leith and took a ship somewhere – then maybe after a year or so I could send for my sister to join me. Then I could still look after her. But if you were alive, you would try to stop me, wouldn't you? You'll say you won't: you'll tell me you'll let me go, and then you'll run after me and stop me. You're bigger than me,' he added, head on one side, assessing the opposition. Just at present, Murray felt that being bigger only made it more likely that Abernyte would hit him when he fired, however much his hands were trembling. 'I'm glad I brought the pistols. I wasn't sure at first, you see. I haven't fired a pistol before, but I'd seen how to load one so I knew what I was doing.'

'Who did you steal them from?' asked Murray, deciding that his best hope was to play for time. But Abernyte shrugged.

'It was all so crowded down there, I have no idea. They don't match, anyway, but I thought I would need two,' he added, glancing down at them. 'They're heavier than I expected.'

'Yes, your hands will be getting tired.' That might have been a mistake: Abernyte shifted the pistols as though it were time to get on with it. Murray said quickly: 'How do you think it will feel? Will it be different? You've only stabbed people before, haven't you?'

'I hit Mrs. McGregor with a plank,' Abernyte corrected him solemnly. 'But yes, the Ochills were both – I stabbed both of them. I don't think it will matter,' he went on. 'I don't feel so angry with you, you see. To stab someone – I mean, I thought about it, afterwards, after I'd killed Ochill – to stab someone I think you need to be angry with them.'

'And you were angry with Ochill,' said Murray. 'About the book of poetry?'

A sharp hiss emanated from Abernyte's suddenly clenched teeth. He nodded, stiffly.

'Yes …' Murray tried to find a new subject, but everything in his head was the book of poetry, Isobel and Augusta. Abernyte had turned a nasty shade of red. Murray began to pray.

A door slammed, somewhere on the attic floor. Running footsteps echoed, more than one set. Murray gasped in surprise. Abernyte paled, but kept his gaze fixed on Murray. His hands shook violently now, and it was quite clear that he had every intention of finishing what he came to do before he was stopped. He pulled both triggers.

Carr appeared at the end of the corridor, panting. He seemed not to see Murray and Abernyte, but ploughed on. And behind him came Smith and Matthew.

Time seemed to stand completely still, and Murray had leisure to watch the whole tableau before him. Smith and Matthew, each of them fixed and determined. Carr, panicking. Abernyte, horrified. And the pistols, apparently useless in his hands. Both guns had jammed.

Abernyte threw them on the floor, shoved past Murray, and ran, just as Carr cannoned into Murray, knocking him to the ground. Smith and Matthew skidded to a stop.

'Go after him!' cried Murray, trying to get up from under Carr's weight. 'After Abernyte!' He pushed Carr to one side, seized the two guns and shoved them in his pockets, praying they would continue to be useless – better to risk that than to have them fall into the wrong hands just now. Then he ran after Smith, Matthew and Abernyte. He could ask questions later.

Smith and Matthew had not set off as quickly as they might have. Whatever reason they had had for running up to the attics, the idea of chasing Abernyte was new to them and they had paused, briefly, to make sure they knew what they were doing. Murray caught up quickly, but Abernyte was already at the top of the far stairs, and before they were anywhere near him he had disappeared down them. It seemed an age before they reached the top step, and followed.

Murray tried to review his knowledge of the Palace in his head. This was the staircase that led down to the top of the Grand Staircase. A few steps along the cloisters and Abernyte would be at the main entrance. Who would know to stop him? And if he escaped, as he probably would, where would he go? Leith?

At the foot of the spiral, he paused, remembering the last time he had come down here. It would be a remarkable coincidence if the King were passing again, but just in case, he opened the door with care. There were no Royal Archers now guarding the staircase, and no Celtic Society members rearranging their plaids. Murray ushered Smith and Matthew out in front of him, and stopped abruptly as they stopped in front of him.

'What's going on here, then?' came a familiar, nasal accent. Townsend, the Bow Street Runner, stood broadly at the top of the Grand Staircase, blocking their way. 'I've heard about you two – a couple of ruffians running about the Palace, with His Majesty only a few rooms away! What do you think you're doing, the pair of you?'

Murray pushed through.

'We're on the trail of the murderer,' he began.

'Oh yes?' said Townsend. 'What, still? I tell you, we get things done quicker in London.'

'Well, we won't get it done at all if you don't move out of the way, please,' said Murray. 'He ran through here just now. I'm surprised you didn't see him.'

'I didn't see him,' Townsend confirmed, unmoving. 'I'm beginning to wonder if he exists at all.'

'Mr. Townsend,' said Murray with emphasis, 'the very best way for us to cause you the least bother would be for you to let us past – now.'

Townsend thought about it for a long moment, then shifted his weight a little to one side.

'If you're leaving,' he said, 'make sure you're not going to come back any time soon.'

'Oh, and here,' said Murray, pulling a pistol carefully out of each pocket, 'you'd better take these. I believe a pickpocket lifted them earlier, so I'm returning them to you for safe keeping.'

Then he ran down the stairs after Smith and Matthew, along the cloister and out on to the forecourt. It was almost empty now, with a lone figure in a wheeled chair sitting by the central flower bed.

Blair waved excitedly when he saw them, and began an elaborate series of wild gestures. Murray thought it would be quickest just to go and hear what he had to say.

'A man! Young man with dark hair! He went that way! He didn't have his glasses on, though,' Blair added sadly.

'That's Carr. He's innocent – the publisher's clerk. We're after Abernyte. Did you see when he left the gateway – did he go right or left or straight ahead?'

Blair scowled.

'He went left. Definitely left.' He bounced in his chair. 'I wish I could go after him!'

'I'll push you, sir,' said Smith, 'but I doubt I could do that and run at the same time. Not on this gravel, anyway.'

Murray opened his mouth to say something, then realised that Smith was almost completely out of breath. He needed to slow down, and Blair was a perfect excuse. He looked at Matthew. The boy nodded, ready to go on.

'Come on, then,' said Murray.

'Where are we going, sir?' Matthew asked, hurrying after him.

'I'm fairly sure,' said Murray, 'that he's heading home.'

'But he's the murderer, sir, isn't he?'

'Yes, he is. He's killed three people so far, and tried to kill me.'

'Then … wouldn't he be better to run away, sir?'

'I think he is running away,' said Murray. 'But I think he wants to say goodbye to his sister, first.'

'That's – that's not very wise, sir, is it?'

'No, not at all,' said Murray. He had slowed to a walk. He sensed there was less urgency now: Abernyte might not even realise he was still being pursued, and that was probably a good thing. If he relaxed, he would be easier to catch. He would not wish to do anything to harm his sister, and he would have to give up and surrender himself quietly.

Chapter Forty-Four

'WHAT A CHARMING room you have here!' said Isobel. 'So airy and light.'

Miss Abernyte smiled, looking about her. The room was in fact rather bare, but comfortable enough. What furnishings there were were of good quality, but considerable vintage.

'Thank you. Though sadly we had to part with many pretty things, at least we were able to keep some of our books.' She gestured with her good hand at the shelves fitted in alcoves on either side of the fireplace. 'I think they make a home, but perhaps that is my fancy.'

'Not at all,' said Isobel firmly, and Mrs. Helliwell murmured agreement. 'Books are essential furnishings – not to mention company and entertainment.'

Miss Abernyte nodded, toying with Isobel's card, which she had received from the maid. The maid had then brought tea, poured it, and disappeared. Whatever Miss Abernyte's disabilities, it seemed she could manage to entertain guests alone.

'I'm afraid I'm not quite sure to what I owe the pleasure of this visit,' she said. 'You are – Mr. Murray of Letho is your husband? He called to see us, bringing us sad news, unfortunately.'

'Of the death of Mrs. Ochill, yes,' said Isobel, sympathetically. 'I believe you had all been good friends, when you were neighbours?'

'The stairs in the Old Town are intimately constructed,' said Miss Abernyte, with a smile. 'We were rarely without visitors, which was of course a delight for me as I don't often leave the house.

Yes, the Ochills were frequently with us.'

'It is such a blessing to have good neighbours,' said Mrs. Helliwell. 'And did Mr. Abernyte find them just as congenial? Men are sometimes less apt at making friends than we women!'

'He – he liked them very much, I believe,' said Miss Abernyte.

'You must have been very sorry to hear of Mr. Ochill's death,' said Isobel, 'and then to lose Mrs. Ochill.'

'It was indeed quite a shock,' said Miss Abernyte, and bit her lip.

'A very unfortunate couple, it seems. Strange that she should vanish, just as she was growing successful in her writing,' said Isobel, gazing up at the books on their shelves. Some were old, in the matching bindings that perhaps old Mr. Abernyte had ordered for his library. Others were newer, perhaps saved up for from their modest income. Try as she might, she could not see any volume that looked at all like Mrs. Ochill's *Gaelic Garland.*

'Perhaps she felt unsure of herself, managing as a widow on her own,' said Miss Abernyte after a moment.

'Perhaps. Though even if she felt she must leave, you would have thought she might have told you where she was going. But before that happened, you must have enjoyed having such a celebrity as a neighbour,' said Isobel. 'Do you read Gaelic, yourself?'

'I – yes, a little,' said Miss Abernyte. 'Where we were brought up it was the native tongue, you understand.'

'On the west coast, I think my husband said?'

'That's right, yes.'

'It must have been quite lovely,' said Isobel with a smile.

'We miss it very much,' said Miss Abernyte, 'but there is little work there these days, so when my father – when we had to leave our home, we came to Edinburgh.'

'Very sensible,' said Mrs. Helliwell. 'And now Mr. Abernyte has a fine position, I believe, and here you are in comfort.' She smiled, too, in her best minister's wife fashion. Isobel wondered if they were wasting their time. Was Charles right about Robert Abernyte? And if he was, did Miss Abernyte know what her brother had done? The woman was uneasy, certainly, but when two strangers appear at your door and come in to talk about the misfortunes of your past, it would put anyone on edge. Perhaps they ought to leave. But then, if they were right, and if Charles was successful, Miss Abernyte would shortly be receiving some very bad news. Perhaps they should stay.

'I suppose Mr. Abernyte must be out at work?'

'Yes, indeed.' Miss Abernyte cleared her throat, and took a sip of tea. 'He is very fortunate in having found so good an employer, but of course the hours are quite long. He has many duties to perform.'

'Including dealing with those poor tenants at Holyroodhouse, is that not so?'

Miss Abernyte looked at Isobel in surprise, but before she could respond, they heard the front door open and shut again. There was a long moment of silence. Isobel felt her heart gallop, and glanced over at Mrs. Helliwell. That did not sound like someone bearing bad tidings of Robert Abernyte. That sounded like Robert Abernyte himself, coming home.

'Robert?' Miss Abernyte called out.

'Yes! Just a moment, Chrissie.'

'We have guests, Robert.'

At once, Robert Abernyte poked his head around the parlour door. Isobel supposed, looking at him, that usually he was quite a handsome young man, but just now he was flushed and sweaty, his hair sticking up where he had pushed it from his brow. He stared at the two visitors.

'Good day to you,' he said, and came into the room properly.

'My brother, Robert Abernyte,' said Miss Abernyte. 'These are Mrs. Helliwell and Mrs. Murray, from Fife.'

Isobel rose to curtsey, doing her best to look self-assured. Mrs. Helliwell managed much better, she thought.

'From Fife?' asked Robert Abernyte, finding a small smile of welcome to use. Then he blinked. 'Did you say Murray?'

'That's right, Mr. Abernyte. My husband is Murray of Letho, in Fife.'

'Then – but –' Robert glanced around, a little wildly. 'Where is he? He cannot be here, not already!'

'Were you expecting him?' asked Isobel.

'I – I left him at Holyroodhouse,' said Robert, still looking about as though Murray might be concealing himself somewhere in the small room. 'So he cannot be here,' he added, half to himself.

'Will you sit and have a cup of tea, Robert?' his sister asked. 'Call for Minnie to bring another cup and saucer.'

'No, no, I must not,' he said. 'I must be going, at once. Though perhaps I should write a note …' He looked about him as if he had no idea where he might find paper and a pen. 'But then … no, I shall send it later. I promise,' he added, though it was not clear where the promise was directed. 'Chrissie, I must go. I'll be back late, though. You mustn't worry. You won't, will you?'

'If you're sure, Robert …'

'Yes, Chrissie, it has to be done now.' He sighed sharply, and took her good hand. 'I'll see you again,' he murmured, almost too low for Isobel, shamelessly watching, to hear. 'I'll write.' He squeezed her hand, and looked past her, out of the window to the street. Then he leapt back, almost knocking over the tea table.

'Too late! Too late!' he gasped. He stared about the room again, but this time he was not looking for hidden visitors. Instead, he reached into his coat pocket, and pulled out a knife. And in a moment, Isobel found herself on her feet, with Abernyte's strong left arm around her, and the blade to her throat.

'This is the place,' said Murray as they reached the Abernytes' front door. 'I don't think I'll bother with the formality of knocking, just this once. Would you rather stay outside, Matthew? I don't know how dangerous this might be.'

'I'll come in, sir, if I can be of use.'

'Very well. Stay behind me as much as you can.'

The door was, as Murray had expected, unlocked, as most doors around here would be. Inside the flat there was silence, but an air of expectancy with it: this was not an empty house. Murray hoped he was right and that Robert Abernyte had come here: he had no wish to frighten Miss Abernyte if she were at home with only the maid, or worse, on her own. But a small sound from the parlour, its door ajar, reassured him: it had been the least squeak of alarm, quickly suppressed with a cross, tutting sound. Two people at least were here, and one was telling the other what to do. He frowned. He had not thought that Abernyte might threaten his sister, but if his sister were likely to give him up to justice, then perhaps he would. It seemed unlikely, though. So what was happening in the parlour?

He stepped forward smartly, and kicked the door open, not too hard, just hard enough so that he was not centrally in the doorway when Abernyte saw him.

'Charles!'

'Isobel!' His jaw dropped. What was Isobel doing here? And Mrs. Helliwell? And then, of course, he saw what was happening, and that Robert Abernyte had a tight grip on his wife and his knife at her throat.

'You want to get away, don't you?' Murray asked quickly. 'It won't be so easy if your nice blue coat is covered in blood, will it?'

'I have a cloak,' said Abernyte. 'And I know knives. I know what I'm doing with knives. Not like guns.'

'Isobel, are you all right?' asked Murray. A stupid question, but he wanted to hear her voice.

'Yes, of course, Charles. Quite all right.' Her eyes flashed at him, and he thought she might well be having words with him later. He prayed there would be a later.

'Be quiet,' said Abernyte, nudging her with his knee.

'Mrs. Helliwell? Has he mistreated you?'

'Not at all, Mr. Murray.' Mrs. Helliwell was breathless, but clearly unharmed. That was something.

'Perhaps you would allow Mrs. Helliwell to leave, Abernyte.'

'I don't think so,' said Abernyte. 'Stay where you are, Mrs. Helliwell.'

'Very well. I'm quite comfortable here. I can just finish my tea, see? Quietly here.'

'Not quietly enough,' said Abernyte, annoyed. 'Do as you're told.'

'And Miss Abernyte,' Murray continued politely. 'You seem very much unsurprised by all of this. Perhaps you knew what your brother had in mind this morning? Killing me at Holyroodhouse?' He could try to seize the knife, he thought. But what if he misjudged it? What if the knife went into Isobel's throat? The more he thought about it, the more his confidence ebbed.

'Leave her out of this!' cried Abernyte. 'It's got nothing to do with Chrissie!'

'Ah, but it has, hasn't it?' Once again, Murray found himself playing for time. What he hoped would happen in that time, he had no idea. Where was the maid? Would she help him, or her employers?

'It has nothing to do with my sister,' Abernyte insisted.

'If you say so,' said Murray. 'But it was my impression that she wrote a fine book of poetry, in English and Gaelic, and Ochill stole it so that his wife could claim credit. Is that not the case?'

'Robert!' cried Miss Abernyte in alarm.

'Chrissie, no. It's all right, Chrissie. I'll make sure it's all right.' He gave his sister a long look, as if willing her to be strong. Then Murray saw him flex his knife hand. He drew a deep breath.

Before he could do anything, something shot past him like a firework exploding, and there was a whirl of movement in the middle of the room. Miss Abernyte screamed. Robert tumbled to the floor, clutching at, but missing, Isobel's skirts as he fell. The knife bounced off a chair, and was snatched by quick hands. Matthew stood over Robert Abernyte, watching him like a sparrowhawk.

Mrs. Helliwell seized Isobel, and supported her as she turned to Murray and sank into his arms. Only for a moment, though: she straightened herself and returned to stand with Mrs. Helliwell, allowing Murray to help Robert up and hold his arms close behind his back.

'Rope, please, Matthew, if you can find some.'

Matthew hurried out of the room, returning almost at once with some thick twine. Murray held Robert's arms while Matthew tied some fine knots to secure him.

'And now, Matthew, I need you to run back down to the Palace, and get a message to Viscount Melville. Tell him it's a little belated, but we have his murderer for him.'

Chapter Forty-Five

'MY DEAR,' SAID Blair, clutching Isobel's hand, 'are you quite sure you are well enough to go?'

'I wouldn't miss it for the world!' said Isobel firmly. 'And there is nothing wrong with me. There is not even a mark on my neck to illustrate the dramatic tale!'

'What a shame,' said Murray with a grin. 'You'll not be able to tell it, then.'

She made a face at him.

'I'm not sure there will be much opportunity for tale-telling, anyway,' she said, peering at the mirror once more to check that the feathers in her curled hair were at just the right angle. Whether or not they would be by the time she and Mrs. Helliwell reached Holyroodhouse and the King's Drawing Room, no one could know. They were pearl-white, as was the fur trim on her eau-de-nil silk gown. Mrs. Helliwell was in a russet concoction, blushing pink from all the unaccustomed fuss over her costume. Both garments had been pulled together urgently by a skilled dressmaker with an eye to last-minute invitations, but looked, to Murray's eyes, wonderful. 'From all that you tell me of Saturday's Levee, it will be one long, suffocating queue from door to door, and we'll barely catch sight of the King.' But her eyes danced with excitement, all the same.

'At least you'll be first in the queue: we'll be there before anyone else,' said Murray. 'You can stake your claim on a place in the Long Gallery, while I go and talk to Viscount Melville.'

'Well, don't be late to present us,' said Isobel. 'That would be mortifying.'

Robbins appeared at the drawing room door, and approached Murray.

'Mr. Hepburn is in the parlour, sir.'

'Thank you, Robbins.'

Downstairs, Hepburn was standing by the window, fingers knotted behind his back, shoulders tense. He turned at once when Murray came in, knocking a small ornament off a nearby table. He bowed and picked it up.

'You wished to see me, sir?'

'I did, Hepburn. I don't think I'll be detaining you long, but I should like an explanation. What did you think you were doing when you installed that block and rope contraption inside the gateway?'

'I – I didn't, sir!'

'Were you trying to prove that the Scots could not arrange an event like the King's visit, for the sake of Mr. Mash?'

Hepburn turned pale.

'It didn't even work,' he said softly. 'And when I told Mr. Mash what I had tried, he was furious. Said I could have killed the King. I didn't think so, for the rope was too short, I thought.'

'I'm not so sure,' said Murray. 'I was up there, and it looked just the right length for regicide to me.'

'You saw it?'

'I stopped it.'

'Oh … Oh, that's probably just as well.'

'Just as well that you didn't kill the King? I should think so.' Murray looked at him. He was not an impressive specimen, despite his gold ring and his fine boots. If Mr. Mash were basing his impression of the Scots on him perhaps he was not far wrong. 'What are your duties today?'

'None, sir. Mr. Mash does not want me.'

'Then stay here and don't get into any more trouble,' said Murray. 'There will be more required of you later.'

Hepburn, looking defeated, slumped against the windowsill, and Murray left him there.

The invitation for the two ladies to attend the King's Drawing Room on Tuesday had come late on Saturday, after Robert Abernyte had been taken away to the Tolbooth and a brief account of the matter sent to Viscount Melville. Lord Melville, however, had not been available until this morning to hear everything at first hand, and he had asked the Murrays and Mrs. Helliwell to be at the Palace by half past nine. Refreshments, he had intimated, would be available, which was just as well as the King would not start to receive his illustrious female visitors until a quarter past two.

Melville, along once again with the Duke of Atholl, received them in a small parlour. The Duke looked tired, but made much of the two ladies and their valiant part in the arrest of Robert Abernyte. Mrs. Helliwell and young Mrs. Murray behaved with aplomb, and when ushered away to their tea and bread and butter left well pleased with the occasion. Isobel was already planning humorous sketches of it in her head, and Mrs. Helliwell looked forward to dropping mention of it into conversation with her husband over the breakfast table.

'And so,' said Melville, seating himself once again on a red silk-upholstered armchair. 'Glengarry had nothing to do with anything.'

'Not according to young MacDougall, my lord, no. Though I'm not sure who was paying MacDougall.'

Viscount Melville and the Duke of Atholl exchanged glances, and Murray thought he caught a smile on both their faces.

'I have my suspicions,' said Melville, then shrugged. 'I think Stewart of Garth wants an eye kept on Glengarry throughout the visit. And who would blame him?'

'It seems more than prudent, my lord.'

'But now to the actual guilty party. Robert Abernyte has admitted to murdering both the Ochills and the woman McGregor, as you said. He would have been a young, impulsive man when he killed Ochill, and of course his father was not long dead, a bankrupt, I believe. Was it political, in the end?'

'Not at all, I believe, my lord.'

'Then what?'

'Ochill stole a manuscript from Chrissie Abernyte, and passed it off as his wife's own work, having it published.'

'And Abernyte killed him, rather than say anything?'

'Ochill convinced him that no one would believe two youngsters, alone in the world – well, with a dying mother – and one of them a crippled girl, at that. Mrs. Ochill had always wanted to be a poetess. Ochill made it happen. He does not seem to have been a pleasant man, but he was devoted to his wife.'

'So Abernyte killed him. Money in it too, I daresay. What then?'

'Mrs. Ochill, of course, knew what had been done. Of course she knew that the poems were not hers. When her husband died, she found out – I'm not sure how – that Robert Abernyte had killed him because of the poetry book. She fled, fearing for her own life – justifiably, as it turned out. As soon as Robert found out where she had gone, he managed to kill her, too.'

'The man can certainly bear a grudge,' remarked the Duke.

'He's quite an emotional young man. And very much devoted to his sister,' said Murray.

'Did she know of the matter, do you think?'

Murray hesitated.

'I did not ask, your Grace.'

'No,' said the Duke after a moment. 'Probably just as well. I gather he stole pistols?'

'He did. He thought he had locked me in a room in the attics, and that pistols would be the best way to deal with me as I could hardly be taken by surprise like the Ochills. He thought he knew how to load them, but as it turned out he made a bit of a mess of it.'

'Lucky he didn't blow his hands off,' said the Duke.

'Indeed, your Grace. Instead the pistols just did nothing. He threw them down and ran. He had talked of fleeing straight to Leith, but he could not resist going to see his sister once more.'

'Which is where Mrs. Murray and Mrs. Helliwell come into it,' said Melville. 'They seem remarkably unscathed, I'm pleased to say.'

'They are both strong women,' said Murray, quietly proud of them. As for what Matthew had done … The boy had not, fortunately, received an invitation to the King's Drawing Room. He would, however, be made a gift of five guineas, partly from Melville and partly from Murray himself.

'Will you look after it for me, sir?' Matthew asked, on receipt of the money. He had seemed surprised and gratified, but had remained quite calm.

'You don't want to spend any of it now?'

'No, sir. I'll save it for – for when it might be needed.'

'Very well. I'll write out a receipt for you.' Murray did so, while the boy waited. 'What you did was extremely courageous, Matthew – and not a little foolhardy.'

'It needed to be done, sir. I don't mean – I mean he was watching you, but he wasn't watching me. It was easier for me, sir.'

'Nevertheless, you know that I am more than grateful. Thank you again.'

'Sir.' Matthew bowed, and left the book room. Murray took the little stack of coins, and placed them in a drawer in his desk. Matthew was a strange boy. Murray wondered if they would ever discover his story.

'And what about Carr?' asked Blair. They were in the drawing room after dinner. Every detail of the King's Drawing Room had been talked out, but would no doubt furnish conversation for years to come. Isobel had already sketched a dozen figures.

'The Duchess of Atholl had a red velvet tartan petticoat! And Lady Scott was all in gold! You would have loved it, Papa,' she said happily.

'I'm sure I should have – gold! But what about Carr? What was he doing at Holyroodhouse? Why did he run away? Where did he go?'

'I believe he is back at his desk at Hutcheon & Purvis,' said Murray, with a shrug. 'As to what he was doing – well, there is no evidence left of it, so I shan't be pursuing the matter. We might want to look for a different publisher, though, my dear Isobel, as you suggested. It would be awkward to return there.'

'Do you think Hutcheon was involved?' asked Isobel.

'I don't, no. I'm not sure how Mrs. Ochill came to have one of the handbills, but I don't think Mr. Musgrave was as careful a guardian of them as Carr expected. Was it he who tried to get into Mrs. Duguid's house and steal it back? Or was that Hepburn's first feeble attempt at contacting his cousin? I'm not sure.'

'And I don't suppose we'll have much to do with Hepburn now, either,' said Isobel.

'No …' Melville's men had removed Hepburn, and his belongings, during the course of the day. Murray was not sure what would happen to him. He found he did not much care.

'I gather there was some fire damage to one of the attic

rooms of the Palace,' said Blair innocently, going back a stage.

'Mr. Carr came in very useful at just the right moment,' said Murray, 'and also helped me to work out what Robert Abernyte's motive was. A fire? Really?'

'Ha!' said Blair, grinning. 'I shall find out one day!'

'I daresay you will,' said Murray, smiling back. 'You always do.'

Historical note:

Anyone wanting to find out more about the remarkable visit of King George IV to Edinburgh in 1822 can do no better than to read John Prebble's book, *The King's Jaunt*. I have had far too much fun weaving Murray's story into the actual history of the event as presented by Prebble, which really didn't need anything added to it for entertainment and intrigue. Glengarry did act in a very peculiar fashion throughout. Ewan MacDougall did at least at one point succeed in stopping him. Glengarry and Garth did not get on at all. I have taken liberties with the ground floor, mostly, of Holyroodhouse, and thoroughly recommend a visit there to see it in its current form.

L.C. 2025

About the Author

LEXIE CONYNGHAM IS a historian living in the shadow of the Highlands. Her historical crime novels are born of a life amidst Scotland's old cities, ancient universities and hidden-away aristocratic estates, but she has written since the day she found out that people were allowed to do such a thing. Beyond teaching and research, her days are spent with wool, wild allotments and a wee bit of whisky.

We hope you've enjoyed this instalment. Reviews are important to authors, so it would be lovely if you could post a review where you bought it!

Visit our website at www.lexieconyngham.co.uk. There are several free Murray of Letho short stories, Murray's World Tour of Edinburgh, and the chance to follow Lexie Conyngham's meandering thoughts on writing, gardening and knitting, at www.murrayofletho.blogspot.co.uk. You can also follow Lexie, should such a thing appeal, on Facebook, Pinterest or Instagram.

Finally! If you'd like to be kept up to date with Lexie and her writing, please join our mailing list and claim your free copy of three novellas here:

Murray of Letho

WE FIRST MEET Charles Murray when he's a student at St. Andrews University in Fife in 1802, resisting his father's attempts to force him home to the family estate to learn how it's run. Pushed into involvement in the investigation of a professor's death, he solves his first murder before taking up a post as tutor to Lord Scoggie. This series takes us around Georgian Scotland as well as India, Italy and Norway (so far!), in the company of Murray, his manservant Robbins, his father's old friend Blair, the enigmatic Mary, and other members of his occasionally shambolic household.

Death in a Scarlet Gown

The Status of Murder (a novella)

Knowledge of Sins Past

Service of the Heir: An Edinburgh Murder

An Abandoned Woman

Fellowship with Demons

The Tender Herb: A Murder in Mughal India

Death of an Officer's Lady

Out of a Dark Reflection

A Dark Night at Midsummer (a novella)

Slow Death by Quicksilver

Thicker than Water

A Deficit of Bones

The Dead Chase

Shroud for a Sinner

Murder on the King's Jaunt

Hippolyta Napier

HIPPOLYTA NAPIER IS only nineteen when she arrives in Ballater, on Deeside, in 1829, the new wife of the local doctor. Blessed with a love of animals, a talent for painting, a helpless instinct for hospitality, and insatiable curiosity, Hippolyta finds her feet in her new home and role in society, making friends and enemies as she goes. Ballater may be small but it attracts great numbers of visitors, so the issues of the time, politics, slavery, medical advances, all affect the locals. Hippolyta, despite her loving husband and their friend Durris, the sheriff's officer, manages to involve herself in all kinds of dangerous adventures in her efforts to solve every mystery that presents itself.

A Knife in Darkness

Death of a False Physician

A Murderous Game

The Thankless Child

A Lochgorm Lament

The Corrupted Blood

A Day for Death

Orkneyinga Murders

ORKNEY, C.1050 A.D.: THORFINN Sigurdarson, Earl of Orkney, rules from the Brough of Birsay on the western edges of these islands. Ketil Gunnarson is his man, representing his interests in any part of his extended realm. When Sigrid, a childhood friend of Ketil's, finds a dead man on her land, Ketil, despite his distrust of islands, is commissioned to investigate. Sigrid, though she has quite enough to do, decides he cannot manage on his own, and insists on helping – which Ketil might or might not appreciate.

Tomb for an Eagle

A Wolf at the Gate

Dragon in the Snow

The Bear at Midnight

The Fate of the Sea Stag

Alec Cattanach

HITLER MAY HAVE declared war, but police work continues in Aberdeen. Detective Inspector Alec Cattanach, torn between his work in the city and his love of the countryside beyond, has to deal with new crimes and old, regardless of the bombs and the blackout.

A Vengeful Harvest

The Gowden Wifie

The Journals of Dr. Robert Wilson

After Waterloo, and his service with the Honourable East India Company, Dr. Robert Wilson decides to travel east. He is accompanied by his secretary, Gil Archibald, who has his own reasons for the journey. With neither able to tell the truth to the other, how will they cope when faced with murder?

The Business in Blandyce

Other books by Lexie Conyngham:

Windhorse Burning

'I'm not mad, for a start, and I'm about as far from violent as you can get.'
When Toby's mother, Tibet activist Susan Hepplewhite, dies, he is determined to honour her memory. He finds her diaries and decides to have them translated into English. But his mother had a secret, and she was not the only one: Toby's decision will lead to obsession and murder.

The War, The Bones, and Dr. Cowie

Far from the London Blitz, Marian Cowie is reluctantly resting in rural Aberdeenshire when a German 'plane crashes nearby. An airman goes missing, and old bones are revealed. Marian is sure she could solve the mystery if only the villagers would stop telling her useless stories – but then the crisis comes, and Marian finds the stories may have a use after all.

Jail Fever

It's the year 2000, and millennium paranoia is everywhere.
Eliot is a bad-tempered merchant with a shady past, feeling under the weather.
Catriona is an archaeologist at a student dig, when she finds something unexpected.
Tom is a microbiologist, investigating a new and terrible disease with a stigma.
Together, they and their knowledge could save thousands of lives – but someone does not want them to …

The Slaughter of Leith Hall* and *The Contentious Business of Samuel Seabury

'See, Charlie, it might be near twenty years since Culloden, but there's plenty hard feelings still amongst the Jacobites, and no so far under the skin, ken?'

Charlie Rob has never thought of politics, nor strayed far from his Aberdeenshire birthplace. But when John Leith of Leith Hall takes him under his wing, his life changes completely. Soon he is far from home, dealing with conspiracy and murder, and lost in a desperate hunt for justice.

Thrawn Thoughts and Blithe Bits* and *Quite Useful in Minor Emergencies

Two collections of short stories, some featuring characters from the series, some not; some seen before, some not; some long, some very short. Find a whole new dimension to car theft, the life history of an unfortunate Victorian rebel, a problem with dragons and a problem with draugens, and what happens when you advertise that you've found somebody's leg.

Printed in Dunstable, United Kingdom

81898212R00180